Praise for Margaret Campbel

"Ever since *My Lady of Cleves*, Margaret Campbell Barnes has been one of the most reliable of England's historical novelists."

—*Chicago Tribune*

"Mrs. Barnes has found a rewarding field in English history, retelling royal lives with sympathy and skill."

—*New York Herald Tribune*

"Barnes vividly depicts Anne's hopes and fears in an age where royal marriages were brokered like a cattle fair, and beheading could befall even a Queen."

—*Publishers Weekly* on *Brief Gaudy Hour*

"This novel is rich in detail and flows beautifully, letting readers escape into Anne's court and country life. It is a must read for those who love exploring the dynamic relationships of Henry VIII and his wives."

—*Historical Novels Review* on *My Lady of Cleves*

"A highly enjoyable book and definitely something to check out for fans of Tudor-era historical fiction."

—*Devourer of Books* on *King's Fool*

"A wonderful historical read and well worth curling up with for immersion into another world."

—*Medieval Bookworm* on *The Tudor Rose*

"Margaret Campbell Barnes truly deserves the accolades given her. Read this work, and you will see why."

—Bookloons on *Within the Hollow Crown*

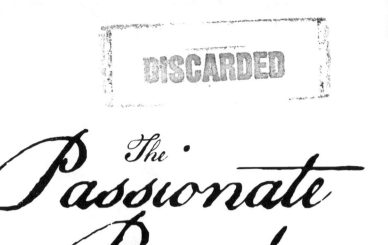

The Passionate Brood

A Novel of
Richard the Lionheart
and the Man Who
Became Robin Hood

MARGARET CAMPBELL BARNES

sourcebooks
landmark

Published by Sourcebooks Landmark, an imprint of Sourcebooks, Inc.
P.O. Box 4410, Naperville, Illinois 60567-4410
(630) 961-3900
Fax: (630) 961-2168
www.sourcebooks.com

Originally published in 1944 by Macdonald & Co. Ltd. as *Like Us They Lived*.

Library of Congress Cataloging-in-Publication Data

Barnes, Margaret Campbell.
  The passionate brood : a novel of Richard the Lionheart and the man who
became Robin Hood / by Margaret Campbell Barnes.
     p. cm.
  1. Richard I, King of England, 1157-1199--Fiction. 2. Robin Hood
(Legendary character)--Fiction. 3. Great Britain--History--Richard I, 1189-
1199--Fiction. I. Title.
 PR6003.A72P37 2010
 823'.912--dc22
                          2009051070

          Printed and bound in the United States of America.
             VP 10 9 8 7 6 5 4 3 2 1

Also by Margaret Campbell Barnes
Brief Gaudy Hour
My Lady of Cleves
King's Fool
The Tudor Rose
Within the Hollow Crown
Mary of Carisbrooke

To the memory of my elder son

Lieut. Michael Campbell Barnes

Royal Armoured Corps

The Plantagenets

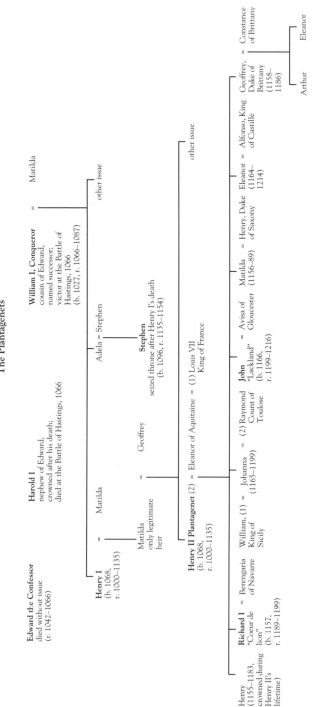

This chart shows the characters and relationships integral to the story and does not attempt to provide a complete genealogy.
Bold indicates a ruling king.

Author's Note

I N WRITING THIS STORY of the young Plantagenets I have used
modern dialogue, with the result that their fooling, their quarrelling, and their love-making sound much like those of any
other family. For this I make no apology. Since they must have
spoken in a Norman tongue quite incomprehensible to us, it
seemed more sensible to translate their imaginary conversations
into twentieth century English rather than into some pseudo-
Elizabethan jargon—though trying, of course, to keep their
thoughts within the limitations of their times.

Through their deeds and reactions and affections it is possible
to come to know these twelfth century people; but few of their
actual sayings have come down to us. When writing a novel about
Tudor or Stuart characters there is usually a wealth of letters,
contemporary memoirs, and authenticated remarks which can be
woven into the narrative; but, apart from a *chanson* or two, the only
well known words of Richard Cœur de Lion are those unfortunate
ones used when he was in the throes of collecting money for his
Crusade—"I would sell London if only I could find a buyer!"

Yarmouth, Isle of Wight

Contents

PART I

Oxford

Chapter One

BLONDEL DE CAHAIGNES WAS fifteen and homesick. It was four days since he had parted from his parents, and the life he had shared with them in their unpretentious manor seemed like a lost world. Of course, he had wanted to come to Oxford to serve in the royal household, and the journey up from Sussex had been more exciting than all the rest of his life put together. He had slept a night in London and ridden over the new wooden bridge across the Thames and seen the Conqueror's Tower and Edward the Confessor's Abbey at Westminster. But as the gentle hills which had sheltered his childhood gave place to flat and unfamiliar river country he had begun to realise how much his future happiness depended upon the kind of man whom he was to serve as page. And this Richard Plantagenet had been abroad so much in his duchy of Aquitaine that no one seemed to know much about him, except that he was tall and ruddy and turbulent like the rest of Henry the Second's sons.

It had been dark when Blondel arrived at Oxford Castle, and he had been packed off to bed without ceremony in the Constable's room over the gatehouse. And now the old farm servant who had accompanied him had gone back to his pigs and his plough, and the last link with the rural manor of Horsted de Cahaignes was broken. Blondel had waked to find the whole castle astir and had dressed hurriedly, wondering if his new master had already asked for him. But the Constable only laughed. "Duke Richard and his foster brother were off to Banbury fair two hours ago," he said. "And what's more they've taken the whole pack of clamouring pages with them, so it looks as if you'll have to lay the King's table."

"The wild way things go on here, it's a good thing the Queen *has* come home again!" added the Constable's wife, coaxing the boy to eat some breakfast.

Blondel knew there was scandal in the royal household; but he knew it only with the uncomfortable, unacknowledged awareness of youth. So he made no answer but stood by the windlass that lowered the great portcullis, staring out enviously at a dusty road which he imagined might lead to Banbury. How much more fun to go to a fair in good company, he thought, than to begin one's new duties all alone! But, being a conscientious lad, he lingered for no more than a few seconds to view the enchanting picture framed in each sunlit arrow-slit as he descended the dark spiral of the stairs.

As he pulled aside the leather curtain at the end of the hall his heart beat hard against the velvet of his fine new coat. In his inexperience he expected to find the King and Queen of England sitting there with some of their family grouped about them, just as everybody sat and talked and worked in the hall at home. But the great hall of Oxford Castle was deserted save for half a dozen hounds stretched about the central hearth and the servants who were strewing fresh rushes on the floor and setting up trestles for the midday meal. Blondel did not yet know of the Tower room where the young Plantagenets really lived, and he was too unsophisticated to take it for granted that at this hour of the morning the King was usually with his mistress at Woodstock.

The hall seemed long as a cathedral to a country boy walking the length of it under the servants' curious gaze. He was overawed by the tall torch sconces and banners and tapestries, and when he reached the King's table at the far end he stood rather desolately regarding a pile of freshly laundered napkins, stacks of plates, a large finger bowl, and a great gold salt cellar.

He was still wondering what to do with them when a heavy door banged somewhere up in the gallery that ran round the hall and two girls came out of one of the small rooms built in the thickness

of the second storey wall. One of them was golden and the other
dark. Seeing a stranger in the hall they stopped on their way to the
turret stair, and in his embarrassment Blondel seized the nearest
pile of plates and began doling them out along the table. The girls
leaned over the edge of the gallery to watch him and the dark one
laughed contemptuously. "Just look at that fool of a page putting
a wooden platter for Richard!" she said carelessly, so that he could
hear. "We shouldn't tolerate such service in France!"

"Well, thank goodness, this is England!" countered the other
one. "And, anyhow, he is new." There was something gallant and
arresting about her clear voice and, sensing Blondel's discomfiture,
she immediately included him in the conversation by calling down
to him pleasantly, "You're my brother's new page, aren't you? What
is your name?"

Although no more than a year or two his senior, she seemed to
him quite grown-up. The thick plaits hanging like red-gold ropes
on either side of her slender breasts confirmed his guess that she
must be the popular Johanna Plantagenet, who rode and swam
and hunted almost as well as her brothers. Blondel held his head
high and answered her with grave courtesy; but his sensitive face,
framed in a formal straight-cut bob of fair hair, was still hot with
humiliation.

"It must be horrible having to leave home and begin life all over
again among strangers!" she said. And because her lively interest
in people killed formality and the haughty, dark girl had shrugged
herself away up the turret stairs, Blondel found himself asking this
Plantagenet princess which plates he ought to have used.

Instead of calling to one of the servants to instruct him she
came down into the hall herself, attracted by his ingenuous smile.
"One of the other boys should have stayed behind to show you!"
she exclaimed indignantly. And—princess or no princess—she
tucked up her long green velvet sleeves and herself showed him
how to lay the family table. "Those wooden platters are for the
people at the trestles—squires and bailiffs and shire reeves and so
on," she explained. "The servants will see to them. Put pewter for
the family, always. Unless someone special comes, and then we

eat off the gold. But we do not have many banquets since poor
Archbishop à Becket's death." She picked up a long rye loaf and
with quick, capable fingers showed him how to roll a piece of bread
in a napkin for each person.

"I was wondering what to do with all those napkins," he
confessed. "We do not use many at home."

The youngest daughter of Henry of Anjou and Eleanor of
Aquitaine was too great a personage to make him feel small. "Then
your sisters must be very lucky people!" she laughed. "We have to
embroider the tiresome things during the long winter evenings.
Now put a knife at the left of Duke Richard's plate in case he wants
to divide his meat. You will like working for him, Blondel."

"I'll do anything—anything…It's just this waiting at table…"
muttered the boy, without looking up. When one's heart is
an aching tenderness for home, kind words are difficult to bear
without tears.

"Oh, it's quite simple really," she assured him. "The servants
will bring all the dishes to that door. All you have to be careful
about is not to slop water over people's feet when you hold the
finger bowl for them as they go out. My eldest brother's page ruined
a new pair of shoes for me only yesterday."

"At least I shan't do that," vowed Blondel, with a smile. "I often
wait on my father's guests at home. But then he is only a knight.
Here at court, where every other person is a prince or a duke, I am
afraid of serving the wrong one first."

"Well, the King sits here—when he is at home," said Johanna
sliding into her father's great carved chair at the middle of the
table. Henry the Second was a broad man, and she did not nearly
fill it; but she and the jester were the only people who dared sit
there at all. She often did so to annoy her young brother, John,
or to scandalise, the stolid Saxon thanes, taking care to vacate it
the moment she heard her father's voice rapping out orders on the
stairs. But to Richard's new page she looked wonderful enough to
sit on the throne at Westminster. He stood at gaze across the long
oak table while she stretched an arm this way and that, introducing
him to the imaginary company of her relatives.

"The Queen here on his left, of course. And my three brothers in order of age. Henry, Duke of Normandy, on the right. Remember to bow to him, Blondel—he is almost as important as the King. Then your own duke, Richard of Aquitaine, there. And Prince John at the end. Robin and I sit where we like. You will see a lot of Robin. He is your master's foster-brother, and when Richard is in England they are inseparable."

"I've already *heard* a lot of him," volunteered Blondel. "My father's labourers say he is going to make them freemen with fields of their own."

Although she had no particular interest in unwashed serfs, Johanna looked unaccountably pleased. "So they talk about him right down in Sussex, do they?" she said, her fingers drumming abstractedly on the carved lions that formed the chair arms. Her mouth was smiling and her green eyes wide with some dream of her own from which, presently, she pulled herself back to her present good deed. "Prince John is about your age," she continued briskly. "You'll have plenty of fun with him."

"I believe I must have seen him while I was dressing," recalled Blondel, to whom the bleak events of exile were beginning to assume a more homely guise. "He was down in the bailey imitating a fat monk who had just fallen off his mule."

"I'm afraid the fat monk was his tutor," explained Johanna, "and he fell off because John had been poking chestnuts under his saddle." She spoke with the full severity of one who had only recently given up abetting him in such pursuits.

"And who was that other lady? The one who called me a fool?" Blondel's reminiscent laughter had turned to a scowl. "Is she your sister, Madam?"

"God forbid! She is Princess Ann of France. Both my sisters are married and live abroad, but Ann Capet has lived with us since she was quite small because it has been arranged that she shall marry my brother Richard. So she always sits next to him—here." Johanna Plantagenet flounced out of her exalted seat to jab an explanatory fork into Ann's bread; and the inelegant force with which she did so suggested to his quick intelligence that she coveted the place for herself and met with a sharp reprimand from someone behind them.

Blondel turned quickly to find an elderly woman bustling into the hall with some expensive-looking white material trailing from her arm. The pleasant, work-lined face was creased with anxiety. "It's the only fork in the Castle, child!" she expostulated. "And God only knows what that finicking French Madam will say if it's broken!"

Johanna withdrew the rare implement more gently, and the three of them examined a bent prong with consternation. Louis of France had sent it specially for his daughter, and she always used it at meals—an affected foreign fashion against which the younger Plantagenets frequently sharpened their ribald wit.

"I could take it down to the armoury and get it straightened out before she comes back," Blondel offered, with the resourcefulness which was to serve them so well.

Johanna regarded him with gratitude. "This is Blondel de Cahaignes, Richard's new page, Hodierna," she said.

The woman looked him up and down with shrewd, bright eyes that seemed to be assessing something less apparent than his good breeding and good looks. "Do you know anything about sick nursing?" she asked surprisingly.

"Why, no—" began the boy. He had always supposed that to be work for women and monks.

Hodierna jingled the iron keys that hung against her dark woollen gown. "Then I must show you how to mix herbs and make a soothing posset."

His young dignity was up in arms immediately. "I hardly suppose my duties will include…"

But although she looked like some sort of upper servant, she caught him up sharply. "Your duties are more important than you realise, young man. You will have to learn to do a great many more things than these other idle popinjays who expect to become useful squires by holding a hawk or strumming a lute. Those Saracens are cunning dogs."

Blondel began to laugh. "But I don't suppose I shall have the luck to go crusading—at any rate for years and years!"

"The Duke of Aquitaine is sure to go," said the woman with finality. She gathered up her costly material, and Johanna slipped an arm round her ample waist. "Hodierna is your master's foster-mother," she explained laughingly, "and if I know anything about her she will hold you responsible for his least little finger until the day of his death!"

The two of them went upstairs together, the young Princess protesting that she had done nothing but try on new dresses since her mother's return. And before going down to the armoury Blondel waited, fork in hand, for another glimpse of her where a turn of the turret stair opened to the gallery above. He was, of course, her slave for life.

Chapter Two

ETWEEN THEM, HENRY OF Anjou and Eleanor of Aquitaine must have owned half the castles in Western Europe. But because they had begun their married life by being so ardently in love they needed to have one in particular which they called home. So after Louis of France had been persuaded to divorce Eleanor, and Henry by inheriting the throne of England had healed the scars of civil war inflicted by his mother and dead Stephen, they decided to live their private lives at Oxford. Their children were born there and filled the grim castle walls with quarrelling and laughter.

They were a passionate brood—four strong sons and three fair daughters—all inheriting their father's ruddy energy and their mother's beauty. Henry adored them, but neither they nor Eleanor could hold him after the first ten years or so of marriage. The prodigality of happiness she radiated satiated him. To a man of his restless energy new, hardly-won success must always be sweetest. So he rode abroad in search of fresh romance and met Rosamund de Clifford.

To give the man his due, it was business as often as pleasure that accounted for his frequent absences. He worked indefatigably for England. And when he did ride wearily into Oxford he noted with a jealous eye Eleanor's influence on his growing sons, and began to resent the careless spells she cast upon all who came beneath her charm. "Statesmen and scullions, she bewitches them all!" he grumbled, trying to curb the frank indiscretion of her witty tongue. But Eleanor of Aquitaine was of too high a metal to be silenced by any man. When her elder sons made trouble for their father on the continent she was caught trying to join them disguised as a man. So the epic of the Angevin love story ended by the King sending her to live in a separate household at Salisbury.

During the dead days after her departure it was Hodierna who noticed the quenched look in her children's eyes, and who tried by simple coaxings and scoldings to counteract the frequent rages of the conscience-stricken King. High up in the tower, where she had minded them when they were small, her care out-lived their childhood. She herself had been widowed just before Robin's birth, and Eleanor had had her brought to the Castle, where a son had been born to each of them on the same day. So the Tower room was her mute gift of gratitude to Eleanor. Nothing in it was changed. And when at last the Queen came home from Salisbury, although her eldest son Henry was nearly twenty and Richard and Robin were over six feet tall, their feet still came hurrying up the familiar turret stair. Back from Normandy or Aquitaine, home from hunting or merely bored by the company in the hall, some of the Plantagenets were sure to be in the Tower room.

It was a place where they could discuss their betters and pursue their individual hobbies in private. Not only was privacy rare in a royal castle, but, as young John Plantagenet always pointed out, the higher one went the more light one got. Down in the dungeons there was no light at all, the guardroom on the ground floor had arrow slits, and the bedrooms on the second floor had only narrow, deeply embrasured windows. But the Tower room was high enough to be safe from snipers, and if you were young enough not to mind climbing up past the garde-robe passage and the gallery, you had the best of it.

The walls were not blazoned with banners like the hall, nor warm with glowing tapestries like the Queen's bower, but the living sunlight streaming through a double-arched, unglazed window could turn the rushes on the floor to ripe corn gold. And never, all their lives long, did the Plantagenets quite lose that lovely, light sense of floating straight out to the blue sky through its blunt-headed Norman stonework as they came breathless to the top turn of the dark stair.

When Hodierna and Johanna came up with their dress length they found Henry, the King's heir, using this excellent light to study some fortification plans. Instead of studying his Latin young John lay sprawled on the floor, shying chessmen at a wounded dove; and Ann—who was not yet a Plantagenet—was at her everlasting embroidery. "It amazes me how you can waste so much time talking to the servants, Johanna!" she remarked, virtuously finishing off the centre of a yellow fleur-de-lis.

"The poor page was homesick," said Johanna. "Don't you remember how you cried when you first came?"

Henry picked up a notched stick and began making some measurements on the parchment he held before him. "And our pages are scarcely servants," he pointed out. "Their fathers are usually gentlemen who have done us some service." Ann's superiority always amazed him because it impinged on his own prerogative.

Johanna draped a long train of white lamé from her boyish hips and began peacocking up and down with her head screwed round backwards to see the effect. Unfortunately for her dignity she tripped over one of John's neglected books and rounded on him with sudden annoyance. "Can't you let that miserable dove alone?"

But John—that "after-thought" of their parents' cooling passion—took a deformed delight in cruelty. "'Tis mine," he said, shying white bishop and red knight in quick succession. "Richard's falcon caught it yesterday. He threw it aside to be killed."

"Richard kills, but he doesn't torture," retorted Johanna.

John grabbed the poor creature by a fluttering wing and rolled over on to his stomach so that the back of his head made a splash of warm copper colour against the grey stone flags. "Look how neatly the falcon picked out one of its eyes!" he invited, still spattering his Norman with the blunt stab of occasional Saxon words, as they all did in childhood. "It would be amusing to put out the other and see if he walks round in circles."

"How would you like to be blinded?" reproved Hodierna absently, her mouth full of pins.

"My tutor says the Huns used to blind all their boy prisoners. I could do it with this," went on John, coolly drawing his new jewelled dagger from his belt.

"Drop it, you disgusting little beast!" ordered Henry, kicking at him tolerantly with his soft leather boot. He understood how the least important member of a family must want to shock people into paying him some attention from time to time; but Johanna, unable to bear the bird's squawking terror, swooped down on its tormentor like a fury. Ann watched the undignified scuffle with quiet disdain, her needle suspended until the dagger went ringing across the floor.

"The King had it specially made for my birthday!" raged the boy, groping for his newest treasure among the rushes.

"It's a pity he never made you obey!" cried Johanna, seizing the strategic moment to release the dove. Leaning from the window, she watched its triumphant flight into the blue. How fine, she thought, to be absolutely free like that! Free to go out into the world and make one's own life like a man. Freedom, she supposed, was one of the few things worth fighting for. Why, only yesterday Robin had been saying that even the peasants wanted it. Being a woodman's son, he should know. But, being Richard's foster brother, he should also realise that princesses hadn't half as much liberty as peasant girls'. If only they had she would willingly have risen early and ridden to Banbury fair with him as he had wanted... Well, he would soon be back, and perhaps he and Richard would take her hawking. She came stepping down from the window seat stretching her arms with vast contentment. "How peaceful it is when the King is away!" she yawned.

Hodierna glanced forebodingly at her happiness. "Peaceful?" she sniffed, biting off a thread. "Why, when a pack of wolves used to howl round my old cottage it was peaceful compared with a family party of Plantagenets!"

"Don't pretend you don't like us!" teased Johanna. "And you know very well that your precious Richard is the most quarrelsome of us all."

"It's lucky for him, now his hellish temper has provoked rebel-lion in Aquitaine, that our amorous father still philanders at Woodstock!" remarked Henry. "Particularly lucky as rumour has it that the King is tiring of the lady."

"Who cares?" shrugged Johanna, submitting to the fitting of a sleeve.

"The Queen, probably," suggested Ann.

"Do you suppose she is jealous of this woman they call 'fair Rosamund'?" asked John, who had recovered both his dagger and his good temper. "Have you ever seen her, Henry?"

"Once—at a tournament. She is certainly fair."

"So is mother," said Johanna, defensively.

"But no longer young," observed Ann, her red mouth mocking primly in her pale, heart-shaped face.

"You might have grown up less objectionable, Ann, if he hadn't sent her away to Salisbury as soon as he was reasonably sure she wouldn't bear him any more contentious, red-headed sons," said Henry.

"Stop talking like that in front of your sister!" Hodierna told him sharply, much as she used to when he was small. But Ann, whose window looked down on to the herb garden, began giggling. "My dear Hodierna," she said, "it is high time King Henry married your precious innocent to some possessive foreign princeling! She has the warm kind of colouring that enslaves handsome commoners."

Hodierna muttered something in Saxon, a language which Ann felt it would be vulgar to understand. "After all, I'm not much older than Johanna, and I've been engaged to Richard for years," she pointed out.

"And look like being engaged to him until you're buried!" retorted his sister. She was ashamed of her rudeness as soon as John sniggered; but Ann goaded her deliberately and always made her feel a hoyden. It was the sickening way she boasted about French culture and ate with a fork and—most of all—her infuriating habit of referring to England as "this island." Like Henry, she could say disagreeable things pleasantly, which left forthright Johanna at a disadvantage. Fiddling with some scraps of silk to keep her angry hands from slapping

Ann's sallow face, she added, "Anyway, I'd rather marry a handsome commoner than a king's son who didn't want me!"

Henry joined in their feminine dispute with lazy amusement. "My dear Johanna, has it never occurred to you that Ann's wedding may be delayed less because Richard doesn't want her than because the King does?"

Ann's needle jabbed at a harmless *fleur-de-lis* with venom. "How clever some of your stupidest remarks sound!" she mocked.

"Perhaps he will build her a secret bower like Rosamund's?" suggested John hopefully.

"Now, by all the saints!" laughed his eldest brother. "Who talks to a brat like you about secret bowers?"

"I think it's so clever of him!" went on John, unabashed.

"No wonder you and he dote on each other, but I think 'cunning' is the word you mean," corrected Henry, tilting back his chair and treating his long, elegant limbs to a good stretch.

John sprang to his feet, his handsome face aflame. "And don't I need cunning?" he demanded. "With not a duchy left by the time I get born so that I have to be brought up by a lot of mouldy priests? All our parents' possessions divided between you and Richard and Geoffrey? Normandy, England, Aquitaine, Guienne, Anjou, Maine—" In a worthy gust of Angevin rage, he rapped out each name on the table with his over-worked dagger.

His family remained unmoved. "Poor little Lackland!" laughed Johanna, regarding the effect of her fashionably low belt with approval. "Perhaps if you go on being charming to the King he will give Ann to you instead of to Richard, and then you will get a good slice of France."

"Ssh! The Queen is coming up the stairs," warned Hodierna. "For Our Lady's sake, talk about something else."

Henry was quick to take up her cue. "If you care so much about a bit of land, why not go on a Crusade and make yourself King of Jerusalem?" he suggested, with loud casualness.

"Because fighting isn't much in John's line," jeered Johanna.

John thrust out his tongue at her. "We can't all be Richards!" he shouted back from his favourite corner of the window seat.

Chapter Three

A T THE TOP OF the turret stair the tall, white-haired Queen stood for a moment to regain her breath, her scarlet under-dress still lifted a little with both hands. She surveyed her family with a humorous quirk of finely marked brows. "Still quarrelling? What a brood!" she sighed.

They rose to greet her and Henry, with his easy grace, pushed forward the well-worn chair he had been using. "It must be because you yourself went crusading, Madam, before we were born," he suggested.

"His father's ability and my beauty—what a king he will make!" thought Eleanor, with an impersonal sort of satisfaction. Aloud she said, "That was before your father and I got our divorce, dear Ann. When I was young and *ravissante*." She always tried to be particularly nice to Ann to make up for Richard's indifference.

Johanna thought that her mother looked like some exquisitely painted picture with the arched window behind her and the slender gold circlet holding her flowing wimple in place. She leaned over the back of the chair and said, with a provocative grimace at Ann, "Richard still thinks you're the most beautiful woman he's ever seen!"

"If he does it must be because he looks only at crossbows and catapults," laughed the Queen.

Crossbows and catapults were an obsession with Henry too. "If he hasn't much time for women, I must say he has some pretty sound ideas about fortifications," he said, hunting out one of

Richard's plans. "Just look at this curtain wall with which he proposes to strengthen the Tower of London!"

Eleanor of Aquitaine regarded it with a reminiscent shiver. "I suppose the Londoners think we ought to live there like your grandmother, Queen Matilda. But I always found the bedrooms so gloomy."

Henry passed the drawing on to Ann. He resented the way in which she emphasised her fiancé's gaucheries and ignored his touch of genius. "Your brother Philip always says Richard might have made a fortune as an architect if we hadn't been born into the kind of family that is expected to butcher Saracens for nothing," he told her.

"Tell us about the Crusade *you* went on, Mother," urged Johanna, heading him off from technicalities. It was bad enough having to listen to endless discussions about curtain walls when he and Richard were together.

"You were all brought up on it till you know it by heart," objected Hodierna, who alone guessed that the Queen had found the steep, winding stairs a strain. "Far better help me with this seam."

But Johanna had no use for needlework. "Don't you remember— in this very room?" she coaxed. "The brazier would burn low, throwing long shadows like tall horsemen on the walls. Your voice was like a harp, with memory plucking at the strings. You made everything sound exciting—the heroic things and the ludicrous things, the important people and the pathetic ones—so that it all became part of us and somehow made us different from other families. And after you'd gone downstairs we always got out of bed and acted the part about the siege. The table was Jerusalem, and Henry used to make the rest of us take it in turns to be Saracens. Except John, of course—he was always asleep in his cot and had to be the baggage waggons."

Eleanor had only to close her eyes to repeople the room again with her absent sons and daughters; she was soon back at her spells again. The spell of adventure she had laid upon them all. All except John. He had been quite small when she went to Salisbury. Too small, as Johanna had just said, to be even a Saracen. And so the King had kept him. And he was growing up full of common sense, and quite English.

"Well, St. Bernard came preaching. Isn't that how it always began, Hodierna?" She settled herself comfortably in her chair and smiled affectionately at the woman who had shared so much of her family life. "He told us how a handful of knights were still holding out in Syria. How the Saracens had driven them out from Jerusalem and taken the Holy Cross. It made all our tournaments and dancing seem so trivial that we all wanted to go."

"You had only just come to Paris then as a bride, hadn't you, Madam?" encouraged Hodierna, beginning to baste her seam.

"And my first husband Louis was a monkish sort of man who felt he ought to do something about the infidels being in all the sacred places. So we set sail with all his troops and horses and supplies, and my ladies and the dower chests—"

"And the poor devils of French archers had to swelter through the sand with your baggage when they might have been shooting Saracens!"

"But, Henry, it was my first honeymoon!"

John, sitting cross-legged on the floor in front of her, gave a hoot of disrespectful laughter. "Catch Henry taking women on a Crusade when he and Richard go!"

"Catch you going on one at all!" retorted Johanna, who had always entertained secret hopes that they might invite *her*.

Eleanor regarded her youngest son with puzzled disapproval. To have given birth to someone beyond her comprehension was disconcerting. And then there was Robin, spending half his time studying astrology and wanting to experiment with a lot of new-fangled notions for improving the conditions of the poor. In her young days things had been much simpler. A man either wanted to go to war or was a craven, just as a woman wanted babies or was wanton. "We women used to send our distaffs to the young men who didn't want to fight," she recalled.

It was Ann who gathered up the fraying threads of the spell and handed them back to her with French politeness. "And you really saw Jerusalem, Madam?"

"Yes, Ann," replied the Queen, grateful for her pretty deference. "Perhaps you will, too, when you and Richard are married. And I hope you will not be as disappointed as I was. It isn't a golden city at all, you know. Only dreadfully hot and dusty, with all the holiest places built over and quarrelled over until the spirit of them seems to have been trampled into the inhospitable sand." She lifted one of her beautiful hands to the light, turning it about absently, so that prisms of colour flashed from her costly rings. "Like a great love all marred and twisted out of recognition by jealousy," she added sadly.

"The way so many human loves are spoiled," said Ann.

The Queen looked up at her sharply. Ann was so much more mature in some ways than her own children that one could not afford to indulge in significant similes. "That was how I came to part from your poor, pious father, my dear," she went on lightly, although it was of her second husband she had been thinking. "If I smiled at another man, he mistrusted me. He thought that to be gay was to be immoral. Besides, I wanted children."

"When he married again he managed to have Philip and me," Ann reminded her, knowing very well that it had been the contrast of Henry of Anjou's hot ardour that the Queen had really wanted.

Eleanor could not gainsay it. "Your mother must have been a marvel!" she said politely, and looked with pained surprise at Henry when he burst out laughing. "Well, perhaps it had something to do with it that Louis and I were first cousins," she allowed. "Anyway, that is why the Pope let me marry again." And she had married the fierce, ugly, red-headed man half the women in Europe wanted. The man with a name like a poem—Henry Plantagenet, Count of Anjou. She sat there, with her lovely jewelled hands in her lap, smiling back at the scandalous conflagration there had been. Then added briskly, as if to shield their young eyes from the blaze, "When the usurper Stephen died I came over here, of course, and helped your father make a united nation out of all the Saxons and Normans who were turning England into a slaughter house."

"And in return he sent you away from us," added his heir cynically. It was true that he and Richard had been abroad in their duchies most of the time, but whenever they came back they had missed her badly. If the hard-working King had hoped to bring them to heel with the spell-maker safely shut up, he had succeeded only in widening the rift he was so pathetically anxious to bridge. Save in warmth of colouring and temper, they were never his.

"It was partly my own fault," admitted Eleanor. "I probably meddled too much in his affairs, and he was furious because I refused to take Aquitaine from Richard and give it to John."

"In which you were legally right," contested Henry.

But Eleanor shrugged those lonely years of stagnation into the past without rancour. She had her children, strong and splendid as the passion from which they had sprung, and she was too proud to let the world guess that her love for her husband had out-lived neglect, or that she cared so much about his lovely mistress Rosamund. "At least your father knows that men are muddlers when it comes to arranging marriages," she said lightly. "So now I am here to talk to Johanna."

Henry could be depended upon to handle a delicate situation with tact. He put away Richard's plans and picked up some samples of a new type of arrow his fletcher had just sent. "Come on, John. Let's try these out before Richard and Robin get their hands on them," he invited, leading the way up another turn or two of the stairs to where a little iron door gave access to the gatehouse roof. Ann pushed aside her embroidery frame and followed them, whispering to Johanna as she passed, "I told you so!" Hodierna, too, laid down her scissors but the Queen motioned to her to stay.

Johanna stood alone by the window trying to assimilate the full significance of her mother's words. "It is I this time!" she thought, remembering how one after the other her elder sisters and Geoffrey had gone. She heard the iron door clang behind her brothers and Ann, and by leaning out she could see the three of them spacing themselves out like a happy frieze of Youth along the battlements. The flight of their arrows and the strong wind in their hair gave them an ethereal, transient quality. Already their voices as they shouted to each other were light, unreal, far off. A sudden desolation gripped her. She felt that she must follow them—mingle carelessly with them again—or some part of her would die.

Even when Hodierna reminded her that the Queen was waiting, Johanna withdrew her shoulders from the window embrasure with a reluctance that caught at her mother's heart. More than all her daughters this youngest—vivid, headstrong, generous—was the replica of her own girlhood. "You have such a wild, carefree life with your brothers," she sighed. "Nothing important seems ever to have happened to you before!"

"Important?" Johanna swung round on the two women, her hazel-green eyes wide with fear. Suddenly she was down on her knees, her hands urgent upon the Queen's. "Madam, what are you trying to tell me?"

"That the King has arranged your marriage." Eleanor had had to say those words to her two elder daughters, Matilda and Margaret, who were always languishing to the minstrels' love songs and speculating about every young gallant who came to court. It had not been so difficult then because she had known that both of them would be helped over the moment of parting by thoughts of their new importance and the dresses in their dower chests. Whereas Johanna sprang from her fondling hand as unprepared as any boy, and quite disinterested in the wedding finery her old nurse was preparing.

"No—no! I can't! Not yet," she stammered. "I haven't finished—playing." She knew it was a silly, immature sort of thing to say, and her hands made a pathetic groping gesture that included all the everyday things of her life, as if she tried to draw the familiar walls about her like a cloak.

"I know, my little love," said the Queen gently. "I remember the morning when they told me the same thing. The scent of the almond trees—the white doves fluttering against a blue sky in sunny Provence—and I had to leave it all for the cold, grey North and a man I had never seen."

"But I am so young!" breathed Johanna.

Eleanor smiled a little, comparing her with Ann. "'Tilda and Margaret were both mothers at your age!" she scoffed kindly.

"Remember, my dear, the King has been very patient because we all hate parting with you."

The girl stood almost listlessly for a moment or two. "Who—who is it?" she asked presently. Although she asked it as if the matter were of quite secondary importance, the words fell poignantly into the pleasant stillness of the room.

"The King of Sicily."

"*That* sickly old horror!" Johanna's voice croaked into sudden harshness like John's, which was beginning to break. But no gentle woman, according to Eleanor's code, could indulge in a scene. "Quiet, Johanna!" she remonstrated firmly. "You must always have known that we royal women are just political pawns. You don't suppose I wasn't terrified when I heard I was to be Queen of France, do you? And after all, Sicily is a pleasant place to live in, your new relations are half Norman, and probably William is too weakly to be unkind."

But far from being soothed, the girl was swept by sudden outraged anger. Frustration beyond her understanding shook her body. At seventeen all her blood was beating passionately to the beckoning rhythm of life. "Kind! Unkind! What does that matter?" she cried incoherently. "I wouldn't care if he struck me—if he took me by force—but I wanted a man—"

"We all do," murmured the astonished Queen, thinking perhaps of the monkish Louis.

But Johanna's young, self-betraying protest swept on. "A tall fierce-hearted, adventurous man like Richard. Someone strong enough to compel my desire, to—to lift me down from the saddle the way Robin does…" Frightened by the emotional momentum of what had hitherto been romantic fancies, shocked into realisation that they had all centred in Robin, she ran to his mother and flung herself sobbing into Hodierna's arms.

Her old nurse held her close, comforting her as no one else could, petting her with foolish, homely endearments. "It is like the way you used to cry out for something in the night, my pretty. Just another impossible dream. But you always forgot about them in the morning, didn't you, my poppet?" And across the bright, stricken head she held so tenderly to her bosom Hodierna met the Queen's surprised, questioning look, and nodded.

"It certainly was time Henry found her a husband!" thought Eleanor. "But I wish he had forgotten his foreign diplomacy for once and found her a young one!"

Chapter Four

BLONDEL DE CAHAIGNES' FIRST morning at Oxford was anything but dull. He had already laid the King's table and been sent to gather up the Duke of Normandy's arrows when John Plantagenet came rushing down the Keep stairs shouting to all and sundry, "They're coming back from Banbury! I was the first to see them from the battlements."

Instantly the whole Castle came to life. The inner bailey, drowsing before high noon, suddenly became alive with grooms and baying hounds and servants waiting to unload the pack horses. In the great kitchen the cooks hurried on the midday meal. Caught up in the general excitement, Blondel dumped his arrows on the first bench he came to in the armoury and ran out again into the sunshine, almost cannoning into John. They eyed each other with approval. "If you're Richard's new page, I'd nip in and hold his bridle before the others get a chance," advised the youngest member of the family in his most engaging manner. "He likes brisk service."

Blondel grinned his thanks and dived under the elbows of the waiting grooms just as Richard and Robin came riding in. They were followed by a bunch of chattering pages and the Steward of the royal houschold, who had taken the opportunity of replenishing his stores. Blondel looked quickly from one to the other of the two tall, bare-headed young men and found that except for their height and a certain similarity of gesture they were not in the least alike. If Richard looked the stronger of the two it was because he lacked Robin's sinuous grace. His comely head was capped by the smooth family auburn, while brown hair curled strongly from Robin's thoughtful forehead. There was no mistaking which was the Plantagenet so—although there was plenty of competition— the new page slipped in first to hold his master's horse. "Stout work!" approved Richard, amused at his enterprise. "I suppose you are young de Cahaignes?" And Blondel, who had spent so many anxious hours wondering what this man would be like, looked up with the appreciative smile that always lightened the solemnity of his face like sudden sunlight warming a grey mere. He was aware of three things he liked—virile warmth, a fine voice, and a sort of careless arrogance. He was too young to see latent cruelty in the firm mouth and in the lazy green eyes; but he did notice that Richard's uncorrupted Norman sounded almost like a foreigner's compared with Robin's or John's, and that his great horse stood a hand higher than any other man's in the courtyard. And although the other pages were full of all they had done and seen at the fair, Blondel ceased to envy them.

When the horses had been led away Richard and Robin stood by a flight of stone steps slaking their thirst while John plied them with questions. Half the garrison seemed to be crowding round, eager for news, and Blondel marvelled at the homeliness of it all and at how little it differed from home-comings at Horsted. Robin was telling them how he and Richard had put a fortune into the fair people's pockets by entering for a competition in the wrestling booth.

"Robin won, of course," interpolated Richard, lifting his face from a second mug of ale. "He threw me twice."

"I had to," explained Robin, "or the old hag would have got a ducking."

"What old hag?" asked John.

"A fortune teller at the fair. Richard promised to keep his men off her if I won."

"She was a witch," averred the men who would have ducked her.

"I doubt if there be any such thing!" scoffed Robin.

"But some of us old 'uns have seen 'em up to their devilry," persisted a gnarled old man-at-arms. "I tell 'ee, Sir, there be women who have power to cast spells on a man and make him do all manner of things against his conscience."

"Then every pretty girl I kiss must be a witch!" laughed Robin.

Blondel was so interested in the conversation that he forgot he was among strangers. "Surely there are witches aren't there, Sir?" he asked, appealing to his Duke.

But Richard was not to be drawn. "I'm sure I hope you're right, Blondel," he laughed, handing the boy his empty mug. "Because this one promises me all sorts of impossible fame."

He went indoors and called for a wash and then, inevitably, he and Robin and John went tramping up the turret stair, and the Tower room was complete, holding them all again. All but Matilda and Margaret who were married, and Geoffrey, Duke of Brittany, who had died just before his little son Arthur was born. Eleanor's best-loved son was telling her how good it was to have her back and Robin—who seemed older than any of them because he thought more for others—was showing them a ridiculous fairing he had brought for Johanna. He and John set it up on the table—two cleverly carved wooden knights, less than a foot high, who pranced and couched their lances in mock combat when one pulled the strings. But, to his surprise, instead of exclaiming, "Oh, Robin, how adorable!" Johanna thanked him with a preoccupied politeness which made the thing seem tawdry instead of droll. Johanna, who was usually such a satisfactory person about presents!"

Ann had taken up her embroidery again. The Plantagenets' demonstrative delight in each other made her feel an outsider, and she considered it bourgeois.

"What an industrious chatelaine you'll make!" praised Richard, trying to make amends for having forgotten to bring her anything from the fair. But the thought of her industry seemed to cast a gloom over his future. How much more fun, he thought, if she plagued the steward for parties and joined in forbidden boar hunts like Johanna! He kissed the cool cheek Ann offered him and, as an antidote to her gentility, took Hodierna into a bear-like hug.

"Fond woman, when are you going to make me that magic suit of mail?" he demanded.

"When I've found the herb that's proof against poisoned arrows," promised Hodierna. It was an old bargain between them. One of those threadbare inanities upon which family life is built.

"You're not even looking for it," he scolded. "Just wasting time on all this woman's gear." But as he disentangled the handle of his hunting knife from a froth of clinging white stuff Johanna said tonelessly, "It's my wedding veil."

Richard dropped the stuff as if it had burned him. "My dear infant!" he muttered, suddenly sobered.

Living less carelessly from day to day, Robin had always known that this must happen. That was why he always bought her amusing fairings and never brooches, as a lover might. And now his heart bled for her, understanding her desolate preoccupation.

They all stared at her expectantly, but when the words came she felt that she was explaining about someone else. "I know now why we have Mother back. The King wants me to marry William of Sicily."

"The swine!" ejaculated Richard.

"Which?" enquired Henry.

"Both, for that matter." Richard stood in the middle of the room, frowning and furious. "Mother—Henry—it's damnable!" he burst out. "Selling a girl to that mouldering old deathshead for the sake of a Mediterranean alliance!"

Robin stood dumbly torn. Months ago he had had to make out the marriage contract from the King's dictation. It meant the immolation of Youth's fires, but there was nothing he could say without criticising the man who had given him everything.

With a wild gleam of hope, Johanna caught at her brother's arm.

"Oh, Richard, can't you persuade him—"

Richard shook his head regretfully. For the first time he wished that he had tried to keep on better terms with his father. "Not I, my dear. Nor Henry." Untouched by the issue that absorbed them all, John kept importuning him to look at his new dagger, and as Richard took it he ruined the boy's hair and suggested good-naturedly, "Try John here. He has the royal favour."

"You're right. He almost rivals Rosamund!" broke out Henry bitterly.

They all knew that jealousy was his particular demon and that ever since Ann's brother, the Dauphin, had been crowned prospective King of France, Henry had been sensitive about the insecurity of his own title, but the unexpected outburst shocked them to silence. Richard swung round, the little jewelled knife clenched in his hand. "Shut your foul mouth!" he muttered threateningly.

"Why?" argued Henry, with cool disregard for his mother's feelings. "Doesn't everybody know the King is at Woodstock?"

As if by accident Robin moved between them, and Eleanor tapped angrily on the floor with her scarlet shoe. "Henry! Richard!" she cried, with weary disgust. "Must you be for ever snarling like curs over every stale bone?"

The moment of tension was snapped by the unexpected appearance of Blondel. He had found his way to their aerie because the whole place was seething with news which he felt that they should know—and which none of the other pages dared tell them. "The King has come home," he warned breathlessly, from the stair head.

"From Woodstock? Already?" exclaimed Ann, rising involuntarily in a cascade of scattered silks.

"I must go and see the servants," said the Queen, who always remembered to order a bath and the special dishes that he loved. But Blondel barred her way, white-faced and resolute. "Do not go down now, Madam," he begged. "He is in one of his rages. He…"

"What is it, Blondel?" she asked quietly, steadying him by her own perfect composure.

He dared not look at her. "This woman they call Rosamund has been murdered," he blurted out.

"Murdered!" The sinister word was echoed round the room.

"At last!" added Eleanor, triumphantly.

It was Ann, the quick-witted, who implored her to be more careful what she said. Her own trembling mouth was half hidden by horror-stricken hands.

"How?" Henry wanted to know.

"Poisoned, Sir."

Young John, eaten by morbid curiosity, pulled at his new friend's sleeve. "But hadn't he hidden her in some cunning bower?"

"I heard people down in the hall talking about it. It seems some malicious person had the wit to unravel a thread from the silk of the embroidery she was carrying—just as you might from those silks milady Ann has let fall."

"How damned ingenious!" exclaimed John.

"So ingenious that people will probably say it must have been by order of another woman," speculated Henry.

"Someone who was jealous?" suggested Ann.

"They're saying—" began Blondel; then stopped short, abashed at finding himself the centre of their interest. It seemed fantastic that he—the new page—should already be playing a role in this Plantagenet drama. He went down on one knee with his burning face hidden against the scarlet of the Queen's skirts. "They are saying that you yourself had most cause, Madam. Some malicious gossip has spread it all over the town—" he reported shakily, and was thankful when a concerted murmur of indignation stemmed his words.

"He will send her back to Salisbury for this!" wailed Johanna.

"Now, by God's heart, hasn't he insulted her enough?" cried Richard, making for the stairs. But the Queen herself was there before him. She winced at the muttered guardroom oath with which he cursed his father, but countered it with laughter. It was not the first time she had averted something approaching parricide by bringing her family's heroics down to everyday sanity.

"What *can* you see to laugh at, Madam?" reproved Hodierna.

"The silk, my dears!" explained Eleanor, looking back at their shocked faces. "What an old fool I've been all these years not to think of it!"

Richard stood nonplussed.

"You heard what she said?" asked Ann, when they had finished staring after the Queen, and the sound of Blondel's following footsteps had died away down the dark turret.

"Of course we all heard," retorted Hodierna, turning back to her work. "And we all know it's only people with something on their consciences who need guard their tongues."

"Besides," added Henry, moving lazily from the window, "if that malicious sort of gossip means anything you had as much cause for jealousy yourself."

The French girl, conscious of the shrewdness of his glance, began putting away her embroidery. "Sometimes I hate you so much, Henry, I hope you will die young!" she said, with one last vindictive thrust of her needle.

He smiled imperturbably and, crossing to the littered table, began playing with Hodierna's great shear-like scissors. "I don't mind going when the Almighty sees fit to oblige you, of course," he drawled. "But poisoning, I'm told, is becoming quite a pretty art in France!"

They were always sparring like that, but Richard became aware of some unusual tension. "What the devil d'you mean?" he asked, pushing between them.

Henry dropped the scissors and the light, mocking tone he always adopted with Ann. He surveyed his brother through narrowed eyes, half affectionate and half contemptuous. "To be blunt, my blind armament builder," he explained suavely, "it's high time you asked the royal old rip for your betrothed."

"God damn your insolence!"

Ann screamed as Richard lunged at him, trying to choke the words in his throat. The heavy oak table crashed against the wall, dragging work and scissors with it. The women crouched against it. Although of lighter build, Henry held him off with the cool, maddening smile on his bruised lips. Richard's eyes went light and golden as an angry, watchful cat's—the way they always changed in battle. Their auburn heads swayed levelly, and they struggled in silence save for their panting breath and the shuffling of their feet among the rushes.

When Johanna could bear it no longer she slid from the protection of Robin's arm. "Stop them now!" she begged, and he intervened instantly, dodging their blows with the litheness of some wild forest creature and parting them with such superior strength that he flung each of them to a different corner of the room.

"He's stronger than either of you!" yelled John, dancing on the stone window seat in an ecstasy of excitement.

"I ought to be strong," smiled Robin, almost apologetically. "My own father bequeathed me the muscles of a lumberer, and your father had me taught how to use them."

"Then is it because you're half a peasant that you use them only to protect old women and to keep the peace?" asked John, jumping down to start one of those interminable arguments which helped them all to bridge over the embarrassment of their ill-controlled passions.

Robin laughed his great, carefree laugh, and Richard joined in sheepishly. Johanna rescued her wooden knights and Ann her silks. Henry's first thought was for his precious plans; and even while he was wiping the blood from his mouth he remembered that there was something he wanted to ask Richard about that clever curtain wall.

"Peace!" snorted Hodierna, beginning almost automatically to put her Tower room to rights again. "I doubt if you crazy Plantagenets know the meaning of the word!"

Chapter Five

THE CURFEW HAD CLANGED from the Keep, echoing through the barbican as the drawbridge was raised for the night, and down in the town the friendly fires were damped out one by one. The King would soon be coming to bed. His servant moved softly in the bedchamber, turning back the crimson covers and setting flaming torches in two tall sconces. He opened the exquisitely illuminated missal on the prie-dieu between them, and put out a pair of riding boots for the morning. And outside, in the great hall, the King's eldest son waited.

"How long is he likely to be, Gregory?" he asked, with a touch of subservience. For after all, the incorruptible body servant of a king knows more secrets than his sons.

Gregory came down the two shallow steps, carefully closing the heavy oak door behind him. "He should be to bed early, Sir. What with his having to be up early for the assizes, and to-night being Friday—"

"I wonder what he confesses?" speculated Henry.

Gregory never speculated about his betters. Perhaps he had no need to. Instead, he crossed to the window with the dignified tread of the perfect indoor servant. Looking down on to the courtyard of the inner bailey, he was able to offer definite information. "Prince John has persuaded him to play a game of darts. It is getting dark, but I think the King must be staying to see your brother hit the bullseye."

"Then it looks as if I shall have to kick my heels here half the night," yawned Henry, stretching them towards a dying fire on the central hearth. To his annoyance, he soon perceived that he would have to kick them in company, for as the departing Gregory flattened himself politely against the serving screen, Richard and Johanna came strolling into the hall.

"Quite a deputation to-night!" remarked Henry, observing that the annoyance was mutual.

Whenever the Plantagenets wanted anything they waylaid their father at this hour when he must pass through the hall to bed. Short of climbing the half flight to the Queen's room and passing round the gallery and down by the garde-robe turret on the opposite side, he could not escape their importunities. And coming at the end of a hard day, their tactics seldom failed to enrage him.

"What do *you* want?" enquired Johanna, coming to warm her capable little hands.

Henry reiterated his constant grievance. Ann's brother Philip, who was still only a spotty weed of seventeen, had been crowned in Paris. "And if the heir to the French throne is crowned during his father's lifetime," he argued, "why can't it be done in this benighted island?"

"You're beginning to talk like Ann," said Johanna. "And what does your token crowning matter, anyway, compared with our Mother's freedom?"

"Don't worry!" he reassured her. "The King won't revenge Rosamund's death on her."

"But Blondel told us what the people are saying and that he is in one of his rages. He hasn't seen anyone but Gregory since he came in."

"Yes, he has. He's with John now, playing darts. And I rather fancy the rage was partly eyewash, my dear. He had to blame somebody."

"You think he was getting bored with this bower business and wasn't altogether sorry?" asked Richard, in the impersonal way in which they always discussed their father's love affairs.

"And probably knows the real murderer. What is *your* grievance, Johanna?"

"Sicily, of course." She looked covertly from one to the other of them. They'd ruled their duchies on the Continent and been in battle, but she knew that in their hearts they were still half afraid of their affectionate, tyrannical father. "I wish you two would let me beard him first before my courage fails!" she sighed. It was a rule of their own making that they should do so in order of age, and she did not for a moment suppose that Henry would waive his priority.

"And get the old lion thoroughly roused before I ask for Ann," teased Richard, who would probably give way to her.

"Why do you want Ann?" she asked, momentarily side-tracked from her own troubles.

Richard laughed shortly, staring into the fire. "I don't—particularly. But no man likes to look a fool. She and I have been betrothed since we were about six, and he still won't let me have her. Besides, I suppose I shall have to marry *someone*, and at least I've known Ann too long to have to pay her silly compliments."

Johanna regarded him with puzzled concern. "But you don't love her."

"My dear Johanna," remonstrated Henry, kicking the embers into a blaze, "I should have thought that after learning your own fate you would realise that the last place one looks for love is in a marriage of our kind!"

It seemed unbelievable that they should accept it so casually, like having an ugly dance partner or a fever; while to her it was everything—and final. But then, of course, for a man it was so different. "Oh, well, you can always shut her up in one of your grimmest castles with her everlasting needlework and ride off on a crusade or something. And I suppose her dowry would come in useful," she agreed.

"If I ever get it!" said Richard. "I'm sure the King is holding up my marriage because of John."

Johanna went and sat by the narrow window from which she could watch the filial little scene in the courtyard. John must have said something excruciatingly funny because the page who was scoring was doubled up with laughter, and even the servants were tittering as they stooped to pick up the darts. Although he often got them punished, they liked him because he listened to their gossip and mimicked the priests and learned professors who thronged the town. He had none of his brothers' fierce, competitive pride, and his cheerful acceptance of defeat in the darts contest had flattered his middle-aged father into the mood of jocular indulgence natural to his leisure hours. "What has John to do with it?" she asked.

Richard came and set a foot on the window seat beside her. The supper torches had almost burned out and a full moon rising above the river threw a bar of silver across the floor. "Don't you see, Joan," he said, beginning to talk in the intimate way she loved, "that if Henry got killed and Ann and I had children, they would come between that little lap-dog and the throne?"

"If Henry got killed?" Her startled gaze wandered to the fair, clever face of her eldest brother thrown into relief by the flickering firelight.

"Modern warfare is such a gamble," he pointed out. "I once saw six knights wiped out by one stone from a catapult."

Johanna was too absorbed by a new idea to care about war statistics. Her gaze came back to the beloved face so near to her own. "Why, if Henry got killed you would almost certainly become King of England! 'Richard the First.'" She savoured the title slowly. "Doesn't it sound strange?"

"Not very," answered Richard lightly. "You see, I've had to think of it before—when Henry and I have been at each other's throats, mostly. It's the one thing that's restrained me from killing him when he's being clever."

He threw an apologetic smile over his shoulder and Henry—who was only half listening—grinned back without resentment. "Most ambitious men wouldn't let it restrain them!" he remarked absently.

For the first time Johanna saw these two brothers of hers not merely in relation to herself, but in relation to the world. Not just as Henry and Richard, who had played at "Christians and Saracens," but as people of great potential importance. She realised that the knowledge of their destiny must always have been in their hearts, setting them apart even from Robin, and that the loneliness they shared forged them together more strongly than their feuds of temperament drove them apart. "Don't you want to be king, Richard?" she asked.

The silvery half-light seemed to have softened his hard young face into unwonted thoughtfulness. "Robin thinks that kings are consecrated to their countries and ought to stay and look after their people instead of fighting abroad. And I want to lead the most efficient, best equipped crusade—"

The word "crusade" always provoked attention. "How you do listen to that madman's ideas!" interrupted Henry.

"So many people say mad when they mean new," snapped Johanna, getting up from the window seat. "Of course, Robin's kind of cleverness is quite different from yours. Much kinder, and more constructive."

Henry listened to her vigorous attack with lazy amusement. When she blazed into defensive anger like that she was quite a little beauty.

"When I *do* get my crown, I suppose you'll be wheedling me into letting you marry a tall, dark commoner," he teased, remembering Ann's spiteful innuendoes.

"It will be too late then. I shall be Queen of Sicily. Oh God, I wish I were a goatherd!"

"You'd hate their smell," he reminded her.

Johanna began pacing the floor as she and Richard both did in moments of strong emotion. "I shall tell the King I *won't* be sold like a slave to an old horror whose touch must be revolting. I'll tell him I won't be a helpless brood mare in a horrible volcano-ridden country—"

"Go to it, girl!" urged Richard, taking up a spectator's seat on one of the retainers' long tables as firm, familiar footsteps approached from the bailey steps. He had hardly said the words when the leather curtain by the serving screen was jerked sharply aside and Henry the Second stood, thick-set and capable, against a wall tapestry woven by generations of Plantagenet women to immortalise the exploits of his ancestors. At forty, there was nothing romantic about this Angevin who had once fluttered the dovecotes of Europe. His short, serviceable riding tunic was still dusty from the highways, and only a heavy-jowled bloodhound followed at his heels. With a shuddering breath his youngest daughter got up and ran to him. "Oh, Sir—" she entreated, from obeisant billows of green velvet at his feet.

"My little maid! What brings you here so late?" His deep, husky voice was kind. He stooped to raise her, caressing her cheek with strong, spatulate fingers.

It was his wrath the others feared but, being a girl, she found his kindness more difficult to bear. "This marriage—" she began bravely.

He looked pleased. "So your mother has told you our wishes? And I suppose you are wanting some new gowns and pretty gewgaws?"

Scorn of the way John traded on his affection made her slip from the comforting approval of his arm. "No, Sir. It isn't that. Because I won't—won't—"

"Be sold like a slave," prompted Richard, from his seat in the shadows behind her.

Half over-hearing him, the King turned in quick irritation and caught Henry making a gesture of ribald encouragement. His eyes were growing angry in his weather-beaten face. "My confessor is waiting, and I must get some sleep," he snapped, crossing the hall towards his bedroom.

He was going, and no one else could help her unhappiness. In her urgency, Johanna clutched at his arm. "Oh, please, please! It has all been so wonderful. The hawking on the dear English hills— the minstrels singing in the lighted hall—the fun we had when the river froze at Christmas," she implored brokenly, clutching pictures at random to illustrate the short book of her life. "Don't send me away! Don't make me marry a stranger!"

The King stopped in his straddling stride to stare down at her in amazement. The baffled, rather pathetic amazement of a parent seeing for the first time a stranger where his child has stood; humiliated, perhaps, by a glimpse of the pity with which the child has been defending him against the discovery for years. "Tch! A pack of whimsies!" he exclaimed, taking refuge in the thought-saving clichés that each generation in turn mouths at the next. "You modern girls, with your cruises to Palestine, and your hair worn without a wimple, and your new notions about choosing your own husband! I can see we have allowed you to run wild too long. It's high time you settled down with the man provided for you like your sisters before you."

The rare tears fell unheeded from her hazel-green eyes. "If I may not choose," she begged, "at least find me someone who would care for the same sort of things! Someone—younger."

"There is my friend, Sholto of Navarre," ventured Richard, who never could bear to see a woman cry.

His father turned on him with all the pent-up aggravation caused by his quarrelling on the Continent. "Are you presuming to teach me my trade? You who, with your brothers, have turned Normandy and Aquitaine into a bear garden!" he raged. "How would an alliance with Navarre help to preserve the balance of power in Europe? You irresponsible young egoists see no further than your own petty piece of the pattern; while all my life I have been preventing bloodshed by balancing power, no more able to relax than some miserable juggler in full gaze of a fair."

The querulous note of a strong man ageing had crept into the King's arresting voice. A few grey hairs had already begun to soften the aggressive colour of his hair from which his children had inherited only enough for beauty, and the energy it betokened had driven him so hard that both work and pleasure had begun to take their toll. "You think only of war, but diplomacy is the key to progress. And I ask you, where would diplomacy be without daughters?"

He turned to the one still to be bartered, not unkindly, but as if he had forgotten her tears in the vortex of things that really mattered. "Get back to your mother, girl," he ordered, "and tell her that if she cannot manage this wedding without any more fuss she may as well go back to Salisbury."

"Oh, no—not that. I will obey you," promised Johanna.

As soon as she was gone the King rounded sternly on his sons. His hot eyes glared at them, but subconsciously it was Eleanor whom he blamed. "And you two? What do you want?" he barked.

"To be crowned now—in your lifetime—like Philip Capet," said Henry.

"Full control of my lands and revenues in Aquitaine so that I can afford to marry Ann," demanded Richard, sliding off the trestle to join him.

"Lands! Lands! Lands! Till there's not a mouldering manor left for John." Reluctantly, their father came back and sat in the chair Henry had vacated. "And all this insubordinate talk about marriage...One wants to marry and another won't." He slumped a little in the chair, and his favourite old hound flopped heavily at his feet. "I am getting on for fifty now, Henry, and weary of it."

"The more reason, Sir, why you should pass on some of the responsibility to me." Henry spoke with cool restraint, but Richard was still raw from seeing Johanna hurt. "You sent me to fight for my possession of Aquitaine when I was no older than John," he stormed, "and if you will not let me rule it independently and get married, by God's beard, I will do homage to Louis of France!"

The King leaned forward, his hands clenched so tightly on the arms of his chair that the strong, golden hairs on the backs of his hands seemed to bristle with rage. "So that's how you spent your time abroad? Plotting with that young fop, Philip, against me?"

Although the feudal laws were on his side, Richard had the grace to look ashamed. "Don't I owe France fealty for it since I had it through my mother?" he argued.

"And don't you owe me some sort of reverence? How many times have I explained that with Ann in our hands still unmarried we can make better terms with France? You shall have her as soon as these disputes about her dowry are settled."

The King realised that Richard's heritage was responsible for his continental outlook and he was making an effort to be friendly to his sons. After all, he never *intended* their conversations to be unpleasant. Sometimes he overheard scraps of talk when they were with their mother—thoughts tossed as lightly as shuttlecocks and caught with inconsequent laughter, while they grouped themselves comfortably round her chair. He would have liked to talk with them easily like that, but when he tried they stood defensively polite, or drifted away to some aerie in the Tower. Only John seemed to understand his longing and stay. And John, in consequence, learned a good deal—for Henry the Second of England was a knowledgeable man, with sound civic sense. He had given opportunity of learning to them all. Already the philosophers and scientists and men of letters he had gathered together were making Oxford rival the universities of Paris and Bologna; but it was characteristic of his domestic disappointments that only Robin, the woodman's son, had profited by it. Robin studied astrology and invented all manner of useful devices for his countrymen. He had even written a book. A brilliant book about the works of nature which he loved, in which he tilted against cruelty and superstition.

When the King worked like a galley slave to give the Saxons a fair deal, rising at dawn to ride from town to town until he knew more than most of his subjects about the price of pigs or the prosperity of his ports, Eleanor laughed down her aristrocratic nose and said he was turning the English into a nation of shopkeepers. But Robin understood the international importance of trade and the social necessity of satisfied peasants. Consequently the King often wished he had been born authentic Plantagenet and kept him with his sons, hoping he would influence headstrong Richard.

But Richard seemed interested in nothing but sport and war. He was the most difficult of them all. And the most popular. He was generous, direct, and dependable—but gullible. Yes, easily gullible. The King roused himself from his reverie with a queer, secret smile. "And, I suppose, in the meantime, some of us will have to join a crusade," he said tentatively.

The magic topic, used to distract their attention, brought forth an even more startling result than he had expected. After a short silence Richard confessed with nervous aggression, "I have already taken the Cross, Sir."

The King stared as if he had not heard aright. "Without our consent?" he exclaimed. And Henry, who seldom showed his anger, said sharply, "You've stolen a march on me!"

Defiantly, Richard told them how Bishop Bartholomew had been preaching on the steps of the cathedral as he came through Tours, how his moving words had recruited hundreds and how he himself had impulsively taken the vow.

"Crusades cost money," objected his father.

"There are always women's jewels and the Jews," said Henry. "I shall go and raise some money in Normandy and come with you."

They were both amazed how well their father had taken it. "I might help you," he offered thoughtfully, seeing in it a cure for their discontent.

"That's generous of you, Sir!" said Richard, all harshness immediately forgotten.

"Better fight the Saracens than make a shambles of Europe with your quarrelling!" chuckled the King. He heaved himself out of the chair stiffly as a middle-aged man will who has spent many hours in the saddle; but when crossing the hall to his bedroom, he squared his broad shoulders as if to cast off the burden of his family's importunities before going to his own still vigorous life. "You must both have patience," he adjured, with a hand on the latch. "Put off the expense of marriage until you come back, Richard. Ann will be safer here."

"We certainly don't want any women on a crusade," agreed Henry, remembering all the cumbersome things his mother had taken.

"And this question of a coronation can wait, Henry, if you are seriously preparing for the Holy Land." Standing in the narrow archway of the door, the King looked back at them benignly and bade them good night.

They bowed formally. The door closed behind him, and he was gone. And they found themselves—as usual—no better off than they had been before.

Chapter Six

ENRY LOUNGED BACK TO the hearth, shoving the sleeping
hound aside and tipping himself backwards in the chair his
father had just vacated. "The old fox is still too cunning for
us both," he said, watching a spiral of smoke ascend to a louvre hidden
in the blackened rafters. "He threw you a cunning bait, Richard."

"A bait?" repeated Richard vaguely.

Henry shrugged impatiently at his density. "You—battering at
the walls of Jerusalem. And Ann—here."

But Richard only stared at him across the smoke. "By Heaven,
Henry, you don't really *believe* that poisonous old scandal, do you?"

"Didn't she show a pretty venom when I suggested that she had
no cause to love the fair Rosamund? Hoped I'd die young because
I've the wit to see things."

"You'd see mud on poor old Becket's shrine!" muttered Richard.
But clearly the old rumour had been bothering him.

"Well, there's no particular virtue in being entirely devoid of
subtlety. It leaves you straightforward fellows so defenceless. Why,
even Robin says it shamed his nice Saxon susceptibilities to see
Norman morality making such a fool of you!"

"Robin said *that?*"

"Funny that a peasant's words should always have more power
than mine to move you!" remarked Henry with bitterness.

"This time they'll move me to the King!" swore Richard, always
dangerously swift to act on an emotion.

With an agility usually camouflaged by a show of elegant indolence, Henry sprang to bar his brother's way. "Don't be an idiot! You daren't disturb him at his prayers."

The word 'dare' was always a goad to Richard. "What better time to get the truth?" he snapped.

Henry had not meant to provoke him into doing something to his own detriment. Ann was not worth it. "Does it matter so much?" he temporised. "I was only half serious—"

But because Robin had minded, the truth seemed to matter urgently.

Henry spread both arms across the door. "Remember, Dickon, even when we have taken up arms against him, the King always wins!" he warned, using—in his rare sincerity—his brother's boyhood name.

But Richard had out-grown submission and bade fair to become a better soldier than any of them. "We'll see," he said, shoving him aside.

For good or ill someone had forgotten to shoot the bolt. It yielded to Richard's shoulder so that he almost stumbled into the room. And what the two of them saw set an end to all need for speculation. It gave them their fill of truth. By the tall sconces at the foot of the bed stood the King, with Ann of France in his arms.

Filigree fragile she looked against his powerful breast, the torch light making a raven river of her unbound hair. For a full moment of loathing Richard watched her. Her head was flung back in laughter—malicious laughter, at his expense. "But you are clever—clever—to let him go on his old crusade—" As the door swung inwards, letting the chink of light widen to the whole intimate scene, her caressing voice came softly across the bedchamber. And then, suddenly, she was tensely aware of them. Aware of Henry, looking over his brother's shoulder with a contemptuous sneer. But most horribly aware of Richard, powerful and handsome, with hatred growing in his fierce eyes.

More slowly, warned from his ardour by her unresponsive body, the King himself became aware. He turned and saw them, and his embrace slid from her. "More of your insolence!" he stammered.

"More of your Rosamunds!" shouted Richard hoarsely.

Immobile, each chained by intensity of emotion, they held the moment of stark drama. Richard arrested on the threshold, his hands still clutching the door jamb as if their strength must be restrained from murder; the girl drawing back with trembling fingers pressed to her mouth, her august lover shrunken and silent; Henry, alone unscathed, turned fastidiously from the ugly discovery of his father's shame. He had always deplored Richard's passion for the truth.

Of course, it was the woman who invented first. "You must be drunk or crazy, Richard, to speak to your father like that," she said, trying to draw a tattered dignity about her. "I came to him only for comfort."

"You looked sad!" jeered Richard, remembering her laughter, and that other sniggering laughter which must have rippled from it down to kitchen, street, and guardroom.

She had the audacity to come to him, warm from his father's fondling, and try to tempt him back into blindness—and it was not self-protection alone that prompted her. All through her girlhood Richard had been there, casual as any brother, and his preoccupation with masculine affairs had bored her. Never once had she roused passion in him. But now, for the first time, she saw in the blaze of his betrayed anger the kind of lover he might become. All her sex subtlety called her fool, finessing for the flattery of a middle-aged man's intrigue when ready to hand was an incomparable mate. "You are always so cold to me, Richard," she accused. "And now I hear rumours that you intend to go crusading. Do you suppose that it means nothing to me that you have not asked me to come with you? To-night—in desperation—I came here to persuade the King to let us marry."

But Richard, who had come to ask that very thing, pushed her roughly from him. The belated invitation in her eyes made him feel unclean. "I want no man's leavings on my plate!" he told her.

Seeing the morsel he coveted so spurned stung the King from his confusion. "Only the rashest of your mother's whelps would dare so far!" he said thickly, the veins swelling at his temples.

But Richard's rage was beyond caution. "Keep your tongue off of her!" he said. "She is finer than all of us. Fine enough to laugh when you tried to pin on her the poisoning of your other mistress."

"Be quiet, you fool!" his brother warned.

"Oh, I've been fooled all right!" agreed Richard, laughing mirthlessly. Once and for all he would lay this foul thing, and there would be no more hateful secret laughter. "It is Ann—Ann who is young and scheming—who had more cause to poison Rosamund de Clifford," he accused.

Her pitiful pretence crumbled before his frenzy of disgust. "Send him away! Send him away!" she kept whimpering, cowering with covered eyes.

"He shall go before daylight!" vowed the King, pealing the great bell beside his bed.

That sobered Richard. "Back to Aquitaine?" he asked.

His father laughed harshly. "To plot against me again with Louis and Philip? By our Lady, no! You're too much your own master there. I'll have you sent to Navarre—a chivalrous court where you may learn less boorish manners."

Here in England his turbulent sons were still puppets in his hands. He turned to his table and wrote with bold, angry strokes, and they waited in silence while he set his seal. "Send a messenger with this to Dover immediately," he ordered, when Gregory came hurrying in. "Tell him to give it to Mercadier, the man in charge of my new castle there. He is to have the Cinque Ports prepare a ship to take the Duke of Aquitaine to Spain." It was all settled before the sand could run down in the hour glass.

Ann curtseyed low before her royal lover but he gave no sign that he had seen her. She passed between the two brothers on her way to the gallery stairs, and Gregory permitted himself the pleasure of shutting the King's door with finality behind her. "Better wake one of the grooms and tell him to have horses ready for the coast," Richard called after him, hating the man for what he must have seen and heard.

"And will you not want a squire and some of the pages to go with you?" suggested Henry.

Richard thought a minute. Knowing how the whole pack of them would be sniggering about this in the morning, he recalled the trustworthy face and sudden smile of the lad who had run so eagerly to hold his horse. "No. I'll take that new fellow, Blondel de Cahaignes, and no one else," he decided.

"He is very young, Sir," pointed out Gregory, with the decorous liberty of an old family servant.

"All the better. He won't have had time to pick up all the family scandal," said Richard grimly. "Tell him to pack my gear."

"Well, anyhow, it must be worth a compulsory change of air to have told that little trollop what you really think of her!" consoled Henry, when he and Richard were alone.

"I am finished with women!" growled Richard.

"You mean, you haven't yet begun!" rallied Henry, drawing him back to the dying fire. In spite of the curfew he threw on fresh logs and made a cheerful blaze. No English law was going to make him go to bed at dusk like a ploughboy. "You know, Dickon, it may be quite amusing in Navarre," he prophesied. "They have the best music and dancing and tournaments in Europe. None of our haphazard sort of mêlées. Properly run tournaments with judges who mark each point and all the competitors drawn by lot so that you might get a chance to try those muscles of yours against men like de Barre and the Lusignorts. And you know how well you got on with Sholto when he was here."

Richard considered the prospect. Sholto, the King of Navarre's son, had been a good sportsman. There was nothing very exciting happening in England these days, with everything so well ordered and peaceful; and only a wide stretch of sea, he felt, could wash out the foulness of Ann. "I shall see those new crossbows Sholto was always bragging about," he said, surprised to find himself talking about such trivial things so soon. Of course, if he had loved Ann it would have been different…

"Like Robin's ingenious cranes, they should come in useful for our Crusade," Henry was saying, skilfully doctoring the hurt he had caused.

Richard's thoughts easily projected themselves into the future. After all, life was just beginning and there were plenty of splendid things left. He saw himself cutting a fine figure in the famous lists at Pamplona—impressing experienced knights with his armament plans—leading a conquering army through the gates of Jerusalem. "If only I'd a couple of Arab chargers and a two-handed sword!" he sighed.

Although the Plantagenets had plenty of land and castles, their upbringing, compared with some of the princes of Europe, had been spartan. They lived hard. And Geoffrey had taken some of their best trappings and accoutrements when he married Constance of Brittany and went to rule Anjou.

"Ask young John to lend you that new dagger of his," suggested Henry.

"I'll probably look fool enough without it!" laughed Richard ruefully, and looked up to see Johanna standing at the foot of the gallery stairs. The colour was drained from her cheeks, and she had hurriedly thrown a miniver cloak over her bed robe. "Oh, Richard, is it true what Blondel says?" she cried. "That father is sending you to Navarre?"

"Quite true," he admitted. "He was furious. Our amiable pleasantries are probably already being repeated in the guard-room."

She threw out her arms in exasperation. "But why did you have to infuriate him *now*? So that you won't be there to say 'Goodbye'—when the ship takes me to Sicily?"

Richard regarded her remorsefully. "I am afraid I didn't stop to think about that. I had just found that bitch Ann in his bedroom."

"Richard! Will you still have to marry her?"

Richard shrugged the ugly matter aside. "Blondel and I start at dawn," he said. "So you and I will have to say 'Good-bye' now, my sweet."

"If it hadn't been for Blondel coming to tell me I should have gone to bed without knowing, and then…" There was a slither of soft slippers across the stone floor as she flung herself into his arms. "Oh, Richard! Richard!" she sobbed brokenly. "If only—the same ship—could take us both!"

Henry wandered to the window and began plucking at the strings of a lute someone had left there, while Richard jerked forward the chair and drew Johanna on to the arm of it. Very gently he stroked the waving bronze of her hair, so identical in colour to his own. "Perhaps one day we *will* sail together on a great warship," he comforted. "Your old Sicilian is sure to die of apoplexy when he sees you're a red head, and then I can come and carry you off on my way to Palestine."

"You always m-make an adventure out of even the h-horridest things," she sniffed, from the warmth of his comforting arm.

"Every day *is* an adventure for those who choose to meet it so. And my old witch prophesies plenty of excitement for both of us," he reminded her. "But first, I suppose, we have to win our spurs. You, when you step ashore in a strange country and have to be a credit to us. And I, in the lists of Navarre, when some knight who has fought from end to end of the Holy Land comes charging down on me and my knees are knocking against my poor horse's ribs with fright, and even the leopards on my shield turn white—"

"Richard, *you're* not really afraid?"

"Hideously."

Johanna sat up straight to stare at him in perplexity. "But no one except Robin can beat you at tilting!"

"No one *in England*," he said. "Though if you must know, Joan, it is not so much the tilting as the dancing that unnerves me. Sancho said they have more formal social occasions in Pamplona."

"Better teach him that new measure Ann was showing you," suggested Henry from the window seat.

Johanna slid to those restless feet of hers, her heartbreak momentarily forgotten. "Yes! Yes! How did it go, Henry?" she cried eagerly, picking up the heavy folds of miniver.

In his clear tenor he began to hum an infectious little dance tune, picking out an accompaniment on the lute. Johanna kicked aside the rushes to try over the steps. "Come and try it!" she urged, dragging Richard from his chair; and blunderingly, he let her guide him through the opening movements of a masque.

"Don't look so solemn about it, man!" laughed Henry, to whom such accomplishments came easily.

"And even if you *don't* do it very well, you're so ridiculously good-looking all the ladies of Navarre will want to dance with you," encouraged Johanna.

"Until all six foot of him lingers on their feet!" laughed Henry.

It was long after curfew, and the servants were coming in from the barns and kitchens to sleep. Before huddling themselves in their cloaks around the hearth, they stood in grinning groups assisting at the lesson. Sometimes they offered criticism, sometimes they applauded. The doings of the young Plantagenets were the high-lights of life to them.

"Not so bad!" decided Henry, when his brother had conscientiously mastered the steps. He winked at Johanna as he laid down the lute. "Now I come to think of it, didn't Sholto say his sister Berengaria was quite a little beauty?"

Richard let go of Johanna's hand as if she had the plague. "God help me!" he exclaimed. "Shall I have to dance with *her*?"

PART II

Navarre

Chapter Seven

KING SANCHO OF NAVARRE'S tournaments were famous throughout the civilised world. His hospitality was so lavish and the standard of tilting so high that all the most celebrated champions in Europe angled for invitations. Competitors with feudal responsibilities in cold climates were only too glad to take an annual holiday at his sunny southern court. At his laden board they met everybody who mattered; and such was the enthusiasm of the Spanish populace, the blaze of heraldry, and the stir of trumpets in his lists that even seasoned warriors could recapture something of the din and stir of battle at Pamplona.

It was fun for their womenfolk as well. Most of them were related by marriage, which made plenty of matter for a good gossip and, while lending half an ear to their husbands' everlasting sports talk, they could note what kind of wimples were being worn in Paris or Milan.

Probably the only woman who was bored was Berengaria. She was tired of being Queen of Beauty and having to crown the victors. Of course, she had only to look in the metal of her mirror to know that she was beautiful; but then, being Sancho's only daughter, she supposed that she would have been chosen had she been as ugly as a witch. Her flower-decked pavilion always looked down upon the same scene. The tiltyard thronged with people. The townsfolk crowded round the barriers of the oblong lists, leaving a gap at either end for the competitors, whose tents stretched like a field of gaily striped mushrooms to the castle walls. The groups of men-at-arms looking down from the battlements.

The guests were much the same this year as last. The same banners floated from the King's stand, the same kind of rose garlands decorated her own. Her ladies had been making them for days, and she was weary of the sight of them. Berengaria loved roses best in a garden, and hated the way Isabella and Henrietta crushed them with eager elbows as they leaned over the balcony, showing off their bright new gowns.

All the forenoon she had sat opposite to her parents, smiling at the victors and saying the right thing to important guests as they strolled past between bouts. And now the heat and clamour had given her a headache. The herald's shrill trumpeting had become an agony. She still listened politely each time the Marshal called the names of fresh combatants, but once all eyes were upon them in the lists she took the opportunity of moving farther into the shadow of the awning and surreptitiously reading an illuminated book of poems.

"Why don't you watch, Madam?" asked her youngest lady, to whom it was like all the minstrels' tales come true.

"Because I hate the sight of blood, Yvette," confided Berengaria. Not for worlds would she have had Isabella and Henrietta overhear confession of such weakness. From the front of the pavilion scraps of their conversation drifted back like a thin dissonance through the deep harmony of the words she was reading.

"That scarred knight with the black plume fought all through the last Crusade. I asked him if the Saracen girls were really so beautiful—"

"Look, Henrietta, there goes my handsome Sicilian! How he kissed me last night!"

Their voices were drowned by a fresh fanfare. This time even the booming voice of the Marshal was inaudible through the cheering of the crowd. A knight spurred across the lists, making sparks fly as he pulled his charger to its haunches before the King. Without looking up, Berengaria knew it must be William de Barre, back from the Holy Land. De Barre, making a spectacular entrance.

How she loathed the man! A proud, hard-bitten champion, who went from one tournament to another winning all the prizes.

"What do you suppose he does with them all?" Yvette was asking.

"Distributes them among his women!" Isabella told her succinctly.

At least, thought Berengaria, there is one prize he will never win. Although of bastard blood, he had had the temerity to ask for her in marriage, and it said much for her father's tolerance that he was still invited to compete. She wished that Raymond of Toulouse or someone could unhorse him. "How uninterestingly alike they all look in their armour!" she yawned. "This is the last bout before dinner, isn't it, Henrietta?"

"Yes, Madam. And if Sir William de Barre wins he will meet Count Raymond tomorrow in the final bout."

"Of course he will win," said Berengaria. "There is never anything new in these tournaments."

"There is a new foreign knight, Madam," reported Isabella, over her shoulder.

"He's riding in now. On such a sorry charger!" laughed Henrietta.

Yvette turned eagerly to look. "He is so tall!"

"And awkward," scoffed Isabella.

"And red-headed," added Henrietta. "And instead of a proper heraldic device there's just a silly sprig of broom stuck in the helmet his page is handing up to him."

Berengaria put down her book. "If he wears broom he must be my brother's friend, Richard Plantagenet. I hear he arrived late last night from England."

"That is the odd shaped island where they have fogs, isn't it?" asked Yvette, staring inquisitively at his back. "Is it true that all the men there have tails?"

The older girls' laughter covered her with confusion. Berengaria laughed too; but then she always took the trouble to explain. "Of course not, child! That's only some silly legend left over from the Dark Ages. These Plantagenets are Dukes of Normandy and Aquitaine as well as kings of England, and their mother was once

Queen of France. So you see, this young man's elder brother will be quite an important person one day."

"Well, nobody seems to know this one now," remarked Isabella, pertly.

Yvette leaned over the balcony. "He looks quite embarrassed," she murmured compassionately. Having come straight to court from her convent school she could sympathize with his embarrassment.

"Throw him your new Damascus girdle, Isabella!" giggled Henrietta.

"And have it trampled in the dust!" Isabella was not the sort of wench to back a loser. She fastened the jewelled thing more securely about shapely hips that had snared a rich Sicilian. "What chance has a raw young man like that against *real* crusaders?"

Berengaria sprang up. Indignation always had the power to override her gentle diffidence. "Is that the kind of hospitality Navarre shows to strangers?" she demanded. "How do you know he may not some day fight Saladin as well as any of them?"

By stretching out a hand she could almost have touched his shoulder. He sat his horse quietly just below her pavilion, watching his adversary's impressive showmanship. For days he had been horribly sea-sick in a single-masted galley. His arrival had been spoiled by disappointment at finding his friend, young Sholto, away; and he had not yet had time to get to know anyone else. Unfamiliar surroundings and the babel of an incomprehensible tongue confused him. "Just my luck to arrive late and get drawn against their champion in my first round!" he thought, remembering his prophecy to Johanna.

The crowd loved the way the veteran crusader loosened an experienced arm in a series of clever practice thrusts and made his mighty stallion rear and stamp to show off his fine horsemanship. Certainly, man and horse together were an impressive sight. The last word in armour with ringed mail from thigh to toe, scolloped saddle trappings of crimson leather, and a gorgeously plumed ceremonial heaume held by an obsequious squire. In the hurry of his expulsion from England poor Richard had brought no heaume at all—just a plain, tight-fitting battle helmet, a steel haubert considerably dented in the frequent wrangles for his heritage, and one slender stripling of a page.

All the same, the King of Navarre's daughter, who had been brought up to love fair play, plucked a pink rose bud from the wreath she wore and, in full view of her father's subjects, threw it deliberately—not to the seasoned warrior—but to the unknown competitor. It struck with a soft plop against his clean-shaven cheek, and he turned angrily, quieting his startled horse.

"He is quite handsome!" exclaimed Isabella, and the others laughed at the chagrin in her voice.

"I threw it for Sholto's sake," explained Berengaria, in case they might think that she too had noticed the fact.

Richard stared up at her with little gallantry. It was his first big tournament. Queens of Beauty, he had always supposed, were heartless and vain like the lady in the minstrel's ballad who threw her glove among the lions. Probably those giggling girls leaning over the balcony were out to make a fool of him because they knew he hadn't a dog's chance. Young Blondel, quick to cover his discourtesy, saved the blossom from an impatient hoof and handed it up to him.

Trumpets blared and de Barre bellowed a challenge. With a vicious spur he urged his stallion to the attack. And still the tall Norman stared rather incredulously at the dusty petals in his mailed palm.

"Oh, hurry, hurry!" breathed Berengaria.

Richard looked up then and grinned reassuringly. So it was true. Someone wanted him to win. The slender rose girl with the kind eyes who looked as if she had walked straight out of the lovely Provencal legends his mother used to tell. He leaned to Blondel for his shield, and the Spanish sunshine glinted on the gold leopards snarling across its blood-red surface. Like a lean, crouching leopard himself, he balanced his lance to get some favourite grip, then clapped down his vizor and charged.

Towards him in a cloud of dust thundered his man. Even to Richard's optimistic mind it looked as if such a mountain of steel and muscle must mow him down. "God help me not to disappoint that rose girl!" he prayed, swerving in time to take a glancing blow that, at full force, would have felled an ox. The force of it shook his confidence. This was the real thing. "Just because I'm supposed to be pretty good at home—" he thought, picturing his pride humbled in the dust before all this assembly of international sportsmen. King Sancho's shout of "Well saved!" helped to steady him.

As he wheeled his horse, Richard overheard a critic by the barrier say, "Hopelessly outclassed in weight and experience, of course, but he has youth and speed..." Acting on the hint, he used both to forestall by the fraction of a second each cunning ruse of his opponent. The Frenchman no longer fought contemptuously. In the second encounter he paid Richard the compliment of fighting furiously. He had seen a favour flung by a girl whose high birth had put her out of his own reach, and he was out to kill.

But Richard's eyes had gone light with the lust of battle, his brain cold as ice. He settled closer in the saddle to enjoy the one kind of game at which he was master. The spectators began to shout wildly each time he dodged death, but he was no longer conscious of them. Concentration had come back to him. His whole world was whittled down to one arena where two horsemen wheeled and thrust. Yet, fantastically enough, part of his mind was back in England where he had practised these very strokes beside the placid Thames. If only he could believe himself back there, delivering them as coolly and unhurriedly as he had then, he felt that he might win. It was Robin's voice—a thin, controlling memory—that gave him patience and precision now. "Wait, man—wait! Any fool can strike. It's choosing the moment that counts." And then Robin himself—part of the placid river and the sturdy oaks—showing him that clever counter-thrust. "Let the other fellow go all out. And *now*—when he has over-ridden himself—"

In each encounter Richard's timing was perfect. The intoxication of success was upon him. He felt the crowd with him at last. A lovely crowd, appreciative of all the finer points, and generous in praise. His famous adversary was tiring. Past the peak of his prime and a gross liver, de Barre must have realised that he could not stay another round against such fitness. He came on like a maddened bull, blind with rage. Now—now was the moment. Richard stood in the stirrups and drove his lance home with all his strength.

Berengaria covered her face with her hands. She could not bear the sight of blood. She heard a crescendo of hoof beats, the crash of steel and splintering wood. A sibilant intake of breath passed like the rustle of stiff ripe corn across the crowd. The silence that followed was split by a man shouting hoarsely, "My God, de Barre is in the dust!"

"Only his armour saved him!" chanted the delirious crowd.

"The lance broke against it with such force that it slid down and pierced the Plantagenet's own horse," moaned Yvette, in a sick, shuddering heap at Berengaria's feet.

Seasoned crusaders leapt to their feet and women wept hysterically. Lusty men-at-arms cheered and countrymen threw their capuchins in the air. When Berengaria dared to look, the great, invincible de Barre was lying in the middle of the tiltyard. His heaume had fallen off, its fine plumes matted in a stream of blood flowing from the belly of his opponent's horse. As he rolled on to his back the muscles of his bull neck bulged obscenely from the restriction of the gorget that had saved him. And standing over him was the tall Plantagenet, swinging a great two-handed sword. He had pulled it from the vanquished Frenchman's scabbard. Mercifully for de Barre, King Sancho's baton clattered into the lists before the point had time to reach his throat. Richard lowered it reluctantly. It was just the kind of sword he had been coveting, and would make a good souvenir of a splendid fight.

Chapter Eight

AFTER THE SPECTACULAR BOUT in which the great de Barre
was brought low all was clamour and confusion. People
shouted and took up their bets and jumped the barriers.
Heralds and judges vied with each other in proclaiming names and
achievements of the morning's victors. A whole army of grooms
seemed to spring into the lists, and quite important people helped
to lift the vanquished champion from the ground. "Just as well I
didn't finish him off!" thought Richard. "But no man ought to have
a neck like that." Now, just why had he hated it so? Something to
do with a girl…He was still leaning on the tall sword feeling oddly
tired when he became aware of a pleasant, stocky young man who
was wringing his hand and wishing him luck in the next bout.

"I am glad it will not be until to-morrow!" panted Richard. "Do
you know this Raymond of Toulouse I have to tilt against next?"

"Quite well."

"Is he anything like this one?" Richard waved a vague hand in
the direction of the group gathered round his late opponent.

"God forbid!" The words, were said with such amused friendliness that Richard laid aside all defensive pretence. "What I mean
is, have I a chance?" he asked simply.

"I'd say it ought to be a pretty good fight," laughed the young
man. "You see, I *am* Toulouse."

Involuntarily, Richard shot out a hand. "Splendid!" he cried,
and would have liked to stay and talk. But a squire was already

at his elbow, respectfully summoning him to the King. He could see the Queen's women, like a bright parterre of multi-coloured flowers, beckoning to him with their handkerchiefs. The sweets of victory awaited him. But first he stooped to gentle his dying horse. "You carried me well, old friend," he whispered. At sound of his voice the poor beast whinnied pitifully, and he bade Blondel have it put out of pain.

Elation was tinged with gaucherie as he approached the royal stand. But a new world was opening before him. A world in which he was somebody, apart from his title. A world full of friends. Richard rose to their approval with youthful flamboyance and, to his relief, found that most of them spoke Norman-French. Men stretched across each other's shoulders to grip his sword-hand, and women threw him flowers. "Where did you learn that counter-thrust?" asked the jovial king, and Richard found himself telling them about his small military successes in Aquitaine and about Robin's prowess in England. Friendship with Philip of France might be a profitable business proposition, he reflected, but a few words of praise from Sancho of Navarre set the seal on a sportsman's record.

"Time to collect your laurels, mon brave!" Toulouse reminded him. Friendly hands pushed him towards the Princess's pavilion. He took the short wooden steps at a bound and stood smiling down at her. "I cannot reach. You will have to bend down," she reminded him, under cover of the cheering.

"I am already at your feet," swore Richard, dropping to one knee. "Without your rose I'm sure I couldn't have tackled that blustering son of Mars!"

From beneath demurely lowered lashes, her brown eyes laughed down at him. "Why, I thought you were sent here to learn pretty speeches!"

"I suppose some busybody had to tell you that!" he muttered, hating his father for the humiliation.

Berengaria was quick to set him at ease. "I assure you that no one outside the family knows the King of England was—displeased. A pity he did not see you just now. He would have been very proud. I wish you good luck against the Count of Toulouse."

"I shall need it, Madam," he said, as he rose to face the cheering crowd. "Unfortunately, I shall also need a horse."

They spoke to each other formally, going through the ceremonial motions required of them; but the cheering was gradually dying down. The eventful morning was over. The royal party began to drift back towards the private apartments for a meal and the noonday siesta. Berengaria should have followed them, but she made a gesture of dismissal to her ladies. "Go and get the head groom to ransack the stables for the best mount he can find for the Duke of Aquitaine. I fancy my brother's roan mare might be up to his weight. And fetch our visitor a cooling drink, Yvette."

Left alone among the flowers and the banners, they turned to each other in smiling relief, formality falling from them like a discarded cloak.

"So you are Berengaria?"

"And you are Richard?"

"I've heard quite a lot about you."

"When Sholto came back from England he nearly drove me insane with the repetition of your name."

"I know, for instance, that you adore dancing and that you fell shamelessly in love with the Archbishop of Rheims when you were six—"

"And I know that you are always inventing hideous war machines, and that when you were twelve you created a vast hue and cry by shutting your small brother up in a dungeon, and then going out hawking and forgetting all about him."

"He was supposed to be a captured Saracen, and anyhow he has a morbid interest in dungeons," laughed Richard. Shopkeepers and housewives were hurrying home through the barbican to their affairs in the town and a group of children and holidaymakers were gathered round a travelling puppet show by the gate. Berengaria drew him to the wide wooden rail of the balcony beside her, and Yvette brought him a drink. Laying aside his laurels and helmet, he pulled off a gauntlet and stretched his long legs at ease. "To the Queen of Beauty!" he said, lifting the goblet.

"You were wounded!" cried Berengaria, seeing a long red gash on his uncovered wrist.

"Oh, that!" He examined it with mild interest. It was the first time he had noticed it. "Must have been a splinter from the broken lance."

"But there's blood."

"My page will bind it up presently," he assured her carelessly.

"But afterwards is no good.'"

He did not want to waste time now fussing about bandages, but Berengaria insisted, "Fetch me some water and a napkin, Yvette," she ordered; and when they were brought she firmly overcame her aversion, cleansing and binding the gash as carefully as if it had been some deep seated wound. Richard watched her ministrations with amusement. He was not accustomed to being fussed over by women. "One of these days, Richard Plantagenet, " she warned, between anxious pullings and twistings, "you will leave a wound too long—and it will fester. And then perhaps—you will die." Her dark head was close against his breast and, looking up to meet his amused grin, she became aware that her preoccupation had landed her almost in his arms. At such close quarters he was disturbingly attractive. "Oughtn't we to be joining the others now?" she said hurriedly.

Except for grooms rubbing down the horses and the people gathered round the puppet show, the outer bailey was deserted. Even Yvette was half way to the drawbridge that divided it from the inner bailey—a charming, childish figure carefully balancing a basin. But Richard was exceedingly comfortable where he was. "All I need now is rest and quiet—and pleasant companionship," he bluffed gravely.

"But you said yourself it was only a scratch." She tried to pull him to his feet, but he only imprisoned her little hands and sat there, laughing. "Oh, Richard, we *must* go!" she urged. "My parents will be wondering—Look, here's Raymond coming for me."

They could see him crossing the drawbridge. He paused to question Yvette, who pointed back in their direction. Berengaria picked up her beautiful white dress and ran to meet him; and Richard had perforce to stride along beside her, wondering why he had ever liked the man.

"Is my mother angry?" she panted, pink cheeked.

"Livid!" teased Raymond. "But seriously, my dear, you ought to come in and rest."

"I will," she promised meekly.

"There is sure to be an interminable banquet, and then all the music and dancing."

Their air of friendly intimacy drove Richard to an unprecedented expedient. "Will you dance with me to-night, Berengaria?" he asked abruptly. "I'm afraid I dance very badly." Henry and Johanna would have given their ears to hear him.

"As you may remember, I dance rather well," the Count reminded her.

"I will remind Henrietta about it," laughed Berengaria. "For myself, I prefer a beginner with the saving grace of modesty."

The two men stood side by side to watch her go. When she had waved from the bridge Raymond noticed the bandage. "What's the damage?" he asked. "Nothing bad enough to keep you out of the final, I hope?"

"Lord, no! But Berengaria insisted upon binding it," bragged the morning's victor.

"She would, bless her!"

"Do you infer that she makes a habit of binding up men's wounds?" enquired Richard, stiffly.

Raymond tried not to smile. "I wouldn't say that. But she's ridiculously tender-hearted with people whom she *likes*." He disarmed Richard's scowl with a humorous shrug. "Like the rest of you, I am her slave," he explained. "But I also happen to be her cousin. So you needn't murder me *outside* the lists."

Richard felt a graceless fool. He grunted an apology and hailed Blondel from the direction of the stables. "He's been seeing about my poor beast," he explained. "I'll be getting my mail off and have a wash."

"Come and use my tent," invited Raymond. "It's bad luck for you Sholto being away."

Richard was only too glad to accept the invitation as the Keep was packed with visitors.

"There were a good many things I should have been glad to ask him this morning," smiled Richard, as they strolled through the lists to the tents at the far end. "For instance, why do all the men who've been crusading wear a sort of white surcoat over their armour?"

"Because of the sun out there. The steel gets unbearably hot. Haven't you been here before?"

"No. The place amazes me. It's all so different from how we live." He looked at the sentries slouching in the shade and noted that the drawbridge was obsolete. "I keep wondering what they'd do if they were besieged," he said. "Do you suppose they grow flowers on the battlements?"

"Not quite," smiled Raymond. "But you must remember they haven't had a war down here for years. That's why they are all so delightfully civilized. The King has time to see that you don't really kill de Barre, and Berengaria reads books."

In his cousin Sholto's absence, the Count of Toulouse was roped in for a variety of hospitable duties. "Hi, there, Nando!" he shouted into the interior of his tent, before hurrying off on some other social errand. "Wake up and fetch the Duke of Aquitaine some water."

Nando was fat and the well was in the Keep. He didn't see why the Duke's own energetic page shouldn't get it, but Blondel was already on his knees struggling with leather thongs. Besides being unbearably set up about his master's victory, he had the soul of a budding poet and understood that any man to whom a beautiful girl throws roses wants to meet her at dinner looking his best. He seized the filled ewer from the sulky young Spaniard and poured its contents over his master's naked body, then requisitioned for him one of their host's clean shirts and set Nando to polishing the Plantagenet leopards. And all the time Richard—usually the soul of good-natured indifference where clothes were concerned—cursed and fidgeted and fussed. "These cloth chausses are too clumsy to the leg…I need another shave…

Nobody wears a nose piece to his helmet nowadays. Take the damn thing off. I'll go bareheaded…"

"What a pig to work for!" remarked Nando, when at last they had cleaned him up and sent him forth fit to feast with ladies. Had either of them understood more than six words of the other's language it would probably have started a Toulouse versus Plantagenet fight before the final.

Chapter Nine

THE BANQUET, AS RAYMOND had prophesied, was interminable. At any rate, it seemed so to Richard. Being only a second son, he was placed at one of the side tables between Henrietta and a fat bishop; whereas Raymond of Toulouse sat at the family table with the principal guests. Not only was he Berengaria's cousin but his province adjoined Navarre. Richard found it tantalizing to hear their laughter and not be able to join in their jokes. His own conversation in Spanish was as limited as Blondel's, so he was glad when the servants began clearing the tables. "What is this game they are preparing to play?" he asked Henrietta, when King Sancho had risen and the trestles were set against the wall.

"'Hoodman Blind,'" answered Henrietta, explaining it in dumb show. "You know. The one where all the men wear a capuchin back to front and have to catch a girl. I'm sure to get caught with a dress that rustles like this."

But Richard did not avail himself of the hint. He borrowed Blondel's capuchin, cut two holes in it and managed to steer a tolerably straight course through groping men and shrieking girls to the window recess where Berengaria sat talking with Raymond.

"My quarry, I think!" he interrupted in a muffled voice, seizing her wrist.

"Really, Richard!" laughed Berengaria.

"A little too swift to be plausible, my friend!" accused Raymond, releasing him from the hood and poking two searching fingers through the holes.

"Don't tear it any more, Toulouse," besought Richard, smoothing his ruffled hair. "I borrowed it from my page."

"That nice boy with the long lashes?" asked Yvette, who was standing beside them.

"I can't say I've noticed his eyelashes, but he seems pretty capable."

"I must mend it for him," she promised, rescuing the thing from Raymond.

"Do you always cheat at games?" asked Berengaria.

"I had to get away from a repulsive bishop and a girl who giggled."

"I have to put up with her all day," said Berengaria. "*And* with this incurable chatterbox. She has nearly exhausted me talking about your fight."

Face to face with her new hero, Yvette became covered with confusion. "At least she speaks very good Norman," commended Richard.

"She went to school in Normandy. What was the name of the place, Yvette?"

"Fontevrault, Madam."

"Fontevrault!" repeated Richard. "Where the nuns grow such beautiful roses, and the Abbess is a delightful old aunt of mine with hands like a carved ivory saint. Were you happy there?"

"Oh, yes. You sound as if you knew it well. Have you been there often?"

"Never in my life, Yvette," he said, smiling at her eagerness. "But I shall one day."

"How do you know, Sir?"

"Because we Plantagenets are all buried there."

"Of course, I remember. Rows of richly carved tombs with a lovely chantry—"

"Then I hope you won't go for a long time!" Berengaria shivered involuntarily, in spite of the heat. "These games get so frightfully rough and noisy," she added, seeing de Barre's bulk approaching them through the crowded hall. "Shall we go outside until the dancing begins?"

"Aquitaine wants to know if you grow flowers on the battlements," said Raymond, batting the eyelid nearest to Richard.

"We might, if it wasn't for the Captain of the Guard," laughed Berengaria. "But I have a rose garden under the chapel wall. Would you care to see it?"

"Anything connected with roses, after this morning!" declared Richard. "And perhaps while we are out there you could show me that horse you promised to lend me for to-morrow?"

Berengaria spread palms that appealed expressively to high Heaven. "How *English*! Did you hear, Raymond? A girl offers to show him a rose garden and all he is interested in is a horse!"

"Well, show it to him. Then I can tell your mother quite truthfully that you are looking after the comfort of one of her guests," said Raymond, preparing to head off the advancing de Barre with an irritating enquiry after his wound.

❧

It was cool and peaceful in Berengaria's rose garden. The chanting of Compline mingled pleasantly with the evensong of birds. A westering sun reddened the housetops of Pamplona and made the tents and banners set up round the lists look all aflame.

"I felt such a fool down there this morning," said Richard, producing her crumpled rose bud from his wallet. "Why did you throw me this?"

"For the hospitality of Navarre," said Berengaria, sitting down on a low wall.

"I had hoped it was because you liked me." Like the rest of men who had done well, he was in the mood for fighting his battle over again. "Anyhow, it made all the difference," he said, pacing up and down before her. "What with a hostile crowd."

"Not hostile. They just didn't know you."

"Well, they got to know me before the finish. After I winded him they veered right round, didn't they? I suppose it *was* a pretty good fight to watch."

Berengaria did not rise to his boyish bragging. Probably she had to listen to a surfeit of it at tournament time.

"Didn't you enjoy watching it?" he insisted.

"No. I hated it. Your poor horse—"

"Oh, I see. You would sooner it had been I?"

But Berengaria was bad at hurting people, even when they deserved it. "How can you be so stupid? The humiliating fact is," she confessed, with a conciliating hand on his arm. "I hate the sight of blood."

He stared down at her in surprise. "But you bound up my wrist."

"I know. One has to be bigger than one's dislikes."

"Even without a cheering crowd? Unilluminated sort of courage. Like Robin's. Mine is a cheaper sort."

"Who is Robin?"

"My foster brother. You are rather like him. You do the same sort of things—not because you want to."

"Want to! A woman has to forget the things she wants to do if she has the misfortune to be born a king's daughter." Berengaria spoke bitterly, looking back at the lighted windows of her stately home. A slim, horned moon rode in silver serenity between two turrets and a young soldier with a lute chose that moment to begin serenading one of the maid servants in impassioned Spanish. "The people have stolen our private lives," went on Berengaria, with low vehemence. "Now, while we are living them—and afterwards when they hand us down to posterity neatly labelled with the verdict of popular prejudice. Oh, I know they enjoy staring at us, poor things. But we have to pay for their cheers with ceremonial weariness and for our picturesque lives with miserable marriages!"

"That's what poor Johanna says."

"She was still struggling with Latin verbs when Sholto was in England. But he said she was like a flame. I see now what he meant."

"He probably meant she was an undisciplined young hoyden. Hawking and deer hunting aren't enough for her. She wants to do everything that we do. I verily believe she would go to war if our parents would allow it. You should see her in a borrowed suit of John's trying to stick a boar!"

"Surely your father doesn't let her?"

"He is away from home a good bit. But he nearly caught her once when riding past us on his way back from some musty law court or other, 'Who's that new blond page over there?' he asked. Robin pretended she was his. He had the presence of mind to clout her over the ear and send her back for a brace of birds. So she got away with it without a beating."

"Robin sounds a dear! I hear Johanna is to marry the King of Sicily. How she will miss you all!"

"She will probably have sailed by the time I get back. It will be dreary without her. Even the scullions adore her." He roused himself from the gloomy prospect to chase a little lizard from the vicinity of Berengaria's foot. "Have they chosen a husband for *you* yet?"

"They are still haggling about my dowry as if it were of more importance than my disposition."

"Who is the lucky man who will get both?"

"I don't know yet. Does it matter very much?" She looked away towards the Pyrenees, outlined against a last pale streak of sunset. "Just the name of some politically desirable state for which I must desecrate my most sacred dreams!"

"Suppose it were some man you could care for?" suggested Richard. Having a sister of his own, he realised how unfair life could be for a girl.

But Berengaria was not to be comforted. "Suppose that moon up there were to fall!" she scoffed.

"But there must be some ordinary, decent princes about," he urged. "Fellows like Sholto or—or myself, for instance."

"Modest, aren't you?" laughed Berengaria. "And anyhow Philip of France won't let you dodge his sister, and my father wouldn't hear of a husband for me who wasn't at least *heir* to a throne."

"I could go home and murder Henry," he offered obligingly.

Berengaria's pansy brown eyes were mocking him again. "It's just sweet of you, Richard. But I'm afraid you'd make a very bad murderer."

"What! Didn't I show you this morning that I can strike?"

"Yes. But you'd probably strike in the middle of some market place and then tell the world how beautifully you'd done it."

"You *do* seem to have summed me up rather well!" he laughed ruefully.

"So well that I even know you entertain your *special* friends with songs you have composed yourself." She leaned over the garden wall and beckoned to the disappointed serenader. "If you want your wench to get some time off after the party, Cervantes," she bargained, "come here and lend us your lute!"

The love-lorn young man came eagerly.

"I'll wring Sholto's neck for this!" muttered Richard, red to the ears. But she pushed the lute into his unwilling hands. "You owe me a song for the rose," she insisted.

"In gratitude for that I would have spared you the pain of my voice," he grumbled. But there was nothing else for it and, however unworthy the song, he knew there really wasn't anything wrong with his voice. In his nervousness, the few elegant ballads in his repertoire eluded him, so after plucking uncertainly at the strings for a few moments he plunged full-throatedly into some doggerel that had become a guardroom favourite at home.

> *"Give me a sword of shining steel,*
> *A camp fire and a song,*
> *And I will strew with Saracens*
> *The plains of Ascalon."*
> *"Give me a horse and—"*

"But that's all about war!" interrupted Berengaria, both hands clapped to her ears.

Richard stopped, affronted, the lute swinging from his hand. "Of course. Of what else should a fellow sing?" he demanded.

Berengaria uncovered her ears and began picking delicately at some moss in a crevice of the wall. "Men *have* sung about me," she said, smiling up at him from beneath dangerously curled lashes.

"Oh, you mean love songs? I never tried to make any." He ambled about among her roses, twanging the long suffering instrument uncomfortably. Out of the tail of his eye he could see its ardent owner grinning, and it riled him that such a slip of a girl could tease him so. "Very well, how is this?" he asked, brightening with sudden inspiration. He came back and struck an attitude beside her, burlesquing the Spanish lover. To the same old guard-room tune he sang,

> *"Give me a lute and I will show*
> *How kind your small hands are!*
> *Give me your heart before I go*
> *Dear lady of Navarre!"*

Berengaria sprang up, clapping her hands delightedly. "Not so bad, Richard! Not so bad! It seems you are learning quite a lot in Pamplona."

Richard said nothing. Somehow the mockery had faded out of the last two lines of his parody. He knew that he *was* learning something new—the best thing in life probably—something he had scarcely believed in. Something so elusive and beautiful that a man could go on working and fooling for years without experiencing the thrill of it. Until one day some woman smiled at him so that, without touching her, he could feel her taking possession of him, body and soul. And then all his conceits and infidelities would be jettisoned, leaving only humility and desire…

"Don't stand there dreaming!" badgered Berengaria, with the cruelty of unawareness. "Give the man back his lute and come and show me if you can dance as well as you sing."

He knew very well that anything more than friendship between them was forbidden, impossible. He must make this growing attraction stop now before she, too, got hurt. "I told you—I dance very badly," he said gruffly.

But she caught at his resisting arm. "I'll try to bear it with that unilluminated courage of mine!" she promised gaily. She had forgotten all about her headache, and he had forgotten his horse.

They danced until de Barre glowered and the King called her to partner a proud prince of Aragon. "Afterwards perhaps?" whispered Richard, letting her go.

"There are so many important people!" she sighed.

If he had had any sense he would have abandoned hope and responded to Henrietta's roving eye. But what had first love and a Spanish summer night to do with common sense? And what Plantagenet, having held perfection in his arms, could cure himself with second best? He was still mooning after her from a window embrasure when his page came looking for him with an urgent message.

"The Duke of Aquitaine—where is he?" he was asking right and left as he pushed his way through the crowded hall.

Either people did not know or he did not understand what they told him until a girl said in Norman, "Over there, by that window. Glaring at every man who speaks to my princess."

Blondel resented the implication that his master, who had scored in the lists, could be a wallflower at a party. "Nonsense!" he said. "Half these man-snatching Spanish women would give their girdles to dance with him!"

"I am a Spanish woman myself," said Yvette, drawing up her five foot nothing of offended dignity.

"But you speak Norman. And what are you doing with my hood?"

"I was going to mend it."

For the first time he really looked at her. A flaxen girl with blue eyes and a dimple, rather like the thanes' daughters with whom so many Normans intermarried at home—only much more animated. "That is exceedingly kind of you," he said. "And I'm sorry if I was rude. It's pretty harassing looking after an impetuous man in a strange country and I don't know anyone yet, except the Count of Toulouse's fat page."

"And *he* won't put himself out much to help you."

They stood smiling at each other, jostled by the shifting crowd, until the memory of his errand drove them apart "A message from *Normandy?*" repeated Richard, bestirring himself as soon as he was told, and following Blondel out into the dark courtyard. "It must be from my brother Henry."

Chapter Ten

YVETTE ROSE AT DAWN to darn Blondel's hooded cape. The nuns of Fontevrault had taught her to sew exquisitely. All the same, she had barely finished by the time Berengaria had begun to dress for the final day of the tournament. And Berengaria was almost as fussy about her colour scheme as Richard had been about his clothes the day before.

"I look hideous in this gold surcoat!" she declared, flinging the costly thing across the ladies' bower.

"But the Queen had it made specially. She said for anyone dark and pale—"

"I am not pale," snapped Berengaria.

It was true enough. There were roses in her cheeks that morning. So patient Yvette brought out the blue brocade.

"Not that. I hate it!"

"But only yesterday morning you said—"

"Yesterday is not to-day. Besides, it needs a fastening. I suppose you spent the time mending that page's hood?"

What with unaccustomed late hours and her mistress's rare displeasure, poor Yvette was near to tears. "I did it in my own time, Madam," she said.

"Oh, I know. I'm sorry, Yvette." On her way to the window Berengaria stooped to kiss the girl. She could see the people of Pamplona flocking to the lists and little puffy white clouds drifting lazily across the blue sky. It was a long time since she had felt so excited about a tournament. "After all, I think I'll wear the white again," she decided.

Her youngest lady fetched it joyfully. "I'm so glad. I love you in that. And everybody said yesterday they had never seen you look so lovely."

Berengaria picked up her mirror to make sure. Exile, dowries, marriages—what did they all matter? They were a long way off. Whereas here was to-day—and to-morrow and to-morrow. "I must look my best for the final bout," she explained, dividing her attention between mirror and window like the luckless Lady of Shalott. "Look, the people are taking up their places already, and the grooms are bringing out some of the horses. Your Anglo-Norman page is down there, with that roan of Sholto's. I'm so glad someone remembered about it. And Nando is leading a pack horse. I wonder what that is for."

"Someone going away perhaps," suggested Yvette, down on the floor with her mouth full of pins.

"Not just before the best joust of all, surely!"

"I do hope the Duke of Aquitaine will win again!"

"You little traitor!" laughed Berengaria. "Why, only the day before yesterday you were backing my cousin."

"Blondel says there is only one better all-round sportsman in England. He is very handsome, don't you think, Madam?"

"Very," said Berengaria, smoothing a delicate eyebrow.

"And his voice—" Yvette gave a tweak here and there to the white samite.

"Dios mio!" laughed Berengaria, pirouetting for a final inspection. "I'm afraid it might beguile a girl into all kinds of foolishness."

"And then, of course, his hair—like pale gold!"

"Pale gold? But it is almost red!" Yvette sat back on her heels to stare and Berengaria, red with confusion herself, put down her mirror with a bang. "Oh, go and finish your mending, do!" she ordered, realizing that they had each been thinking of a different man.

"It's finished, Madam. Blondel said he wanted it this morning," said Yvette, stifling her mischievous laughter. She jumped up to take a swift peep from the window. "Do you think I might take it down to him?"

"Oh, I suppose so," smiled Berengaria indulgently. "I shall have to wait here in any case until Isabella and Henrietta come back from the garden with the fresh rosebuds for my wreath."

Left alone, she turned back to the window, humming a half-remembered tune. Raymond was down there, punctual as usual, standing in the middle of an animated group discussing some last minute alteration with the Marshall. She could see Yvette run past him with scarcely a glance, making for the patch of shadow where Blondel and Nando were holding the horses. The tall roan was stamping impatiently for her rider and Berengaria found herself sharing the same impatience. Any minute now he would come out into the courtyard, striding with that long, soft tread of his, beckoning arrogantly for his page. "Give me your heart before you go—" sang Berengaria, realizing suddenly what tune she had been humming all morning, and stopping abruptly at the sound of hurrying footsteps on the stairs. "Well, Isabella," she called over her shoulder, "have you stripped all my best bushes?"

There was no answer—only that long, soft tread behind her. She turned swiftly, with tumultuously beating heart. "Richard! What are you doing here?" she cried; for rarely did any man less nearly related than Raymond find his way to the room she shared with her women. But, taken off her guard like that, there was no mistaking the joy in her voice.

He came straight to her, taking both her hands in his. "I had to find you," he said urgently. His face was set and white beneath the southern tan, and she noticed that he wore a plain and serviceable riding cloak. "Where is your armour?" she stammered. "Are you not going to tilt?"

He hardly seemed to hear her. "I had to come here," he reiterated. "They meant to be kind down there. But they talked and talked. And all the time I was planning how I could see you before I go."

"Go!" she echoed, all those sunny to-morrows drifting out of sight like the little puffy, white clouds. When he let go her hands she felt weak and empty.

He began padding back and forth. "It's about Henry," he said, in a stunned sort of way. "You remember what I said jokingly about murdering him? I little thought then…God forgive me! That was only last night, wasn't it? And after I left you I heard that he is dead."

"Dead! Oh, Richard, how terrible!" She stood desolately in the middle of the room, crucifying herself with his hurt as some women can—imagining how she would be feeling had it been *her* brother who was dead. Presently she said gently," I am so sorry—so grievously sorry. Can you tell me about it?"

He stood looking down at the gay pageantry of Pamplona. Competitors and crowd, officials and servants—all the supernumeraries who were to have formed a frame for the uncertain issue of his fight. The medley of their voices came up to him, far off and shrill like the shouting of children playing on the seashore. Tents and trappings and gowns were so many gaudy blotches against the sombre background of his thoughts. He hated them because he no longer had any part in them. "Henry had gone to Normandy to raise some money for our crusade," he was saying woodenly. "It seems he caught some sort of fever…Anyway, he will never come crusading now."

Sensing her dumb participation, he turned with a reassuring smile. He was never one to unload his burdens on to any woman's love. "Oh, you needn't be too sorry for me! Anyone will tell you we quarrelled like curs. Aquitaine and Poitou have been laid waste by our disputes over patrimony. But he was one of us. Cleverer than I, of course—and much more fit to rule. And a good fighter, God rest his soul!" He crossed himself, standing quiet for a moment in prayer or thought.

Berengaria yearned over his bright; bent head. "Why must you go immediately?" she asked.

"Because of my lands," he said crisply.

He was so oddly compounded of sentiment and common sense that she found herself saying with an almost motherly smile, "They won't run away."

"No. But they can be given away."

"At least wait until after the tournament."

He shook his head obstinately. "King Sancho has excused me, and your cousin understands. By the time I get back my father will probably have had John crowned."

She had never seen that harshness on his face before. It made him look older and square-jawed and somehow frightening. "But your own father, Richard! Surely you can trust him?"

Probably she pictured him as some genial counterpart of her own parents. She had never known a harsh word. She had never seen disillusionment widening with the swinging inward of a bedroom door. Ah, well, he couldn't tell her about that…Better she should think him unnatural, grasping…"I never wanted to be King of England," he said slowly. "But now—don't you see the difference it makes?"

"I see that you are now a very important person," she said soberly.

He beat palm with fist, staring at her as if the whole of life were opening up before him. "Important enough to make it possible!" he cried.

Berengaria was too honest to pretend to misunderstand him; but, woman-like, she wanted confirmation. "To make what possible?" she asked.

He seized her hands impulsively, drawing her towards him. "To keep our private lives. To have happiness, love, ecstasy—like any common craftsman. We're both young, and you're so beautiful. Can't you see that I am hungry with love for you, Berengaria?"

"So soon?" she whispered laughingly.

"Almost since I first saw you, I suppose—with your soft skin and your roses. Oh, I know I can't expect you to care like that about me—in a day, or a few hours. But at least I could save you from marrying a lustful beast like de Barre or some senile old death's-head like Sicily."

He was so impetuous that in order to think she freed herself and turned away. "Oh, Richard, don't torture us both!"

"Then you *could* care?"

She answered him obliquely. "There is always Ann."

For him there would always be just two kinds of woman. The wanton, behind closed doors, and the soft-eyed saint bending above him with giving hands. Ann's laughter had done that to him. And even Berengaria would never be able to give him back belief in any imperfect, household mate between.

"Ann be damned!" he stormed. "Nothing will make me marry her now."

"But what about your father and Philip?"

It was true that his father might no longer force him to marry Ann, but he would probably do his utmost to prevent a union with Navarre. But with Berengaria caring—and he could swear she did— Richard's natural optimism knew no bounds. "By God's throat, I'll bribe Philip somehow!" he cried, and took her in his arms.

He had so little time and no legal claim—nothing but passion with which to bind her. Briefly, fiercely, against the dividing years, he kissed her. Instead of international pledges and discussions about dowries, he held her against his heart and felt her unresisting body his. In that quiet room he staked an impossible claim against the diplomatic scheming of all Europe. Raging against leaving her, he knew that unless he was acknowledged heir to England he would not be considered important enough to get her. He hoped desperately that she would wait until his despotic father gave up some of the power. Had he been more experienced, he would have known that the very incompleteness of this hour might hold her. When other suitors came she would make comparisons. She would remember his unfinished kisses and care only that his hands were tender and his young mouth hard.

"They are coming back with my roses," she whispered at last. "They mustn't find you here."

"If only I were free to begin negotiations with your father before I go! But I am afraid Philip will be still more tenacious of me as a brother-in-law now."

"I will talk to my father. You know how kind he is. I will beg him at least to let me wait—"

Reluctantly, Richard released her and drew on his leather gauntlets. "It may mean years. You know I'm pledged for this next crusade?" He took a turn across the room, tramping unheedingly across her scattered finery and coming back to take her shoulders in his gloved hands. "Listen, sweet. If ever I sent for you would you have the courage to come?"

"Come where?"

"God knows! England, Cahors—the Holy Land, perhaps?"

She smiled through her tears. "You know it isn't my kind of courage—but I expect I should."

"You are wonderful! I suppose a man oughtn't to think of dragging the woman he loves about the world like that? You're so little, and you hate the sight of blood."

She met his searching gaze with assurance. "When a man hands a woman back her dreams she does not count the material cost."

"It may be harder than you think," said Richard, with rare prescience. He took her in his arms again, but their kisses were tormented by the sharp edge of parting. "Sholto will send me news of you," he said. "And I shall always wear your favour against my heart."

Because he was going she had to tell him what she had really thought about his fight. "I was so eaten with pride in you I think God must be punishing me now. I even made up a name for you." Standing on tiptoe she reached up and said it against his lips. "Richard Cœur de Lion."

He laughed and held her close, trying to curb his strength so that he should not hurt her. "It is a fine name—Cœur de Lion," he said, without a thought for how it might echo and re-echo through the years.

PART III

Dover

Chapter Eleven

DOVER WAS A PROUD town in the Spring of eleven ninety. The royal leopards flew from the new castle on her white cliffs, and the pride of England's navy rode the blue waters of her bay. Not merely the converted fishing fleet levied from each of the Cinque Ports in case of invasion, but twin-masted war galleys with castles for the bowmen built fore and aft, and the broad, red cross of Christendom flaming across their sails. For Richard Cœur de Lion had succeeded his father as King of England and was off on his crusade at last.

Dover was a busy town, too. There were soldiers carrying dunnage to the waiting ships, mettlesome horses being coaxed down the slipway, and sailors drinking and singing wherever the sign of a bush proclaimed that alewives brewed. Down the narrow, salt-tanged streets swaggered knights and pages from all parts of England. The harbour was thronged with laughing harlots and weeping wives.

And it looked as if Dover would soon be a very impoverished town, for Richard himself was in the Reeve Hall collecting money for the crusade. People kept passing in and out of the wide door. They went in laden with this world's goods and came out light with exultation about the world to come. He was persuading all men to the cause of his sincerity, and robbing the women of all but chastity by his charm.

In his late twenties Richard was in his prime. He had lost the first slenderness of youth, but nothing of its enthusiasm.

His body was fit and strong as any blacksmith's. During the six months he had been king he had, of necessity, acquired poise. Not the easy grace of his brother, Henry, perhaps; but a grave, considered courtesy which made a decent enough cloak for his incurable impetuosity.

"And is the new King such a fine figure of a man as they say?" the women, leaning from their windows in Reeve Hall Street, wanted to know.

A painted hussy prinking her way between the houses looked up and laughed. "For myself, I'd as soon sleep with one of those stern stone statues at Canterbury," she shouted brazenly. "But did you see Prince John?"

They did not deign to answer her but craned their necks, with the half-envious curiosity of honest women, to see how she was snapped up by a roystering group of sailors at the corner of the market square. "Aye, I saw him, and I hope he won't stay long!" sighed one of them who had four growing daughters.

"The King's foster-brother is inside there," announced the local miller, emerging from the Reeve Hall. "I told him I'd 'a been able to bring more'n two pieces o' siller if most folks weren't compelled to cart their corn to Canterbury 'stead of grinding local. 'Just to put money into the church mills,' I ses; and he promised to see the thieving old Abbot about it."

A hook-nosed cobbler looked up from the open front of his shop. "They say this Robin saved some of the Jews the Londoners beat up at the Coronation."

"He was always kind to us when he came to the assizes with King Henry," remembered an old market woman.

Anxiety wiped the excitement from their patient faces. "If Robin sails too, what shall we do?" they asked each other, thinking of the jocund Prince John and the long, hard winter.

Since his father's death Richard had been quite glad to have John around, and even Robin—who hated this begging business— had had to admit that John had managed it quite successfully.

"Suppose we just sit here and nobody brings anything?" he had objected, knowing how his fellow Saxons loathed foreign wars.

"Then I shall disguise my page as a converted Moslem and make him bring one of the crown jewels—just to get the thing started," said John. "They'll turn out like sheep."

"Playing up to mass hysteria!" Robin had grunted.

"And would you say that women get this mass what-is-it worse than men?"

"Probably."

"Then what a blessing Richard is that rare aphrodisiac—a bachelor king!"

Robin had laughed and given in. "Not much scope for him with you about!" he had pointed out, trying not to wince as John tried on his brother's crown.

So there they all were in the bare Saxon hall. Richard himself, resplendent in his new crusading outfit, sitting in the shire reeve's chair. Robin making an inventory of the gifts people brought because he was the only one of them who could wrestle with accountancy. John perched conversationally on the edge of the fast-filling coffer, and Blondel—now an efficient young squire—ushering in the important and helping out the poor. And sometimes, Richard felt, the spirit of his brother Henry trying to get back to them now that the great day of adventure was at hand. The veil between them wore so thin at times that he felt he would only have to turn his head to see him lounging somewhere in the shadows and to hear his pleasant, lazy voice saying, "Not so bad, Dickon...But I ought to be leading this expedition, you know... Did you manage to get rid of that trollop, Ann? And was there good sport in Navarre?"

And all the time a stream of people passed through and had to be thanked. Monks from Canterbury and parish priests with their altar plate, well-to-do shopkeepers with their money bags and family parties come to Dover to see the King. The local miller had parted with his two pieces of silver, and the fletcher's Norman wife had bounced in with her second best jewels. Coming in from the sunlit street, she had stumbled; and Richard himself—glad of an excuse to stretch his legs—had helped her to rise. "Madam, your generosity has helped to launch another Christian ship," he said, his spacious gesture towards the masts just visible above the harbour wall making her feel herself a shareholder in their enterprise.

He was so exciting, so virile, seen close to like that. And yet there was no woman in his life. Officially, of course. But it was ridiculous to suppose him celibate…her erotic thoughts wandered on…It was gracious of him to come down to the town, but it would have been interesting to have seen inside the castle. She wished she had brought some of her best jewels. Her husband, the fletcher, was doing well out of the holy war, and her plump fingers began fidgeting with the new necklace he had just given her.

"I'm sure so white a throat needs no adornment," whispered the King's attractive young brother at the psychological moment. And before she knew it the pearls were in the coffer, and the polite young squire was bowing her out.

"How much are they worth?" enquired Richard crisply, before her simpering face was well out of sight.

John was already testing them with strong, white teeth. "A hundred shillings, at least. And she'd have given you her ears as well if you'd asked for them. You know, Richard, some of these middle-aged women are so consumed with curiosity about your private life that you ought to let them look over your bedroom at a shilling a time."

"They are welcome to if it would bring in a bit more," laughed Richard.

"Or how about paying less for your arrows?" suggested Robin, who had been turning up her husband's exorbitant charges in the shire reeve's account books.

They became aware that Blondel was gesticulating with urgent whispers from the doorway. "That reluctant knight I told you about, Sir, who wants to get out of his vows. Crossing the street now…"

"With a rich miniver coat and an invalid's litter," supplemented John, leaning backwards so that he could see.

Robin consulted the mighty tome before him. "Dugorge was the name. Sir Gawaine Dugorge. He's down here in Doomsday as having hogged the lands of at least three Saxon thanes."

"Then he should be good for four or five hundred," assessed Richard.

Sir Gawaine was fat and florid and made great play with a staff and his squire's arm. Richard greeted him with an assumption of hearty good comradeship, enquiring after his wound; and the embarrassed knight, who had never been to war, had to admit that he suffered merely from the gout.

"Now our old nurse makes a very potent compress of neats-foot and liverwort for that—" began the irrepressible John. And the four of them listened with covert amusement while the poor craven explained just how bad his gout had become of late.

"I know. I know. Since seeing my ships actually ready to set sail," laughed Richard contemptuously. "I've noticed they *do* have that effect on some people's ailments. Well, well, in the circumstances we might persuade our good bishop to remit your holy vows. For a consideration, of course. Now, let me see—the loss of such a valiant companion-in-arms might be estimated at four hundred shillings, should you say, John?"

"Make it five hundred," urged John promptly.

The man's florid complexion faded to an unhealthy putty colour. "But, Sirs, I am a comparatively poor man! "

"Not half so poor as those three thanes you robbed, I'll warrant!" said Robin, poking the knight's flabby paunch with a fresh quill he was cutting.

"But five hundred! It is hard—"

"So are the plains of Palestine—very hard," remarked Richard, dismissing him curtly as two old ploughmen brought a few groats wrapped carefully in an earth-stained cloth. He leaned forward to take it in his own hands, making it seem precious by the gesture. Because they had never in their lives been out of Kent, he pulled a map across his knees and traced for them the way he meant to sail. They forgot the toil that had bent their backs in the service of the soil. Their fine, gnarled faces looked up worshipfully into his. And Robin, standing by, pictured what the lives of such men would be during the hard, lawless winters ahead.

Richard was even trying to sell his parklands. "Have a notice about them put up at the harbour where these prosperous foreign merchants berth, Blondel," he ordered, getting up to stretch himself when the last of the public had gone. "And you, John, can't you hunt up a few more rich Jews?"

"It's the only sport I can give you points at!" grinned John, gathering up his modish riding cloak obligingly. But out in the sunshine with one foot in the stirrup he called back to his brother, "Don't forget, Richard—I'm playing for castles. You promised me Nottingham and Marlborough."

"All right, Lackland. Good hunting!" agreed Richard indulgently; and went to the door to watch the two young men ride up the street—a pleasant-looking pair, the one capable-looking and soberly dressed, the other ruddy and debonair. He saw John turn to catch the eye of a pretty girl sitting on the steps of a house opposite the cobbler's and heard Blondel's quick laughter as her mother pulled her inside and slammed the door.

"Has this crusading fever left you *no* conscience, Richard?" asked Robin, with a smile.

Richard came back to the coffer and, digging a hand deep into its contents, let a cascade of coins run idly through his fingers. "I would sell London if I could find a buyer," he admitted. London, for him, held fewer memories than Rouen or Cahors.

"A little hard—on London!" murmured Robin.

Richard glanced back at the harbour with the eyes of a visionary and the calculating mind of a commissary. "Somehow each of those ships must carry at least forty horses, and provisions for a year. I'm not taking any chances of starving in a hostile country as they did last time."

Briskly, his foster-brother laid before him some parchments. "Well, here are your sailing orders for each captain."

"Good. I'll sign them."

"Rather ruthless, aren't they?" Leaning over his shoulder, Robin indicated a clause in which it was laid down that any man who disobeyed an order should be thrown overboard.

But Richard sealed them firmly. "Good generalship necessitates occasional imperviousness to individual pain," he argued. "To my way of thinking, the man who hasn't courage enough to burden his conscience with occasional ruthlessness has no right to rule."

"And those of us who aren't called upon to bear the burden need not add to it the weight of criticism," apologised Robin handsomely.

Richard locked the great chest and sat down on it, calling for drinks. "It's funny, after sitting at side tables in other men's halls, to have Philip deferring to my military judgment instead of patronising me; and to see the way that young time server, John, follows me about!"

"As long as you realise that he *is* a time-server," warned Robin. "Your father never did, and so his defection from himself to you at the end nearly broke his heart." He came and sat down at the other end of the coffer and a page set wine between them. "What are you going to do about Ann?" he asked. "Why don't you tell Philip straight out you won't marry the girl?"

"Can't afford to now he's king and we're starting off on this crusade together," said Richard. "But guess where that wonderful mother of mine went off to so quietly last month."

"Everybody's been wondering about that—just as you'd been able to make her life so much pleasanter."

"To Navarre!" said Richard, lifting his tankard and smiling happily at the rich redness of the wine, so that it sounded like a toast as well as an answer.

"Navarre!" echoed Robin, with satisfying surprise. "Still finessing at seventy!"

"She is going to bring Berengaria to Brindisi." Richard quaffed off his wine and, reaching for the map that was never far from his hand these days, began tracing a route to the south of Italy. "I shall have to contrive to meet them there on my way to Syria."

Robin sat hugging his knee and staring at Richard's absorbed, bent head. Such extravagant moments always left him a little breathless. He, too, had his dreams but—with the patience of a peasant—he accepted his limitations. It had been so in love. Instead of clamouring for a girl out of his reach, he had striven for self-mastery. Whereas Richard kicked aside obstacles with the godlike impatience of his breed, widening their everyday horizon to a panorama of romance. "And what about King Sancho?" he asked.

"Oh, he is all in favour of it now I have England. And, as you know, Philip would sell his soul for money. If only I were not so damnably hard up just now I might bribe him about Ann."

"But didn't your father leave a pretty useful reserve in the vaults at Winchester?"

Richard nodded towards a convoy of arms and provisions rumbling down to the quay. "I've had to put every penny of it into that sort of thing," he explained.

Having so often acted as confidential scribe, Robin had in some matters been more in King Henry's confidence than his own sons. Because he knew just how many pennies there had been and for what wise improvements they had been saved, he felt that those fine, insatiable ships were robbing England. He kicked at the coffer beneath him with an aggressive heel. "I believe John, in one of his more inspired moments, suggested that you could buy off the King of France with some of this?"

Richard sprang from the chest as if he had been stung. "Does he take me for a Judas, blast him? God's money—given sometimes in spite of grim necessity! You saw those two old men just now. Does he suppose I'd touch it if I were starving?"

Robin began rolling up the map; absently, as if he were trying to tidy his thoughts at the same time. "Yet we all know there *are* plenty of self-seeking humbugs in this," he said, slowly. "People out for notoriety, and bored barons who want to dodge a lot of dull routine duties at home."

"And, unfortunately, I must use them. But to me it's all real. The loyal comradeship—the thrill of adventure. Choosing the job I'm best at, if you like. But there's something more to it than that. A sort of dedication of one's strength, I suppose…" Richard laughed self-consciously. "I'm afraid I'm not very good at dissecting my soul!"

"That's one of the things I love best about you."

The page who was serving them had gone to his dinner, and Richard lingered to refill their tankards. "I never could talk to Henry about it," he said. "Of course, he was just as eager to go. But

I never quite knew what he *believed*. To be a man's friend one must walk more familiarly about his mind."

"Can even the keys of friendship give so much freedom?" debated Robin doubtfully.

"Assuredly," answered Richard. "Why, I can even appreciate your cursed independence about a title. At least it proves there are some men who can't be bought."

Robin flung a melodramatic arm, tankard and all, about his shoulders. "Why, Richard, your new state is saddening you already with horrible suspicions! Or were you just thinking of Ann's accommodating brother?"

"No. Just that however much other men may flatter me you will always be at hand to call me a f-fool!" said Richard, spluttering over his wine with the force of the impact.

"Not that you will ever listen!" laughed Robin.

"No. But I shall always know that you are right."

Hearing a commotion in the street, they turned in time to see John slide from his horse before the open doorway. "I've just rounded up my hundred and fiftieth Jew," he announced from the sunny pavement. "At a castle a hundred that means Nottingham and half the battlements of Marlborough. Bring him along, you fellows!"

Because he was a Jew, Richard did not bother with any formality. "What's he worth?" he asked, going to the window seat to pick up a little model ship he had been making for young Arthur of Brittany, his dead brother Geoffrey's boy.

"A small fortune as a goldsmith and half as much again by usury, no doubt," answered John.

"Half of it will help to victual my ships," said Richard, squinting along the tiny hull to make sure it was straight.

To their surprise the goldsmith answered up in his own defence. "Most of the money I have lent has been to impecunious knights wanting to fit themselves out for your Crusade," he said. "And if you take half my profits it will ruin my business."

"It may save your worthless skin," taunted John. He had helped himself to a drink and would have thrown the dregs in the man's face had not Robin shot out a hand and spoiled his aim. "At least this man works for his keep, and harsh handling can't cow him," he pointed out. "Must he be less generously treated than that lily-livered old humbug with his expedient gout?" He interfered so seldom that the men-at-arms withdrew their grimy fingers from the goldsmith's yellow robe immediately.

"But he's a Jew!" protested Richard, looking up in astonishment.

Robin smiled at him disarmingly, and pointed to the flaming emblem on his new white surcoat. "So was the Man whose cross you wear," he said quietly.

Richard stood staring, the half-made toy in his poised hands. "I suppose you're right," he admitted grudgingly. "Let him pay only a quarter, John."

"May the God of my fathers grant me an opportunity to show the gratitude—"

But Richard cut short the man's thanks. "Better thank my foster-brother," he said shortly. It occurred to him that he had been saying that very often of late.

One of the soldiers touched the Jew's arm, almost respectfully. Both of them waited while he bowed first to the King and then to Robin. John laughed at the pointed omission of himself. "Anyone would think it was I who wanted to spend his beastly money on war horses!" he said, indefatigably refastening his cloak as soon as they were gone. "And thanks to you, Robin, I shall have to go out again to earn a couple of castles fit for my bride to live in while you two are away." Actually, it had been suggested that he should live in Anjou or Maine during his brother's absence, but by feigning forgetfulness he hoped to make others forget, too.

Richard roused himself from an unpleasant reverie. "You still want to marry Avisa of Gloucester?" he asked.

John kissed amorous fingertips to her charms. "Is she not blonde and rich?"

"And the granddaughter of a Saxon thane," murmured Robin, realizing that there was nothing the youngest Plantagenet could possibly have thought of which would ingratiate him more with the people.

"Then I must arrange the marriage before we sail. It's high time you settled down," agreed Richard surprisingly.

John went out grinning covertly because that was all he asked of life, and it was Richard himself who was so incapable of settling down. But at the doorway his jauntiness deserted him. He lowered his voice, passing close to Robin. "*You* know what it would mean to me, leaving England. For God's sake don't say anything that might make him change his mind!" For once he spoke sincerely, appealing to Robin's generosity and admitting his influence. He knew well enough that neither Robin nor Johanna was to be moved by a show of devotion or a sudden desire for domesticity. Richard might allow himself to be gulled, but they always saw his ulterior motives with such uncomfortable clarity.

Robin neither promised nor denied. His eyes were on the beloved figure of Richard. He knew how he was feeling. He had taken up his small nephew's toy again and, for some moments after they were alone, the silence was broken only by the savage whittling of his knife.

"You'll soon be known in every tavern as the King's better self!" Richard began. But it was not like him to be sore for long and after a moment or two he threw aside both bitterness and knife. "I'm starving!" he declared, linking an arm in Robin's. "For pity's sake, let's go and get some food."

As they rode up to the Castle the women of Reeve Hall Street waxed quite sentimental over their close comradeship. "Both of a height," they said, smiling after them, "and so inseparable!"

Chapter Twelve

UP AT THE CASTLE, after the midday meal, Richard drew Robin from the crowded hall. Together they went up a short flight of stairs to the room Henry the Second had had built for himself behind the dais. It was a serviceable, well-lit room. Instead of the central hearth that used to smoke the beams at Oxford, a fireplace had been built into the wall, its wide arch decorated with the zigzag carving beloved of Norman masons. An armoire still held some of the late King's possessions, and before a large work-table stood the massive chair of state from which he used to receive messengers and merchants from his duchies across the Channel, as well as deputations of seamen from the Cinque Ports.

Richard and Robin were particularly intrigued by the small glazed window over-looking the hall. Except in cathedrals, glass was a novelty to them. It had the queer effect of making the people down below look as if they were doing everything in dumb show. Officers, members of the household, guests, and all manner of people who fed at the royal expense were sitting or standing about in groups before dispersing for their afternoon occupations.

"Just look at John!" chuckled Robin. "One can't hear a word he is saying, but I warrant by the way he's prodding that poor hound around he's giving those giggling girls an hilarious account of his Jew hunt."

"Yes. And now he's got to the part where he's mimicking me," said Richard. "Am I *really* as pompous as that?" He took off his crown and strolled over to the open window on the sea side. The harsh screech of gulls and the deep beat of surf made a diapason of invigorating beauty. Sheer down below scarped the white cliffs of Dover, laving the folds of their dazzling skirts in a greenish-blue sea. Seen from such a height, submerged rocks showed like a shadowy brown girdle beyond the flying spume. The impregnable pride of those white cliffs stung sudden salt to Richard's eyes. Like Johanna, on the eve of departure he realised the dearness of England. But there was his fleet in the bay. Thirteen war ships, with fifty galleys and innumerable flat-bottomed boats for conveying the horses.

He leaned out, the breeze ruffling his hair. In the clear midday light the harbour itself looked like some miniature model with black dots of men scurrying back and forth provisioning toy ships. One of the black dots was Mercadier who, at King Henry's order, had shipped him off to Navarre. He was now superintending the lading of armaments, and although the great catapult they were slinging aboard must have weighed several tons, they were handling it as carefully as if it were a baby. A keen fellow, Mercadier. Good, keen fellows, all of them. He must go down presently and help. It warmed Richard's heart to know that they liked to have him there. He didn't just stand about, wasting their time, like some royal personages; but was often able to make practical suggestions. And since the day he had lifted a crossbeam no one else could shift, they sang more lustily when he was about and strained their muscles to live up to his amazing strength.

With such willing work they should be ready to put to sea by mid-Lent. Disputes, deferment, and disappointments were done with at last. Life had never seemed so good. Richard hummed a stave of a song. "Now if I were a mason—" he began, looking down with a critical eye upon some feature of his father's fortifications.

"Oh, spare me!" laughed Robin, bisecting an apple with his splendid teeth.

Richard drew his mighty shoulders back into the room. "What I *really* wanted to talk to you about was this question of a title," he said, "You can't go about the world for ever labelled just 'the King's Conscience' or 'the Friend of the Unfortunate.' Nor just 'Robin.'"

"It's a good enough name," asserted its owner, with his mouth full.

"I know. But only *one* name. We Normans always have two."

The familiar harangue left Robin unimpressed. "I will take my father's name as well and call myself Robin Neckham if you like, but I don't need a title," he reiterated stubbornly. Ever since Richard's accession he had been dodging one. He felt that it would set him apart from his own people.

"Oh, I know you're a better man than most of us without one," agreed Richard, with a friendly grin. "And here at home everybody knows that to slight you is to slight me. But abroad—with Philip of France and Leopold of Austria and all the haughty hangers-on they'll be bringing—" He spoke almost diffidently, watching the flight of a gull with exaggerated interest. "You know, Robin, this is the first time I've been in a position to offer you anything—and it might make things out there a lot easier for you when you're trying to persuade them to use this new crane you've invented for our sieges."

"Generous red-head!" Robin's jeering voice was rough with feeling. Tossing aside his apple core, he clapped a hand to each of Richard's shoulders, swinging him round so that he could look levelly into his eyes. When at last he let his hands fall reluctantly to his sides, it was as if he released something unspeakably precious. "But I am not going crusading," he said, turning away.

"Not *going?* You not going?" echoed Richard, rubbing a shoulder where his ringed mail had been pressed painfully into his flesh.

Robin stood by the table, blindly turning over the captains' orders which he had brought up from the Reeve Hall. He knew the words by heart; but he saw the captains, a gallant company, sailing away without him. "Do you suppose the Queen will send me her distaff?" he asked flippantly.

Richard watched him, frowning uncertainly. "Don't try to be funny, Robin—at a time like this—"

Robin put down the parchments and faced him. "On the contrary, I was never more serious."

"Serious…" With a flurry of white and crimson, Richard was beside him. "Am I mad? Or have we travelled so far apart in thought—or what?" he demanded incredulously.

"No. It is just that you were wrong about friends walking familiarly in each other's minds. You see, although you and I have lived, eaten, joked together whenever you have been in England, we must still conserve two separate consciences in the sight of God."

"But we've always talked about this…"

Robin smiled sadly. "You talked—and I listened. Dreading this inevitable hour."

Richard's fair skin went red with anger. "You mean, you let me talk my heart out about the battles I meant to win, the castles I meant to build. While you sniggered secretly, like Ann. You let me prattle about my life's dreams—damned funny, I expect they were—about things I'd never have told another living soul. And all the time…"

Robin put an arm about his shoulders, shaking him gently. "My God, man, you don't think this decision of mine was easy, do you? But England will have to bleed for this crusade of yours. One of us has got to stay."

"Isn't John staying?" Richard shook off his arm impatiently, and began pacing up and down with emphatic, Latin gestures. "And am I not buying his loyalty with the lands he always lacked? You heard him making some ridiculous wager about it this morning. Nottingham, Derby, Marlborough—all the western counties—"

"He covets land so much it might have been wiser to listen to Longchamps, Bishop of Ely, and send him abroad until your return."

"It seems so unnatural to turn him out, and it will be pretty lonely for my mother without any of us. After all, if John marries and settles down—"

"He'll offend the barons just as he infuriated the chieftains when your father sent him to Ireland."

"He was younger then," said Richard testily. Like the rest of the family, he was rather tired of hearing about their youngest's delinquencies.

"But he still mocks at the things most people hold sacred."

Richard felt he was being side-tracked into a discussion about something of minor importance when his mind was seething with something that concerned himself. "Henry always said that was a kind of complex due to Becket's idea of bringing him up for the priesthood," he explained hurriedly.

"Henry was probably right. But that hardly explains about more secular things—like play-acting with your crown, for instance."

"Oh, that!"

Robin was shocked by his indifference. "Even your father, who would have given him your inheritance, never let him touch the crown of England!" he remonstrated.

"But it isn't," laughed Richard shortly.

Robin felt himself behaving like a peasant—being heavy and tedious. He lifted the circle of gold reverently from the table, turning it so that each big jewel caught a prism of richly coloured light. "You mean—this is fake?"

"We never take the real one round the country." Richard spoke impatiently, his mind on the main issue of their argument. His family use of the word 'we' seemed to exclude Robin, and the fact that John must have known it all the time made him feel a fool. "I never coveted it, as you know, until I met Berengaria," went on Richard. "But at least I have the grace to remember that it must be very precious to you Saxons because it belonged to Edward the Confessor." He sat down again in the late King's chair, thereby quite unconsciously stressing still further the purely private nature of their equality. "To counterbalance John's levity I could leave William Longchamps as Chancellor," he said, drumming thoughtfully on the arms. He had never attempted to hide the fact that he trusted Longchamps of Ely more than any of his English councillors and that in itself was sufficient to make the Bishop unpopular.

"Is it wise, Richard?" Robin debated, as they often did upon such matters. "He is devoted to you, of course. But you know how the people call after him in the streets 'bandy-legged little foreigner'."

But Richard had been called upon to bear too much. The difficult decision Robin had been digesting for weeks was still new and sour in his mind. The state chair creaked beneath his anger. "Now, by God's wounds, you're trying to taunt me with my own Angevin blood!" he cried.

Robin stepped back. His whole manner changed. Richard had never spoken to him like that before. They frequently cursed each other roundly, but without the hurt of misunderstanding. "Anyone would envy rather than taunt you, I should think, Sir," he said, with cold formality. "But because I was born plain Saxon I can't help seeing things through their eyes. And my curse is that the gift of learning your father gave me lays upon me the obligation to use my tongue in their defence. They don't want war."

"But they gave their money," protested Richard.

Having been made to feel momentarily like any other subject, Robin was able to see an every-day companion from a new angle. "Don't you know that you are a very glamorous person, Richard?" he said, smiling in spite of himself. "In every age some dominant leader like you bewitches nations into war. It's so fatally easy."

"Easy!" snorted Richard, who had been working harder than any of them to get it going at all.

"All the trappings and excitement, I mean. If only someone could dress up Peace as gorgeously people might realise that there's plenty of adventure in building a bridge across the Thames as your father did, or planning a town that wouldn't burn like dried tinder. They might even see scope for devotion in fighting the plague. And cattle and crops, you know, often call for as much courage as any visionary crusade."

"You call it visionary! To get back the Cross from the hands of Saladin? To drive out the infidel dogs whose unbelieving breath defiles the Holy City?" cried Richard, using in all sincerity the claptrap phrases of recruiting priests.

But Robin shrugged his shoulders. Like John, he was too insular to be much moved by them. He had lived among people to whom such phrases were a cult, but it was Hodierna who had really brought him up. And in spite of his strength and hardihood he had read and studied deeply. "Why must the women and children of this country starve to secure a plot of sun-scorched land that grows no corn?" he demanded. "A relic that strains the credulity of any thinking man?"

"Now *you are* blaspheming against the things which others hold sacred!" accused Richard. Clearly he felt as badly about it as Robin had felt about the mishandling of the crown.

"Oh, Richard, I know these things are sacred to you," said Robin, sweeping aside a pile of parchments to sit on the table beside his chair. "But to my practical mind they are—just things. How can the spirit of Christianity be confined within any one city? How *can* it sanction so much suffering?" He spoke quietly, urgently, striving for complete mental clarity between them. "You can't suppose I wouldn't give my right hand to be beside you in the bloodiest fight," he went on, seeing the bleak look on Richard's face. "But it seems to me there will be far more urgent crusading to be done here at home. Hodierna has often told me about what went on during the Civil War. She saw children starve to death and her young sister dragged by Stephen's soldiers to the streets. It's things like that that hold me back."

It was things like that that were unanswerable. Richard sighed, seeing the rent in their sympathies widening past repair. He got up heavily, and stood helping himself absently from a platter of fruit. "I always counted on your coming…" he said, half apologetically.

"I too have had my disappointments," Robin reminded him.

"I know. If only I had become king when Henry died I might have been in time to save Johanna from that travesty of a marriage."

"Even so it couldn't have made any difference to me—a peasant—and I was vile enough to be glad it *was* a travesty." With so many conflicting loyalties, Robin always found it difficult to speak about the matter. Even now, he changed the subject "What I meant was I had always counted on your carrying on the great work for my people which your father began."

"My father!" Richard threw his apple untasted to the circling gulls. "Bah, Robin, don't preach!"

"The wrong he did you blinded you to his wisdom," Robin persisted. How often had he seen him sitting at this very table, choleric and conscientious, working when he might have been hunting—never too tired to explain his system of economics to any youngster who was genuinely interested! Because he had known no father of his own, Robin's hand pressed gently on the chair back where that greying red head had so often rested. "*He* saw the opportunities of peace," he said. "Not many men would have had the energy to take over an island full of wrangling breeds and weld them into a united nation."

"Are we a nation?" enquired Richard negligently, picking over the fruit. "Or just a pack of mongrels?"

"Norman initiativeness grafted onto Saxon solidity," elaborated Robin. "Have you ever thought what a driving power that might become? Fit to dictate a policy of peace and freedom to the world."

There was something inspiring about Robin, standing tall and straight beside the state chair. Besides the infectious humanity of his own appeal, he seemed to have the shadowy backing of monks and reeves and rulers who, down the ages, had done their imperfect best for England. For a split second it was vouchsafed to the new crusading king to see a shining segment of an unsuspected dream more splendid than his own. Involuntarily, he stood up and took a step forward, as if some imperious voice had called him. "Now you are trying to hold me back too," he said, half eagerly.

For the sake of that dream Robin was exerting all the dominance of his character. His steady grey eyes held Richard's. "You've all the gifts," he urged. "Vision, singleness of purpose, a charm your father never possessed. Why, a man like you—"

But the spell was soon broken. Richard began to laugh self-consciously, holding up a protesting hand. "You over-rate me, Robin! I should grow fat and flabby sitting about in rooms like this, and fly into ungovernable rages with any poor, windy councillor who had the guts to contradict me." At the bare thought he tightened up his sword belt and strode back to the window for another look at his ships. "No," he said, with the decision of a man who knows his own job. "Let me go and spill some of my hot blood killing Saracens and then perhaps I'll come back and do all the things you want."

The eagerness died out of Robin's taut stance. "A man must follow his own conscience," he allowed sombrely. "But it will mean dark days for England." Glancing up at Richard's uncompromising back, he added, "Suppose the Saracens kill *you?*"

"There is always Geoffrey's boy," shrugged Richard. He picked up the little boat he had been making and set it on a chest before the fireplace, picturing young Arthur's pleasure in playing with it. Like most big men, he adored children. "I will get Constance to bring him to England, and have him publicly proclaimed my heir before I go," he said, bending to set the finishing touch of a red sealing wax cross on each billowing parchment sail.

This was a new complication. Robin held the hearts of the people in his hand. Unofficially, he could control and help them. But, without official status, what could he do to protect a small prince from the inevitable jealousy of John? "If Arthur comes over here," he said anxiously, "you had better make me his guardian."

Richard swung round, sealing wax in hand. "John is his *real* uncle," he said sharply.

"But I want to do *something* for you—and I always hate the way he fondles anything helpless." Had Robin noticed the gathering fury on Richard's face, he might have answered more warily. As it was, the storm broke over his unsuspecting head as suddenly as Richard swung round from the window.

"Now, by God's throat, you go too far!" he raged. "Is no man right but you? No Angevin to be trusted?" It was the same old story. The Plantagenets for ever divided amongst themselves, but united against the world. How often in the old days would Henry flay Richard to frenzy with his clever tongue, only to rend the first person who presumed to do likewise! "First you make me out to be a sort of glamorous mountebank, evading my responsibilities in the cause of God," went on Richard, lashing himself into one of his ungovernable rages. "Then you refuse an earldom and in the next breath calmly demand a regency. There are still men who can't be bought, did I say? 'More than any of my blood brothers,' have I called you? By God, you mean to be! My very self, with England's heir in our hands. Why, John—whom you're always warning me against—begins to look a lamb beside such cunning!"

Robin, who had never in his life used his strange position to get something for himself, leaned back against the table and laughed. "Don't be a fool, Richard!" he said.

But Richard rounded on him, all sense of humour and proportion gone. "Don't you know that without the favour of my love it is treason to call me that?"

Robin spread deprecating hands, his wide mouth jibing but tender. "I'm afraid that's a favour you won't find it easy to withdraw from me."

"I could kill you for that!" raged Richard, infuriated by his cool assertion of the truth. "If you weren't"—he had the grace to add—"the only man I haven't strength enough to kill."

Robin ripped open his green leather tunic. His own blood was up. "Strike, then," he invited, almost contemptuously. "By the same line of argument it would be treason to defend myself."

For a moment it looked as if Richard would. He rushed at him, fumbling at his sword, only to turn away with a gesture of clumsy mortification. "No man could have made me so angry," he muttered. "I shouldn't have cared whether they came or not. Only you—you—"

All through their boyhood it had been Robin's role to soothe his rebelliousness about forbidden things. "No need to rage because you can't get what you've set your heart on," he reminded him now. "Hasn't it occurred to you that I *must* come if you command me to?"

"Command!" scoffed Richard bitterly. "Even kings can't command comradeship—kings least of all!" Kicking a stool out of the way, he went to his father's chair and sat down heavily. "Oh, stay safely in England and be damned to you! Only get out of my sight."

Stiffly, a little unbelievingly, Robin bent to pick up his cloak. "Wasn't 'safely' a little unnecessary, Sir?" he asked coldly.

"Quite." Richard bit the word savagely between strong, white teeth. "I no longer care whether you're safe or not, and to prove it I will leave you an outlaw in this cursed country you rate above my friendship."

Robin stopped on his way to the door as if an arrow had struck him between the shoulder-blades. An outlaw. A hunted man with a price on his head. His honour gone and his dreams shattered. Not at any moment in their quarrel had he supposed that it could end like this. His thoughts flew to Johanna—to the Queen and Hodierna—women who had loved him. Richard couldn't mean such cruelty. He turned with a gesture of appeal. He almost offered to barter individual liberty for the romantic figure that had lit up all his life. But Richard wasn't looking at him. He had taken up a quill and was writing a *deed* of outlawry with firm and unrelenting hand.

Robin went out without a word. As he passed through the hall people spoke to him, but he had no idea what they said. Out in the bailey a groom sprang forward to fetch his horse but Robin remembered that the beast was really Richard's, and shook his head. "A woodman's son going back to the soil," he thought ironically, throwing his cloak over his shoulder peasant-wise and making for the woods that lay between Dover and Canterbury. An hour at most, he supposed, and the price on his head would be published on every reeve hall along the south coast. He stopped at the armoury and exchanged his sword for a bow, the weapon of the common people. From now on he—who had shared the home of the proud Plantagenets—was of less account than the pigs that routed along the sides of the road.

Chapter Thirteen

L IKE ALL THE CINQUE Ports, Dover was quickened by contacts
with the outside world, colourful with snatches of foreign
speech about her streets, and entertained with news hot from
the Continent or the East. The top of her quayside wall was worn
smooth by the elbows of the idle. Landsmen gathered there with
envy in their hearts. Touching the fringes of a more full-blooded
life, they forgot their own tedious frustrations. There was always
something to stare at, something to laugh at, something new. Each
incoming ship brought them the intriguing spice of strange lands
and each ship that slid out past the swinging beacon carried their
imagination, entangled in her rigging, to the far horizon.

Having posted up his notice about the sale of the King's parklands, Blondel sat on a bollard in the sunshine, exchanging an
occasional pleasantry with Mercadier's men. Kentishmen had come
in from all the neighbouring villages to see the great crusading
fleet, and the quay was thronged with people watching a great
Sicilian merchantman sliding to her accustomed berth.

Born of Norman parents and brought up in a homely Sussex
manor, Blondel de Cahaignes had never been out of England except
for that wonderful but swiftly terminated sojourn in Navarre. And
now, watching all the bustle of preparation, it seemed part of his
amazing luck that he should be going to Palestine. And not only
going, but serving as personal attendant to the King. Whatever
happened, wherever they went, he would always be right at the

executive hub of things. And, knowing the dynamic personality of the man who had set it all in motion, he foresaw that Richard's presence would turn every incident of the campaign to dramatic adventure. Looking down into the laden holds, Blondel felt the quivering excitement of all unfledged warriors, half fear of being afraid, half exulted determination to out-dare. He would—he must—justify the trust the King had placed in him. "You will like working for him," his 'fair princess' had promised him years ago. Blondel smiled at the inadequacy of the words. The fortunes of the Plantagenets meant more to him now than his own family.

Rousing himself from his dreams, he was amused to find the girl John had ogled outside the cobber's hanging about on the steps beside him. Perhaps it was because his thoughts had been running on foreign countries, but something about her honey-coloured hair and softly rounded profile stirred him to remembrance of a girl who had once mended his capuchon in Navarre. Piqued by the resemblance, he got up and spoke to her. "So your mother didn't lock the door?" he teased.

Seen close to, the girl was flat, fair Saxon. Her momentary eagerness as she turned held some faint resemblance to the lovable animation of Yvette, but in any case it was not for him. "Is he coming down here? Your friend, who rode past with you this morning?" she asked.

"He's pretty sure to come presently with the King."

"Then I think I'll wait," she said, with an anxious glance up the street towards the house where her mother had probably already missed her. "What is his name?"

"John. But if I were a pretty girl I wouldn't waste my time waiting for *him*," laughed Blondel. "He's going to marry a girl called Avisa."

It was good to take a rise out of John for a change. But before he could profit by it a young officer of Mercadier's called out in passings, "Heard the news, de Cahaignes? The King of Sicily's dead."

Blondel spun round, all philandering forgotten. That meant that Johanna was a widow. She had served her sentence as a political pawn, and how they had all missed her! It had been as if some warmth had been withdrawn from life. Surely now she would be free to come home and marry again to please herself! He stared at the Sicilian ship, where there seemed to be a great deal of chatter and commotion about something. A group of sailors, coming across the swaying gang-plank, detached themselves from the rest and approached him. "They told us to come to you because you are of the royal household," said one of them, who spoke both languages. "This half-wit countryman of mine keeps on about some message from the Queen of Sicily."

They were swarthy, laughing men, and they pushed forward an uncouth looking fisherman, even more spectacular than the rest. Knowing no Norman he kept repeating "King—England" as persistently as Thomas à Becket's lovely Syrian mother must have sought her merchant lover with the cry of "Gilbert—London."

"She isn't aboard?" asked Blondel, eagerly scanning the emptying decks.

Her spectacular messenger shook his head until his great round ear-rings danced. Translating his torrent of excited speech, the other man explained that Queen Johanna couldn't get home at all—that William's younger brother, Tancred, wanted to marry her and was besieging her with his affections in some tower at Messina. Even allowing for the amorous eccentricities of these Sicilians, it sounded a cock-and-bull story!

But the fisherman, over-joyed at finding someone who appeared to appreciate the importance of his mission, thrust a tiny ring of twisted steel into the young squire's hand.

"A scurvy-looking trinket," observed his bilingual friend. "But he was told the King of England would recognize it."

Blondel certainly did. As it lay in his palm the years rolled back. By some trick of memory the salty South Coast tang began to merge into the aromatic smell of fresh rushes and wood smoke. He was back in the hall at Oxford, a homesick page. Because of the young intensity of his misery at the time, he remembered every detail. That hoop of twisted steel, incongruous against green velvet, upon a girl's comforting hand. A hand that waved this way and that, introducing him to the exalted company he was to serve.

"Your own duke, Richard of Aquitaine, there. And Prince John at the end. Robin and I sit where we like..." The clear, light voice of Johanna came back to him as if it were only yesterday.

He gave the Sicilians some money and beckoned to the fisherman to follow him. As old Gregory was always saying, one never had a dull moment working for the Plantagenets. Blondel was already hustling Johanna's messenger towards the Castle. Because most of the townsfolk were either sleeping off their dinners or down at the harbour, the market square had a deserted look. An old soldier hammering a parchment to the Reeve Hall wall waked echoes from the drowsing houses. The guard stood about in groups watching him, and their officer pounced on Blondel and waylaid him, "You're the King's squire. Did you know?" he asked.

"Know what?" asked Blondel impatiently. All his thoughts were on Johanna, all his desire to tell the King and Robin her news as soon as possible.

"About Robin," said the officer, nodding towards the half-fixed notice.

Blondel became aware of some ominous tension about him. He pushed past the muttering soldiers to read the thing. It was a notice of outlawry, white and unweather-stained, with the royal seal freshly impressed. In the middle, bold and clear, stood Robin's name, and in smaller lettering there followed the usual description of his height and colouring and a proclamation of the price upon his head. The words danced foolishly before Blondel's eyes. They just didn't make sense. Robin, the beloved—an outlaw. Robin, whom he had last seen leaving the hall, his laughter mingling with the King's.

"What is it? Some fool joke?" he demanded, turning to read the scowling faces of the soldiers.

One of them spat into the garbage stream that gurgled down the middle of the street. "You wouldn't call it a joke, Sir, not if you'd ha' been up at the castle. Them Angevin rages..." he muttered.

"They quarrelled," explained the officer.

"But it's absurd, man," persisted Blondel, almost pleadingly. "Robin and the King. Richard and Robin." The coupled names sounded like some modern version of David and Jonathan.

But the price on Robin's head stared down at them for all the world to see. The shame of it brought hot blood flaming to Blondel's face. Every sane and decent instinct urged him to tear the insult down. The old man who was fixing it dealt the wall a final, heavy-handed blow. "A dunnamany times I marked the arrow flights for the pair on 'em!" he grieved, the tears standing unashamed oh his leathern cheeks.

"Why, Giles! You used to be with us at Oxford," said Blondel, recognizing him as he turned.

"Ay. An' I mind the night he was born to Hodierna and the Queen whelped her lion cub. This be a mortal bad day for us, Master Blondel, Sir."

"Where has Robin gone?" asked Blondel tersely.

"He's took to the woods," volunteered a raw young recruit, thrilled at being caught up in such strange events.

The old man trudged off with his hammer and Blondel's gaze followed the direction of the raw archer's nod. The woods stretched dense and dark towards the North. A sombre cloud hung over them, gathering from a clear sky as if to herald some devastating storm; just as human anger seemed to have blotted out some of the shining promise of their enterprise, leaving a sullen canker at its root. Johanna's appeal for help might have healed it, but it had come an hour too late.

Bewildered and sore at heart, Blondel signed to the Sicilian to follow him out of the town and up the steep cliff path. The castle, which he had left resounding to a clatter of preparation, seemed wrapped in gloom. The breeze had dropped before the approaching storm, and the standard with Richard's three crouching leopards hung listlessly from the Keep. All bustle and excitement had burned themselves out. Even the servants had ceased to chatter. The Constable's wife had retired with her women and in the great hall men stood about in furtive groups, from time to time glancing uneasily towards the room above. The very dogs seemed depressed.

Only John, the debonair, looked unconcerned. He was playing chess with Picot, the jester—a misshapen caricature of a fellow sprawled across the dais table. Every man's gaze followed Blondel as he hurried to them. "It's true then, Sir, about Robin?" he demanded, interrupting their game without ceremony.

John looked up, a red knight suspended from his fine fingers. He waggled it resentfully in the direction of the stricken hall. "Judge for yourself, my dear fellow, by the lugubrious atmosphere," he invited. John Plantagenet liked a comfortable atmosphere, and was astute enough to attach himself only to those who could provide one.

Marshalled at his elbow stood the little company of carved white pieces he had captured which Blondel, in his urgency, sent rolling across the floor. "What happened? What did they quarrel about?" he persisted, ignoring the jester's lamentations as he grovelled beneath the table to retrieve them.

"How should I know?" shrugged John.

Because he had the smug look of a cat that has been at the cream, Blondel guessed it had been about John himself. Nothing, he knew, would suit the youngest Plantagenet better than to be the wedge divorcing the perspicacity of Robin from the tolerance of Richard. The King's squire stood uncertainly at the end of the table between Picot and the waiting Sicilian, and looked up at the small squint window above. He had lived so intimately in the service of the family that he could gauge how damnably the man up there must be suffering. "Haven't you been up to him?" he asked, feeling that it was hardly his own place to go first, and wishing with all his heart that Queen Eleanor had not gone off somewhere abroad just when they all needed her affectionate wisdom.

Resuming his game, John swooped down with his victorious knight. "Richard invited Robin up there—not me," he pointed out blandly, surveying his opponent's discomfiture. "Besides, I value my skin. You should have seen him throw the Constable out when he tried to protest about having the notice put up. If you have any sense, Blondel, you'll let him cool off a bit. Who is the exotic-looking brigand you have in tow?"

"He's just come ashore from a Sicilian ship with a message from your sister. King William is dead."

John was all interest at once. He waved aside the unfinished game and swung round on his stool. "Johanna a young and desirable widow!" he whistled. "God, what a day we're having!"

"One of us must tell the King," insisted Blondel.

"Send the brigand. He looks tough," suggested John flippantly. "Come to think about it, Blondel, if only old William had been accommodating enough to die a day or two earlier Johanna might have married Robin before all this rumpus."

Blondel was uncomfortably aware that everybody in the hall was watching them, waiting for them to act. "Do you believe that she loved him?" he asked, lowering his voice. He had heard it rumoured, of course. But a royal household is always rife with rumour, and at the time he had been too young to comprehend.

John smiled up at him, indolently jiggling a couple of chessmen between cupped hands. Even when he had been sixteen he had wormed out other people's secrets. "I watched them say 'good-bye' in the herb garden—after you and Richard had gone to Navarre," he said, his blue eyes narrowing the way they did when he wormed his way down into the dungeons to watch some unfortunate felon take a turn of the thumb screw. "It must have been hell for Robin. The man's no monk, and she did her best to seduce him. In her innocence and her misery she—"

"Well, anyhow, Tancred wants to marry her now," interrupted Blondel, turning abruptly towards the stairway arch. John was an amusing enough companion until he started dissecting sex emotions. He got up from the table and followed now, not because he had any particular feeling for Johanna, but because he was intensely interested in people's reactions.

The threatened storm had broken and a rising wind made the heavy door at the top of the short stair difficult to open. Through the unglazed window in the outer wall they could see the rain lashing a white-capped sea. A distant mutter of thunder came to them, accompanied by the restless tramp of Richard's feet.

A tornado of destruction seemed to have swept King Henry's pleasant workroom. Chairs were overturned and parchments scattered in all directions. As the door swung open Richard pulled up short between window and table. His face was ravaged by rage and grief, his voice thick as a madman's. Seeing Blondel edge cautiously across the threshold, he picked up a massive stool by one carved leg and began swinging it threateningly round his head as if it were a battleaxe. "Get out!" he shouted above the storm.

It was not the first time Blondel had seen a royal Angevin rage; but the late King, being of shorter stature, had never looked so terrible. Facing a charge of Saracens with whirling scimitars, such as he had been picturing down at the harbour, would surely seem child's play compared with this! He was in the habit of obeying the King's lightest command, and his heart beat hard in his breast. But he held his ground gamely.

Richard glared at him like some dangerous, wounded beast. "Didn't I tell that damned Constable I'd break every bone in his body if he whined to me about his love for Robin?" he roared. "You can spare your breath, all of you. From now on, no man shall so much as mention his name in my presence."

"It's not that, Sir," corrected Blondel obstinately. "I've an urgent message from our lady Johanna."

The name seemed to catch at some shred of Richard's everyday sanity. He stopped brandishing the stool.

"We only came to tell you that our jovial brother-in-law of Sicily is dead," drawled John, from the comparative safety of the doorway.

"Dead?" laughed Richard crazily. "Then I warrant she'll be taking the next boat home to hold a thanksgiving service!"

"But she is imprisoned in a castle at Messina, Sir, where they are trying to force her into a second marriage with the new king, Tancred." Blondel spoke with deliberate loudness, and Richard's upraised arm fell slowly. The stool went crashing unheeded to the floor. "What's that you say?" he asked, like a man waking from a drunken stupor; but interrupted before his squire had finished explaining. "My good Blondel," he protested impatiently, "what fantastic waterfront tales have you been listening to? People don't imprison Plantagenets!"

"She sent a ring, Sir."

"They always do!" scoffed Richard.

But when Blondel handed it to him he moved to the light of the window, turning the little hoop of steel between strong fingers. "By God's beard, John, it's true!" he called incredulously over his shoulder. "Don't you remember my twisting this for her out of Henry's outgrown mail that day you broke the doll Becket brought her from Canterbury? You were furious, because he hadn't brought you anything."

John glanced at it from a discreet distance. "I remember the licking Robin gave me," he admitted dourly.

But Richard—who remembered the excitement that always heralded that mighty prelate's arrival, his brilliance and his lavishness, and above all King Henry's joy in him—was deeply touched. "Imagine a girl keeping a thing like that all these years!" he said. He went back to the table and sat down, laying a hand on his squire's shoulder in passing. "I'm sorry, Blondel," he said simply.

In spite of anxiety for Johanna and grief for Robin, that brief, kindly pressure seemed to readjust Blondel's world. Unobtrusively, he set a drink at his master's elbow and straightened some of the signs of his violence.

"Send this Sicilian fellow up," ordered Richard curtly, already ashamed of his rage. "And for God's sake, John, stop lounging there quizzing the rest of us as if we were some sort of show, and come and make yourself useful. Having been educated for the church, you are better at languages than I."

John came pleasantly enough. "If what the man says seems to be true, I suppose you will sail at once?" he asked; and because he stooped obligingly to gather up the scattered parchments, Richard failed to notice the satisfied smirk spreading across his handsome features.

"And Heaven help Tancred's volcano-ridden island when I get there!" he snarled. "Daring to detain a sister of mine—"

"*And* her dowry!" John reminded him. "With that she could have afforded to marry almost any man she fancied—to make up for the way her desires must have starved with William. So let's hope Tancred hasn't been *too* pressing. Not that it would matter so much—*now!*" he added negligently.

Richard glared at him as the implication sank in. Already he had begun to be ravaged by remorse about Robin—and now there was Johanna's lost happiness. After the Sicilian had been interviewed and rewarded, he sent for Mercadier and the captains of his fleet. They came crowding into the little room, their cloaks dripping raindrops to the floor. Clearly and concisely he gave them their orders. They were to weigh anchor at dawn and set their course for Sicily.

"But I thought you had arranged to meet Philip at Marseilles?" ventured John, comfortably aware that nothing this side of death would hold his brother back now.

"He'll have to meet me at Messina instead," barked Richard; and before they were in their beds he was out in the bailey mounting his swiftest horse.

"At least let me get you a cloak!" implored Blondel.

"I shall ride the lighter without one," shouted Richard, above the buffeting of the wind.

"If he rides like that he'll go back to the Devil who made his temper!" muttered the Constable, watching the sparks strike from his horse's hooves in the darkness beneath the barbican.

But Richard was already swallowed up in the blustering wildness of the night—riding towards the woods as unsparingly as he swept across a tilt yard—unarmed and uncloaked, soaked to the skin like any serf. Bare-headed and sore-hearted because, in the terrible anger he had never learned to govern, he had spoiled the happiness of two of the four people he loved best on earth. Too proud, still, to revoke a decree made in anger—too generous to sail for Sicily without trying to tell Robin that Johanna was free.

But in the deeper darkness of the woods the going was hard; and wet, overhanging boughs whipped blood from his cheek. Hunting by daylight, he had supposed that he knew these pleasant, grassy rides; but now their direction baffled him. He hadn't the woodman's sense. Or was it, he wondered, ripping his flying tunic from a malevolent thorn bush, because he wasn't wholly English? The thought irritated him unreasonably. With all his superior knowledge of the world, he would never know these woods as Robin did.

Robin, who knew instinctively which way a frightened doe would bound to cover—whose green jerkin always merged so uncannily into the forest foliage that the very trees seemed to protect him. Robin, whose lost friendship had felt like the great, sturdy heart of an oak…

PART IV

Messina

JOHANNA PLANTAGENET SLEPT LATE. Because she had been watching most of the night for a humble little fishing boat to cross the narrow straits from Italy, she missed the grandeur of the avenging armada that came for her at dawn. Being a thoroughly healthy young woman, comfortably housed in a massive tower, she even slept through all the clamour of sudden panic and invasion, and began to stir only when the sun rode high in the cloudless Sicilian sky and somebody began banging on her door.

Except to hunch a protesting shoulder and to turn the burnished glory of her head on her pillow, Johanna took no notice of the banging. People had been bringing gifts from her persistent suitor ever since she had fled from his blandishments to this castle at Messina. Unfortunately the castle, like everything else on the island, now belonged to Tancred. But, being the widowed queen of a civilised country, at least she still retained the privilege of a bolt to her bedroom door.

At first this *siege d'amour* had been rather amusing. Johanna knew plenty of marriageable princesses who would give their ears to be shut up in a castle because a rich and romantic king like Tancred wouldn't take "no" for an answer. But she had had ten years of Sicily, and she wanted to go back to England. So as soon as poor William's elaborate obsequies were over, she had made a methodical list of all her possessions and asked her brother-in-law to arrange about transport.

He had been lounging on the moonlit terrace of the winter palace at the time. "Too bad that all my ships should be laid up or at Genoa!" he had evaded politely.

"Not *your* ships, Tancred," she had explained. "I want the ones my father sent out with my dowry when I came." And because he had pretended to have forgotten all about them, she had thrust her list into his hand.

"You haven't forgotten anything, have you, my sweet?" he had teased, in that silky voice of his. "Your ships and that beautiful gold table from the Abbey at Rouen. And your multi-coloured silk pavilion. You know, I always thought that provided one of the few bright spots of poor William's tournaments." He might have been some Semitic merchant picking up bargains in Constantinople, the way his dark eyes snapped over the list of her possessions. A few weeks earlier his dawdling interest in each item would have helped to pass the time pleasantly, but already Johanna's brisk Northern mind had begun to accelerate to the tempo of less leisurely climates, and—with the scent of windswept English heaths almost in her nostrils—it had seemed suddenly repulsive that his clothes should smell of musk and attar of roses.

"Promise me you will have my ships overhauled this week!" she had persisted. But instead of promising anything he had asked her to stay and marry him.

"And save all this packing?" she had laughed. And then, taken off her guard, she had found the heavy Eastern perfume beating down her careless laughter. His full, lascivious lips were bruising hers, his hot hands holding her as if she were some harem favourite. And she had realised that he really meant it.

Lying in bed behind her locked door, Johanna shuddered at the memory of his embraces, but she was honest enough to admit that in the past she had seldom discouraged him. During ten years she had been tenderly compassionate to William—patient with his stricken body and understanding about his embittered mind. But she was no saint...Throughout her exile she had grasped at every compensating pleasure. She had let Tancred make light-hearted love to her from the day she first landed, and had been grateful to him for a hundred diversions. He had been the perfect brother-in-law, taking her to watch the snaring of wild beasts among the rugged mountains and sitting beside her in the multi-coloured pavilion to watch the tournaments. But the men Johanna had been brought up amongst were seldom spectators. They did their own killing, on the battlefield, in the forest, or down in the lists. And that was the only kind of man she had any use for as a husband.

When a whole tornado of blows rained upon her door she got up reluctantly and began to wash in the water from a tall stone jar. She had only to call, of course, and a whole bevy of obsequious servants would come running. But they were Tancred's creatures. Since she had pitted her will against his, he had sent away her own women. So, with independent pride, she preferred to dress herself. And, having been brought up so simply by Hodierna, she found it no very great hardship.

"If it's pomegranates or peacocks you've brought this time, you can take them back to your master," she called, over a bare shoulder. "And tell him that when I marry again it will be to please myself!"

But whoever it was did not go away, and when she had finished sluicing about with the water she became aware of a man's voice, very full of impatience and authority. Definitely no cringing courtier or timid tiring woman. "Tancred himself!" thought Johanna, hastily reaching for her shift. Hurriedly she donned her tight-sleeved under-dress and slipped over her head a becoming *bliaut* with fur-trimmed sleeves. "Break open that door and I'll fling myself down on the rocks!" she defied rather shakily, as the iron bolt shook in its sockets.

To her horror, it looked as if he would drive her to the test. There was a splitting of wood and one of the sockets shot across the floor. Never would she have believed the elegant Tancred capable of such vigour. Fear gripped her—the sex fear that puts even the bravest woman at a disadvantage. "I've sent word to my brother Richard," she confessed, retreating to the window. "When he comes he'll lay waste your miserable towns and harbours. And when he f-finds my broken body down there he'll throw yours to his d-dogs!"

But her invader only laughed at the high-sounding threat and, as bolt and door burst inwards together, he stood flushed with exertion on her threshold.

"Richard!" cried Johanna, incredulously. Comb and mirror clattered to the floor as she hurled herself upon him.

"A fine welcome," he grumbled, licking a bleeding knuckle, "when a man has come over a thousand miles!"

"I thought you were Tancred," apologised Johanna. "How quickly you must have got my message!"

Richard's face was momentarily shadowed by the memory of that shameful night when he had received it. He felt again the goad of Robin's cool laughter, his own suffocating rage, and the wildness of his fruitless searching of the woods. "If it hadn't been for Blondel I shouldn't have had it at all," he admitted.

But Johanna was safely in his arms, pressing against the fine new cross on his breast, her stripling height dwarfed by his maturity. "If that scented dago has hurt a hair of your head—" he threatened, torn between tenderness and ferocity.

Johanna began to laugh weakly at the conventional phrase. It was so like him to use it. He was always too intent upon whatever he was doing to be plagued by a sense of the ridiculous as were she and John. And in his exhilarating presence even her imaginary plight of a few moments back seemed half a joke. "No, no. Tancred isn't as bad as that," she assured him. "Actually, he was quite amusing and kind until he thought he could bluff me into marrying him."

"It took me just two hours to cure him of *that* illusion," swaggered Richard. "You should have seen his toy soldiers run when my bowman cleared the harbour walls! No discipline at all." He surveyed the semi-Oriental luxury of her room with distaste. Like most open-air men, he was awkward in any room that was not sparsely furnished. "Haven't they any wholesome rushes here?" he demanded, stooping to detach one of his spurs from a priceless Persian rug.

"Don't be so old-fashioned!" bridled Johanna. "This is a much finer castle than Rouen or Oxford."

"It *was*, you mean," grinned Richard. "When Mercadier brought a battering ram ashore we made your lover's new ornamental gates look like the Londoners' booths after St. Bartholomew's fair. Didn't you hear all the din?"

Johanna had to admit that she had slept through it all. Surreptitiously, she smoothed the untidy huddle of her bed covers lest he should think that she, too, had grown soft in this pleasure garden of an island. "I sat up late—watching for a special fishing boat," she tried to excuse herself confusedly. "I saw her come in under the horns of a new moon, which is said to be lucky. And now my luck really does seem to have turned. Your ships and my little boat arriving on the same day, and my being a widow. Of course, I don't mean anything against William, God rest his poor cheated body and weary soul! But just that I am free—" Because of the years separating her girlhood from his new air of poise and authority, the rare constraint of shyness gripped her. "It *does* mean that I am free, doesn't it, Richard?" she asked, glancing up anxiously at the stern lines on his bronzed face and wondering if he were so much changed that he would want to make a diplomatic pawn of her as their father had done.

But Richard took no particular pleasure in the power his position gave him over other people's lives. "What else do you suppose I came for?" he said, with a reassuring laugh. "Come and see!"

She followed him to the window, catching her breath in ecstasy at sight of his war fleet in Messina bay. "Oh, Dickon, all the proud ships with sunlit sails—just as you promised! And before ever they went crusading you brought them here for me!"

Although she was widowed and a queen, Johanna slipped a hand into his, with a gesture out of their past. Shyness and submission were wiped out. They stood side by side, these two Plantagenets, drinking in the joy of his creation. Because Berengaria had not yet come, this was perhaps the most perfect moment of their companionship. Each rakish ratline, each arrogant pennant and defiant prow of that crusading fleet satisfied some urge deep down in both of them. There was no question about what it had cost or whether he should have come. How had he managed without her all these years, Richard wondered, when no one in the world shared his reactions to life so completely? "And when I do bring them you sleep like an unimaginative cow!" he said, with the convincing rudeness of family affection.

"I shall never forgive myself!" she murmured remorsefully. "What I would have given to see them come sailing in! The old dragons of England, the leopards of Anjou, and the lovely lilies of France!"

It seemed that her rhapsody about the lilies was a little ill-timed. Letting go her hand, Richard said curtly, "Yes, Philip is here."

"You haven't quarrelled with him already, have you? The whole thing will be hopeless if you start like that—"

"He's so diplomatic," complained Richard, lounging in the warm sunshine by her window. "He and this Tancred have been bowing and scraping to each other already. We Normans and English do all the fighting while the French go and smooth things over in the town and take all the best billets, leaving me to sleep like a camp follower anywhere I can find room."

"You must sleep here. I specially want you to come to dinner."

"Of course, my dear. But if I don't keep an eye on Philip he'll be signing a treaty with the fellow. But I suppose things always *are* awkward," laughed Richard ruefully, "when two men both think they're leading the same expedition!"

"Believe me, Philip's being here is a whole lot more awkward than that!" agreed Johanna gloomily.

"You mean because he still expects me to marry Ann?"

Johanna glanced behind her at the door. It was hanging on its hinges, half open, and she was aware that some of her women, agog with curiosity, had been inventing errands to pass and repass her room. The whole castle was alive with the tramp of soldiers, lay-brothers attending to the wounded and frightened servants passing each other on the stairs carrying all manner of things for the reception of the French king's retinue. The panic of invasion seemed to have shattered all privacy. "Listen, Richard," she said, lowering her voice. "Your mother and Berengaria are here."

He was down from the window step and at her side in a couple of strides. "What? Mother and Berengaria *here*? Already?" he cried deliriously, wasting all her caution. "My dear Joan, you're wonderful"

"A sort of off-set for your war-like fleet," she murmured modestly. "In the old days it was always *you* doing things for *me*, you remember?"

"But how on earth did you manage to get them here?"

"In the fishing boat I was watching for. You see, Mother wrote to me from Brindisi as soon as she heard that William was dead. I gathered that she was staying there more or less incognito. She said she would try to come across and see me and perhaps we could travel back to England together. But she couldn't come until she had despatched a very precious Spanish cargo for you to the East. The vendors were more than satisfied with the deal but there was some difficulty about transport owing to the state of the French market."

"How she must enjoy shaking Europe up again after all those years at Salisbury!" laughed Richard, settling down on the window seat to listen.

"Of course, it was easy to guess what she meant," went on Johanna. "You know the way Mother always gets her scribe to underline all the important Latin words. So I saw how I must have upset your plans, by sending word of my predicament to Dover. The only thing to do was to bribe another fisherman to fetch them both across to Messina."

"How?"

"The Sicilian fishermen spread their nets to dry on the rocks down there," explained Johanna, negligently. "It only meant parting with another string of William's pearls."

Glancing down at the foreshore, Richard appreciated Tancred's carelessness. "You seem to have been very sure of my coming here," he said.

"Have you or Robin ever let me down?" enquired the favourite daughter of Oxford Castle, making him hold her pin box while she braided her beautiful hair. "But I didn't reckon on Philip. We must persuade him to go on ahead to Syria. Can't you tell him he's a cleverer general or a better sailor or something?"

"But he isn't," objected Richard stolidly. "He is sick every time we have a storm."

"Well, at least he is liege lord of half your lands and even you can't go sailing round the world with him and Berengaria, and leave his discarded sister at home!" pointed out Johanna irritably. Men were so exasperating, getting into a jam and then standing round without an ounce of invention waiting for one to get them out of it. After a few moments' devoted concentration, she suggested doubtfully, "I suppose Ann must be getting a bit shop soiled by now, but wouldn't it do if John married her?"

"It might—but he has probably married that flaxen-haired doll, Avisa, by now."

"Avisa of Gloucester? A commoner!" Johanna flared out at him with unexpected bitterness. "And just because he was a man—you let him!" She snatched a final pin from the box and clipped it savagely round the end of a plait. So John, as usual, had managed to grasp at life with both hands. He would keep his stake in England and spend the best years of his life with the woman he wanted. Whereas she…A sudden storm of self-pity swept her because she knew that the first transient bloom must have gone from her beauty. She had kept the fires of youth damped down so long for William. Would she now, she wondered disconsolately, have less to give?

Richard looked at her with understanding. He wanted to tell her about Robin—that it didn't matter now. That nothing would ever matter quite so much for either of them any more. But he could not find the words. He put down her trinket box and turned listlessly to gaze at the fine fleet for which he had fleeced England. Just so had he looked down upon it from his father's room at Dover Castle. There had been sweet-scented Kentish rashes on the floor—and the orders all ready for his captains—and Robin. "But I'm not coming crusading," he had said. "Cattle and crops, you know, call for as much courage as any visionary crusade…England will bleed for this." It was always like that now, he thought angrily. In the moment of success or lovers' meetings a pin prick of memory must come to deflate the high quality of his mood.

But his sister jolted him back to common sense. "You must bribe Philip," she said.

"What with?" he asked succinctly.

"With Sicilian money, of course. Haven't you just beaten our toy soldiers? Aren't you master here? Make Tancred pay a big indemnity for holding me prisoner, and then hand it over to Philip to buy off Ann."

Richard considered the scheme cautiously. "A sort of breach-of-promise settlement," he said, unaware that he was making legal history. "Of course, he'll probably say he hasn't enough ships to go on and begin operations without me—although actually the Venetian and Austrian contingents will have arrived, and I shall probably catch them all up before any of the serious fighting begins."

"Tancred has six galleys of mine," offered Johanna. "You can give them to Philip if you like as my contribution to your crusade."

The mesh of Richard's mail rustled pleasantly as he loped down from the window to hug her. Each was so easily bitten by the other's ideas. "Heaven bless you for your generosity!" he cried, accepting eagerly. "And when am I to see Berengaria?"

"The moment you get rid of Ann," she promised, hurrying him from her room so that she could get on with her preparations for a betrothal party. For what were the affairs of Philip Capet compared with the joy of bringing together the people she loved?

Richard, gathered up his gauntlets, stumbling over a silk-tasselled stool without so much as an oath. "How invaluable you would have been as my chancellor!" he said admiringly. But Johanna was already considering the size of her table and planning where everybody was to sit. "Well, my dear," she answered, with the abstracted forthrightness of her mother, "*somebody* has to be the brains of the family now Henry is gone."

Pausing without resentment on the threshold, Richard carefully reassembled the wreckage of her door. "I forgot to say that your amorous dragon is now bound and the castle all yours," he announced formally. "I shall be proud if you will come down and entertain our allies?"

But poor Johanna had had her fill of foreign kings. She shook her head, laughing. "It is more homely up here, and I can see your splendid ships. We are going to dine up here privately—all of us—instead of down in the hall." She wouldn't ask for Robin by name. She felt sure that immediately he had finished all the aide-de-camp jobs he always did so efficiently for her brother he would come. She kept the thought of it, warm and unexplored, in the background of her mind—the way a woman keeps a long-looked-for letter until her household tasks are done. And because happiness always killed her resentments, she added, "Thank you about the dragon. But don't twist his tail too hard!" Then, remembering a dozen things she wanted done, she hurried out to the stairhead. "Richard! Richard!" she called down after him. "Could you possibly spare me Blondel?"

His head was still visible like a torch in the curved darkness, and as he turned the newel he grinned up at her indulgently. "You know very well he is your devoted slave!" he called back.

Just to hear him bellowing for Blondel as he clanked down the stairs was almost as good as being back at Oxford. Johanna bustled back into the room of her captivity, singing. Instead of presiding over one of Tancred's fantastic feasts in the hall, she was going to give a private Plantagenet party.

Chapter Fifteen

WHEN BLONDEL PRESENTED HIMSELF in the Queen of Sicily's ill-used doorway she stared at him for an uncertain moment across the roses she was arranging, trying to reconcile this grave young man with the engaging lad she remembered. The dreams that used to lurk behind his long lashes seemed to be hidden by a hard-won air of efficiency, and a business-like Norman crop had superseded his thick, page's bob. "Why, Blondel," she exclaimed, "you look so *capable*! Don't you make verses any more?"

But the way he knelt to kiss her hands seemed to give her back the whole of England. As she touched his shoulders, an exasperating mist of tears made his bent head just a blur. It was as if she touched Henry and Hodierna—the carved lions on her father's chair or his favourite wolfhound—the tower room, the sunny tiltyard, and the willows dipping green fingers in the placid Thames. All the things of their old, familiar life. "We were all so happy together—at home—quarrelling—" she said incoherently.

Blondel got up. He was not much taller than she. They stood smiling at each other, level-eyed. "It was so dull after you went," he told her inadequately.

Johanna laughed, turning back to the silver bowl she was filling. "And how is Hodierna?" she asked.

"She isn't there any more," he answered, after a moment's hesitation.

"But Oxford without Hodierna is unthinkable!" As he made no comment, Johanna asked sharply, "She isn't ill, is she?" Her concern for the beloved curse was as real as if she herself had left there only yesterday.

"Oh, no, Madam." Blondel saw the next question framing itself inevitably on her lips. His sensitive mind realised that it must have been in her heart at the nostalgic moment of their greeting.

"And—and Robin?" asked Johanna, carefully selecting a tall red rose.

Dumb with consternation, the King's squire stooped to retrieve her scissors. He—who was never clumsy—fumbled to gain time, recalling John's vivid picture of their parting in the herb garden. Not that John's pictures were always accurate, of course... "Perhaps, Madam, you had better ask the King," he said, hating the stiff sound of his words.

He heard the tall stem snap between her fingers. But by the time he had straightened himself it had been thrust firmly into place—like her burning curiosity. Being the daughter of a great house, Johanna had learned young how to cloak her own vulnerable humanity with gracious enquiries into the concerns of others. "When you came to us as a page you little thought you would so soon be serving a king, did you?" she asked.

"It's like being part of one of those splendid old tapestries about adventures—working for him," grinned Blondel.

"Then there's a very happy episode you can act in to-day," she laughed. She called one of the bustling servants to set the bowl in the middle of the table. Richard and Sholto had both told her that Berengaria loved flowers—and what Berengaria loved was going to matter very much from now on. Even Queen Eleanor would have to take second place. Johanna sighed, wiped her fingers on fringed damask, and went briskly to the window. "Come and look down, Blondel," she invited, pointing out a dilapidated hut where an old man sat mending his nets. "Nobody would believe I had smuggled two ladies in there last night, would they?"

But Blondel had reason to believe her capable of any

hare-brained scheme. "Is that why the old fisherman is blocking up the entrance with his nets?" he enquired.

"And why you, my gallant Blondel, must go down quickly and discreetly to rescue them from such bare entertainment." She picked up a cloak of her own and bundled it into his arms. "Here, take this and wrap it round the younger one," she said, "and—whatever you do—don't go through the hall. You can bring them up by the postern turret and then we must feed them here."

Blondel viewed the fruit dishes and flowers with fresh understanding, and so willing was he to further even her wildest inventions that he found himself half way to the door with the cloak neatly folded over his arm before his quick brain had foreseen a possible difficulty. "Suppose they distrust a stranger and refuse to come?" he suggested.

Johanna smiled down at him from the window step, her hands folded smugly in the sleeves of her *bliaut*. Such service was very gratifying after the careless procrastination of the Sicilians. "They will not hesitate for a moment," she reassured him. "You see, both of them have met you before and one of them is the Queen of England."

Having trained himself to be a sort of human buffer between the family and discomfort, Blondel was badly jarred. "Our Queen! Waiting in that deplorable hovel!" he exclaimed. Like the rest of them he adored Eleanor, and trailed after her with things she had mislaid and tried to protect her from the importunities of people to whom she had been kind.

"I am sure she would wait down in one of the dungeons quite cheerfully if she thought it would profit your master," Johanna assured him. "And I suppose it is fine of the other one," she added, with reluctant generosity—"crossing Europe without ceremony like this—"

Light dawned on Blondel. "You say I have seen her, madam," he repeated eagerly. "May one hazard a guess at her name?"

"Hazard anything you like—except a chance encounter with the King of France!" laughed Johanna, speeding him gaily on his errand.

But when he was gone her mood changed. She turned back to the window, wondering anxiously what Berengaria would be like. She saw Blondel emerge from the postern gate, cross the sands, and slip something into the hand of the old fisherman, who moved his cumbersome nets aside; and presently the little party was picking its way over the rocks towards the castle. No hood ever woven could have disguised the tall, unconcerned dignity of Eleanor—one might as well try to bring in the archangel Gabriel unnoticed, thought her daughter, with a smile. The shorter one, closely enveloped in the fur-lined cloak, must be Berengaria; and the girl with the honey-coloured hair one of her ladies. How beautifully Blondel was helping them over the slippery pools! Once he picked up the little honey-coloured wench bodily and set her down on the other side.

As the four tiny figures grew more foreshortened beneath the walls, Johanna turned back into the room and snatched up a plate. As she peered anxiously into its silver surface she thought, with self-disparagement, "I wonder if she is as lovely as they say? And much more lovely than I?"—forgetting that an ill-reflected Johanna, without colour or animation, was no Johanna at all. But before she could lament for long over the comparison her party was upon her. Her mother and Berengaria and the pleasantly rounded little blonde. Queen Eleanor's hair was a little whiter, perhaps, but by her very erectness scorned the twinges of rheumatism which had driven her to accept Blondel's watchful assistance on the last few turns of the stair. And even a shapeless, borrowed cloak could not hide the perfection of Berengaria's beauty. It was like a fine etching in sepia tinted with the warmth of southern roses.

So much Johanna saw before she and her mother were clinging to each other with the joy of family reunion, which always used to seem so bourgeois to Ann, but which looked so lovable to Berengaria. "My dear, if only you could have come home before your father died! He lost all of you at the last," Eleanor was saying, half her thoughts still with her faithless husband who had suffered so from John's ingratitude. "Your fisherfolk were dears," she announced in the next breath. "But their hut was full of fleas!"

How good it was to hear again the mellow comfort of her voice and to giggle over the inimitable way in which she always repudiated her emotions with a brisk commonplace! "Forgive me—both of you—for keeping you down there," apologized Johanna, disengaging herself breathlessly. "But Philip was here—"

Having got herself divorced from his father before he was even thought of, Eleanor was not likely to be much impressed either by his new importance or by his matrimonial ambitions for his sister. "Philip or no Philip, I should have come up to the castle," she declared, drawing Berengaria to her side. "But these two fainthearts began shuddering when all the carnage started, and I must say Richard made a spectacular job of it. This is Berengaria, Johanna."

Johanna turned with outstretched hands. "You must be very tired," she said politely.

"Not too tired to appreciate your kindness in sending for me." Berengaria's voice was low and pleasant, her French quaintly softened by a southern accent.

The fair girl who had accompanied her lifted the cloak from her mistress's shoulders as if she were unveiling a miniature Venus, and Blondel brought a basin of scented water. Berengaria dipped her exquisite fingers while Eleanor frankly wallowed. "I expect we both smell of fish," she said, tucking back her crisp, windswept curls beneath a snowy coif.

Berengaria looked up across the basin at Johanna and smiled. Like most people who do not smile over-readily among strangers, she disarmed them when she did so. Johanna knew at once that, although this exquisite creature was accustomed to facing crowds with composure, she had shared her own shyness in anticipation of their meeting.

"Then you didn't mind the fish or the fleas?" Johanna found herself asking.

"Either your mother exaggerates or I must have been thinking of Richard," laughed Berengaria, shaking out her crumpled dress.

"I can lend you a fresh one," offered Johanna, suddenly wanting her to be as beautiful as possible for him. "But I suppose it wouldn't fit and—frankly—I haven't anything half as attractive."

"It is kind of you, but Yvette will see to it for me," said Berengaria, introducing the girl. "She is the youngest of my ladies."

"And the nicest, I should think," added Eleanor, touching Yvette's wild rose cheek with an approving finger.

Blondel, helping to brush the dust from Berengaria's skirts, seemed to think so too. And standing patiently between them, Berengaria looked over their busily bent heads to the wonderful panorama of blue and white beyond the bay. "How beautiful!" she murmured, with no word at all about having been hustled in without ceremony by the back stairs.

So she wasn't just a spoiled, sophisticated beauty after all, nor the carping sort of person who would crab all their pleasures as Ann had done. "Then you won't mind dining up here instead of in the hall?" asked Johanna, eagerly. "I thought it would be a pleasure for you and Richard—for all of us—to meet without a crowd of staring people. Would you mind if we don't even have the servants?"

"Lovely!" murmured Berengaria, who had never dined really *en famille* in all her pampered life.

Yvette took up the idea at once. "I could help, Madam, perhaps?" she suggested, seeking guidance from the elderly Queen who had directed them so expertly through divers foreign ways.

"You must be hungry yourself, child," demurred Eleanor. For was not a girl who had been brought up by her own kinswoman, the Abbess of Fontevrault, fit to sit at meat with the highest in the land?

But sentimental Yvette wanted to help with the betrothal party. "I can eat afterwards," she insisted, looking round in a lost sort of way for some less private apartment. Fishing boats, back entrances, kings and queens more or less picnicking on the third floor—it was all so different from anything she had hitherto experienced in her carefully ordered life. Blondel came to her rescue immediately. "Perhaps Mademoiselle will join me in the hall after we have finished serving here?"

Turning from the happiness of their glowing youth, Berengaria touched Johanna's mourning with a little gesture of compassion. "Everyone in Italy is so full of Tancred's romantic behaviour that it is difficult to think of you as recently widowed," she said gently.

"It seems only the other day I was trying to tell her that she was to marry William," sighed Eleanor.

"Was he so very old?" asked Berengaria, thrilling secretly at the thought of Richard's virility.

"Much older than Tancred—and ill," Johanna told her.

"How cheated you must have felt—you who seem so full of life!"

Johanna was silent, touched by her understanding. Then she remembered her laden table. "Let us sit down," she invited. "You must both be famished. We won't wait for the others."

Smiling her thanks as Blondel set her chair, Berengaria noticed that five places were laid. "Who else?" she asked.

"Richard and his foster-brother," said Johanna, her hazel-green eyes bright with happiness.

"Ah, yes, of course, I remember. Ro—bin." The ordinary English name acquired an exciting strangeness from her Spanish tongue. Whereas Johanna merely sat down, Sancho's daughter had an enviable trick of sinking into a chair surrounded by gracefully spread skirts that lent her littleness unbelievable dignity. "Richard used to talk by the hour about his precious foster-brother," she explained. "He said I was like him."

"Like him?" repeated Johanna, seeing nothing comparable between her guest's soft perfection and the resilient strength of Robin.

"Oh, I don't mean in looks!" laughed Berengaria. And, seeing that they were served, Johanna settled herself for a good gossip. "What's this about Hodierna having left Oxford, Mother?" she asked.

"Has she? It's news to me, and I left only a few weeks ago." Eleanor looked up anxiously at Blondel, who was handing her a dish of stuffed olives. "I hope she isn't ill?"

"No, Madam," replied Blondel, signing to Yvette to refill the silver-mounted drinking horns.

All this sea air had given Eleanor an appetite, and it was good to sit down to a properly cooked meal in a civilized room again. "Perhaps she has gone on a visit or to see poor Becket's shrine," she suggested comfortably. "We must ask Richard."

"Will he come soon?" asked Berengaria, her gaze never far from the door.

Johanna's heart was hurrying to the same question, but she had the misfortune to sit facing the window and her mother was complaining—not without reason considering how far she had travelled to fetch him a bride—that Richard ought to have been there to receive them. "It's so like all the boys," she said, insisting upon Yvette pouring herself a glass of wine. "Always remembering something they simply must do just when it's time for a meal!"

"I'm afraid it's *my* fault this time, sweet," confessed Johanna. "You see, I wanted to have you both here as a surprise for him. So I reminded him of an urgent debt he had to pay Philip."

"More expensive war equipment, I suppose," sighed Eleanor, who had been talked out of a good deal of her best jewellery for this crusade.

"Well, no," admitted Johanna. "Just something he didn't want."

Her mother gave a dubious little grunt. "It doesn't sound much like a son of mine—paying good money for something he doesn't want."

"But then, you see," went on Johanna, involving herself still further, "it wasn't *his* money."

Berengaria laid down knife and napkin with a little spurt of laughter. "You are a crazy family, aren't you? In Navarre we have a saying, 'As mad as a Plant—' But she didn't finish what she was going to say. She just rose slowly from her chair as if she were welcoming the whole host of Heaven. Her pansy brown eyes went wide and all the roses of Navarre seemed to warm the creamy pallor of her skin. "Richard!" she cried softly.

Chapter Sixteen

THERE WAS A SUDDEN stir outside the Queen of Sicily's door. Servants scuttled out of the way, holding dishes at impossible angles as they squeezed themselves against stone walls to let the Angevin invader pass. They gazed at him with hatred and awe, for was it not common rumour in every Mediterranean port that he could kill a lion single-handed? But except for his height he didn't look so terrible. He had bathed off the bloodstains of battle and was freshly shaven, pleased with himself and his world. Out of sheer good humour he paused on the top stair to pinch the ear of a pretty serving maid, and his laugh was good to hear as he recounted something sketchily over his shoulder to the companion who followed hard on his heels. "My dear fellow, he'd sell his soul for money," Richard was insisting. "So I told him there were plenty of good nunneries for his sister—"

Their laughter and the firm tramp of their feet came nearer, obliterating the soft shuffling movements of the servants. But they both pulled up short under the spandrel of the doorway, seeing the three women sitting there in homely setting just as Johanna had planned.

"Mother! Berengaria! But this is magic!" exclaimed Richard.

"Johanna's magic," his mother reminded him. And Johanna turned swiftly to reap her reward. Her heart was hammering as it had never hammered for the amorous Tancred or for any other

Sicilian, and her hands gripped the table edge behind her because she had not seen Robin for so long.

But the man Richard had brought with him was not Robin. Johanna saw a stocky man with a blunt nose and a large, humorous mouth. Although, like Richard, he had laid aside most of his war gear, it was easy to guess from his quiet, easy bearing that his shield would bear no insignificant device. All the same, Johanna hated him at sight. Not for any personal defect, but simply because he was not Robin.

How like a man to bring this stranger along, tying their tongues with politeness when everybody knew that she had planned a family party! Didn't Richard ever *think*? Why, they might just as well have dined in hall and spared her mother the stairs!

Actually, Richard *had* thought—wretchedly and hurriedly in the midst of his own happiness. And knowing that she must be expecting Robin, it had seemed to him kinder to bring someone—anyone—rather than no one at all. So when he had had the pleasure of meeting a man he really liked among Philip's supercilious followers he had brought him along as a sort of shield against Johanna's wrath and his own unhealing loneliness.

"I thought you would be glad if I persuaded your cousin to sail with us, Berengaria," he said, avoiding the furious questioning in Johanna's eyes. "Mother, you remember Raymond of Toulouse?"

Eleanor cast her mind back to a time when she had almost despaired of ever having sons of her own. "He insisted upon showing me his toy horse while his father and a tedious procession of nobles were doing homage to Louis," she managed to recall. "It was a ferocious-looking quadruped, I remember, and helped to enliven the ceremony considerably."

Raymond laughed and kissed her hand. "And I was taken home babbling about 'the lovely lady' who had kept me quiet with sweet-meats," he recalled.

"Yet I had to drag him here to dine," complained Richard.

"At least he had that much sense!" thought Johanna, going through the paces of a hostess without enthusiasm.

"I understood it was a family affair," explained Raymond.

And even while he greeted his cousin his brown eyes begged for some sign of welcome from this golden girl who was so ridiculously like Richard.

"All the more reason why Berengaria's family should be represented too," said Eleanor, who could always be depended upon to put people at ease. "What a happy thought, Richard!"

Berengaria loved him for it. None of them would ever know what it had cost her to leave Sholto and her adoring parents and the cultured pleasantness of her home. Johanna's compensating love of adventure was not hers, and from all she had heard of these Plantagenets they would not understand how one could cherish a smoothly flowing family life, unbroken by passionate incident or harsh word. Her hands clung to Raymond's arm, pulling him down to the form beside her. He was a bit of home. And of late Raymond had managed to content himself with the knowledge that he could never hope to be more. But he felt a fool because Richard's sister, whose party it was, sat down at the other end of the form with scarcely a word.

Richard himself was too excited to notice. "I just can't believe it's true!" he kept saying, still standing just inside the door, looking from one to another of his womenfolk. "An hour ago I believed you two were in Brindisi."

"We got tired of waiting," Berengaria told him demurely. Her adoring eyes must have told him much more, for, with a low laugh, he was across the room and had her in his arms with her little pointed chin cupped in his hand. "You're even more beautiful than I remembered," he was saying, his eyes devouring her before them all.

Eleanor leaned forward to smile at Raymond across their unresponsive hostess. "Oughtn't we to go and look at the ships or something?" she suggested, mocking gamely at the loss of her maternal empire. But Richard overheard her and, swinging on his heel, pushed her gently back into her chair. "Do you think I would let you go now when you have been wonderful enough to bring her?" he asked, his tanned cheek resting for a moment against her silvery hair. He slipped into the seat between them and helped himself lavishly to all his favourite dishes at once. And presently—under cover of the general conversation—he produced the wreckage of a rose and placed it carefully beside Berengaria's plate.

"Oh—you've kept it all this time!" she murmured, covering it quickly with her hand.

Richard was thrilled to find he could call the red into her cheeks so easily. In Pamplona it had been he who was confused and she who had laughed. But now, with senses stormed by the unabashed ardour of his full manhood, she was no longer entirely mistress of the situation.

Still watching her with tender amusement, Richard forced open her predatory fingers one by one and took back his cherished tournament favour. As he thrust the withered petals back against his heart, the warmth of his flesh revived some of their faded fragrance, wafting to his nostrils the heady intoxication of his first awakening passion for her. "Until I hold you there," he whispered, his eyes burning her.

And all the while Johanna sat dumbly surmising, hospitality forgotten and food untouched. She saw the four of them as a complete and pleasant square from which her uncertainty excluded her. Suddenly she could bear it no longer. "Isn't Robin coming?" her clear voice demanded stridently across their happiness.

They lifted startled heads from the absorbing topics of reunion. "No," barked Richard, almost rudely.

His mother and Raymond left the reputation of a mutual friend hanging scandalously in mid-air. "You mean—not coming at all?" Eleanor asked incredulously. She too had always taken it for granted that love necessarily included understanding, and this had been her undoing with Henry of Anjou.

For the first time since they had sat down Johanna's attitude became less rigid and withdrawn. "Oh, Richard," she said, letting her upturned palm fall pleadingly across the table, "you haven't quarrelled with *him*, have you?"

"He thinks we're a lot of bloody foreigners!" he muttered, shamefacedly.

Eleanor's wise old eyes searched his face. It had always been an

open book to her in which both good and bad intent were under-
lined as uncompromisingly as the important words in her letters.
And this in spite of her almost idolatrous love for him. "My poor
Hodierna, who loves you both!" was all she said.

"Hodierna could have stayed at Oxford," he said. "She chose
to follow him."

"Where?" demanded Johanna.

Richard shrugged with an exaggerated assumption of indifference—a nasty, Gallic gesture he had caught from Philip. "How
should I know? Except that he stayed in England," he answered
stubbornly. "He traded on my love—letting me down and then
criticizing everything I did. So I outlawed him."

Both the Plantagenet women smothered a cry. Eleanor sat
unconscious of a hand that still covered her parted lips, watching
Johanna's overturned wine spread like a bleeding wound across the
cloth. Johanna pushed back the form she had been sharing with
her unwanted guest. In so doing she caught the end of her sleeve
clumsily on one of the jewels studding his sword belt, and when
he bent to unravel it she tugged it blindly from his grasp, scarcely
aware of his courtesy. "How could you? Oh, how could you? I must
send him a message—somehow—" she cried incoherently, turning
away to hide her distress.

To hide how much he cared, Richard laughed boisterously.
"Better send him your distaff!" he scoffed, washing down his food
with Tancred's choicest wine.

Johanna swung round on him like an angry, spitting cat; but
Eleanor lifted a restraining hand. She was very angry with him
herself. "Richard, that is unworthy of you!" she said quietly.

He knew that it was, but no man enjoys being reproved before
his future wife. And here was the inescapable memory of Robin
making a churl of him again and spoiling all his best moments.
"Well, if he didn't want to come with *me* at least he might have
changed his mind if he heard we were sailing for Sicily," he said
sullenly. What he implied in self-defence was scarcely true, because
probably Robin hadn't heard until after they had sailed. "But that
was no fault of mine," thought Richard, reliving that hellish night

when he had combed the Kentish woods so ineffectually. And anyhow, he felt, it was illogical of Johanna to blame him instead of Robin. But there she stood with her back to them, staring unseeingly at his beautiful ships and tearing her silk headdress to shreds in a miniature edition of his own Angevin rage. Except that being a woman and a hostess cramped her style a bit, he supposed, with brotherly satisfaction.

Blondel and Yvette had slipped away so tactfully that no one had noticed the moment of their going, and the Count of Toulouse got up and moved nearer to his cousin. Loves and loyalties, rancours and shifting passions incomprehensible to either of them had been tossed about familiarly as shuttlecocks. To understand them, Raymond supposed, one must be born in the bosom of this charming, turbulent family—which, thank Heaven, he was not! "Everything they do turns to drama," he said under his breath, and Berengaria felt she must somehow ward off this strange destiny to which she would so soon be joined. She had never seen this Robin about whom they were all wrangling, but she knew how Richard loved him, and palpably he had power to move them all. She looked down at the clenched fist lying on the table beside her and ran a tentative finger down the back of it, smoothing the strong reddish hairs. "Didn't you say, Richard—that day at the tournament—that there are two sorts of courage?" she reminded him.

Richard turned at the touch of her hand, but it was quite clear from his blank stare that for the moment he had forgotten she was there. Although he was hers there would often be moments when, like Ann, she would be made to feel an outsider. But—unlike Ann—she would always have power to reclaim him with a touch. His hand closed over hers now, and he smiled down at her reassuringly. "I am sorry, Johanna," he apologised at once. "I spoke like a fool—because I was hurt—forgetting that you loved him too."

If the words elucidated things a little for Raymond, somehow they jarred him badly. He had thought of Johanna as someone coming through widowhood into untrammelled freedom. She had stood apart, battling with disappointment and hurt pride, and it was her turn for play-acting now. "I was rather young then, wasn't I?"

she said negligently. Stepping down from the window embrasure, she flicked her skirts at a grey Persian kitten Tancred had sent her and laughed when it bounced after her along the floor. And just to show them that there were other men in the world besides Robin, she sat down next to Raymond and began deliberately trying to attract him. She appeared to have forgotten that he had come uninvited to her party and she neither knew nor cared that he was far too fine to endure being made use of.

Richard accepted her attitude with relief. "And what about you, Mother? Are you coming on with us to look up all those Syrian lovers of yours whom old Louis waxed so jealous about? Just to show Raymond he's not the only old campaigner present."

"Don't be ridiculous, Richard!" laughed Eleanor. "You know very well if Henry had lived to run this crusade with you instead of Philip he wouldn't have allowed any women at all. But if you can't do without them"—she moved aside a spray of roses in order to nod pleasantly to her future daughter-in-law—"well, at least let them be young and beautiful." The gallant old Queen sighed, remembering perhaps what fun she had had at Antioch; then added briskly, "Besides, I had better go back and keep an eye on things in England."

Richard got up and rinsed his fingers, drying them thoughtfully. "Perhaps I should have been wiser to send you officially as my regent," he said.

But Eleanor's eyes twinkled. She knew how the irascible little Longchamps would resent such an appointment. "I will just go back as the besotted old watchdog I've been for you ever since you were breeched," she decided.

"But I thought you had another son to keep an eye on England, Madam?" said Raymond, politely extricating himself from Johanna's embarrassing attentions.

"That's just why," they told him cryptically.

He shrugged helplessly. "Mad—quite mad!" he murmured, catching Berengaria's amused glance.

Richard clapped him on the shoulder and invited Berengaria to come and look once more at his wonderful ships. She loved the way they sparkled in the afternoon sunlight, painting deep purple shadows on the water; but they meant nothing to her, rope by rope, as they did to the understanding of the island-bred Johanna. Secretly, she wished she could be done with ships and spend her honeymoon peacefully on dry land. But at least they were bigger than the uncomfortable little fishing boat and no one, she supposed optimistically, could be sick or frightened with Richard on board.

"Look, the French fleet is beginning to weigh anchor," cried Johanna, curling herself up on the window seat with the unstudied ease of a boy.

"Oh, good!" breathed Berengaria, feeling released from the untiring tentacles of Ann.

But Richard did not seem to think it so good after all. "Philip has more ships than I," he remarked, watching them sort themselves out from the Normans and the English.

"That must be unbearable for you!" mocked Eleanor, still sitting at table peeling a pear.

The others laughed but Richard continued to scowl, counting them as they moved majestically towards the open sea. Already a following wind was billowing out the golden lilies on their sails. Berengaria squeezed his arm. "You are thinking, aren't you, that but for me you would be in virtual command of both fleets?" she asked, a little forlornly.

"No, no, of course not," he denied hastily, realising with a momentary stab of dismay that his thoughts would never be quite his own property again. "But I must push after him soon. I can't let all Europe say I left him to raise the siege of Acre single-handed."

"I am ready to start whenever you like," she offered.

Richard took both her hands between his own the way he did when men swore fealty to him. "I shouldn't think any man was ever so blessed in his womenfolk," he said, smiling down at her tenderly. "But the devil of it is we shall have to sail separately."

"W-why?" faltered Berengaria.

"Well, my sweet, now that we are together at last it is already April. And you must see that, as a soldier of the cross, I cannot marry in Lent."

Berengaria gave a little gasp and sat down beside Johanna, staring at him. Here was a complication which had never occurred to her. In the gay, go-ahead court of Navarre her education had been intellectual rather than religious, so that the ruling of the church seemed harsh. She had come so far and given so much for Richard's sake, and already their barely tasted romance was turning into disagreeable reality. She saw herself tossing about indefinitely on rough seas, without either the comfort of her home or the thrill of a husband. She felt like crying, but supposed these strong-minded Plantagenet women would only despise her for it. Instinctively, she turned to her cousin—the one person who was always so reliably sane.

"Raymond, what do *you* think?" she asked, almost beseechingly.

Raymond was a crusader too, and recognised the unseemliness of a royal marriage feast in Lent. But recognising also the pathetic signal of her fluttering lashes, he suggested something soothing about a message to the Pope.

But Richard was adamant. Besides being a crusader, he was deeply and simply religious. Plenty of people, he knew, were going to the Holy Land because they loved adventure. They could not love it more than he. But the very simplicity of his nature made it possible for him to keep his real goal quite clearly before him. Focusing his vision upon the far-off end of endeavour, he could always see the red cross of Christendom crowning the hills of Jerusalem. He wanted that more than anything in the world. He saw himself on his knees offering it to Christ. The gift, of course, would be Christ's—but his—Richard's—would be the power and the glory. And this splendid goal was coming nearer and nearer until soon, he felt sure, it would be a definite fact for all the world to see. He was not to know that only the hardness and heartbreak of the task could ever teach him to want Christ to have the city, without caring whether it were Richard Plantagenet or some other who gave it to Him. Even though by that time he himself might have become the greatest crusader of them all.

Berengaria shivered a little, as if recognising in his stern adherence to his vows a fanaticism that could out-grow love, just as Richard detected in her something of the tolerant humanitarianism which had seemed to him almost pagan in Robin. But in the high noon of their love these things were as yet but unlengthened shadows. Berengaria knew only that she had keyed herself up to surrender to his frightening but delicious urgency and now found herself in the humiliating position of rebelling against his continence. Sancho the Wise had taught her to respect the mental processes of all sorts and conditions of men, and she herself was too fastidious to pit her physical lures against a man's conscience. But the fact that their marriage was to be delayed through no lack of ardour did not make things easier for either of them.

"You can sail in the Bishop of Beauvais' galley and we will be married in Syria at Easter," said Richard.

"That will be best, I suppose," agreed Berengaria. Then, remembering Eleanor—that tower of strength—would be going back to England, she added involuntarily, "But, oh, Richard, I shall be so lonely!"

Johanna turned suddenly from her contemplation of the fleet. "I will come with you," she offered.

They stared at her in surprise.

"I thought you said you were counting the days to get back to England and the hawking and the comfortable green hills?" said Eleanor.

But all savour had gone out of these things. How could one bear the sight of beech trees without the sound of Robin's voice or come home from hunting without the kindness of his smile? "It will probably be more amusing in Syria," said Johanna casually. "And in spite of Tancred I am still a respectable widow, so I shall be able to chaperon the bride-to-be."

"Would you really do that for us?" Richard wrung her hand as if she were a man, and Berengaria kissed her. "It is going to be wonderfully different for me having a sister!" she said gratefully.

Raymond wanted to tell Johanna that she had won her spurs like a good knight—coming through suffering and humbled pride to courage and generosity. He wanted to beg forgiveness for looking on her humiliation and to cry aloud that she was beautiful. But because he could not bear her smiling at him cheaply he was dumb.

Gallantly, she threw off the fetters of her resentment. "So it has all come true!" she cried, going to her brother with a radiant smile. "The splendid ships and the shared adventure. All that your old witch promised us, Richard."

"Even to the charmed life, I hope," he laughed, putting his home-made ring back on her finger next to William's costly one.

"Did she really promise you that?" Berengaria didn't really believe in witches but, after seeing the arrows that had whistled about his head that morning, she was ready to grasp at any sort of assurance.

"There was a proviso, of course," admitted Eleanor, wiping her fingers after her fruit.

"There always is," laughed Raymond. "It lets the old witch out if anything goes wrong."

But Eleanor was quite serious about it. "Because Robin made him save her from a ducking or something, she says no one can kill Richard so long as he fights in a just cause."

"And you couldn't have a juster cause than crusading, so why worry?" said Raymond cheerfully.

Eleanor rose from the table and kissed Richard on either cheek. Tall as she was, she had to reach up to place her hands on his shoulders. "So God will keep you, my son, for my old eyes to see again," she prophesied resolutely.

Richard's hands closed hard over hers, and Berengaria created a diversion in order to leave them alone a little longer in their world which she was so soon to invade. "My dower chests!" she exclaimed. "They are still down in that verminous hut."

"Blondel will have seen to them," Johanna assured her.

"And I do hope Yvette will be happy. Both her parents died of the plague, you know."

"No need to worry about her. Yvette is such an attractive little person, Blondel won't miss the opportunity of seeing to her too."

Richard came and slipped an arm through Berengaria's, drawing her towards the door. "Let us all go down and bait Tancred now those Frenchmen have gone," he suggested.

But Raymond lingered a moment with Johanna. "Thank you

for offering to sail with my cousin—and for your party," he said. Evidently, Johanna was beginning to realise how badly she had treated him, and to cover her embarrassment he went on lightly, "This Blondel of yours sounds invaluable. I remember how he requisitioned one of my best shirts for your brother at Pamplona."

For the first time Johanna looked at him with real friendliness. "Come to think of it, I don't know what we should do without him," she laughed. "He is the perfect squire. Mends all the things we break and finds all the things our mother loses. In fact, if Richard himself got lost I imagine Blondel would find him."

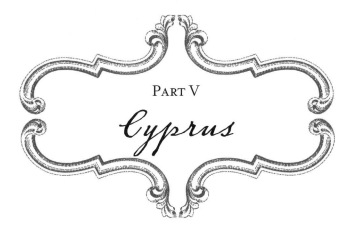

PART V

Cyprus

Chapter Seventeen

RICHARD AND BERENGARIA WERE not married in Syria after all. The ships which had looked so fine off Dover and Messina were tossed about like cockleshells on an angry Mediterranean for weeks. Only the riding light of Richard's red-sailed flagship by night and the coercion of his cheerful voice by day kept them together in any semblance of a fleet. Battered by the storm and beaten out of their course, some of them finally found shelter under the lee of Cyprus.

If Richard had profited by what his elder brother had said about bringing women, his great galley *Trenchemer* and several of his troopships could probably have made Beirut. But news came that Isaac Comnenos, the thick-lipped, plausible little emperor of the island, was plundering the Bishop's ship as she lay helpless off Limassol and trying to persuade him to bring the European women ashore. Berengaria and Yvette were by that time far too sea-sick to care what happened to them; but Richard could remember laughing over Picot's bawdy stories about Isaac's overcrowded harem, and his voice became full of profanity instead of cheer. He put the *Trenchemer* about, called for landing parties from the rest of the ships, and treated the inhospitable port of Limassol much as he had treated Messina.

Isaac fled inland to the hills and for three whole days Richard fought up and down the island until he caught him and sent him back to the coast in chains. And then quite suddenly he had time to notice that the spring flowers were in bloom and that it was no longer Lent. After fighting the sea for three weeks and the Cypriots for as many days, he ought to have been too exhausted to do anything but sleep. But instead he decided it was time to get married.

Riding down from Mount Troodos with a following of weary knights, he turned in the saddle to grin persuasively at his gifted squire. "Make me a song for my wedding night, Blondel!" he ordered.

"Considering the bride's beauty, you'd better make it pretty amorous!" advised Barbe Vidomar, the black-visaged Count of Chalus, enviously.

"And considering the bridegroom's long Lenten fast, Blondel, you'd better make it before to-morrow night!" chuckled jolly old Sansterre of Mortaine.

Pursued by a gust of their friendly laughter, the prospective bridegroom spurred on ahead across the sandy plain. The storm seemed to have spent itself with his battle rage and the peace of eventide hung over Cyprus. Flat on the rim of the Mediterranean he could see the walls of Limassol. Caravans of haughty camels padded past him bearing the wealth of the Levant to Nicosia, and shepherds led their patient, black-faced goats to folds at scattered farms. "This is really the beginning of the East," exulted Richard, catching passing glimpses of olive-skinned women preparing an evening meal in the walled yards of their little flat-roofed homes.

Some of his men were already fraternising with the Greeks, dallying with dark-eyed girls as they drew water from the wells and quenching their thirst from native pigskins. Some were merely rowdy and others were quite openly looting. Once or twice, in the short twilight, men hurtled almost under his horse, chasing some dusky beauty. It was amusing to hear the jackdaws imitate their tipsy laughter and the shrill, inviting screams of the girls. Had Richard been engaged on some stern campaign he would have controlled them with iron discipline; but here on this lovely, lazy island after their cramped tedium aboard ship, he shut his eyes to it.

Only once did he interfere—and his interference cost England a queen.

As he rode into Limassol he saw a girl run from the shelter of a house pursued by two English archers. She neither screamed nor giggled, but ran with the grace of a deer along the narrow street towards him, eluding their grasp by inches. From the shadow of the city gate Richard watched the chase dispassionately, much as he might have followed the cunning of some hard-pressed deer. She ran so close that he could hear the quick sob of her breath, and when one of the soldiers grabbed away her cloak he noticed that she was little more than a child. Instantly, his gorge rose.

"Get back to camp or I'll slit your throats!" he thundered. At the sound of his voice both men slunk away up some back street as if they had seen the devil, and the girl was left, panting and dishevelled, leaning against the city wall.

"You got what you asked for, hanging about the streets when men have done fighting," Richard told her sharply, "Go back to your father's house."

She raised beseeching, dark-lashed eyes. Even in the half light he could see that she was slender as one of the young palm trees that grew on Troodos, and that her small breasts were still pulsating like the heart of a frightened animal. "My father has been taken prisoner," she said.

"Well, haven't you a mother—or some woman to look after you?" he asked irritably. But her answer came pat. "They are all with your soldiers"—and that seemed to make it his responsibility. He could hear Mortaine and Barbe of Chalus and the rest of them coming along the road behind and was in no mood to be chaffed on the subject of knight-errantry as well as matrimony. Almost angrily he stuck out a foot. "Jump!" he ordered. And light as this-tledown she set her bare foot upon his mailed one and let him pull her to the saddle before him. With a click of his tongue he set the great war-horse in motion again towards the Emperor's citadel where he had taken up his abode. As the girl swayed against his shoulder she smiled up at him shyly, her teeth like small square pearls in the childish oval of her face. "I saw you wade ashore waving your great battle-axe. Is it true that you killed a lion?" she asked naïvely.

Perhaps Richard was flattered that she knew him. "I'm afraid I've never met one," he laughed more amiably. "What is your name? And how is it you speak French so well?"

"My name is Ida, and we had French tutors when we were small."

Now that she was so close he noticed that she smelled sweet and that there were silver bangles on her arms. "I will have you taken home," he said.

But she shook her head so that the top of her short, dark curls brushed his cheek. "My home has been taken over by a thieving Anglo-Norman," she told him fearlessly.

"Find me the man and I will punish him," he promised.

"What would you do to him? Slit his throat?"

He shook her in the crook of his arm as one shakes an unmanageable child and told her not to be such a blood-thirsty little wretch.

"But you said—just now—to those English pigs—"

"Only to teach them not to frighten pretty little girls. I can't afford to kill my best archers. But if you think you can describe the undisciplined swine who looted your home and turned you out on to the street—"

Ida turned in his arm, examining him impudently with smiling, sloe-black eyes. "He's tall and strong enough to take whatever he wants," she enumerated in her quaint, broken French. "His hair is reddish—his nose a soupçon too long perhaps—and his mouth? Oh, yes, that is very well. It is firm and hard and, like all the accursed Normans, he keeps his lips shaven—"

"That's enough!" laughed Richard, jerking his cheek from the liberties of her exploring fingers. "I'm glad I picked you up if you're Isaac Comnenos' daughter. And sorry," he added, more soberly, "about your home."

"I don't mind much," she shrugged, staring disdainfully from her high perch at the pink-faced foreigners guarding its gates. "He ran away when you offered to fight him for it—and, anyway, I always hated him."

"I didn't exactly dote on *my* father," admitted Richard, wondering what sort of woman had helped the old Levantine to produce anything so refreshing.

Casting about in his mind as to what he should do with her, his eyes lighted thankfully upon Johanna returning from an evening gallop with Raymond, whom he had left in charge of the garrison at Limassol. "The sands-are marvellous!" she called to him, her fair skin aglow with exercise. "We've been exploring a place farther round the coast called Famagusta."

"There's a really useful harbour there," Raymond told him, as they rode into the Citadel courtyard. "Deep enough water for our biggest ships and facing Beirut."

"Good. I must take a look at it," said Richard. "Where is Berengaria?"

"In Isaac's garden. Of course, if she'd known you were bringing home a native beauty—" Johanna was all curiosity about the refugee on her brother's saddle, but the Count of Toulouse cut short her laughing indiscretion by lifting her down from her horse. Even if he wasn't tall and good-looking like Robin, he made a pretty good job of it.

Richard put Ida down and rode closer to them. "It's the old Greek's daughter," he explained. "I caught two of our fellows chasing her like a common troll. I wish you'd take care of her for me, Joan."

"She seems to make a habit of taking care of people for you," grumbled Raymond. But Johanna looked compassionately at the lonely little figure surrounded by Plantagenet possessions in her own courtyard. "Oh, well, I suppose it must be rather grim for her the way we've spread ourselves in all the Comnenos' best rooms," she conceded reluctantly.

"Being a princess of sorts, she ought to make a useful hostage," Raymond reminded them.

Richard had already thought of that. "Give her everything she wants but don't let her stray again," he said, dismounting and beckoning to the girl to join them.

She came with the docility of a captive and a grace achieved only by those who go barefoot. She knew they were discussing her, these two powerful men and the straight-limbed Northern woman who rode astride. "Here is a lady who will look after you, Ida," said Richard, unaware that—having just escaped from life in the women's quarters—this was the last thing she wanted.

She hung back, staring at Johanna with hostility. "Who is she?" she asked suspiciously.

"My sister, Queen Johanna of Sicily," he answered curtly. "And you will obey her."

The girl's manner changed instantly. She touched one of Johanna's burnished plaits with a conciliatory gesture. "Her hair is the same colour as yours. I shall like her," she said.

"There's a second-hand compliment to give anyone!" laughed Johanna. "Let us go in, Ida. I need a bath after my ride, and we will see if we can find some of your women and clothes and things."

Before going in Ida turned to thank Richard for bringing her home. "But your heavy Flemish horses are too clumsy for this kind of country," she told him. "When you cross to Syria you will find their hooves sink in the sand. I will give you Fauvel—the Arab gelding my father ran away on."

Surprised at her perspicacity, Richard bent down and kissed her lightly. "Thank you, my dear," he said gravely, winking across her head at Johanna, who knew he had already taken the horse.

With a casual "good night" to them, she drew the little hostage indoors. Raymond swore softly. Just as he was beginning to make some headway with his suit, Richard must needs turn up with this new toy. What with weddings and dower chests, Johanna had had little enough time for him these last three days and now, he supposed, she would always have the wretched little Cypriot in tow. He turned to tell Richard what he thought of him. "Didn't you *see* how the little cat sheathed her claws the moment you said Johanna was your *sister?*"

But Richard had disappeared. He had probably forgotten their existence. With long, eager strides he had made his way to the deserted garden behind the women's quarters. Although officially of the Orthodox church, Isaac had planned it harem fashion with a fountain splashing in the middle and shady colonnades where he could walk with his favourites. The semi-Eastern twilight was short and the cypress shadows long, and Berengaria sat in her filmiest samite gown on the low coping of the fountain. "Wherever two stunted flowers manage to raise their heads above the sand, there I shall always be sure of finding you!" laughed Richard triumphantly.

She turned before she could hide her passionate joy.

"Enchantress!" he muttered, pulling her close against his hungry body. Because he had taken her off her guard Berengaria returned his kisses without pride or prudence. All her senses answered his. For days she had been mad with anxiety and longing and now, suddenly, he had lifted her into this ecstasy of happiness. She did not foresee that if she married him most of her life would be brief Heavens between one battle and the next. She only knew that it is given to few women to have so fierce a lover.

"If people tell you there have been other women, forgive me," he said after a while. "I don't even remember what they looked like…It didn't seem to matter…No one has ever made me feel my body was theirs before!"

Considering his rank and vigour, Berengaria was intelligent enough to see that it could hardly have been otherwise. "I shall mind only those who come after," she said, exulting in a comradeship that drove him to complete candour.

"Little fool!" he whispered. "How could they?" And then, with lips urgent against hers, "Need we wait for Syria? Can't we be married here—to-morrow?"

Berengaria pressed both palms against his racing heart, trying to free herself enough for thought. "You know how I love this island—and fierce, impatient red-heads!"

Richard released her to capture both her small marauding hands. He—who feared no man—was almost afraid to let her know the devastating power she had over him. "And you won't mind not waiting for a cathedral—and Philip of France—and all the conventional trappings?"

Berengaria shook her small, dark head. "There was a time when I should have—but now those things don't count." Her brown eyes looked deep into his tawny ones, giving him truth for truth. Her body was soft with surrender, her lips a lure he dared no longer dally with. Because of Ann's perfidy he wanted to keep her sacred. So he turned away abruptly and started shouting for the servants.

"Bring lights into the hall—and fetch me the Bishop of Beauvais," he ordered. His voice rang to the vaulted roof, full and round with happiness.

Berengaria could have followed, but she wanted to keep the bloom of her happiness unbrushed by other contacts. Richard's cloak lay where it had fallen when he took her in his arms. She picked it up and wrapped herself in it, fancying it still warm from his body, and sat there by the fountain until the stars pierced the black velvet of the Cyprian night. She could hear them planning her wedding. Richard's crisp voice and the Bishop's suave one. Other people were sent for—Raymond, Blondel and Mercadier. The marshal and steward were wakened and given orders. Through the branches of an acacia shrub Berengaria could see them all moving about in the lighted hall—the Bishop's fine gesticulating hands—a sleepy cook with straw still in his hair passing the open doorway—someone's shifting sleeve or the flash of a ring and, from time to time, the warm glow from a torch illuminating her lover's head. "Heavens!" she thought, with a little tender smile, "doesn't the man ever sleep?" Irrelevantly, she fell to wondering how many men he had killed that morning—and now to be discussing colour schemes!

Once, when they started talking about clothes, she nearly went in and joined them. But, partly out of curiosity, she wanted even the setting of their wedding to be Richard's. Their voices droned on. She forgot even to listen. She was spent with emotion, living again through each of Richard's kisses. She might have sat there half the night if Yvette had not found her. "Suppose you caught a chill before the wedding?" she scolded.

"Don't be a motherly little hen!" laughed Berengaria, snuggling closer into the King's cloak. Yvette was all pleasant curves and young importance these days, finding herself the only lady-in-waiting to a future queen.

"It's only because I love you, Madam. And because I promised King Sancho—"

"I know, you funny child! But you won't have to feel responsible much longer. Richard Plantagenet and I are going to be married to-morrow."

"Oh, Madam!" Yvette lifted her frivolous skirts and executed a jolly little *pas seul* between the long, slim shadows of the colonnade. But her excitement was mostly for the wedding itself and for the new blue gown she was to wear and because she was to dress the bride. When she thought, in her innocence, about the irrevocable intimacy of their married life she stopped dancing and shivered with foreboding. "Blondel only just saved your rose from being trampled on—that day in the lists—and really your heart lay there too," she said, with apparent irrelevance.

But Berengaria had no misgivings and—whatever happened—she would have no regrets. To be loved by Richard was worth everything. "Ever since he came laughing up the pavilion steps, thrilled with himself and his blazoned leopards and his ridiculous sprig of broom, I haven't been able to *see* any other man. I tried—for years—after he went, because I thought they would never let me marry him…"

They sat talking of love for a while, forgetful of all difference in age and rank, until Berengaria suffered herself to be put to bed and went to sleep for the last time a maid, hugging her happiness.

Then Yvette picked up the King's cloak and, very properly, returned it to the King's squire. Guided by the spasmodic notes of a lute, she found him on the battlements composing a wedding song. He was just as anxious about it as she was about the bride's veil, so he insisted on trying it out on her. She hadn't a note of music in her honey-coloured head, but she said quite kindly that she was sure the song would be a success, and in return for her encouragement he told her how plucky he thought her to come so far from home.

"*Me* plucky!" protested Yvette. "Why, I'd die this very minute if I saw a snake. I dreamed about them for nights when I heard we were coming to the East. But you bustle about quite cheerfully, don't you, even when you feel like sobbing because nothing's unpacked and everything feels so strange?" Her blue eyes opened wide the way he meant them to. "However did you guess?" she asked. So he told her the story of a homesick page who was laughed at because he couldn't lay a table properly, and then comforted by a kind princess.

"You adore the Queen of Sicily, don't you?" said Yvette, making nasty little discords on the strings of his lute.

But instead of committing himself, Blondel drew her- to the west side of the battlements, and showed her how the same stars must be shining over Navarre. "Look up and count them!" he teased. And when she looked up like an obedient little goose, he kissed her round, astonished mouth.

Chapter Eighteen

THE WEDDING, AS RICHARD planned it, was unique. Not in the least the kind of affair either of them had expected, but much more original than the marriages of any of their friends. Instead of walking in stately procession up the aisle of some cathedral with music and incense soaring to the dim vastness of the roof, they were married quite simply in the small, dark chapel at Limassol. Instead of rows of staring subjects there was room for only their relatives and intimate followers and friends. And if Berengaria *did* cry secretly on Raymond's shoulder before the ceremony because her beloved parents could not be there, her heart must have been warmed by the shouts of welcome that went up afterwards when her husband led her out into the sunshine.

Berengaria never forgot that scene. Companies of armed knights, each with his squire and richly caparisoned horse, out-blazoned the stained glass of any cathedral with the colours of their heraldry. Austere, white-robed Templars stood waiting before the sombre chapel, leaning on the tall swords they had dedicated to the protection of Christ's pilgrims; and behind them, rank upon rank, were massed the archers and sappers and men-at-arms. Their upturned faces seemed to stretch away to an azure sea where the dragon of England flew from a score of mastheads. Like a proud jewel in the midst of them rode the *Trenchemer*, with her blood-red sails, and closer to the palm-girt shore a new ship had anchored, glittering with the five golden crosses of the Holy City itself. For by a lucky chance Guy de Lusignon, King of Jerusalem, had landed that very morning to welcome the Anglo-Norman contingent.

"Trust a Plantagenet to produce some sort of pageantry!" whispered Berengaria, squeezing the arm she held so formally. And, seeing that the stage was so well set, Richard insisted upon having his bride crowned there and then before them all.

"But where are the crowns?" whispered the agitated bishop.

"At Westminster and Rouen, I suppose," remembered Richard.

So the Count of Chains, who collected antiques, very obligingly produced a circlet of Roman gold and Berengaria was crowned with that. All through the ceremony she kept thinking how different Richard looked. She was so unfamiliar with his public manner as a king that by the time she came to take her oath of allegiance she felt as if the urgent Richard she loved had gone away and left her with some dignified and rather terrifying stranger. But when she knelt before him he held her trembling hands firmly between his own and—proud daughter of Navarre as she was—she saw in him attributes to which she could give wholehearted homage. And once the solemn moment was over she discovered joyfully that both he and Johanna discharged most of their public duties to a sotto voce accompaniment of racy private remarks which promised to dissipate the dullness of all formal occasions.

After the coronation Richard had barrels of wine rolled out to the troops, and a great wedding feast was served in Isaac's hall, with the doors set wide to the splashing fountain and the colonnade. "The poor cooks must have worked all night!" exclaimed Berengaria, delighted with the fairy-like effect of the iced cakes and fantastic sugar castles they had produced. And the steward had certainly commandeered the resources of the Comnenos' cellars.

Blondel's song was a vast success, and Yvette was sure no bride had ever looked lovelier than her mistress in her stiff white samite gown and the exquisite veil which she herself had embroidered with tiny silver hearts copied from the arms of Navarre. In place of Philip, the King of Jerusalem proposed the bride's health. "To Berengaria, Queen of England and Cyprus, Duchess of Normandy,

Aquitaine, Anjou, and Maine!"—the proud titles rang out as he lifted poor Isaac's goblet.

"Am I really all that?" she laughed, when the cheering of her guests had died down and the servants had begun to bring in the dishes.

"You don't look big enough to be," teased Richard, stooping to kiss the top of her head.

"You'll find he conquers an odd island or two for you any day he feels like it," said Johanna.

"I suspect that both these little skirmishes of mine, here and at Messina, were child's play to the fighting you veterans have had in Palestine," grinned Richard, handing a tasty bit of chicken breast to de Lusignon. "Actually, old Comnenos ran away."

"And I thought you promised him faithfully you wouldn't put him in irons," reproved Berengaria, suddenly remembering their imprisoned host with compunction.

"Neither did I, my sweet," declared Richard, his splendid teeth making short work of a wing. "Ask any of 'em."

"Your new husband always keeps his word, my dear," Raymond assured her. "He had silver chains specially made for him."

"Just the foxy sort of humour that would appeal to John!" reproved Johanna, through their heartless laughter.

"Well, can't we have the poor man up to eat some of his own food instead of languishing on bread and water down in the dungeons?" begged Berengaria, who could not bear to think of anyone going hungry on her wedding day.

"He isn't exactly on bread and water, and I don't think it would be wise," smiled Richard. "But I tell you what we will do, my dear. We'll ask his daughter to come and dance for us." He looked along the many tables for her but Johanna explained that when Ida had heard it was a wedding feast she had refused to come.

"They will probably take it as a deliberate insult," warned de Lusignon. "Only the paid dance girls perform in public here, you know."

But Richard had already given the order. "Oh, she's only a child and she likes dancing," he said carelessly.

"Children grow up quickly in this climate," observed Raymond.

His remark was justified when Ida came into the hall. She had removed all trace of angry tears with a sophisticated touch of kohl; her slender arms and ankles tinkled with bracelets, and the vivid Damascus silks she wore were the envy of the three Western women. She came submissively to Richard, but her dark eyes searched savagely for some flaw in Berengaria's beauty.

"Since you won't eat with us," ordered Richard suavely, "I should like you to dance for our guests."

The girl recoiled as if he had struck her. De Lusignon quite expected her to refuse. But she had seen Berengaria's hand creep restrainingly to Richard's. "I would sooner he had me whipped naked before them all than be spared through that woman's intercession!" Ida told herself, in the hysterical exaggeration of her first young passion. Besides, she had wanted to dance for him and here was her opportunity. She looked round disdainfully at the perspiring acrobats clearing their paraphernalia from the centre of the hall and saw rows of amused or admiring faces turned towards her and the stern, aesthetic countenance of the Templars who, according to the rules of their order, did not look at her at all… "But I will make them!" she thought, piqued by their indifference. She smiled up at the bridegroom sitting among his principal guests on the *dais*. "I promised I would dance for you—didn't I—that night when you carried me home on your saddle?" she said, spitefully glad that Berengaria should hear.

She called something in Greek to the native musicians and they played a pastorale on their pipes and zithers. Without fuss or self-consciousness, she began to dance to the fawn-like melody…"She's quite good!" they all agreed, pleasantly lulled by the innocuous measure, and out of the corners of her kohled eyes she noticed some of them who fancied their virtuosity beating time a little condescendingly. Here was an opportunity to befool those men who had humiliated her country, using the only kind of weapon she knew. She snapped her fingers to a pot-bellied little man who had played for years at her father's orgies and he changed the tune to an obscene little nasal song. His beady eyes twinkled as his soft, fleshy palms beat out the rhythm on his drums and Ida gave Berengaria's wedding guests a dance of the back streets and the brothels. Those who had glanced casually between mouthfuls at the jaded antics of the mountebanks and conversed through the customary minstrels' songs laid down their knives, watching the allure of Ida. Because she was young and supple and well-born she stirred men's senses as no hardened harlot could have done. And because she brought to the age-old gestures of enticement something of the freshness of a mountain stream, even white-robed monks forgot their vows. As she turned and swayed to the wicked rhythm of the drums, she watched the Templars' faces. But she danced primarily for Richard, and many of her countrymen—standing about with the sullenness of the vanquished—spat their disgust.

Richard had seen plenty of varieties of the dance in Raymond's ports of southern France and—as always—the hot, insistent undertone of the drums was the mysterious heart of the East calling to him. But he sat frowning, feeling it was all wrong that this lovely, undisciplined child should be dancing before them—and angrily aware that she had taken a rise out of him. The girl was making herself as insistent as the drums, and he regretted trying to subdue her. Berengaria and the convent-bred Yvette, he could see, were painfully embarrassed; and when the girl had gone Johanna said bluntly, "Well, with all our dower chests of fashionable new clothes we cannot compete with *that*!"

The men sitting near them, released from Ida's Circe appeal, laughed a little sheepishly. "I suppose you're keeping her as a hostage?" enquired de Lusignon.

"Looks as if the little bitch 'ud prefer to be kept as his mistress!" guffawed Barbe of Chalus, already in his cups.

"I wish you would let the girl go!" sighed Berengaria, ignoring his provincial coarseness. "She is going to be a grave responsibility." As if to dismiss the subject, she turned graciously to de Lusignon. "I shall always boast to all my friends that we had the King of Jerusalem at our wedding," she told him. "And I know you are the one person in the world whom Richard has been aching to talk to."

Inevitably the two men fell upon the subject nearest their hearts and, with a dozen different knights joining in, poor Berengaria's wedding feast soon degenerated into a council of war.

"Have you ever seen Saladin?" those fresh out from Europe wanted to know.

But even the most seasoned Templars seemed never to have done so. "He is one of those leaders who know the publicity value of an elusive personality," said de Lusignon. "But he has more than once given us Christians a lesson in chivalry."

"Does he still cut in when our men are on the march?" asked Raymond, who had served as a very fledgling knight under de Barre.

"Lord, yes! It's simply uncanny how the hills look bare one minute and his ferocious hordes are upon you the next, picking off half a company before our heavily equipped fellows can close their ranks."

"You'll come to hate those bare hills, Sir," a gnarled old Templar told the tall Angevin leader of this new crusade.

Richard drank in their words. This was the real thing at first hand. "I remember my mother telling me how lightly the Saracens were mounted, and I used to plan how—if ever I had the luck to get there—I would sacrifice speed to security by making my men march in close formation," he said.

"The difficulty about slow marches across those plains is the provisioning," pointed out Raymond, "How are you going to make the water last out?"

"I should hug the coast. Not waste a single man or horse for porterage who could be used for fighting." Richard was all eagerness, expounding his pet theory. Fruit dishes and finger bowls were pushed out of the way, and every available knife pressed into service to form a rough map of the Levant. Men rose and leaned across each other's shoulders to look. "It always seemed to me that Louis and his crowd neglected their naval strength. We've got plenty of ships. Why can't we arrange for them to call at each port regularly with supplies?"

"Shounds all right," admitted Chaïus. "But given the foul storms we've had, how many weeks d'you sup-poshe it'll take them to come from France or England?"

"Only a drunken fool would expect them to come from there!" barked Richard, always rattled to rudeness by the way the impertinent little curmudgeon crabbed all his best ideas. "Look, here's Cyprus." He planked down a plate in the middle of the coastline of knives. "An admirable permanent base—and mine."

Raymond backed up the new idea with enthusiasm. "There's an excellent harbour further north at Famagusta. It would pay us to leave a garrison and fortify the place."

"And when you've got your supply system working regularly?" prompted Mortaine.

"I'd force the enemy to play my game. Keep away from the hills where he has all the advantages and concentrate on the coastal towns. Mew him up and—" Richard caught a Templar's sceptic eye and stopped short. "God's heart, what must you think of me, ranting away in front of a lot of experienced crusaders like this?" he laughed, reddening like any schoolboy and subsiding into his chair.

But Guy de Lusignon had begun to see in this powerful redhead's enthusiasm new hope for his jaded supporters. He was willing to try anything to get back his throne. "Go on," he said quietly, waving Richard back to his improvised map. "Your idea certainly holds new possibilities."

Men came from other tables, crowding round. Berengaria saw their tense faces. Squires with famous names and rich merchants' sons, their smooth, young faces shining with eagerness—the sex appeal of Ida forgotten as they reached for the Fata Morgana of fame. Scarred old war-dogs like Mortaine listening tolerantly. The servants moving softly. The torches burning low and no one daring to change them. Johanna, listening intently, eaten with family pride. The round wonder in Yvette's blue eyes. She herself, a bride, half proud and half resentful. And in the middle of it all her handsome lover, whom men already called Coeur de Lion, telling them how to plan a campaign.

"You see, we've better battering rams and scaling ladders," he was explaining with engaging diffidence. "And I feel that, considering their superior numbers, we ought never to risk open engagements on the plains until we've taken most of the key points along the coast. The fact of the matter is, my brother Henry and I were always terribly keen about armaments. People used to tell us the walls of Jerusalem were almost impregnable, so I spent years studying architecture under Maurice, the man who was building Dover castle for my father. He helped me to make calculations and get out designs for a sort of super catapult. I tried it out at the siege of Taillebourg."

"What's it like?" demanded Lusignon.

"Well, it's mounted on the usual kind of wooden platform on rollers."

"They waste too much time where you have to bridge or fill in a moat," objected Chalus.

"No need to do either," said Richard, too carried away by his subject this time to resent the interruption. "This model of mine has sufficient resilience to sling stones from the *far* side of the widest moat into the best battlemented bailey ever built. By means of a heavy beam twisted so tightly between two sets of ropes that it generates a tremendous force—but I'll show you. Mercadier has brought one ashore,"

He pushed back his chair, and they would have streamed out after him like hounds on a scent had not Berengaria caught at his arm. "Oh, Richard," she protested, "not *to-night!*"

Richard smiled down at her. "I will come back soon, sweet. But de Lusignon knows the actual walls of Jerusalem and can give me expert advice—"

"Once he's got somebody worked up about his old war machines he'll probably forget to come back at all!" warned Johanna.

So Berengaria was firm. "No, Richard. You've fought ever since we landed. Yesterday you were travelling down from the mountains, and last night you sat up arranging all this." She waved regretfully towards the remains of the iced castles and all that was left of her banquet. "It was so beautiful," she sighed. "But what was the good of it if you've forgotten so soon that we are married?"

Everybody laughed and the eager youngsters tried to look as if they didn't mind her breaking in upon their apprenticeship to fame. Richard put an arm round her and said she was perfectly right. He even seemed to enjoy the novelty of giving up his bachelor freedom. He had not yet learned that marriage, unlike his casual loves, could clash with his career.

Perceiving that the party was over, their guests began to drift tactfully away. The King of Jerusalem kissed Berengaria's hand. "We must see your stone-slinger in the morning," he called to Richard, "and wish you an envious good night."

Johanna kissed her new sister-in-law on both cheeks. "May you always get your own way as easily!" she whispered.

Yvette ran on ahead to put out her mistress's night wrap and Blondel shouted to the Comnenos' major-domo for torches to light the bride to bed. Richard lingered over a last drink with his sister and Raymond, talking over old times.

"D'you remember that awful night at Oxford when it all came out about Ann and I tried to teach you to dance?" asked Johanna. "And Henry teased you about Sancho's sister? And you said, 'God help me, shall I have to dance with *her*!"

"He didn't need to dance," recalled Raymond, wishing himself tall and carelessly attractive.

"Funny!" mused Richard, setting down his empty cup. "If it hadn't been for Ann I should never have gone to Navarre!"

When his shadow had passed out of sight on the curved wall of the stair Johanna looked round at the disordered hall and sighed.

"Come out into the garden," suggested Raymond. "There is nothing so depressing as the dregs of a party."

"Except the dregs of one's life," said Johanna. As she passed out into the garden she thought of the mockery of her own marriage. Of William's consideration and his impotence. She brushed roughly past a trailing vine, hating its exotic beauty because her heart was hungry for green hills and the deep, dappled shade of beech trees. "Robin—Robin—" cried the ghost of her happy childhood. She could almost feel the wind in her hair, hear the scuffle of her flying feet searching for him around the battlements. But Isaac's garden was heavy with the scent of spices, and the only sounds were the splashing of his fountain and the distant sweetness of some shepherd's pipe. "What a night for love!" she murmured, glancing up at the landward tower where a light still shone from Berengaria's window.

Most men as much in love as Raymond would have taken up the challenge of her words. But his long friendship with his cousin had made him wise and patient with a woman's moods. He stood in the shadow of a cypress tree worshipping the clear-cut fairness of Johanna's upturned face. "There will be plenty of other magic nights," he said, without touching her. "And if I wait long enough, please God, one of them may be ours."

Chapter Nineteen

"A M I FORGIVEN ABOUT the war' conference?" enquired Richard, grinning down at Berengaria from the doorway of their bridal chamber.

Seeing him there, Berengaria's heart missed a beat.

"I wish I were more like Johanna," she sighed, realising that she had married the kind of man women always *do* forgive. "She adores all this military excitement. But then, of course, she's so like you. Your minds are brave and spacious, and I'm such a home-loving creature!"

She looked anything but homely in the silver lamé wrap Yvette was fastening, and, as always, Richard's pulses quickened at sight of her. "Just the sort of wife a soldier wants as an antidote to war!" he laughed, leaning against the wide, open fireplace. Even in May this southern bride of his liked a fire, and the flickering light behind him made a wavy silhouette of his long limbs. He glanced round at the rich Byzantine furnishings with faint disapproval. "You do realise, don't you, that all the home we shall have for months will be a captured fortress or a camp? Shall you mind very much?"

Berengaria sat down on the end of the low, wide bed and said firmly, "I must get used to it." But she was secretly dismayed by the prospect and, as if determined to cling to the amenities of civilised life until the last possible moment, she picked up her jewelled toilet box and asked Yvette to brush her hair.

"Have you a headache after all that ceremonial pother?" asked Richard. He came and lifted the gold circlet from her forehead and pulled up a stool beside her. "I'm sorry we couldn't get you a better crown," he said, twirling Chalus's circlet between his knees. "I shall have to make up for it with a grand coronation for the benefit of my Saxons."

He was so dear and unemotional and natural, making it easier for her to get used to having him wandering about her bedroom. "Tell us about England," she said, trying to keep her voice from trembling with shy awareness of their thrilling new intimacy, "Yvette used to believe that curious legend that all the men had long tails!"

Her youngest lady laid down her brush protestingly. "Oh, Madam, I was quite a child then!"

"You are not much more now, are you?" teased Richard. "And, anyway, you've got it all wrong, Yvette. What most of us islanders suffer from is short tempers. And sometimes they hurt damnably." He sat staring into the fire while she put away the stately wedding dress and turned down the bedcover which Eleanor had embroidered and brought from England.

"I think I must have read everything ever written about your island and driven people crazy asking questions about it," Berengaria was saying. "So I don't imagine I shall feel strange." By a process of wishful thinking she skipped the months when he would be fighting his precious crusade and thought only of the time when they would be living in what Yvette called "a proper country" again. "After all, I already know most of your family."

"Except John and—Arthur," agreed Richard.

Berengaria guessed that the second name was only a substitute. She always knew when he was brooding about Robin, and now it occurred to her that he must have been wishing him there all day just as she had wanted her parents. She would have liked to comfort him, but somehow did not dare. She thanked Yvette a little absently and bade her good night.

"Good night, Madam—and Sir," added Yvette, not quite sure whether she ought to curtsey twice.

Richard swung round on his stool. Her naïveté never failed to amuse him. "Come here, Yvette," he said, feeling in the wallet of his belt for a string of quaintly carved beads he had chosen specially for her. "I want you to wear these for taking such good care of my bride. I shall tell King Sancho you are worth all the staid old court dowagers he could have sent."

"Oh, Sir!" gasped Yvette, breathless with delight.

"Blue as your eyes!" he said, getting up to fasten the beads himself. "And now go and tell Blondel I shan't want him any more to-night, and when he sees how pretty you look I expect he'll want to sing you that absurdly sentimental song all over again!"

"Oh, Richard, why put such ideas into the girl's head?" laughed Berengaria, when the door had closed behind her excited flurry of thanks.

"For my romantic young squire to make them sprout, my dear. You don't want her to mope in the Holy Land, do you?" He came and lifted the thick waves of her hair, letting them run like a silken ribbon over his hands. "Beloved, I've never seen you with it loose before. It's like a lovely sable cloak."

"What is John like? And who is Arthur?" she asked hurriedly, seeing that they were alone.

"John? Oh, the same as most spoiled youngest sons, I suppose," answered Richard, jerking a cushion to the floor at her feet and resting his head against her knee. "And young Arthur is my nephew. You'll like him, Berengaria. His father, Geoffrey, was the one who married Constance of Brittany and got killed in a tournament, you remember? He came between my other two sisters and Johanna, so Arthur is my heir." He reached up for one of her hands and kissed the small, soft palm. "Until we have sons of our own, witch woman."

Berengaria leaned her cheek against the top of his head, building homely castles in the fire. "I hope they will all have auburn hair," she said softly. "And I want a daughter as vital as Johanna. Do you think the English will like me, Richard?"

"How could they help it, sweetheart? Haven't all my family fallen in love with you? And the young pups of pages and the tough archers and even the King of Jerusalem himself? And isn't that swine Chalus ready to stab me any dark night?" Richard twisted himself round until his arms were about her waist. In the shifting firelight he seemed as young and eager as the day he first loved her in Navarre. It was as if he had shed the years of ugly fighting against his father and brothers—the months of responsibility and king-hood. "You look like a little silver statue—sitting so up right—on that great bed," he said unsteadily. His eyes were warm with passion, his lips demanding. "I've waited such years—wanting you …"

Suddenly they were clinging to each other, laughing between their kisses.

"To think that I might have married Ann!"

"And that I might have let them give me to Philip or someone… And never known that marriage could be like this. It has been unendurable, this waiting—"

But Berengaria held him off a little longer, knowing intuitively that once she had given him everything he would never be so utterly hers again. "Tell me some more about our next coronation," she coaxed. "We've had so little time to talk about our own affairs."

Richard obeyed reluctantly, settling his head more comfort-ably against her knee. "The men will shout themselves hoarse, I suppose, because you are beautiful." He began intoning the words as if they were a rather boring sort of saga. "And the women will bring you their troubles because you are kind—"

"And the children?" asked Berengaria, bending to smooth out the cross lines from his firm, freshly shaven face.

He looked up and laughed immediately. "Oh, they will strew flowers before your feet because they are adorable anyhow."

"I shall like that."

"And we shall go in a state barge to Westminster," he went on, warming to his theme.

"What is this West-min-stair?" interrupted Berengaria, wanting to picture it all just as he did.

"Just a little riverside village near London. Not big like Paris or Pamplona. But Edward the Confessor built an abbey there. The man who willed his Saxon crown away to my grandfather, you know."

"Or William of Normandy *said* he did," corrected Berengaria, whose history lessons had been less biased.

"Well, anyhow, it's a beautiful abbey. I shall be insuperably proud when you walk up that exquisite nave with the priests chanting at the High Altar and all the people cheering and the bells ringing."

Berengaria shifted his head from her lap and stood up. Through the open window she could see her honeymoon island sleeping under the stars. Only the shepherds seemed to be awake, huddled over little wood fires in the fields beyond the land gate. The call of their reed pipes came softly through the scented night. "But in our hearts we shall both be thinking of Cyprus," she said.

"Our private lives which we have managed to keep for each other after all." With one of those lithe movements so surprising in a man of his height, Richard was beside her.

She turned in glad surprise. "You remember my saying that?"

"I remember everything," he assured her.

"My telling you that it didn't matter whom I married? That we were just political puppets. And my bitterness. After I had met *you*—" Because they were so crazily in love it mattered supremely that he should share the memory of its beginning.

Richard shook her gently. "Didn't I tell you, despondent woman, that there would be some decent princes—like me?"

"I admired your modesty, of course," laughed Berengaria, her voice low with happiness. "But I never really believed I should get one." From the lovely security of his arm she watched the leaping flames light up the emblems of England and Navarre on the coverlet of the bed. Richard's blood-red leopards and her own silver hearts and stag. Somehow Eleanor's embroidery seemed to make a reality of their love affair, turning it into the accomplished union of two great dynasties, whose offspring might write their deeds across the face of Europe. It seemed to weight the rapture of their love with responsibility—to make it less their own—and for a moment Berengaria was afraid.

But Richard caught her to his heart. "Do you believe now—and now?" he demanded exultantly, between the passion of his kisses.

"I believe in the goodness of God!" breathed Berengaria, yielding to the urgency she loved. "And to think that the poor scriveners of history will coldly record that in eleven-ninety-one Richard I of England married Berengaria of Navarre!"

But Richard was scarcely listening or heard only the beat of his own blood. He reached up and threw the last torch to the hearth. It hissed into the heart of the fire, sending up a shower of sparks. By their light he unfastened the silver lamé wrap and Berengaria smiled up at him from the sable mantle of her hair. "God's heart, how beautiful you are!" he cried, lifting her in his strong arms to her lawful place upon the Plantagenet bed.

PART VI

The Holy Land

Chapter Twenty

BERENGARIA'S HONEYMOON LASTED FOR only a week. For seven days Richard held up his crusade and forgot everything in the world but her. They rode together to the snow-capped mountains where goats and peasants cared nothing for their rank, and rested in valleys where bright-green lizards scuttled between the sun-baked rocks. He teased and worshipped her by turns, and she made him talk about Oxford and how he sometimes hated himself for the way he had quarrelled with his father, and about Henry and Robin and Hodierna until she knew him, the way women must, right backwards to his boyhood. They were utterly sufficient to each other, and because they were war-time lovers each moment was precious with the poignancy of parting. "Whatever happens, this one short week will have spoiled us both for any lesser loves," Berengaria consoled herself, when it was over.

That last evening at Limassol she felt as if she were deliberately releasing him from her enchantment and giving him back to his world. He seemed to have forgotten his grief for Robin in the manifest happiness of a man possessing both the woman and the work he loves. During their brief honeymoon he had discussed with her the advisability of leaving Guy de Lusignon in charge of Cyprus until Jerusalem should be retaken, and all that last afternoon she had willingly played her part in the formal ceremony of handing over the island. Immediately after a hasty supper Richard was off to the harbour with Mercadier preparing for embarkation and Berengaria loyally slipped away. Having married a public hero she must school herself to share him. But when they were up in her rooms packing Yvette, glancing down at the busy quay, exclaimed: "Just look at the Cypriot princess hanging about barefoot like any peasant!"

Berengaria's heart warmed to the antipathy in her voice, but she treated the youthful criticism much as she used to treat the uncharitable remarks of Isabella and Henrietta. "If we lived in this climate and had such lovely feet I expect we should want to go barefoot too," she said, moving to the window.

And Johanna, sorting out some gay Syrian embroideries, remarked good-naturedly, "With her mother dead and her father in prison, Ida is little better than an orphan. I expect she is waiting to say 'good-bye' to Richard."

She evidently was. She lurked in the shadow of the harbour wall until he left Mercadier and waylaid him as he came up the slipway alone. Berengaria saw her sudden tears, her feigned start of surprise, and the appealing gesture of her clutching hands. She couldn't hear what either of them said, of course, but she saw Richard bend to comfort the girl. "How can men be fooled by that baby stuff after the way she danced!" she marvelled. She watched them cross the quay, dodging the burdens of the laden sailors. Ida was all vivacity now, laughing back at him as they climbed a flight of slippery stone steps. Berengaria noticed with annoyance that she had managed to get a sprig of broom from somewhere or other and saw her reach up to stick it in his helmet for luck. Richard seemed inordinately pleased and kissed her for it before they were lost to sight beneath the arched gateway of the citadel. It was all so open and natural, and yet Berengaria was aware of a horrible stab of jealousy.

"Would you like me to arrange for some family of good repute to look after Ida Comnenos after we are gone?" she asked that night when Richard had come to bed.

"No need," he answered, in a matter-of-fact sort of way, "I've decided to take her along."

Berengaria sat up in the wide bed and stared at him incredulously. "But surely Guy de Lusignon will keep an eye on her," she said.

"Both, I fancy!" Richard unbuckled his sword belt and threw it across the end of the bed with a short, significant laugh.

"Whatever do you mean?" protested Berengaria.

"I oughtn't to have made her dance that night. Of course, the poor child didn't actually *say* he'd been pestering her—"

"Of course not. She just brought you a bit of planta genista and pawed you and cried—"

Richard looked up in bewilderment from the chausse he was bending to unlace. He had never before heard that sharp note in Berengaria's voice. It was the nearest they had ever come to a quarrel and he hadn't an idea what it was about.

"At least she might have managed this 'whither thou goest I go' business without dragging poor Guy into it!" The new Queen of England thumped a pillow and lay down again. Did the conceited little hussy really imagine both kings admired her? Actually, if the King of Jerusalem had shown signs of admiring *anybody* it had been herself. Berengaria pulled herself up with shamed amusement. "Mother of God, what's the use of being an educated woman if loving a man makes one think like a fish-wife?"

She let Richard finish undressing in silence but when he had stamped out the torches and taken her in his arms she turned her face from his kisses. "Richard, *must* you bring that girl?" she begged, with persistent foreboding.

"Who—Ida?" By the light of a rising moon Richard was amusing himself making a pattern of her dark hair on the pillow. "You look like an angry Medusa!" he teased, spreading it in snake-like waves, above her heart-shaped little face. But Berengaria was not to be fondled out of her answer. "I'll see she isn't any bother," promised Richard. "But if I leave any of the Comnenos tribe at large here, de Lusignon will probably have more bother with the natives. You see, sweet, I can't afford to leave much of a garrison." He was so obviously indifferent to the girl's charms that Berengaria snuggled luxuriously against his shoulder and went to sleep calling herself a fool.

They sailed next morning and in six months news of the fall of Acre was ringing round the Christian world. The name of

Richard Cœur de Lion was on all men's lips. For although Philip of France and Leopold of Austria and the rest had done the spade work, everybody knew it was he who had brought genius to the enterprise. By capturing a heavily armed supply ship vital to the beleaguered garrison he reminded them that, besides Angevin anger and Plantagenet pride, the blood of Norse pirates ran in his veins. The sight of his victorious fleet must have been like wine to the jaded crusaders blockading Acre, and his personal courage and tireless enthusiasm certainly inspired a more vigorous and concerted attack.

During those months of hard and brilliant fighting Berengaria saw little of him except in the company of other men or when he was too tired to talk. He spared neither himself nor her. He would clank into their tent, bloodstained and begrimed, and almost before Blondel could unharness him he would fling himself across the bed and sleep. Sometimes, when things went well, he would make love to her—fiercely, exultantly, unaware that although her body responded ardently her mind was still recoiling from the bloodstains. If she knew that Richard was leading some fresh attack the long, grilling days of suspense drained her of any emotion at all, so that living up to the cheerful confidence of the two Plantagenets was all effort and pretence. She would stand at the tent door watching for Richard's conspicuous figure among the crowd of armed men and horses that milled about the walls of Acre, knowing that only some sort of miracle could defend his recklessness. Or she would go and try to cheer the wounded, all the time cowering from the sound of men's approaching feet lest they should be bringing him back to her dead. She knew that his men had orders never to let her stray within range of the enemy's bows, but it was the arrows that rained round *him* she feared.

"But, beloved, don't you remember I bear a charmed life?" he would say laughingly to comfort her whenever she begged him to be more careful. And he came back to her unscathed from such bloody encounters that by the end of the siege she had almost come to believe in Robin's witch.

When at last he went down with fever Berengaria was almost thankful, thinking she would be able to nurse him and keep him safely to herself. But long before he was well enough to sit a horse he had himself carried on a litter to direct the sappers and the battering-rams. And just as he ignored a mounting temperature he had singleness of purpose enough to ignore the jealousy of Leopold and Philip. Inevitably he dominated every scene, unconsciously dwarfing other men. Some of them hated him for it. Most of them would have followed him to hell. For there was a glamour about Richard in those days which was almost like a visible flame.

The war-weary army of occupation, only longing to get back to their homes in Europe, had naturally welcomed any driving force likely to curtail the interminable siege. And men of his own expeditionary force who had leaned across each other's shoulders to listen at Berengaria's wedding feast saw the campaign of the dinner knives coming true before their eyes and felt the solid comfort of supplies from Famagusta warming their bellies for the fight. Acre, the first of Richard's key ports, had fallen. Haifa was their next objective. Then Jaffa, the port of Jerusalem itself.

Chapter Twenty-One

A S SOON AS THE crusaders had actually taken possession of
Acre the European women were able to spend the cooler
parts of the day sitting on the walls. There was more air
up there and they were glad to get away from the stifling streets
where gaunt olive-skinned women and their half-starved children
wrung poor Berengaria's heart. "If only this dreadful hammering
would stop!" she sighed, moving further into the shade of a little
crenellated watch tower as the pitiless sun began to climb.

"But Richard must repair the fortifications," said Johanna,
letting a bandage she was rolling trail in the dust. There was dust
everywhere, and flies and heat, but it didn't seem to affect her. She
had the Plantagenet vitality that throve on discomforts.

Berengaria looked out over the endless plain ridged here
and there with grey-green vineyards. Behind her on the western
side of the town their ships lay motionless, mirrored in a molten
sea, while immediately below her the men mending the main
land gate shouted to each other in an unintelligible medley of
Norman and Saxon which was beginning to become a language.
Berengaria sighed again, wondering if she ever *would* be able to
understand them.

Johanna gave her a quick, anxious glance. She noticed that her
pallor lacked the inward glow that used to warm it.

"At least you need not worry about Richard now," she said
comfortingly. "You know he's down there outside the walls having

the time of his life showing them all what a marvellous mason he would have made."

"But those poor wounded—"

"The Hospitallers will look after them."

"But they are my people now, and it takes a woman—not sexless monks—to sew comfortable bandages and talk to them about their children and picture their homes. Some of them suffer so horribly—Richard says the Saracens are using poisoned arrows now."

"He ought not to let you visit the wounded. He's so used to that sort of thing he doesn't realise how it affects you. Robin's just as tough but he would have *thought*—" Johanna stopped abruptly. She was trying hard to forget Robin these days. She tumbled the last of her ineptly rolled bandages into a basket and sauntered across to the battlements. Sick nursing bored her anyway. All her kindnesses were gay, spontaneous, and consistent with her own immense enjoyment of life. She did not know the kind of queen Berengaria meant to be. Besides, she could hear Raymond talking to someone round a bend of the wall. "Well, don't wear yourself out," she said. "There's Ida eating sweetmeats further along the city wall. She'd probably like to be asked to do something. One can't help feeling sorry for her—a hostage away from home."

"Yvette is still further from *her* home," observed Berengaria, tearing some of her best head veils into strips for dressings.

But freedom was the breath of life to Johanna, so she had to champion the Cypriot girl. "But don't you see, Yvette is *free*? She's in the middle of her first love affair. She has congenial work, and she adores you."

Berengaria looked up, surprised by her vehemence. "Judging by the way Ida hangs about Richard, her life scarcely seems devoid of emotional interest," she remarked dryly.

But Johanna wasn't listening. Raymond and Blondel had suddenly appeared round the corner of the watch tower swathed in masons' aprons, their faces white with dust. "You look like a couple of death cart men!" she told them unkindly.

"I feel like one of the corpses!" groaned Raymond, sitting on some fallen masonry to mop his forehead. "If anyone had told me

I'd be talked into leading a repair squad in this climate! But what else can we do when Richard himself is showing archers how to hew stones? For God's sake, someone, send for a drink!"

"The King has issued orders that everyone, irrespective of rank, is to work six hours a day mending the walls before we go," announced Blondel, letting a basket of tools slide gratefully from his sweating shoulder.

Johanna sent a page scurrying for wine, and Berengaria put away her work with a strained sort of smile. "A few weeks ago you were risking your lives to *destroy* the walls," she reminded them. "That is where war is such waste!"

"Waste!" exclaimed Raymond indignantly, through an inadequate handkerchief with which Johanna was endeavouring to remove some of the grime from his sunburnt face. "My dear Berengaria, how can you talk of your husband's achievement like that? It was the rest of the crowd who were wasting time out here all winter, and along comes Richard and takes the town almost as soon as he lands!"

Richard himself appeared at that moment at the top of a scaling ladder set up from the fosse below. "To hear you talk, my dear fellow, anybody would think I took the place single-handed!" he protested, swinging a leg over the battlements. "What about the French, the Austrians, the Venetians, the Genoese, and all the rest of our noble allies?"

"Well, what about them?" jeered Raymond. "I didn't see old Leopold do much except hoist his standard from the watch tower after you had mopped up this ward of the town."

Richard glanced up with tolerant amusement at the Austrian standard drooping listlessly above them. There was so little breeze that it might just as well have been embroidered with leopards or fleurs-de-lis or unicorns for all anybody could tell, so it didn't matter much. And in any case his attention was immediately distracted by a pull at his elbow. He had no sooner straddled the battlements than Ida had joined the friendly little group. She had brought him a basket of nectarines and oranges temptingly arranged on cool green fig leaves.

"A good thought, Ida! If I'd have known you had anything so delectable I'd have come and sat over there!" exclaimed Raymond.

"The Count of Toulouse would have to be very thirsty before he preferred *my* company to yours," she said to Johanna with teasing shrewdness. Richard, who was learning matrimonial wisdom, picked over her basket for the choicest fruit and carried it across to his wife.

"She hasn't eaten anything this morning," Johanna had to say, drawing attention to her pallor.

"It's this pestilential heat," said Raymond.

But it wasn't only the heat. Berengaria felt sick—swooningly sick. She did not want other people to know—to whisper and to guess her secret. She wanted to tell Richard some lovely time when they were alone. When the Syrian night was warm about them like a cloak, shutting out war, and the stars were shining the way they did over Cyprus. "I shall have a better appetite when all this starving garrison is set free," she said evasively.

"It won't be long now, my dear," Richard assured her. "Almost the best part of this victory will be getting back our own prisoners in return." He made the page pour her wine first and, steadied by it, she followed him to the battlements. With Johanna and Raymond and Blondel they leaned against the parapet watching the new portcullis being lifted into its grooves by powerful pulleys. Its cruel iron teeth grinned defiance to the surrounding plain. "I shall feel happier about pushing on to Haifa when that's fixed," said Richard. From their vantage point they could see most of the battered roofs and minarets of the city, and it was obvious how much the Norman trebuchets and other war machines must have contributed to the final capitulation. They began assessing the damage and fighting their battles over again. "I suppose your precious new catapult was responsible for that, Richard?" said Raymond, pointing out a nasty crater in the bastion immediately below them.

"Why did we bring the stones for it specially from Sicily, Sir?" asked Blondel.

The proud inventor explained how the volcanic nature of the rocks there made them splinter more easily and so become a much deadlier weapon. Fragments from one stone might kill as many as a dozen men, he told them.

And all the time Ida hovered on the edge of the group. She hated the way these fair-skinned crusaders discussed things with their women. They seemed to share so many interests with them besides sex. Yet it seemed to her that a virile red-head like Richard could not possibly be cold. She stole a glance at the firm, full contour of his lips and was consumed by a desire to find out. Her gaze passed contemptuously to the pale bride by his side. Unaware that she was being observed, Berengaria drooped from her usual dignity, a hand pressed to her side. To anyone bred to the gossip of a harem it was easy enough to guess the cause. A savage triumph tingled in Ida's undisciplined blood. Soon this exquisite wife of Richard's would be plain and clumsy. She pulled the gaudy sash more tightly across her own svelte hips, prepared to do anything—however spectacular—to attract his attention. Driven by the same devil that had made her dance desire into the chaste Templars, she swung herself over a machicolation of the battlements and with sure, bare feet clambered out across the bastion at which they were all looking.

"Come back, you little fool!" called Raymond, and Blondel—who was standing nearest—made a grab at her. But she eluded him and stood defiantly at the downward slope of the bastion with the first breath of wind from the far-off Lebanons moulding her barbaric draperies about her lovely, slender limbs. She had regained their attention surely enough when suddenly she began pointing excitedly into the bowl of the crater, which was invisible to them. "It is true what King Richard said about the stone," she cried. "The hole is full of dead. A dozen at least. All blasted with splinters. An arm here…A leg there…" She clambered round the rough edge of the crater like a mountain goat, swooping suddenly to scoop up something. "And here's a head!" Turning with a flashing smile to Berengaria, she held the horrible thing aloft by its matted hair. The half-decayed face of a Saracen stared up at them with bird-pecked eyes and agonised grin.

Berengaria stifled a scream. Too late she flung both hands across her eyes. Not for worlds would she have looked upon that hideous thing. She made a blind fending motion, as if to drive the sight of it from some frightened child. "Please, please, Richard," she moaned, "have it covered up quickly."

Richard had his back to her. He did not see her sway, nor Johanna's arm go round her. He and Raymond were already over the battlements examining the crater with experienced eyes. They saw only the obvious cause for her distress. "Quickly is the word in this climate," agreed Raymond, holding his discarded apron to his nose.

Berengaria begged Johanna not to make a fuss and went to sit in the shade. The whole world seemed to have gone black and the sunlight to have turned cold. "I must forget it," she told herself, staring resolutely in the opposite direction at the sea. "Even Ida couldn't have been wicked enough to hold the dreadful thing up purposely…" Everything going on around her seemed unreal and negligible. She saw Richard lift the girl back on to the wall—saw him standing with a carelessly, approving arm still about her shoulder telling her her quick eyes had probably saved the garrison from fever. Then he was arranging with Blondel about a burial party and a squad to fill in the masonry.

"Most of the men are packing up for the march or trying to get the land gate finished before nightfall," Blondel reminded him.

Richard scanned the hive of industry he had recently left. "Well, what are those Austrians doing over there dicing away the coolest part of the day?" he demanded irritably. "Send some of *them* for picks and shovels."

Blondel went reluctantly. It wasn't the first time he had been sent with high-handed messages to foreign contingents, and he knew their trick of pretending not to understand one's smattering of their various languages. Moreover, he had hoped to clean himself up and spend the noon rest hours with Yvette.

Chapter Twenty-Two

WHILE BLONDEL WAS GONE to round up some of the Austrians the others stretched themselves in the shade, talking in a desultory sort of way. It was almost time for dinner and the midday siesta, and they were all rather sleepy. Nobody but Johanna seemed to notice Berengaria's silence.

"What do you wager old Saladin won't send our men back after all, Richard?" said Raymond, shying a stone at a sun-bathing lizard.

"I gave him till sunset," yawned Richard.

"But last time he let you down."

"We hadn't a whole town full of his people as hostages then."

Berengaria had managed to get a grip on herself, but her thoughts kept wandering off on inconsequent excursions, one thing suggesting another. She was trying to picture Richard as a boy. Eleanor had told her how furious his father had been because he would draw castles instead of doing his Latin. And when they were in Cyprus he himself had said, "When Thomas à Becket gave me my first pony, Robin and I took turns charging the Oxford boys with a tent pole." Odious little savages! But after all, one wanted a boy to have spirit. Berengaria drowsed a little, leaning against Richard's shoulder, dreaming of their son.

She was roused by her improvised pillow being jerked away and her husband's voice demanding sharply, "Well, where are they? Didn't you give them my orders?"

Blondel had, and was still sore at the memory. "They say they do not speak Norman and they take orders only from the Duke of Austria," he reported.

Richard sprang up with an ugly oath. In two strides he was verifying the unbelievable. The Austrians were still grouped picturesquely under the trees. It was a jolt to his self-esteem. "The insolent swine!" he muttered.

"They are in the right, Richard. Don't take any notice of my squeamishness," begged Berengaria, feeling that it was all her fault. "If you can't spare the men I'm sure it would be better to leave the bastion than to provoke bad feeling with our allies."

"I think I'm beginning to hate them rather more than our enemies," he admitted, with a rueful laugh.

Hearing approaching footsteps Johanna looked round the angle of the north wall and came strutting back to them with blown-out cheeks in ludicrous imitation of a fat and pompous figure only too familiar to them all. "Here comes the Duke himself—breathing fire about it!" she warned, hastily reseating herself between Raymond and Blondel to watch the promising encounter.

"Humour him, Richard!" whispered Berengaria. "It saves so much trouble in the end."

Ida took up a good position on the steps of the little watch tower, and as the footsteps came round the corner they all settled into hushed expectancy, leaving Richard the centre of the stage.

Leopold of Austria was a consequential little man, utterly devoid of humour. He was naturally kind and conscientious, but an unprepossessing exterior had given him a sense of inferiority which made him bumptious, and coming breathlessly into the midst of these good-looking, casual foreigners he was at his worst. When he had panted indignantly up the land gate stairs to give the King of England a piece of his mind, he had hardly bargained for the whole family. Their levity and habit of understatement confused his precise mind, and because he was really a very lonely man he sometimes found himself glancing enviously over the edge of his own dignity at their easy comradeship. "What is this I hear?" he demanded, strutting straight up to Richard and puffing out his cheeks just as Johanna had done. "You order my soldiers to make walls?" Actually, he had a sneaking admiration for this tall, energetic leader of the Normans and English but, being vaguely aware of the amusement of their audience, he spoke more truculently than he had intended.

Richard was positively ingratiating. "Good honest work!" he enthused, ostentatiously rubbing the dust from his own fine, swordsman's hands.

"Almost as fascinating as planting bulbs, don't you think?" chipped in that vivid, irrepressible sister of his, in revenge for many an hour's boredom hearing about the Duke's hobby.

Leopold acknowledged her presence with a stiff little bow.

"Flowers," he said sententiously, "are a fit occupation for any peoples. But mending walls—"

"I admit I might have asked you first," apologised Richard handsomely.

Anyone who understood him knew that apologies did not come easily from the Angevin; but instead of accepting it and so ending the matter, Leopold must needs labour the point with Teutonic thoroughness. "If I want a castle built, I do not lay the stones myself," he explained complacently.

"Then you miss a good deal of fun," said Richard shortly.

Johanna tittered and immediately sought to cover her lapse by making violent signs to Ida to hand the Duke some fruit. He was hot and thirsty, but it seemed incompatible with dignity that two important people should discuss the affair while sucking oranges and, before the ladies, he wasn't quite sure what to do about the pips. Moreover, he was embarrassed by the fact that this disinherited hostage of theirs, waiting on him in her Eastern finery, was in fact his own sister's child. "I do not see how one can mix fun with war," he said gravely.

Richard, who was never preoccupied about dignity, helped himself without embarrassment to another nectarine. "No, no, I could hardly expect *that* of you," he agreed blandly, spitting the stone expertly over the battlements. Leopold glanced round the little group with puzzled, short-sighted eyes. He was never quite sure whether these pleasant, easy-mannered Normans were making fun of him or not. Recognising the slow sincerity of the man, Richard met it with plain speaking. "But at least you must see how important it is to leave behind us a chain of strong fortresses in good repair all along the coast?" he appealed.

"Without them we shan't be able to get supplies of that succulent veal you like so much," added Raymond.

The Duke loved his stomach, but he loved his dignity still more, and this relative of the charming new English queen was always ragging someone. So he decided to ignore him. He looked down at the sweating workers at the gate and felt hotter than ever. A mad, mongrel race working with cheerful profanity in such a climate! "Then let your men finish the repairs since they do not seem to mind," he compromised. "What need is there to disturb mine?" The words were euphemistic. Everybody knew that once those stolid Junkers of his had settled down to their drinks he would have the devil's job to make them obey. And the comparison did not improve his temper.

Richard still tried persuasion. After all, the cause was always more to him than the means. He winked at Berengaria and set his elbows companionably on the wall alongside his sulky ally. "Do them good, Leopold!" he laughed. "Just look at them lolling down there in the shade stuffing olives. They're getting too fat for their armour."

"And all bemused by the lovely veiled ladies!" drawled Raymond lazily.

They were all so used to chaffing each other, but unfortunately the pompous little Austrian couldn't take it. He was one of those tiring people for whom one must weigh every word. He killed light-hearted conversation by taking it literally. "What have their morals to do with you?" he demanded, glaring at the laughing Frenchman.

Poor Raymond was nonplussed. It was Richard who answered. He suddenly stopped being either funny or persuasive. "Nothing, thank God!" he admitted sharply. "But the discipline of my army has everything to do with me. And I consider it of the utmost military importance that Acre should be left in sound and sanitary condition and that the troops should have regular employment while we are stuck here waiting for Saladin to carry out the terms of surrender."

But Leopold was considering nothing but his own importance. His short, fleshy neck was almost purple. "*Your* army!" he fumed. "Mein lieber Gott!"

"Yes, mine," snapped Richard, all his virtuous patience exhausted. "Mine every time we are in a tight corner. Mine whenever hundreds of lives depend on one man's decision—which none of you ever seems to have the guts to make. French, Germans, Austrians, Venetians—all the hang-dog pack of you are glad enough to obey me then. And I say that when you cannot be fighting you shall build."

"It is an indignity—" spluttered the Duke, almost speechless.

But Richard cut him short as if he were a junior squire. "I see no indignity in keeping oneself physically fit and using one's muscles on any job that comes along." That was his philosophy of life—his and Robin's—and he knew that Berengaria found it good. Hadn't they all a full size task pushing on to Haifa without this exasperating idiot holding things up? Why should his own men have to start out tired because some other contingent had let the climate turn them rotten? It was perhaps unfortunate that at that very moment a breath of hot, sand-laden air should stir the standard above them, filling out Leopold's emblems for all the world to see. The sight of them at such a moment inflamed Richard's annoyance. "And another thing," he went on, "since we're discussing those lily-handed henchmen of yours down there, I'd like to know what part they took in subduing this ward of the town that you should have the effrontery to set up your personal bit of heraldry here?"

Perhaps Leopold had hoped the breeze wouldn't lift just then to draw attention to it. But it had given him such pathetic pleasure to have it put there. Every time he looked at it from his lodgings in the opposite tower it made him feel he wasn't such a bad general after all. Of course, he had had no idea that the family of the partner who had played him to victory would choose that very spot for their sun lounge. "It was agreed that we should share—" he muttered, momentarily shamefaced.

"Yes—share," agreed Richard grimly. "As I will make your men share the drudgery and dirt." He made a motion as if to hail them and his audience sat enthralled, backing him with silent fervour. Goggle-eyed pages had already spread the news that the King of England and the Duke of Austria were quarrelling and the armies themselves were taking sides. The English stopped hammering to listen to the sound of angry voices on the walls. They were spoiling for a fight—and not with the Saracens this time. And now their King wasn't going to stand any nonsense either. Only Berengaria, while loving Richard for his indignation, saw the folly of it.

"You wouldn't dare!" blustered Leopold, into the tense silence.

He couldn't have said anything more unfortunate. It sounded like a challenge before the two watching armies. Richard's eyes narrowed savagely as a cat's, and Johanna and Blondel—who had had their entertainment and enjoyed it—realised that this was the moment when Robin should have intervened. In the old days at Oxford he would have sauntered on to such a scene with a friendly grin and a well-timed joke calculated to keep his foster-brother's dramatics within the bounds of common sense. His unostentatious control had been so unfailing that they almost looked round for his comforting presence, but there was no one now to avert a tragic finale. Berengaria half rose, sensing the moment; but, being a woman, lacked both the casual manner and the right remark.

"Dare!" barked Richard, swinging round on his ally. "By God's wounds, that's a word no man uses to me twice!" Lithe as a man half his weight, he sprang on to the coping of the little tower, catching at the fluttering ends of the banner. Steadying himself by an iron window bar, he leaned far out and scores of men below craned their necks to watch him. They saw the flag staff bend like a bow to his strength and the flash of his great, two-handed sword as he slashed away the silk. It slithered like a lifeless woman to the battlements, sinking into helpless folds with a rustling sigh, and as the tall Angevin stepped backwards he trampled it unintentionally with his dusty, mailed feet. The Austrians on the other side of the fosse rose and shook their fists with anger, but their abusive shouts were drowned by the derisive guffaws of Englishmen whose comrades had been killed taking that very bastion. Richard knew their temper well enough. They wanted to see either their dragon or his leopards flying there. They were coming to blows with the Austrians about it. He sympathised with every blow but for discipline's sake he shouted for a red cross crusading standard and ordered one of them to run it up. "This isn't a private war," he snarled.

Poor Leopold flung himself upon his torn standard, grasping it clumsily with gloved hands. "Ach, meine estande so dishonoured in the sight of men...Give it to me!" he cried, trying to pull it from beneath Richard's heel.

But Richard stood firm. He might have been the boastful young redhead astride his first pony challenging the youth of Oxford with a tent pole. "Fight me for it, then," he laughed contemptuously.

Leopold looked up enviously at the splendid figure outlined against the sky. "You know very well I am not strong enough," he said, with a kind of dignity. The very simplicity of his avowal made them all feel vaguely ashamed.

Richard jumped down awkwardly. "Oh, go and dice!" he muttered, walking away without even looking at the man. Berengaria was right, he supposed, simulating great interest in the way a man from the *Trenchemer* ran up the Red Cross. Few things are worth the wear of anger. He saw her white, unhappy face and felt about as heroic as a chidden page boy. Out of the tail of his eye he could see the wretched Duke gathering his raped standard to his breast and kissing it. The others averted their eyes, embarrassed by such an orgy of Teutonic sentiment. But they could not close their ears to the irritating guttural Norman of his parting shot. "You do well to remind me that now we fight under a common banner. But if ever the good God should put you in my power afterwards, Richard Plantagenet, you will pay for this deadly insult!"

He went trailing his soiled heraldry towards the land gate stairs. "A pity, after we all tried so hard to be pleasant!" sighed Johanna, rather over-awed for once.

Raymond got up and stretched himself. "I'm sorry, Richard," he apologised, "about the veal and the veiled ladies..."

The tension was broken. Blondel gathered up his tools, and Ida left her grandstand on the tower steps. Her dark eyes sparkled as she danced a sort of fandango round Richard. "You are so much bigger than my pompous old uncle that you can afford to spit on his most sacred things!" she exclaimed exultantly.

Richard stared at her sombrely. Her bold admiration was balm after Berengaria's distress, but her words reminded him of something Robin had once said about John. "I suppose it *was* sacred to him," he said regretfully.

Across the girl's bobbing head he sought his wife's opinion. She looked so frightened he thought she was going to faint. Pushing Ida aside, he went to her at once. And Berengaria, who was so seldom demonstrative in public, clung to him shuddering. "Oh, Richard," she sobbed, through an inexplicable storm of tears, "you have made an enemy for life!"

Chapter Twenty-Three

ALL THROUGH THE BREATHLESS afternoon Johanna made her sister-in-law rest. They were housed in the harem part of a rich sheik's house, but the fountains had long since ceased to splash in the neglected garden, and the stench of narrow streets seeped in through the heavy lattices. Yvette moved quietly about the darkened room trying to ward off the mosquitoes, and Berengaria lay staring at the high-pitched ceiling because every time she closed her eyes she saw the dreadful face of the dead Saracen.

From outside the high wall of the house came the shuffling of hurrying sandalled feet as the people of Acre suffered themselves to be rounded up with the gaunt remnants of their heroic garrison and herded towards the land gate to join Saladin's unsuccessful relief forces In the hills. They would have to leave their battered homes, but at least this Cœur de Lion, so terrible in battle, had promised to spare their lives. "And Allah be praised, it's the turn for the English guard to-night!" croaked a wizened old water-carrier. For they had come to know that the long, lean archers—so much like themselves in some ways—were good fighters but bad haters. Once you were taken prisoner they didn't kick you or mock at your misfortunes but joked with you in their rough, incomprehensible way and as likely as not threw the children a bit of their rations. But all the same the citizens of Acre spat at the shadows of the conquering Infidels who climbed to the city walls towards sundown to watch the exchange of prisoners.

Berengaria got up and called for her bridal dress and her make-shift crown. It would be a formal occasion and Richard would want her to be there to welcome his men. As people made way for her through the streets, conquerors and vanquished alike eyed the sinking sun and said, "It won't be long now!" The only dour faces to be seen belonged to the garrison to be left behind.

A cool evening breeze was blowing off the sea as Richard received his Queen at the top of the steps. "Come and see the Saracens marching out," he invited, leading her to their usual vantage point. There seemed to be an endless procession of them streaming from beneath the great portcullis, most of them shuffling beneath pathetic bundles. Their camels and donkeys had long ago been eaten. The men were bound together with ropes but even that indignity could not quench the fiery pride in their sunken eyes. "What hundreds of them!" murmured Berengaria compassionately.

"Three thousand, my dear," Richard told her.

"Can't we do something for the women with their poor, wizened babies?" she suggested. Richard loved her for her compassion. He was far more interested in seeing her in her wedding dress than he was in the Saracens. The wind had whipped some colour into her cheeks and he thought how lovely she looked with a long white veil floating out behind her thick, dark plaits. But he would probably have sent the women some extra goats' milk if Raymond, coming down from the watch-towers, had not reported that there was no sign of any prisoners on the mountain road.

"They'll probably come winding out from that rocky canyon presently," said Johanna uneasily. "Richard gave Saladin till sunset, you know."

"The sun is making a gold path across the sea," remarked Ida. The glow of it suffused her young, lineless face, warming the smooth olive skin. Like most women of her race she would probably be fat at thirty, but at seventeen she was ravishing. Berengaria, watching her, lifted an exploring finger to her own face for the first sign of a wrinkle.

Her cousin's good-natured face was set and dour. "De Lusignon was telling me the other day that if ever he got any prisoners back the devils had blinded them," he blurted out to all and sundry.

"Oh, no, Raymond!" beseeched Berengaria, as if he could avert it.

Richard looked from one to the other of the men about him with frowning uncertainty. "You really think Saladin may trick me? Send us back a band of blinded men?"

As Raymond did not answer he turned to Mercadier. The hirsute old campaigner shrugged. He had been out here before as a young hired mercenary. "If ne sends them back at all," he said. "An Arab has no sense of time, you know, Sir. Next week—next month—whenever he happens to remember."

"Remember!" snorted Richard. "But he can *see*. Isn't his own garrison lined up and waiting down there? And aren't those hills simply swarming with Saracens watching everything we do?"

Leopold, who had been talking in an undertone to Philip of France, turned to savour Richard's discomfiture. "Watching, yes—and laughing," he sneered. "At the omnipotent English lion."

"No man makes a fool of me and gets away with it," growled Richard.

Egged on by other foreign leaders, the little Austrian felt safe enough to bait their successful rival. "Make him obey your orders then, the way you try to make us," he jeered.

Richard ignored their enmity. He had bigger things to think about. It was one of those moments for a quick decision. What was it he had said to Robin back in Dover? "A man who can't burden his conscience with occasional ruthlessness hasn't the right to rule." And Robin had agreed with him.

"And if Saladin won't obey you can punish him—with three thousand Saracens in your power," prompted the Cypriot hostage at his side, forgetting how lenient he had been to her own countrymen.

Richard looked across the empty plain and struck palm with fist. "And by the foot of God, I will!" he swore.

Ida gazed up at him as if he were some superman. Her eyes burned with excitement. "You will really blind them all?" she asked.

He pushed her out of the way and strode to the top of the city gate. "Of course not. I don't torture people," he said grimly. "But when I must, I kill."

The girl clapped her hands as if he had offered to take her to a mumming or a bull fight; but Berengaria ordered her to be quiet. She caught at the King's cloak as he passed. "For pity's sake, Richard, what are you going to do?" she cried.

Apart from the cruelty of it, Raymond judged that such a wholesale massacre would be bad for Richard's reputation. He put himself in his friend's impetuous path. "Heavens, man, remember most of them are bound!" he warned, lowering his voice so that their whispering allies should not hear.

But it began to look certain that the Christians had been fooled. "If we let Saladin get away with it once he will do it again," pointed out Richard, and Chalus and Burgundy and most of the French nobles agreed with him. There was only one man who could prevent his vengeance now, and he was an outlaw in some English wood. "Line up the prisoners on the plain and surround them," Richard shouted down from the gate head.

His own men moved reluctantly to the order, but the envious leaders of his allies, to whom a few hundred Saracens meant no more than so many sheep, rejoiced covertly over a story that would discredit him in the eyes of the world.

Raymond put his broad shoulder like a shield between Johanna and the proposed carnage. "It's the sort of thing John might have done," she moaned. But Berengaria, the timid, forced herself to look as long as there was any chance of averting it. She saw the reluctant English, standing in a hesitant circle with drawn blades and the sudden doubt and terror of the huddled captives. Most clearly of all she saw the piteous, upturned faces of the women, their swaddled babies clasped like little mummies beneath their dull blue veils. "You gave them till sunset," she insisted clearly.

Richard laid a hand on the great portcullis chain while he waited. A ruby set in the back of his leather gauntlet gleamed like blood in the roseate light. Berengaria watched it pale, afraid to look behind her towards the West.

"Perhaps Saladin will send a message," suggested Blondel.

But Islam mocked in silence from the hills.

Ida stood beside Chalus, erect as some mystic priestess, watching the last rim of light kiss the sea. Suddenly she lifted both arms and her bangles jangled together like clashed cymbals. "The sun has set!" she called shrilly.

The short Eastern twilight was upon them. All men's eyes waited on Richard. "Separate the women and children," he called to Mercadier, who had gone down. "And then kill the rest."

Berengaria saw the women try to shield their bound husbands and lovers with their own bodies—saw them being dragged away. And compassion meant more to Berengaria than being sorry. Cherished daughter of Navarre as she was—and intellectually Richard's superior—she threw herself down on the dusty stones and clasped his knees. "Richard, Richard, I implore you—by our love…" she cried incoherently.

But Richard disengaged her clinging hands. His mouth—of which she knew only the tenderness—was a merciless line above the hardness of his jaw. "God's breath, d'you suppose I enjoy this butchering that you must try to make it harder?" he asked roughly.

Johanna came and pulled her to her feet. She felt that Berengaria's prayers only underlined her brother's cruelty and was angry with them both. "Robin would have known how to stop you!" she told him. He turned on her fiercely and a flame of Plantagenet fury licked round them, momentarily scorching their mutual love. "Curse your interference!" shouted Richard. "Why must you remind me of him now?" But even the memory did more than Berengaria's prayers. For a moment he seemed to hesitate, but Leopold chose the pregnant moment to make some stinging comment about "the only man who had guts to make and stick to a decision." Even Raymond had to admit that reprisals were justifiable. So Richard drew his sword and with forced cheerfulness called to Philip and Leopold to come down. He knew they would be only too glad to see him shock some men's consciences and, having given an unpopular order, felt that he himself must be the first to strike.

They could not do other than follow him, and all the sight-seeing crowd trooped after them. Only the King's squire remained unnoticed with the women. His princess needed him. "Help me with the Queen," she had whispered, under cover of the general excitement. Between them they carried her into the little watch-tower and laid her on a rough camp bed used by the officer of the watch. For Richard's sake neither of them wanted people to know that she had fainted.

"Where is Yvette?" asked Blondel, hastily improvising a pillow out of the old crescent standard that Leopold had had hauled down.

"Down in the town still superintending the packing," Johanna said. He sent a passing man-at-arms in search of her, but she must have been on her way because before they could send for her she appeared in the narrow doorway. "Oh, my poor beautiful!" she cried at sight of Berengaria. She took charge at once, loosening the Queen's dress and telling Blondel to take off the tight, makeshift crown. "She hadn't been well for days," she said, "and you know how she hates all this moving from camp to camp."

Reacting to her ministrations, Berengaria began to stir. "Richard?" she murmured questioningly. Then her dark, curled lashes fluttered wide and her pansy-brown eyes darkened with the horror of remembrance.

"He didn't mean to hurt you, Madam," apologised his squire. "He was just mad with rage…"

Berengaria knew he was more concerned for the king's credit than for her hurt, but loved his loyalty. She lifted a limp hand and touched him reassuringly. "I know, Blondel," she said.

The bare, vaulted room beneath the flagstaff was only big enough to hold the four of them. The city wall seemed quiet and deserted. Normally the Moslems would have been at prayer, but suddenly the evening stillness was rent by piercing shrieks. Yvette straightened herself beside the low bed. "What's the matter? What are those people shrieking for?" she asked, looking from one to the other of them for enlightenment. The shrieks were followed by a dreadful, long-drawn wailing and, as no one answered her, she went briskly to the door. But Blondel was quick to bar her way.

"It's nothing fit for your pretty eyes," he said, holding her fast in the gathering gloom. He had bent to kiss her before a movement behind him reminded him that Ida was still watching the last of her hero's vengeance. Glancing over his shoulder, he added disgustedly, "She egged him on to do it—she and the Austrian!" And Yvette, beginning to understand something of what had happened, clung to him gratefully. It seemed that only in such stark moments snatched from war was their love destined to unfold!

Inside the watch-tower Berengaria turned her head wearily so that the end of one heavy plait dropped with a soft plop to the uneven floor. "Although he will never admit it, Richard will be sorry for this all his life," she said.

Johanna ranged back and forth across the little room. It was her personal shame. "It's as if he'd smeared an ugly stain across our escutcheon," she said. But she had promised to let Raymond take her to one of Chalus's amusing parties, and so she was only too willing to forget the incident when Berengaria professed herself better and said she would rather be alone.

Knowing how she hated a fuss, they all took her at her word, and presently she sauntered out on to the wall…It was pleasantly cool now, the stars were beginning to come out, and the scene of the recent reprisals was mercifully shrouded in darkness. Music and laughter were already bubbling from a large lighted house in the best part of the town, drowning the muted lamentations from the slums round the harbour. Ida was nowhere to be seen, and the fitful strains of native music suggested that she too had gone to Barbe of Chalus's party. She and Barbe got on well together, and it was guard-room gossip that she sometimes condescended to dance for him.

Berengaria was in no mood for the monotonous nasal music of the bazaars, which was becoming such a rage with the younger crusaders. She waited, thinking of her loved ones in Pamplona, until Richard came to her for comfort as she knew he would. Even in the darkness she could see the tired lines on his face, but there was none of the elation with which he used to return to her from battle. "Are you going to forgive me?" he asked.

"A great deal more readily than you will forgive yourself, I expect," she assured him, trying to speak lightly.

Richard looked up in quick contradiction. "My roughness to you in front of all these people, I mean. Not this necessary reprisal."

"Can't you see that my feelings were nothing compared with the suffering of those women? Besides, I knew you didn't mean it. You were furious because what Johanna said was true." Berengaria broke off suddenly and pulled away her hand. "Oh, look!" she cried. "Your sword is dripping blood on my wedding dress!"

He had forgotten the thing was still in his hand, and he wiped and sheathed it, hastily. He could have kicked himself. Particularly just now, when he wanted to please her…"I couldn't give an order which I wasn't prepared to carry out myself," he muttered, going down on one knee to dab awkwardly at her shimmering skirt. When he stood up he was gauche and smiling, unsure of her response. "Can't we kiss and be friends?" he pleaded.

He would have pulled her against the hungry hardness of his body but she made a slender barrier of her hands. "No—no—I can't…" she stammered breathlessly. It hadn't occurred to her that he would want that.

But he wouldn't let her go. "You've been avoiding me for days," he accused, half angrily.

"And you've been far too busy to care," she flashed back. If only he hadn't been so busy—if only she could have told him her secret then—perhaps he would have seen to it that to-day's distressing events hadn't happened!

But he mistook her resistance for some lover's hurt at being slighted. He wasn't humble enough to be very sensitive to other people's moods. "Well, now at last I have a few hours' leisure," he said complacently. "You know we shall have to start at dawn, so let's forget the whole bloody business and make this last night in Acre ours." He pivoted with her in his arms, tilting up her chin so that she faced the velvet sky. "Look, my beloved, the same stars are coming out that used to shine on Cyprus. I can see them reflected in your eyes." Unfortunately, he could also see the vague outlines of a burial party shuffling through the sand and hear the mournful creaking of their carts. He turned in sudden loathing from that side of the wall. Down in the town, as if by contrast, men were celebrating. So why not he, the conqueror of Acre? "Come down, witch woman, and make me forget that madness!" he urged, his natural directness making him betray his shame.

Berengaria knew his need but scorned to give her body as a drug. "Those poor women," she excused herself, looking from stars to darkened slums. "They will always come between us…"

But Richard's hands were roughly urgent. "What are any other women to me," he protested, "unless you have grown cold?" Never in his life before had he been thwarted by a woman he desired. And here was his own wife shuddering from him as if he had the plague. Although she was shivering she freed herself deliberately from the warmth of his cloak and the comfort of his arms. "Cold?" she repeated tonelessly. "Yes, I suppose I *am* cold. But it is my heart shivering—as if someone stamped clumsily across a little grave…" She looked at him with wide, fey eyes and behaved so strangely that Richard let her go. "Rather a sudden indisposition, isn't it," he remarked, with scepticism.

"I really do feel ill," she assured him more naturally. "Please believe me. It isn't just because—because of what you did—"

"I am sorry," said Richard sullenly.

Berengaria moved blindly towards the top of the stone steps. "I'm going down to Johanna. I think I shall sleep with her," she said. She didn't even wish him "good night" because she didn't want him to see the tears coursing down her face—tears of desolation because the stars were shining and they were alone and she had no secret to tell him now.

Richard made as if to follow her. He was worried about her, remembering how upset she had been about that pompous Austrian ass. He thought she was probably in for fever. If so he'd have a litter made for her. However ill she was, he wouldn't leave her behind. She had been an angel to him when he was ill, and to his wounded men. He specially appreciated that. They were ugly sights, some of them, and he remembered how she had always hated the sight of blood. Come to think about it, what a life for a woman! A far cry from binding up a scratched wrist at a tournament. And now he had pestered her. Richard turned back from the top step. After all, perhaps she would be better with the women. He wished he understood them better. Johanna, of course, was forthright and strong. She'd been brought up among brothers and if you did anything she didn't like she just flamed out at you like another man. You knew where you were with her. But he was beginning to find out that Berengaria, for all her gentleness, had queer, obstinate principles. The sort of thing he had quarrelled with Robin over. "A man wants a good wife," he thought with a touch of John's cynicisms "but not necessarily one who wants to make him into a good husband!"

He wandered into the watch-tower, stumbling over a bundle of something on the floor. It appeared to be some sort of flag and he could just make out the Moslem crescent. Remembering the affair with Leopold, he picked it up carefully and put it on the window ledge. After all, those fellows defending the bastion had given their lives for it. As he moved to the window he could hear the rhythm of native drums. They seemed to suit the madness of the night. Christians making merry in one quarter of the town and widows wailing in another. Richard wondered if there was anything he could do about the orphaned children, but the drums began to beat insidiously into his resentful, frustrated blood. As always, they called to his inherent lawlessness beneath the decencies imposed by the discipline of Hodierna and the friendship of Robin. They were the heart of the East, which he had sworn to tame. And hadn't his witch predicted that all his greatest triumphs would be in the East? "Anyhow, I'm damned if I'll go back to a cold bed as if I wasn't fit to live with!" he thought, knowing that such triumphs cannot be won without deeds psychologically suited to one's enemy.

"Here, give me your lantern!" he called to a passing soldier. "And tell Captain Mercadier if he wants me I shall be sleeping up here away from all that hubbub. What've you got on that tray?"

He spent so much time with his army that even the rank and file addressed him without embarrassment. "Supper for the officer of the watch, Sir," the man told him, with a respectful grin.

"Splendid!" said Richard, whipping off the cover and sniffing appreciatively. "Sowerby of York's on to-night, isn't he? Get him something hot from the kitchens whenever he wants it and leave that here for me." The man put food and lamp on a rough wooden table. "And get a fresh plaster for that old wound of yours before we start, Thomas," Richard shouted after him.

"I will that, Sir!" the man sang back. The King had remembered his name.

Richard suddenly realised how hungry he was and wolfed the food standing, washing it down with great draughts of wine. Warm yellow light from the horn of the lantern gave the little stone room a more cheerful aspect, and seen through the narrow arch of the doorway the distant hills looked quiet enough under the winking stars. "Better than all your houses!" thought Richard, as the wine began to warm him. "Many's the night Rob and I have slept out on the castle walls." He began to whistle cheerfully between strong, square teeth, unbuckling his cloak and throwing it across the makeshift bed where its jewelled border sparkled incongruously. True, he hadn't had jewels on his cloak in those days, but he would give them all now to have back the world's best companion.

He had taken off belt and hauberk when he became aware of a girl's voice humming the dance melody of the moment. He picked up his borrowed lantern and to his surprise found Ida still at her favourite niche on the battlements. "My dear child," he said, "I thought you had gone to the party!"

She took the lantern from him and set it beside her on the parapet so that it illuminated her face. "I don't feel like dancing," she said plaintively.

"Then you must be feeling very low!" he laughed. He crossed the wall and stood quizzing her, as she sat with one hand resting against the masonry on either side of her slender knees. "My poor little hostage! It must be very lonely for you. I suppose you think me an ogre for bringing you?"

"I asked you to," she reminded him.

"So you did. Though goodness knows why. You know, I think all that stuff about de Lusignon being amorous was just imagination.

But I shouldn't dance at Chalus's parties if I were you." He warned her diffidently, as he might have spoken to Johanna before her marriage, not certain how much of life she knew.

Apparently she preferred not to discuss the subject. "I am never lonely with you," she confided. "Only with the Queen. She is so fastidious and she doesn't like me."

Richard's eyes twinkled at her shrewdness. "The Queen has beautiful manners," he said gravely. "I expect she thinks we both behave like uncouth savages at times. That putrid Saracen's head, for instance."

Ida dismissed the reminder of her lapse with a grimace. "When you're masterful she doesn't like *you*," she said.

He guessed then that she had been eavesdropping. "Apparently not," he admitted ruefully, moving away from the quick fire of her personal remarks.

But Ida clasped her palms between her knees and leaned conversationally towards him. "Your women are so strange," she said. "Now I adore you when you rage round, killing and cursing, and take what you want."

Richard burst out laughing. The girl was as good as a whole company of paid buffoons. "That's because you have a nasty Eastern mind," he told her, lifting her down from the parapet preparatory to sending her to bed.

To his surprise she would not let him release her. Even after he had set her down she kept her arms clasped tightly round his neck and when he straightened himself she only let them slide caressingly down his shoulders. Her subtle perfume invaded his senses. "And my body?" she asked, with mischievous amusement. "Is that nasty, too?"

It was a revelation to Richard—both her words and the pressure of her perfumed limbs. Caught unawares, he was too surprised to move. After a moment or two he loosened her predatory hands. "No," he said, turning away abruptly. "Your body is very beautiful."

She followed him back to the tower and stood leaning against the open door watching him finish his meal. He jerked forward a stool and concentrated on his plate. Clearly he wanted to be rid of her. "Why do you always treat me like a child?" she demanded.

He looked up with a chicken bone in his fingers and laughed at her. The laughter sounded a little forced, and he was careful to keep his eyes above the level of her petulant mouth. "Well, so you are, aren't you? The brightest young thing about the camp. Heaven knows how we should all endure these solemn Austrians without you!" He spoke boisterously, determined that that moment by the battlements should not recur.

But Ida persisted. Having once tasted her power to disturb him she wasn't going back to any "kind uncle" talk. She picked up his cloak, draping it impudently about herself so that it trailed behind like a bridal train. "I am seventeen," she said, smoothing the rich velvet to her hips. "If you hadn't carried me off from Cyprus I should have been married by now. My father was arranging it."

"Well, I'd better find you a nice, masterful husband," suggested Richard carelessly. He threw down the last bone and wiped his fingers on the guard officer's napkin. Young Sowerby of York would now be able to boast that besides the Queen having lain on his bed the King had eaten his supper.

"I don't want a husband," said Ida sullenly.

Richard got up and kicked aside the stool. He was tired and wanted to get to bed. "Then what do you want?" he asked impatiently.

She stopped play-acting with his cloak and moved into the circle of lamplight, standing before him, barefoot and bangled like some submissive slave girl. Her small breasts pulsed to the quick tempo of her breath. "Are you really so blind?" she asked.

Richard stared at her. Angrily at first and then with quickening blood. He saw the perfection of her youth and for the first time realised her ripeness. She was right—he had been a fool to treat her as a child. She was more like some gaudy tropical blossom, opening in greedy ecstasy to the brief promise of life. With such a warm-eyed wanton in his arms, surely the whole mystery of the East would be his? He passed a hand across his eyes. It must be that damned Cypriot's drums or this seductive scent…"No, no, my dear. We must both be crazed," he said. "It's just because you are very beguiling and I have been a little too kind. You mustn't think we're all like Chalus…"

But she broke in passionately on his desperate reasoning. "Kind!" she cried contemptuously. "D'you suppose my blood doesn't beat with joy when you are cruel too?" She came and threw herself against his breast. "I worship you, Richard Plantagenet. I have worshipped you ever since that night you rescued me from your soldiers and carried me home on your saddle. I thought you were taking me for yourself—the way your men took the other women from my home—"

He took her by the shoulders roughly. "You thought that?" he said, trying to remember the details of that casual ride and recalling only that he had been on fire for Berengaria.

In the shameful recital of her disappointment the girl beat upon his breast with frenzied little fists. "I went *on* thinking it until they told me you were to be married. And then you sent for me, and I saw your pale, cold bride. And you made me dance at her wedding…"

Richard held her wrists with savage strength but she didn't even wince. "You behaved like a common harlot!" he said, remembering how she had danced.

She struggled to free herself, shaking back the curled masses of her night-black hair. "Then do you suppose I should shrink from you because you are strong enough to kill?" she cried. "Don't you believe that I am beautiful enough to make you forget all the sins you ever did?"

Slowly Richard's arms went round her. She was fragrant and supple as a houri. "Beautiful enough, God knows!" he muttered. "But He has my vows of knighthood—and you aren't really a harlot but my defenceless hostage."

Ida Comnenos laughed away his scruples, lifting red lips to his, "I don't want the coldness of your Northern chivalry," she said. "I only want the warmth of your kisses."

With an arm still about her Richard kicked at the door. It swung to with a clang, shutting out the mocking invitation of the drums and spilling the wine as he poured their loving cup. "Then here's to forgetting!" he laughed recklessly.

Chapter Twenty-Four

ROBIN'S WITCH WAS RIGHT. Richard went on from triumph to triumph. Slowly but relentlessly he forged his chain of key points along the coast. Philip might fidget and Leopold sneer because they had to rein in their champing chargers to a crawl. Eager young squires might complain that even the baggage wagons and the cooks could have moved faster. But hadn't Eleanor or Aquitaine—over and over again in the tower room at Oxford—kept her unruly brood enthralled with tales of what happened in the first crusade whenever Louis left a gap? So her son saw to it that there were no gaps. And when a hundred thousand men march slowly like a solid wall there is nothing much that hit-and-run raiders can do about it. The Saracens poisoned the wells and swooped down from the hills a dozen times a day, but French and English, Austrians and Genoese shuffled through the burning sand, some of them with arrows sticking into their shoulders, too tightly wedged between their comrades to fall out by the way. As for the knights and nobles, hadn't Richard predicted that the plains of Palestine would prove hard? They suffered from sunstroke and sleeplessness and thirst, but when at last they marched into Haifa the sight of waiting provision ships stopped all criticism and even rival leaders were content to leave the campaign in hands touched with genius.

From Haifa to Jaffa the going was not so good because stunted woods sprawled down to the sea at a place called Arsouf. Only an optimistic fool could suppose the Saracens would miss such an opportunity. They came snaking down from the hills, grinning with fanatic joy at the funny sight of plated horsemen ploughing their clumsy way on horses almost as encumbered as themselves. With a cry of "Allah Akbar" they charged again and again, severing Christian heads with broad-bladed scimitars. But they had laughed too soon at the clumsy knights—one of whom, at any rate, was more swiftly mounted than themselves and cared nothing about encasing his conspicuous head. The odds were three to one on the Saracens at Arsouf and they fought brilliantly on their own ground, but after the battle riderless Arab steeds were so cheap that an international Christian army made a meal of them.

Camped at last among the pleasant orange groves of Jaffa, the indefatigable Plantagenet let his followers rest. They deserved it and things were going well. But he himself worked like a dog getting everything reconditioned and ready for the final push to Jerusalem.

"Only about fifty more miles, Sir!" Blondel would say of a morning, pouring over their well-worn map. And Richard would think secretly, "If I got on Fauvel now—alone—I could be in the Street of David by nightfall!" But those fifty miles were inland miles, flanked by treacherous hills. The Saracens, he knew, held the road at Ramlah. And never again would he underrate them.

"With any luck we should be in England by next Spring," he consoled Berengaria.

But there wasn't any luck. The weather broke suddenly. The seasons changed with the swift cruelty of the East. Torrential rains washed away the rough mountain tracks. Where men had panted beneath a pitiless sun they almost died of exposure to the wind. And Philip, who had already experienced one winter under canvas, wanted to go home.

"If only you hadn't wasted so much time in Cyprus I might have been back in France by now," he pointed out peevishly, at the end of a particularly acrimonious staff meeting.

"I made up for it when I did come," Richard reminded him good-humouredly, getting up to dismiss the rest.

"A man ought to put his own country first," said Philip sententiously. It was Robin's argument; but at least Robin had been consistent. He hadn't come at all.

Richard gathered up his parchments. "I don't imagine my mother is having a particularly rosy time," he said grimly. "We'd a letter from her this morning, and it appears that John is making things very difficult for Longchamps."

"Then let us go home together," urged Philip.

Richard turned as if he had been stung. Up till then he had taken it as part of the daily grumbling. "Go home? Give up—after all we've done!" he echoed.

Philip lay back wearily against the fleurs-de-lis that sprigged the blue velvet of his chair. He had come as a duty, no doubt, hoping for a swift, showy campaign; and must have hated the way the laurels were snatched from him by a man who was in part his vassal. At home—as a statesman—he shone supreme. "I feel I should be of so much more *use* in France," he excused himself, with rare honesty.

Richard had known him since he was a pale, friendly youth. Because of the glitter of his position he had many a time rated his vain counsel higher than his own father's wisdom. "For Christ's sake don't leave me in the lurch just now!" he implored.

Philip murmured something about money.

"Stay on at my expense," invited Richard, out of the generosity of his own empty coffers. But Philip was obdurate. What was the good of being King of France if one had to eat badly cooked food in a draughty tent?

Even the French nobles were ashamed of his defection and half of them stayed on with the Plantagenet, but it meant he had to feed them. So when the French king sailed he deliberately turned his back on the great blue and gold banners streaming from his masthead and—although he spent years haggling over French soil—he never spoke again to Philip Capet.

Next morning, his army still further depleted by the strong garrison it was necessary to leave at Jaffa, Richard pushed inland as far as Beit Nuba. There were no walls to mend there—nothing to keep cold men occupied. Only a few flat-roofed hovels and torrential rain and ubiquitous mud. For the first time since leaving Dover Richard knew doubt. If only he could hold out and keep his men from cutting each other's throats until the Spring! He sent Raymond back to Jaffa for reinforcements, hoping to come to some sort of winter truce with Saladin.

Berengaria remembered that Saladin's friend, Bohadin, had once enjoyed the hospitality of Pamplona and urged Richard to visit him in the hills. Reluctantly, he put his pride in his pocket and went. "I'd better leave Blondel with you in case I don't come back," he insisted uneasily. But for once Berengaria was the more confident of the two. "They aren't savages," she assured him. "Bohadin is writing Saladin's biography, and he will be most interested to meet you."

When Richard came back some days later he was wet to the skin, shivering with ague, and disappointed because, after all, he hadn't seen Saladin.

"My dear, I am so sorry!" said Berengaria, who also understood the two men's sneaking interest in each other. "Weren't you able to discuss the possibilities of a truce after all then?"

"Oh, yes. This Bohadin seems to be in his confidence. He didn't poison my drinks or anything, and he speaks Norman as if he'd lived in Rouen all his life." Richard's comments were punctuated by the flop of sodden garments to the floor as the pages prepared the steaming bath she had insisted upon. "And you'd never guess the decent thing Saladin did! He had the Holy Rood sent from Jerusalem for me to see. And do you know, 'Garia, they all treated it as reverently as we should. Yet all the time I was collecting money for this crusade I pictured them spitting on it."

"Didn't you know they venerate Christ as a prophet?" smiled Berengaria, knowing how much such a gesture must have pleased him. "I must read you my translation of the Koran, Richard. Parts of it are very beautiful."

When he came for his supper, refreshed and shaven, he lifted her chin with caressing fingers. "And what have you been doing, my love?" he asked.

"Trying to persuade your independent sister to marry my love-sick cousin," laughed Berengaria.

"Then I take it you don't find marriage so bad?" He looked at her searchingly as he kissed her. He often wondered if she guessed about Ida, and had wisely left the little baggage at Jaffa.

Berengaria avoided a direct answer. "If ever a man deserved to be happy, it is Raymond," she said.

"And what does the tempestuous jade herself say about it?" asked Richard, picking over his food. It was so unlike him to be fastidious that his wife watched him with concern. "She wants to get back to England first. Richard, do you suppose Robin really loved her? Except as a sister, I mean. Wouldn't he have come to Sicily if he had?"

"He may not have known about William's death."

"But surely you tried to tell him?"

"My dear woman, I rode hell for leather all through a night of weather like this. But God Himself couldn't find Rob if he wanted to hide in a wood'. And England is full of woods."

Berengaria sat down opposite to him in homely intimacy. "He loved *you*—but he didn't come," she said. "Perhaps it was just that there were things he loved more."

"You talk as if you knew him," said Richard, glancing up quickly from his plate.

"I've been reading his book."

"Oh, that—all about astrology and unsanitary cottages and noblesse oblige."

"I found a copy amongst your things—it was like a friend when you were away fighting—" She never could bear to talk about those lonely, anxious hours. "But Raymond is a relation. And he's here, being much too patient. I wish we could do something about it."

"I have," said Richard. He pushed aside his plate and sat back with an air of complacency, although it is doubtful if his machinations had been prompted by much altruism. "I've offered Johanna to Saladin's nephew."

Berengaria sat staring at him. "I can't believe you're serious—"

"I don't suppose Saladin can either," chuckled Richard. "But Bohadin and the rest of them were tremendously impressed. It ought to flatter them into signing a truce, and if I know anything about Joan she'll go off in a tearing rage and marry Raymond to-morrow."

They couldn't pursue the conversation because Raymond had just returned from Jaffa and Johanna came to the King's tent with him, eager for news. But all Richard wanted to hear about was reinforcements. How many could they spare?

Raymond produced a list which he laid reluctantly at Richard's elbow. "What, only a paltry hundred!" exclaimed Johanna, reading it over his shoulder, and Richard looked up for some sort of explanation. His hands shook with ague, crackling the parchment as he held it. "I know Philip's desertion must make some difference—" he began bleakly.

"I wish to God Philip were the only one!" burst out Raymond.

Richard slid back in his chair, steadying his hands on the arms of it. "What d'you mean?" he demanded.

"It's this sea-board policy," explained Raymond, hating to find a flaw in a friend's best stroke of genius. "You see, Richard, with ships plying all the time between here and Cyprus it's so fatally easy for fellows to slip away when they're fed up. Back to Marseilles or Venice or anywhere."

Richard saw the flaw; but instantly he blamed Philip. "And how long has Capet's craven example been rotting my armies?" he growled between set teeth.

"It seems they've been slipping away by night—in twos and threes—ever since you came up here."

"But what the hell are the staff people at Jaffa doing? Can't they put a stop to it?"

"They do their best," reported Raymond. "But they haven't your pull. They didn't take Jaffa, for instance, by bluffing the garrison into believing they'd an army instead of half a dozen knights at their heels—and that appears to be the sort of joke your queer subjects understand."

"You see, my dear," said Johanna, "they honestly believe your life is charmed so they'd follow you anywhere."

"Then I certainly can't afford to hang about here any longer—rain or no rain," decided Richard. He got up, without his usual alacrity, and asked now many men had died of fever since he had been gone.

"At least a fifth, Sir," estimated Blondel.

"So even if this list of reinforcements were twice as long, we should still lack men as well as money." Richard looked round the little group of intimates whom he trusted. "You know, don't you, that I was fool enough to lend Philip some? I thought I could bribe him to stay—the way I bribed him about Ann. And now, God curse him, he's made off with men and money and ships. And Jerusalem still stands."

It was the first time any of them had heard that note of bitterness in his voice. He had endured jealousies and disappointments and news of treachery at home, and through it all he had kept unfalteringly cheerful. Right from the first they had looked to him for encouragement. When their ships were storm-tossed they had been heartened by the steady light from his masthead. And now, for the first time, it was as if they peered through the hazardous mists of the future and found that cheerful light grown dim.

It was more than Blondel could stand. "Sir, at Arsouf you killed seven thousand and the odds were on the enemy," he reminded his master. "We are ready to start to-morrow—every one of us. The men know that you—and you alone—can take Jerusalem."

Richard would have given anything at that moment for the same conviction. He turned to the only one of them who had been crusading before. "Look here, Raymond, we must decide this here and now. Every day we waste is costing us men and money, and—what with the weather and subsidising half the French army—we can't hold out here much longer. It seems to me the position is this. Either we must push on to Jerusalem at once or we must conclude this truce and turn back and consolidate our position on the coast—with a view, of course, of returning here in the Spring."

Raymond was a good man to appeal to in a quandary because he never let his decisions get mixed up with his desires. He faced

Richard squarely across the table. "In my opinion it's impossible to take Jerusalem now," he said.

Richard took the blow unflinchingly. "Why?" he asked tersely.

"For one thing, it's the wrong season. Every approach would be a quagmire. You'd never get your war machines up there." It seemed so maddening that they should have sweltered across thirsty deserts for months only to be balked by too much water now! "And then," added Raymond, "there's the unique position of the city itself."

"Draw me a plan of it," said Richard.

Raymond looked up in surprise. "One forgets you've never seen it," he said.

But Richard was already helping Blondel to clear a space by the entrance. "Here in the sand—where the light's good," he said.

So Raymond drew his sword and began to trace the Holy City for them on the ground. It cost him an effort of memory because he had been young and careless when he had seen it. He made a mound to represent the Holy Sepulchre and piled up sand for the walls. "Here would come the Jaffa Gate at the end of our road," he said, leaving a space. "And here, if I remember rightly, runs the Via Doloroso from the steps of Pilate's Palace to Golgotha. And here on the far side of the city is the Golden Gate through which Christ rode. It is said that only some great conqueror shall enter by it now." The women seated themselves on stools and Blondel came and looked over their shoulders with the King's half-polished shield in his hands. They all watched Raymond's moving sword- point in spellbound silence, a queer parti-coloured light from the striped tent on their faces and the steady downpour beating overhead. When he had finished his model of the city itself he raised the contour of her seven hills. "You must remember," he said jerkily between his labours, "that not only is Jerusalem set upon hills, she is also surrounded by a bare, coverless plain. And we should be here—" he said, rounding off his effort with a few rough crosses indicating the end of the Jaffa road. "On that plain. Between two hostile armies."

"Why two?" asked Johanna.

"Because Saladin is far too clever ever to allow them to unite."

"He always *has* divided his forces," agreed Richard. "And if only Philip hadn't deserted we could have done the same."

"While we were busy besieging the army of occupation," went on Raymond, "these hills over here would provide excellent cover from which the second army could swoop down, and outflank us. We'd have hardly a withered thornbush for cover, Richard, and the moment you turned to repulse them the gates of Jerusalem would let loose a horde of the garrison on your heels."

Raymond straightened himself and sheathed his sword. One after the other they lifted questioning eyes to the man who must decide. Richard went to the entrance of the tent as if for space in which to think. Outside the usual scene was spread before his eyes. Men gossiping in little knots as they cleaned their accoutrements, grooms whistling as they rubbed down their masters' horses, and, over by the baggage wagons, thin spirals of smoke showing where the cooks were preparing the midday meal. All of them men who had come through hell for him—his men, of whom he was inordinately proud and many of whom he knew by name. He remembered seeing some of them march uncomplainingly, stuck with arrows like the martyred Christopher. He thought of their waiting women and pictured the homes they had set out from—comfortable walled farms in Normandy, heath hovels among the golden broom of Anjou, small wooden cottages beneath the apple trees of Kent. The swift, unobtrusive movement as he crossed himself showed from whence the strength for such a decision was sought. Perhaps in those pregnant moments he made reparation for the murdered garrison of Acre. When he turned back into the tent he had given decent burial to his life's immediate ambition. "I can't juggle with so many confiding lives," he said.

Berengaria's eyes shone with pride and pity. "Oh, Richard," she cried, in that low, vibrant voice of hers, "that was the finest victory of all!"

Chapter Twenty-Five

RICHARD WAS NOT THE sort of man to hold an inquest on a decision once it had been made. "But I'm willing to follow any man who thinks he can pull it off," he compromised eagerly.

Raymond avoided the appeal in his eyes. He had few illusions about his own generalship, and none at all about Leopold's. "There isn't anyone else," he said firmly.

"Then we must draw up some sort of pact about these ports," sighed Richard, trying to talk as if it were just an ordinary routine job—as if to-day were no different from any of the other days since they had landed. "Summon a staff meeting in the town, Blondel," he ordered briskly, "and tell them I'll be there in quarter of an hour. I'll get Bohadin to come to *us* this time."

"Hadn't we better return their hospitality by inviting Saladin's nephew as well?" suggested Berengaria, jogging his memory.

Richard rose to the occasion with a game attempt at his usual cheerful enthusiasm. "That's a good idea," he said. "Then you and Johanna can get to know him. He's a handsome young devil, and knows all there is to know about horses."

They were both watching Johanna with covert amusement. "Do you mean we shall have to eat with him?" she asked, with a patriotic sniff.

"Well, as a matter of fact, my dear," said Richard blandly, "I was proposing that you should sleep with him."

Johanna stared at him uncomprehendingly. "What the

hell—" began Raymond, but Berengaria pressed her foot down hard on his mailed toes. "You asked me to help, didn't you?" she hissed fiercely.

"You see, I was playing for time," Richard was explaining. "So it's tremendously important to keep these Saracens in a good skin. They said their ardent young sheik ought to be married before next Ramadan, and I supposed you'd be wanting another husband soon. Specially as poor old William…"

Johanna interrupted like a whirlwind. "D'you mean you've promised me to a brown man?" She was so livid with anger that she didn't notice Berengaria's twitching lips as she said soothingly, "Just olive colour, dear, like Ida; and they say these sheiks make such thrilling lovers!"

"Weren't those two romantic women of yours, Henrietta and whatever her name was, always hoping to be seduced by one?" put in Richard.

Poor Johanna gazed from one to another of them, bewildered by their heartless indifference. And there was Raymond, who had been professing such high-flown love for weeks, accepting it quite calmly. Why didn't he get up and challenge Richard to single combat or something? Perhaps, after all, he didn't really care. Did any man, when it came to the point? "You must all be mad—thinking I could endure to live mewed up in a harem with stuffy, secret lattices and spiteful little cats like Ida talking sex all day. I'd sooner have married Tancred. What on earth did you rescue me for?"

Raymond, who ought to have been throwing his gauntlet in Richard's smug face, seemed to have withdrawn himself from the argument except to remark irritatingly that he had heard in Jaffa that Tancred had married someone else.

In her flurry Johanna failed to see which way they were driving her. She only knew that it was maddening to be a woman. She had felt all this before, but Richard had been sympathetic then—before he parted from Robin. "You said that this time I could choose!" she reminded him.

"You take such a long time choosing," Richard pointed out, calmly picking up the various parchments he wanted for the meeting.

What was the *good* of choosing, thought Johanna, if you were not sure the man you chose wanted you? One had to have time to go home and find out. And if one married a jealous Saracen one wouldn't go home at all. There would be rocks and sand and horrid little stunted fig trees for ever until one's soul withered for the cool green grass of meadows and the dappled shade of beech trees. "You can't do this to me—you can't," she cried, beating on the table with her capable, horse-wise hands. "You may be head of our house, Richard—but I am Queen of Sicily."

"*Dowager* Queen," murmured Berengaria, going along with Richard to the town.

Johanna could have killed her. She stood and watched them go. They were her companions—of her own generation—and yet they were trying to treat her as if she were still just a pawn. Once a man had power expediency became everything, she supposed, and promises and affection didn't count. Richard cared more about taking Jerusalem than anything on earth. Having been balked, he was ready to offer her on the altar of his ambition. And she would have to pay for his success with the rest of her life. She put her head down on the table among the remains of his meal and sobbed.

It was hard for Raymond to see the proud flame of her courage brought so low, but he had the sense to let her cry. But when at last she looked up and said ungraciously, "You still there?" he came and lifted her into his arms. They were strong and comforting. One felt that what he took he would hold. "You don't have to marry this sheik, you know," he said, smiling very tenderly into her tear-drenched eyes.

Johanna pushed back her lovely, disordered hair. "Richard can't have meant it," she said distractedly.

"Whether he did or not," said Raymond, "you come first with me. I'm willing to risk his friendship if you will marry me. I'm not so young, little love, nor particularly handsome—but perhaps as an alternative—"

Johanna began to laugh at him, as she dabbed away her tears. "That's just the trouble, Raymond. You're world's too good to be an alternative. You stand apart from other men like pure gold. I should probably have married you months ago if I didn't like you so much."

Raymond kissed her lingeringly and without restraint. "*How* much?" he asked afterwards.

"Enough to be quite honest with you—always," said Johanna, her arms still about his neck.

He asked what he had always wanted to. "You still love that fellow in England?"

She nodded.

He released her hands gently and held them between his own. His eyes were deep with understanding. "Isn't it just the remains of calf love?" he pleaded. "I used to feel that way about 'Garia, you know. It became a sort of habit. Wouldn't you, conceivably, feel different about it—kind of flat and cheated—if you went back to England and saw him again?"

Johanna fidgeted with the clasp of his cloak, trying to find the answer for herself as well. "Oh, Raymond, truly I don't know," she said at last lifting the lovely candour of her eyes to his. "All I know is that if he really wanted me he could make me leave you."

It was a grave decision to offer a man, and it would take a bigger man than most to live it out without complaint. "I'll take a risk on it," said Raymond, just as he had said about Richard's friendship. According to his code, the woman one loved was worth the highest stakes a man could pay for her.

He left her and went to find a priest and, as her brother had predicted, they were married in hurried secrecy that night. There was no magic of Cyprian pipes nor any panoply of stars. "Only a second-best night, like her caring," thought the bridegroom, envying Richard's luck. But it was the night he had hungered for ever since he had first seen her, mutinous and abstracted at her own feast because this Robin hadn't come. It would be his fixed intent to kiss that frustration from her lips for ever.

"There'll be no more sheiks or amorous kings or outlaws," he told her with firm tenderness when she waked in his arms next morning.

"I know," said Johanna. In the creeping sunlight she could see it blazoned on the shield hanging from his tent pole. "Je maintein-drai," with a clenched mailed fist surmounting it. It made the flying footsteps of her own girlhood pursuing Robin round the battlements seem a very long way off. She felt comfortable and safe lying there while Raymond dressed—as if the stirrings of adventure were dead.

He came to her, buckling his belt. He looked happy and dear and resolute. "I must go and confess to Richard," he said.

Johanna scrambled up in bed reaching for her wrap, all comfort and security forgotten. "You did it for me. I must come too," she cried. "Just because I'm a woman I can't stay here and hide." And when, adoring her gallantry, he forbade her to come, she flared out at him. "You forget I'm—"

But he kissed the haughty words from her lips. "You are neither a Plantagenet nor a queen this morning," he laughed down at her, "but just the Countess of Toulouse. And we don't let our women go into the front line of battle."

Chapter Twenty-Six

B Y THE TIME BOHADIN came Richard was sweating out his strength on a sick bed at Jaffa. They had brought him down on a horse litter, and this time he had been too ill to care. "England will bleed for this…" he had kept muttering, as if his thoughts had wandered far from his crusade.

"Why must he keep, saying that?" wondered Berengaria. The doctors had gone and Blondel had just brought her a fresh basin of water to sponge their patient's feverish skin. She didn't know what she would have done without Blondel. He was sending a page for fresh palm leaves to keep away the flies. Flies and sand and blood… That seemed to have been the rhythm of life for months. She had almost forgotten what life in a well-appointed castle felt like.

She let the sponge slither back into the basin and straightened her aching back to look round the room, with its bleak paraphernalia of sickness. It was lit by one small window, and the plaster of puddled mud and straw was peeling off the walls in places. The native fire in the middle of the floor appeared to be fed with a repulsive mixture of charcoal and camel dung. And she had willingly exchanged her lovely, cherished life for this.

Because she was tired she looked down at her husband's haggard face, fringed with the ruddy stubble of a nascent beard—at the long, quiescent body that had always been so restless—and wondered almost impersonally what she would do if he were to die. She would be able to go home, of course. Probably she would be expected to marry again. But, however one suffered, life without Richard was unthinkable. Love with any other man would be a stagnation. Remembering his fierce caresses, she knew in her heart that this awful room was a paltry price to pay for any one of them.

Blondel was back with the palm leaves and the monotonous commination went on. "England raped and starved—to buy a strip of sun-scorched land…" The limbs mounding the coverlet stirred. As if roused by some continuity of ideas Richard opened his eyes. "God, I am thirsty!" he said. They gave him some water and he drank greedily, gathering his wits as he stared at her over the cup. Presently he waved it weakly away and smiled at her. "You, my dear! I was dreaming about Robin."

"Yet you seldom speak of him," said Berengaria, restraining herself from laughing hysterically because she had supposed a mere bout of fever could kill him. She wanted to tell him how empty the world had looked without him.

Richard passed a hand across his clammy forehead. It seemed incredible that anything so white and shaky could have wielded the great broadsword propped in a corner. "He's becoming my inescapable conscience," he complained. "Suppose while I'm away—someone murdered Arthur?"

"Why on earth should they?" laughed Berengaria briskly, straightening the bed clothes.

It sounded fantastic, of course, but Richard knew why *one* man might. He could see John now, play-acting in the crown, and Robin feeling as if someone had lifted the chalice off the high altar. But he supposed it was because he was still a bit light-headed.

Berengaria changed the subject abruptly to distract him. "Bohadin is here in Jaffa."

Richard raised himself eagerly. He looked better already. "Then I'd better see him," he said.

"My dear, not to-day. It would tire you far too much."

He looked round for his clothes and saw all the basins and medicines and things. His gaze returned to his wife's face. "It's not I who am tired, lying here all day," he said. "Your dear eyes are all smudged for want of sleep."

They filled with tears at his unexpected tenderness. But the pages were tidying up the room and she laughed away the moment with a triviality. "You wouldn't want visitors if you could see your beard," she said. "Please, Blondel, hold up the King's shield."

Richard explored a reflection which kept getting mixed up with leopards passant. With a tentative thumb and forefinger he stroked his bristling chin. "Umph, I rather like it," he grunted. "What about letting it grow?"

"It would certainly set a new fashion in England, Sir," laughed Blondel, delighted to hear him talking normally again.

"It might if I could persuade John to grow one too." Never having been the showpiece of the family in his youth, Richard was devoid of personal vanity.

It was good to hear them joking, and presently Johanna came in and was surprised to find him sitting up. She had brought one of the new cloisonné dishes piled high with Richard's favourite fruits. "Ida Comnenos sent you this," she said, "and she wants to know when she can come and see you." She set the costly offering on the window ledge where the westering sun struck a gem-like brilliance from the mosaic of coloured metals and warmed the rich, downy bloom of each fruit. It was a gift that caught the eye, lending the shabby little room an illusion of luxury. Richard looked at it and grinned. It was so exactly like Ida. He glanced covertly at his wife who, seeing that he was set on seeing Saladin's envoy, was busy tidying up. "I can't see anyone just now," he said, non-committally.

Bohadin the historian was an impressive figure, with his white patriarchal beard and eyes that burned like beacons of intelligence in his benign old face. When Raymond brought him into the room he seemed to freshen it with a breath of mountain cedars. His spotless white camel-hair burnous shamed the dingy garments of his solitary follower, and Richard—who was all emphasis and movement—thought that his still, contemplative dignity probably served as better protection than an escort. "Allah be with you all!" he said, touching forehead and heart in the beautifully symbolic greeting of his race.

"Just like the oldest of the magi!" thought Johanna, and Berengaria was enchanted with him. She could remember sitting on his knee as a child enthralled by his store of Eastern fairy tales. "My white hairs must have been black in those days," he laughed, when she reminded him of it. If he was amazed at the metamorphosis of a pampered princess, he was too polite to say so. He sent all manner of flowery messages to her father and complimented her on her efficient nursing. And then they got down to the business of the treaty. Because Richard was too weak for legal terms, Raymond epitomized the document for him. "The main point is, of course," he concluded, "that in return for our solemn pledge to withdraw our troops from Jerusalem, Saladin is prepared to leave us in undisputed possession of all the ports we have captured."

"All except Ascalon," Bohadin reminded them suavely. Richard frowned, thinking of his boastful song and how he and his men had strewn those plains with dead for nothing. "We must have *one* outlet for our merchandise," the envoy insisted with a smile, the softness of which deceived nobody. "But if you will agree to this, we are willing to let the truce stand for three years."

"Three years!" ejaculated Richard. Actually, he had not seriously considered a cessation of hostilities lasting longer than three months. He felt flattered that Saladin should have suggested it and wondered for the hundredth time if he had been a fool not to press on to Jerusalem. But perhaps, after all, a long truce would be best. It would give him time to go back to England and see what John was doing, and to find out what Philip was up to on the Continent.

"You have set your heel so hard upon our land," Bohadin was urging, "that only years of seed time and harvest will heal her scars."

Richard loved the warm Eastern imagery. He took the imposing-looking parchment from Raymond and was vexed to find that his hand still shook. He only hoped those sharp-eyed Levantines wouldn't attribute the enraging symptom to emotion or fear, but—being driven to sign the thing—it was characteristic of him to do so with a good grace. "I count it no dishonour to call a draw with Saladin," he said formally. "And I only wish I could meet him!" he added from his heart.

"To prove to you that his own wish is twin to yours, he has sent you something more personal than a parchment," smiled Bohadin, beckoning to his unkempt follower. "This man has almost incredible skill in curing fevers. When he isn't soldiering he spends much time curing the ills of our people."

The man came forward. He was a villainous-looking fellow with an aquiline nose and a bandaged forehead. He peered at Richard out of the one fierce eye that was visible and put a skinny finger on his pulse. Berengaria hoped he wasn't verminous. From the folds of his kaftan he drew a bag of herbs which he began grinding between his palms until they looked like a fine white powder. One by one he let them fall into the water in the King's cup. He appeared to be muttering some incantation; but probably he was only counting them. To European minds the whole scene was suggestive of poison.

Johanna's clear, quick voice cut across the tense atmosphere. "But what can an ignorant soldier do for my brother which our trained Hospitallers cannot?" she asked, voicing the thoughts of all of them.

"Even they had to learn from us how to use poppy juices to put your wounded to sleep before an amputation," Bohadin reminded her. And the herbalist, having prepared his potion, offered it to the King. "Salah-ed-Din himself desires your health!" he said in his own tongue.

"Now that I have signed away the power to fight him, eh, my man?" laughed Richard, who—like the rest of them—had picked up a smattering of Arabic. He was already tired and beginning to feel fuddled again with so many people in such a small room. But to his amazement before he could drink the stuff, his well-trained squire had interfered. "Suppose it's another trick—like the blinded prisoners?" he stammered.

Richard was furious. He was aware that what Johanna called his "dais manner" was slipping away from him and that quick Arab resentment was rising beneath Bohadin's suave manner. "I can see that to set this young man's mind at rest I had better leave my man as a hostage until his patient is better," he was saying stiffly.

"God help him if he isn't!" muttered Raymond, with more fervour than lucidity.

Six pairs of eyes were focused on Richard. To everybody's surprise it was Berengaria whose courtesy snapped next. But then she had the most to lose. It was only a brief half-hour ago since she had looked into a future without Richard and found it desolate. She leaned over the back of his chair, reaching for the cup. "Richard, don't drink it!" she implored, in a voice that cracked.

Richard caught at her hand. All the faces staring at him were merging into a grotesque blur and he felt the need of holding on to something dear and comforting and familiar. "I thought you hated war?" he said. "Don't you know, sweet, distrust is just the diet it fattens on?" He had spilled some of the water by reason of his miserable ague, but he lifted the rest and tossed it defiantly down his throat to finish the argument. He heard the clatter of the horn beaker as it rolled to the floor. Out of the confusion of faces one swam close to his own. It was the fellow with the bandaged eye, and he was looking inordinately pleased. Richard felt a beautiful new coolness creeping through his veins. He was aware that people were drifting quietly out and that his healer had gone to squat humbly in the shadows by the door. Just before he dropped off to sleep he heard his sister laugh in a shame-faced sort of way and say to Blondel, "We must have been thinking of Rosamund de Clifford."

By the time Richard waked the sun was hanging low like an orange over the rocks. The room was very quiet and Berengaria was sitting beside him, her hands folded neatly in her lap. There was something almost severe about her stillness, and the cold evening light from the window was being unkind to the first faint lines about her mouth. Looking at her through lazy lashes, he realised that she had changed since Acre, bearing things with the sort of patience that develops character and weeds the bright, disordered bed of Youth. He remembered how gay she had been at Pamplona and felt responsible for her lost laughter. When they got home he must make up to her for all the discomforts she must have suffered in this make-shift life.

Feeling his gaze on her she looked up and smiled. He was so obviously at ease that there was no need to move. It was one of those leisure hours when people find out that marriage can be something deeper and even more satisfying than a union of the flesh. "And so," said Richard drowsily, rounding off their thoughts with a sentence it had seemed unnecessary to begin, "there seems nothing left but to pack up and go home!"

To Richard going home meant also a confession of failure, the daily grind of council meetings and exasperating discussions about money. But Berengaria conjured up a pleasant picture composed of a riverside village called West-min-stair, Eleanor's welcoming smile, and a pleasant room in Oxford Castle where they all seemed to have lived. "I hope your mother will be pleased about Johanna and Raymond," she said.

"'Joan must be longing to go home," said Richard. "So I'd better arrange for him to take you both back to England."

"Take?" Berengaria gasped. "But, Richard, aren't you coming?"

"There'll be a lot to clear up here," he pointed out evasively. "Suppose I meet you in Rome?" Seeing the consternation in her face, he covered the hands in her lap with his own. "I know you're counting the days for a rose garden and somewhere to hang your clothes!"

But Berengaria's hands were unresponsive. She looked up at Ida's lavish gift on the window ledge and her cheeks flushed hotly. "Richard, you're not staying behind because of that Cypriot girl, are you?" she asked.

Richard laughed comfortably. "Who says I am staying at all?" he countered. "If you must know, Jealous One, I'm going on a pilgrimage—without any women at all. Mercadier can see to all the donkey work of re-embarkation." When Berengaria turned to stare at him he hunched himself up on one elbow, possessing himself of one of her protesting hands and pulling back her fingers one by one so that they snapped like miniature catapults on the embroidered stags and lions. "Listen, my sweet," he went on, with the expansive persuasiveness people always use to cover a very poor case. "I simply haven't the face to skin my poor islanders again for the next crusade, so I thought I'd join one of those parties of pilgrims we are always seeing crossing from here to Rome. I've planned to go through all the principal cities in Europe collecting for it. I ought to get quite a lot out of all those wealthy Byzantines."

Berengaria sighed with relief. He was quite mad, of course—but at least it wasn't Ida. "And do you suppose anyone who has ever seen you would mistake you for a pilgrim?" she asked indulgently.

"Why ever not?"

She looked him over with affectionate amusement. "Well, your height for one thing—and your hair and your incurable swagger."

Momentarily dashed, Richard scratched at his scrubby beard. "I could wear sandals and one of those hideous shovel hats," he suggested doubtfully.

His wife laughed undutifully in his face. He was so dear and irresponsible in this off-duty sort of mood. "You're supposed to be a king—not part of a travelling show," she told him. "And, anyhow, you can't go meandering across Europe now there's all this fresh trouble in England." She could have bitten off her tongue the moment the words had slipped out.

Richard sat up, crusades and pilgrimages forgotten. "What trouble?" he demanded. "Why wasn't I told?"

He was suddenly quite a different person, and it took all Berengaria's inherent dignity not to be afraid of him. "I wouldn't let them worry you," she admitted, "but Blondel was stopped in the street by a Jew on his way to sell jewels in Basra. He recognised Blondel as having been with you in Dover, and told him that it was common knowledge in Kent that the Queen's letters to you had been seized, so he thought you ought to know that your brother has turned that Angevin bishop—William of Some-where-or-other—out of his chancellorship."

Richard tried too late to strangle the coarsest of his guardroom paths. "Go on, what else?" he asked grimly.

"He said John had seized a lot more castles and that he and the barons were on the brink of civil war. Of course," added Berengaria, conscientiously, "he was only a Jew."

But, like most royal personages, Richard had a remarkably good memory. He had a very clear picture in his mind of the only Jewish jewel merchant he had met in Dover, of his dignity and the arresting way in which he had spoken about the gratitude of his race. Gratitude to Robin, really. So Richard had no doubts about the authenticity of the message. England really *was* bleeding for this crusade, and suddenly Jerusalem didn't seem to matter so much. Yet he blamed himself rather than John. "God's teeth, what a fool I was to trust him!" he cried bitterly. Robin had been right…about that too.

Berengaria had that quality—rare in a woman—of letting people follow their train of thought to its conclusion. She made neither comment nor suggestion until her husband had had time to assimilate her news. "If there is going to be trouble of that sort," he decided, "I can't have you landing until I come. Raymond had better take you and Johanna and Yvette to Rome, and you can wait for me to join you overland. Then when Mercadier has cleared up everything here he can call for us with the fleet and we can all go home together. You'd like that, 'Garia?"

Berengaria was amazed that he should still contemplate going on with his money-raising project. "I think you ought to go home at once," she said.

"Now you are talking like Robin," he said irritably.

"It's because we both love you," she smiled. "Of course, Johanna does too—and Raymond. But they're so bemused by your military glory that they don't notice you're being a very bad king." Berengaria broke off with a vexed little laugh, realising what a prig she must sound. "Oh, its partly selfishness on my part, I expect, Richard," she admitted.

Richard drew her head on to his shoulder, kissing her tired eyelids and her lips. "I do understand, darling, about setting one's heart on a thing happening just as one had planned it, because for years I pictured all this—" With his free arm he sketched a gesture intended to include the whole crusade. "And no fight or homecoming has ever been quite the same without Robin." He spoke with intentional lightness. Long ago in his sensitive youth Ann Capet had shocked him into seeing all women either as saints or sinners, and he always felt too iniquitous to make Berengaria his complete confidante. It didn't occur to him that by sharing with her the burden of his sins and disappointments, instead of letting them sour his soul, he might help to dispel the lengthening shadows cast by the dissimilarity of their natures.

Berengaria, born to be a human helpmate instead of the little exquisite she looked, was not deceived by his understatement. "I know, too, what turning back at Beit Nuba must have cost you!" she said.

"I felt rather like Moses after he had seen the promised land," said Richard, with a self-conscious laugh.

She turned against his shoulder, her puzzled eyes searching the dim outline of his profile. "You mean—you have *seen* Jerusalem?" she asked, realising how little of his life was really hers.

The little room was getting dark and Ida's dish of fruit was just a black blotch now against the grey square of the window. Lying there in the half-light with his unfamiliar little beard, Richard looked somehow remote. His long, fine nose and cruel, tender mouth might have been carved in stone—just like an effigy of himself on some cathedral tomb. "Humbly—from afar," he admitted, after a moment or two.

"But you asked Raymond to make that map"

"Oh, I never saw it in *that* way," Richard hastened to explain. "Oddly enough, I never once thought about fortifications." Apparently it had been one of those emotional experiences so moving to oneself, so difficult to describe.

"Was it that day when you'd been boar-hunting, and when you got back to camp and just sat and said nothing, although Blondel sang all your favourite songs?"

"Did he?" said Richard absently. "I never heard him. Everything seemed so insignificant afterwards. As usual, some Saracens came skirmishing down from the hills and let fly at us. We gave chase, of course, and I must have got separated from the rest of our party—"

"Blondel says you always do—"

"Well, you know how fast Fauvel is. And there was one cunning old emir who kept leading me on from rock to rock—"

Berengaria got up in search of a cloak. The nights were bitterly cold. "You know very well they do it purposely to get the reward Saladin offered if you were captured alive," she said, groping in the gathering gloom for the camel-hair burnous Richard had had made for her.

"That wasn't what this one got!" he laughed harshly. Now that he had begun to tell her about it his self-consciousness was dissipated in a sort of inward excitement. He swung his feet to the floor and sat on the edge of the bed, his hands clasped loosely between his knees. "When the going got too rough for Fauvel, I dismounted and scrambled after him to a sort of ledge. A kind of eagles' aerie right against the sky, if you can imagine it. And when I had severed his grinning face from his shuddering shoulders I was so blown with the climb that I stood over him for a bit just resting on the handle of my sword."

Berengaria shivered and drew the soft camel-hair closely about her own shoulders. She could imagine it only too well.

"And when I looked up there was a lovely panorama set out on the far side of the hill. The bare plain was down there, just as Raymond described it, and beyond that some more hills. And in the distance I saw the Holy City."

There was such awed happiness in Richard's voice that Berengaria stood watching him, her face a white disc of arrested interest in the soft folds of her hood. The rich embroidery of the bed cover was all bunched about his knees, and as he leaned forward to throw another cake of fuel on to the fire a dull glow illuminated both his absorbed face and the fierce heraldic beasts. "The sun was setting behind me and the whole plain was bathed in an unearthly radiance," he said, carefully rebuilding his vision for her word by word. "By the light of it I could see the great walls and imagine the exact position of the Golden Gate I had dreamed of setting wide to Christendom. And a little straggle of trees beside the Kedron brook showed the way my Saviour must have walked up the little Mount of Olives." The unaffected simplicity with which Richard spoke of the Christ came almost as a shock to Berengaria. In common with most great leaders whose daily life is a hazard with death, she supposed, his God must be very near—or nothing.

"It was all so remote, unreal, impregnable—shut in like that by the bare Judean hills," he was saying in that vibrant voice. "Somehow, Berengaria, I knew then that I should never take it." He paused for a moment, trying with unpractised mind to express the essence of the experience for her. In his inward searching he was unaware that the sincerity of his words had drawn her close beside him. "It was as if I stood all bloody and sweat-stained with the way I had come to meet the Christ. And he didn't want the proud standards I had mocked or the cities I had sacked nor even the dead Saracen between my feet. But in that high, still solitude He let me look into His heart. And it was full of peace. Enough peace to flood the whole world, I felt—if only men wanted it…" Richard's attitude relaxed with the cessation of mental effort, and his pleasant voice took on the flatness of normal life again. "And so I rode home, my head stuffed with half-understood dreams," he said, almost apologetically. "And the next day I was down with fever…"

Berengaria was kneeling beside him, her eyes sweet with unshed tears. "Poor Richard! And you learning everything that could possibly make you a good soldier ever since you were a boy!" she said, bending to brush her soft cheek against the hardness of his hand. "But even if you never take Jerusalem there are other ways of serving the Christian world. After all, the spirit of Christ can't be walled in any one city. If He died for the grossest of sinners surely it must be wide and pitiful enough to touch good Moslems and Jews? And isn't it, perhaps, a more work-a-day thing than you suppose?" she suggested, lifting her face challengingly. "Isn't it in the hands of people who are trying to heal the sick or carve something beautiful right up in the roof of some cathedral? I'm sure it's in the laughter of children—and perhaps a little even in our own lives."

Richard drew her closer. "Robin had the same sort of idea," he said. "I thought it blasphemy then."

Berengaria hoped that when they got to England Richard would succeed in finding Robin. She had never been jealous of him as she was of Ida. Somehow, one knew that his love was never possessive.

"When you outlaw a man in your country does it mean that anyone can kill him?" she asked.

"Of course. But no one is likely to. At least, I am saved that much contrition! D'you know, 'Garia, Robin's so strong that when we're wrestling he can throw me over his shoulder as easily as that." With one of his old flamboyant gestures, Richard reached for the heavy stool she had been sitting on and lifted it by a leg to demonstrate his boast. It was high above his head before he realised that he was supposed to be ill. As he put it down he whistled softly and their eyes met in delighted amusement.

"Why, Richard, you're cured!" she cried. "There must have been something in those herbs that cooled your fever almost instantly." While Richard stood up flexing his muscles experimentally, she ran to the door and called Blondel.

"That Saracen will be able to go now," said Richard, feeling in his wallet for something to give him. "He *must* have thought us a mistrustful lot!"

With her usual graciousness Berengaria turned to thank the man. But Blondel came hurrying in with a couple of torches and as the shifting lights stabilised they wiped out the shadows behind the open door. Berengaria stopped short. "Why, Richard, he's gone!" she exclaimed.

He took one of the torches from Blondel and held it steadily aloft so that it showed up all four corners. "There is only the window," he said. "But it was getting dark, you remember, and those Arabs are like cats."

"I had forgotten all about him," admitted Berengaria, trying to remember all they had been talking about. "A good thing he didn't speak Norman."

"I wonder?" said Richard, in an odd sort of voice. Blondel had picked up a torn scrap of parchment from the place where the man had been squatting and the two of them were examining it by the light of the torch.

"It looks like part of a letter," Blondel was saying.

"It *is* part of a letter," corroborated Richard. "In Norman. Here's a broken bit of my seal—and my own words 'our dear sister

Johanna.' It's part of the letter I wrote trying to bluff Saladin." Berengaria pressed against his elbow to stare at the incontrovertible evidence. "Then it was Saladin himself?" she marvelled.

"You met him after all, Sir!" said Blondel, knowing well what this must mean to him.

Richard laughed heartily and handed back the torch. "So two of us can play at that game!" he remarked; but he stood for a long time holding the scrap of parchment and staring at the bed where he had lain in his weakness, alone with a woman and the man he had come out here to kill. Having come to the end of his campaign, he let his thoughts review it. It had been good fun, and bits of it had been something that Normandy and England might remember—he was ashamed only about the Austrian standard and the murdered prisoners. All his life his heart would bleed secretly about Jerusalem. But it wasn't so hard to go home now because he knew his crusading could never be so whole-hearted again. The spell Eleanor had woven about his youth was broken. He had come to that moment of maturity when a man finds his religion is personal, but God is universal.

PART VII

Rome

Chapter Twenty-Seven

ERENGARIA HAD TAKEN A villa in Rome. She had been there all the summer because her husband's crazy pilgrimage had ended much as she had predicted. At first Europe had been entertained by rumours of Richard's incredible adventures. He had been heard of posing as a pirate at Ragusa and as a merchant at Corfu, and a party of pilgrims swore to having seen him just outside Venice. Then some ill-judged bravado seemed to have made him change his course in the direction of Vienna, of all cities, where his incurable swagger and an over-lavish tip appeared to have betrayed him into the hands of an officious underling of Duke Leopold. And since then there had been silence. Which was not surprising, seeing that the favourite tale told by soldiers returning from the East was how they had seen the King of England slashing down the Austrian standard at Acre.

As soon as King Sancho heard of his daughter's plight he invited her to come home, but not all the pleasant comforts of Navarre could tempt her from the city where Richard had arranged to meet her. She knew that he must be either ill or in captivity or he would at least have managed to send her some message, and the tearing anxiety she had so often suffered during the crusade seemed brief and bearable compared with the long-drawn-out suspense she suffered now. Each day she tried to pray with something of his simplicity in the splendid churches, but at night she tossed on her soft bed dreaming of damp dungeons. All too clearly she remembered Leopold of Austria saying, "If ever the good God should put you in my power, Richard Plantagenet…"

Gradually, as the months wore on, people began to treat her as if she were a widow. But if there was one thing she was sure of in her half-world of loneliness and uncertainty, it was that Richard was not dead. "I shall know the moment Leopold kills him," she would tell herself fiercely, feeling that something would die in her own heart. Whereas the part of her that had been so starved in Syria was now very much alive. Hating herself for it, she enjoyed the famous pictures and libraries, the cultured, cosmopolitan society of Rome, and the comforts of her own villa. And most of all she appreciated the unselfishness of Raymond and Johanna in staying with her when she felt sure they must be aching to get on with their own lives. "Richard put you in my charge," Raymond would argue with his lovable doggedness, "and it is up to me to see that no one molests you."

"I am nearly thirty," laughed Berengaria. "Who is likely to molest me?".

But one evening when Raymond and Johanna were out riding, her sense of security was shaken. She had had a book brought out to her favourite seat in the forecourt beside a little fountain that splashed pleasantly into a low-walled pool. She had reason to be more hopeful than she had been for weeks because she and Johanna had seen Richard's sword hanging up in an armourer's shop. The owner had told them that some drunken Austrian soldiers had sold it to him with a fuddled story about a giant of a prisoner who had thrown three of them into their own moat before they could get him shut up in Triffels castle. So when the gate bell clanged and there was a clatter of horsemen outside, Berengaria's heart leapt with the wild hope that it might be Richard himself. But one of her hired Italian servants came back to say it was a knight called Chalus.

Remembering how the correct little Duke of Austria used to frequent Chalus's bacchanalian parties, Berengaria thought that at least her visitor might have news of Richard. So she rose eagerly, a finger still between the illuminated pages on the bookstand before her. She had no idea what a picture she made standing in the soft evening light between two dark, tapering cypresses, nor how a flush of anger became her when Chalus seized the unoffered hand lying against the sombre folds of her gown and covered it with hungry kisses. "A much fitter setting for you than the fever-ridden ports of the Levant!" he said, with awkward gallantry. "If I had a beautiful jewel I wouldn't leave it lying about my battlefields."

"No, you would probably keep it locked up," answered Berengaria, with asperity. "Have you brought any news of my husband?"

"I am afraid we must assume that he is dead, Madam," he said ingratiatingly. "The way you have waited for him is profoundly touching, but to a lonely widower like me it seems such waste!"

Berengaria surveyed the man as if he were an offensive groom. He looked strong and cunning with his brutish limbs and dark, hirsute face. She could hear the rough laughter of his men on the other side of the wall and wished that Blondel were about. "What have you come for then?" she asked on a note of fear.

He laughed and came closer so that she could almost feel the heat of his eager breath. "I think you know that I collect beautiful things…"

"Of course," agreed Berengaria, with a hurried assumption of ease. "And we have kept your gold circlet all this time! It is inexcusable of us, particularly as I understand you have a passion for Roman antiques." She would have called someone to fetch it, but he forestalled interruption by reaching impatient arms for the treasure he coveted most. "I have a stronger passion than that," he declared, tearing through polite evasion with rough reality. "I may not be a king or a duke but I can tell you that I am one of the richest men in Europe. I can make up to you for all that selfish Turk-slayer made you suffer. I will give you books and gardens and jewels. And I don't have to leave my women languishing alone while I go begging across Europe. I've all the gold I want—right handy on my own land—"

Berengaria saved herself from the insult of his greedy hands by overturning the heavy bookrest between them and clapping sharply for her servants. "If my husband were here you wouldn't dare to touch me," she said, her voice cold with fury.

"Perhaps not," snarled Chalus, dancing with the pain of a bruised toe. "But we both know that he is dead."

"I will show you that he is not," said Berengaria. When her servants came running she sent one of them for her lady and one for her borrowed crown. To another she said, "Bring the sword you carried home for me from the market-place this morning."

And the man brought Richard's great two-handed sword and placed it across the marble arm's of her garden seat, where it rested like a barrier before her.

Chalus recoiled, gaping at it. "It doesn't prove anything," he muttered. But to anyone who had been through the crusade and seen the weapon so constantly in its owner's hand it was as if Richard himself stood between them. The man who had once sworn fealty to him touched the blunted blade mistrustfully. "It's rusty. The junk man may have had it for months," he pointed out. "Where did he get it from?"

Sitting there with both small hands spanning the handle, Berengaria could almost imagine it warm from her husband's grip. She was no longer afraid. "Triffels," she said, feeling no further need for caution.

"Triffels," repeated Chalus, stroking his horrid little black beard calculatingly. "The Duke of Austria has a fine new castle there, if I remember rightly." As if to hide the idea brightening his shrewd, simian eyes he asked abruptly, "How much did you give for it?" As a collector, he would have liked to possess the Cœur de Lion's sword as well as his wife. The value of it would increase with the years, like the fame of his courage.

"Ten ducats," answered Berengaria, getting up at the welcome sound of her relatives' voices and going towards the gate. "I suppose the jewels were so enormous it never occurred to him that they could be real."

"Funny, part of the regalia of England being sold in an open market as bits of coloured glass!" A good bargain was the breath of life to Chalus, and he went on laughing about it even after Raymond and Johanna had returned from their ride and Yvette had brought him the box containing his circlet. No one invited him into the villa and after their horses had been led away and drinks brought they stood waiting for him to go. His own horses were champing restlessly outside, and even his complacency could not out-sit such aloofness for long.

"I shall be passing through Triffels on my way to Vienna, and I flatter myself I have some influence with Leopold," he boasted, taking leave of his unresponsive hostess. "Is there anything you would like me to say to him?"

If he hoped to trade on the desperate anxiety of this self-contained family, the effect was negligible. "You might ask after his bulbs," suggested Johanna, trying to swing her brother's heavy sword and looking irritatingly like him in her riding kit. They all went on with whatever they were doing and let Barbe of Chalus go out into the hot street, hugging his gold. After all, he was Richard's vassal and a fellow crusader, and had a perfect right to snoop round Triffels if he liked. But they did not tell him that they had sent Blondel on the same errand six hours earlier.

"What on earth did the old money-grabber come for?" asked Johanna, almost before her husband's fat page, Nando, had bolted the gate behind him.

"To persuade me into bigamy," laughed Berengaria contemptuously. "Or he may really have believed that Richard was dead," she added hastily, seeing her cousin's hand fly to his sword.

"If you really want to protect us, Ray, for Heaven's sake don't go out and get murdered by his cut-throats before Blondel comes back!" entreated Johanna, watching their departure from a little pagan temple built in the wall. At first she saw only a jumble of men's heads and horses' flanks and bits of tossing steel. Then she beckoned urgently to her sister-in-law. "Look quickly!" she cried, parting the tendrils of an over-grown vine. "The girl on the little dappled jennet immediately behind Chalus."

As the jennet pricked daintily after his big, black horse, the girl pulled off her shady hat to shake back her dark curls with a gesture familiar to them both. "It's Ida Comnenos," said Berengaria harshly. "And she's going with him to Triffels."

Chapter Twenty-Eight

W HEN BLONDEL SLID FROM his jaded horse in the villa courtyard a week later, he had found Richard. "I didn't actually see him, Madam, but he is alive and well and sends you his undying love," he reported to Berengaria, who was the first to run out to meet him.

All four of them crowded round him while he told how he had borrowed a minstrel's lute and cloak and mingled with the soldiers at the great gates of Triffel's castle.

"And didn't any of them try to stop you?" asked Yvette, bringing him a jug of Tuscan wine.

"They were too stupid to suspect a shabby minstrel singing for his supper," laughed Blondel. "And presently I began to wander round their fine castle strumming snatches of songs as I went. The one that always comes readiest to my fingers is 'Give me a sword of shining steel,' and just imagine how I felt when I heard the words, in good lusty Norman, come floating down from behind a barred window high up in the Keep!"

"Oh, Blondel, what should we do without you!" cried Johanna.

"So there we were, the King and I, singing all our news to each other to the same old tune, and not one of the guards up there with him understanding a word of it."

"You mean he has a guard—all the time?" asked Berengaria, aghast at what this must mean to a man who had never before known restraint.

"Day and night. Six of the biggest soldiers in the Austrian army," grinned Blondel proudly. "You remember, Madam, how he flung the ordinary sized ones into the moat?"

"Did you see anything of Chalus?" asked Raymond. "He called here soon after you left."

"Why, yes, Sir. He came riding through Triffels the day after I arrived. I kept out of the way, of course. But I saw him talking to the Constable up at the castle and pumping the innkeeper. But by midday he pushed on, telling the man his inn was lousy and bragging that he was going to stay with the Duke of Austria."

"Had he a—a lady with him?" asked Berengaria.

Blondel's manner became more guarded. Above the tilted wine jug his questioning glance met Raymond's. "A lady, Madam?" he repeated, his tired face a blank and tactful mask.

But Berengaria would be spared nothing. "The Princess Ida," she insisted, in her quiet, proud way.

Blondel let his empty jug roll across the tiles and rose unsteadily. "When that brazen bitch couldn't cajole the Constable into letting her into the castle she took up her lodging at the lousy Inn," he admitted, with deep resentment. Yvette blushed rosy red for his lapse, but Raymond—who knew what good Tuscany can do to a man who has ridden too far on an empty stomach—laid a friendly hand on his arm as he went indoors to rest. "The King is being treated decently? There's no question of foul play?" he asked, in an anxious undertone.

The devoted squire swayed with weariness, a dusty cloak over his shoulder and his sweetheart in the crook of his arm. "He's being held to ransom," he told them. "One hundred and fifty thousand marks."

They stared after him incredulously. He might just as well have said fifty thousand. "I doubt if there's as much money in all England!" groaned Johanna.

Berengaria paced back and forth between the cypresses. "But there is Normandy. And his own Angevins. Surely they would help to get him back?" she entreated of no one in particular. "And Aquitaine and Maine—and perhaps Navarre—"

But Raymond knew how war-ravaged was Normandy, how strong was the influence of Philip in the lesser dukedoms. And England had been so recently conquered. What, he wondered, would that incalculable little island do? Buy back a king who had drained and deserted her? Or throw off the Norman yoke and back the stay-at-home John, who was all for peace and prosperity and was to all intents and purposes an Englishman? The only thing to do seemed to be to go there and find out. And when a letter came from the indomitable Eleanor saying that she had sold her jewels and pawned her crown to give all the other women a lead, he decided to go at once and help her. He was actuated in this by a desire to please his wife, but surprisingly enough she elected to stay with Berengaria.

"But of course you must go together!" protested Berengaria, rousing herself from an unpleasant mental picture of a disreputable little inn nestling at the foot of an imposing castle. "Blondel and Yvette will be with me."

Johanna stared unseeingly at a statue of some dead and gone Caesar. She could feel them both thinking, "She's dying to go because she's still in love with someone in England." But she didn't want to go—now. So she muttered something about being sea-sick.

"But you never are!" they expostulated in unison. Whereat she threw herself into the arms of her perplexed husband. "If you must know, both of you," she announced, in a voice muffled by the tightness of his clasp, "I think I'm going to have a baby."

So Raymond and Nando went to England without her. And after they had gone Berengaria protested to the Pope about Richard's impossible ransom, and even appealed to Leopold himself. But the Pope was old and tired, and Leopold politely obdurate. Summer dragged into late autumn, and little swirling gusts of wind rustled the curled, dead eucalyptus leaves down into the fish pool, where they floated round and round the fountain like brittle little boats. Johanna's baby was never born and by the end of November she was recovering from a miscarriage. She had ridden too much, the doctors said. It seemed strange to see her slender, restless body so listless. The two women, spent the afternoons in the courtyard, using the last of the sun's warmth to sit where they could watch the gate. "Next time if it's a boy I suppose you'll call him Richard?" Berengaria asked, to cheer her.

"If there ever *is* a next time!" said Johanna, settling herself on the edge of the pool to feed the goldfish. "You remember they said I never should bear children easily." There was no particular regret in her voice. All the angels in Heaven had not sung at her first hope of motherhood as they had for Berengaria during those stifling days at Acre. "It's because she isn't really in love with Raymond," thought Berengaria. She felt sore for him. These Plantagenets could charm the heart out of you, but since childhood she had loved and relied upon her cousin. "You're not still comparing the husband you've got with the one you might have had?" she asked inexcusably.

A fat carp leaped greedily from beneath a large, flat water-lily leaf, and Johanna caught him sharply on the snout with a bit of crust. The red of anger flushed her wonderful skin. "What did you expect when you two jostled me into Raymond's arms with all that pretence about Saladin's nephew?" she demanded. It was the first time she had alluded to their scheming and Berengaria silently saluted her generosity. "We wanted you both to be happy," she said apologetically.

"You wanted *Raymond* to be happy," amended Johanna; but when her basket was empty she slewed herself round on the wall, "Listen, 'Garia," she explained earnestly. "If I knew for certain that Robin didn't want me—that he wouldn't have come to Sicily anyhow—I believe I could love Raymond utterly. He's so—dear. But Robin…"

Berengaria closed her book with a snap. "The man seems to have you all under a spell!" she complained sharply.

"Perhaps he has," sighed Johanna. She sat thoughtfully with the empty basket in her lap. "You see, he showed us England…"

"How do you mean—'showed you England?'"

"We were Normans—top dogs—travelled sort of people. And he made us feel the little island our great-grandfather had conquered mattered more than we did. All the time he was acquiring the veneer of our easy selfishness he was making us care about justice and freedom and the well-being of his fellow countrymen. Because he loved the smooth green hills and little humble villages they came to mean more to us than the broad demesnes of Normandy. To John and me, anyway. There was something in Robin that English people have—a sort of independence of soul…"

They sat in companionable silence for a while. A flutter of white doves strutted about the pavement picking up crumbs, the tips of their tidy plumage gilded by a westering sun. Somewhere indoors Blondel was trying to teach Yvette to play his lute and the spasmodic discords of her uninspired diligence were interrupted by his remonstrances and her laughter. "I suppose this separation would have been much easier for you to bear if you and Richard had had a child?" surmised Johanna.

Berengaria watched the eddying fall of a dead leaf. "I don't think we ever shall," she said.

Johanna had often wondered about that. But it hadn't occurred to her that there must be things which her sister-in-law often wondered about too. Her head jerked up in surprise when Berengaria said, "Ann Capet told me that Richard has a son."

Johanna made a sharp gesture of disgust, and the doves flew back to the roof with a spreading of wings like the sharp click of opening fans. "That is the sort of thing Ann *would* tell you," she exclaimed.

"Then it is true?" asserted Berengaria.

"There was Jeanne de St. Pol," admitted Johanna. "I thought everybody knew about her. My father was furious when Richard tried to make her Duchess of Aquitaine. But he was sent there so young and you can see for yourself how women always—"

"I'm not asking about his *women*," interrupted Berengaria.

Cornered, Johanna said, "They'd a son called Fulk. She took him abroad when she married. The last I heard of him he showed signs of growing into a tall copperknob like the rest of us."

Berengaria closed her eyes, picturing his passionate mouth and slender arrogance. She knew how Richard must have adored him. "It's strange how we attach so much more importance to physical unfaithfulness than men do," she said presently, joining her sister-in-law by the pool. "I never told you, but when you were ill that horrible, Chalus man came back again. He's revoltingly rich, you know, and he offered to pay off Richard's ransom if I'd live with him. And I—just couldn't."

"Garia, you poor darling!"

"I don't see how we're to raise it any other way…I suppose I'm just a fastidious prude."

"Richard would rather *die*!" exclaimed Johanna fiercely. "Don't you know you're the Madonna and all the lilies to him?"

"And yet he can amuse himself with a cheap little—Oh, my dear, don't think I'm stupid enough to mind—much. It's just that I wanted to know—if he'd married Ann or someone—if he'd have had children…" She broke off incoherently, thankful for the distraction of a commotion at the gate.

Above the clanging of the bell and the clatter of hoofs they could hear a man's voice giving orders. "Raymond!" cried Johanna, springing up. And Raymond—at last—it was. With a king's ransom and a letter from Queen Eleanor. He hugged his wife and tossed the letter triumphantly into Berengaria's lap while Nando supervised the entry of a train of sumpter mules so laden with well-stuffed sacks that each mule, silhouetted against the setting sun, looked as if she were in foal.

"You see what a fool John was to scoff at the clergy!" wrote Eleanor. "They can't forgive him for turning out poor William of Ely, but it seems they can forgive a crusader *anything*. So they gave the plate from their altars and wore the soles off their sandals bringing priceless stuff from their treasuries."

It all seemed like some wonderful dream, and Berengaria read the letter aloud to them while the sacks were being unloaded. It told how the peasants had given their pitiful savings or brought a sheep or a pig, and young girls had given the shillings they had saved for their wedding finery and even the children had offered their tiny treasures. "Your mother says she doesn't know what she would have done without Raymond because John just went off to Guildford and sulked. And there's a message for you, Johanna.

She says how sorry she is about your baby…Oh, and Avisa and John have a son!" The next paragraph Berengaria did not read aloud. It was the Dowager Queen's personal message to the woman who had supplanted her. "So now, my dear daughter-in-law, you had better bring that ransomed husband of yours home as soon as possible and begin to raise some of your own. The Tower room is waiting for them—and so is a very lonely old woman who is tired of public life."

It was through a blur of tears that Berengaria saw the mules being led away and the sacks counted. "The whole hundred and fifty thousand marks!" Johanna was exulting.

"In English shillings, of course," smiled Raymond. He tossed one of the smaller bags to Nando. He slit the neck of it and poured a stream of silver pieces on to a marble bench, where Johanna and Blondel fell upon the familiar coins as if they were old friends. "Actually, there are only a hundred thousand here," Raymond said. "The odd fifty thousand went straight to Austria some days ago."

"Queen Eleanor explains about that," said Berengaria, consulting her letter. "She says, 'Even with Raymond's help we couldn't have raised the whole iniquitous amount if someone who *loved* Richard hadn't sent that fifty thousand *anonymously!*'" Her daughter-in-law raised eyes shining with happiness. "She under-lines 'loves' and 'anonymously,' of course," she laughed tenderly.

"Whoever could it have been? We don't know anyone as rich as that!" marvelled Johanna, making a swift mental survey of their friends.

But Yvette, who had been putting some of her finest stitches into a trousseau, was touched most by the thought of the girls who had given the price of their wedding gowns. "What *made* them do it?" she asked, examining the youthful stamp of Richard's head on the face of a coin. "Some of them could hardly have remembered him."

"I don't know, my dear," admitted Raymond, the wonder of it still in his honest eyes. "It was just as if someone had been refreshing their memories—telling them of his good sportsman-ship and his sudden kindnesses—all the best bits about him. They seemed to know all the amusing stories about his boyhood—things even the Queen herself had forgotten."

"You know, for all the English look so stolid and dumb," reflected Johanna, "it's amazing how a man of Richard's dynamic personality can stir them."

"And I should imagine that being profoundly stirred from time to time is good for them," teased Raymond, bending to kiss his Anglo-Norman wife. "If I had to live there all my life, darling, I should never understand them!"

But Blondel stood absently pouring a cascade of familiar coins through his fingers, his eyes warm with memories. "I've seen them when they've penned their cattle and the evening shadows are lying across the South downs. They'll lean on a gate and say, 'That there bain't a bad view.' And what they really mean is, 'That earth I've just furrowed and those fields where my beasts are pastured are the very heart of me, and all down the ages I'll give my sons and my sons' sons to defend it.'" Blondel knew well enough that his own sons would fight for it too, but because he had known Robin he grudged nothing to the land that was absorbing his ancestry.

And Berengaria, reaching out to it as the goal of her desire, said over and over during the next few days, "Richard and I will go home to England for Christmas." Sometimes, however, she qualified it, thinking in the secret places of her heart, "*If that Cypriot bitch doesn't interfere,* we shall go home together for Christmas."

PART VIII

Guildford

Chapter Twenty-Nine

WHILE RAYMOND WAS STILL scouring England helping Eleanor to raise her elder son's ransom, John Plantagenet sat at ease before a leaping fire in Guildford Castle. Tired hounds sprawled at his feet, for the day's hunting had been good. The firelight stabbed at first one ruby and then another in the circlet binding his ruddy hair and, because he had got rid of William of Ely, the Great Seal of the realm gleamed on his finger.

"He might almost be King!" thought Barbe of Chalus, rather overawed at the company in which he found himself. In Vienna and Paris—and even in Rome—he had been treated as a vassal rather than as a visitor. He had not expected England to be either so beautiful or so civilised. In fact, he had always wondered why so many European rulers had coveted the fog-ridden place. But his solitary ride from Dover had been a revelation. All the way from the coast he had seen prosperous towns and well kept priories. Because of the severe game laws, the autumn woods were well stocked with deer, and at sunset each manor looked like a delectable island marooned in a sea of red-gold rye. In a land left kingless for so long he had expected— and hoped—to find lawlessness bordering on civil war. But here were both order and resilience. Although the whole island must have been bled white to pay for a costly crusade and a king's ransom, even the poorest serf, sweating to fill his lord's granaries, seemed to bear his present hardships with an air of patient decency, as if someone he trusted had assured him that better times would come again.

Although this castle in the middle of the Surrey woods was a mere hunting lodge compared with Falaise or Gizors, there was a sort of careless dignity about the hall. Chalus looked round at the excellent tapestries and the silk standard which Avisa of Gloucester, his host's meek Saxon wife, had dutifully embroidered with the single leopard rampant of a Plantagenet younger son. "You are very comfortable here," he remarked, as one man of substance to another.

John yawned amiably, showing scant ceremony to his self-invited guest. "More comfortable than my adventurous brother at Triffels!" he agreed, with a grin. They had supped on wild boar and venison and sweet mulberry tart. The jug of good Kentish ale on the stool between them was almost empty and their speech less wary than it had been before the rest of the company withdrew.

Only Picot, the misshaped jester who was John's shadow, was there to overhear. "Too comfortable to move!" he croaked, hovering round to refill their cups. His words might have meant little or much.

"I've a small son to think of now, you know," said John.

"And I hear the ransom money is coming in more quickly than you—hoped?" probed Chalus.

"It's that damned new brother-in-law of mine—coming over here like a whirlwind of efficiency," complained his host. "Thank God with Richard shut up there's no chance of Berengaria breeding."

"Only bastards," piped the lewd little hunchback, with a speculative eye on their guest.

"A Cypriot hostage your brother has been philandering with begged me to take her along to Triffels; so I left the little baggage on your brother's doorstep and took care to let Berengaria know," chuckled Chalus, betraying by his venom how little success he could have had in that quarter. "For all her chastity, she's got plenty of spirit. So I don't imagine there'll be any inconvenient leopard cubs for a bit."

"Good work!" approved John. "Then it appears you didn't come here just for the hunting?"

But Chalus's private motives were too disreputable to discuss even with John Plantagenet. So he merely remarked significantly, "I saw Philip as I came through Paris."

John's eyes narrowed calculatingly between their sandy lashes. He kicked at Picot's unsuspecting rump, sending him sprawling among the sleeping dogs, and only laughed when a great wolf-hound snapped at his hand, biting it to the bone. "Get us some more ale, you misbegotten dolt, and then clear out!" he ordered.

When the poor, devoted fool had limped away, leaving a trail of blood across the fragrant rushes, John got up and poured the drinks himself. He could be an amusing and agreeable host. Although he bade fair to become stocky like his father, he was slightly taller. Good living had not yet coarsened his body, and rich clothes became him. Not having been born a duke, he was more democratic than the rest of his family. He was popular with shop keepers and could understand the crafty outlook of sheriffs. Riding down the street, he would wave an affable hand to any townsman who happened to have a pretty daughter, and most of them forgave the copper-headed brats he added to their burdens because he granted them trade charters and kept his furious insolence for the barons and the clergy. The presumption of ill-bred, second-rate men like Chalus, which his elder brothers would never have tolerated, merely amused John. "Frankly, I can't make out where all the ransom money is coming from," he admitted, handing the man his drink. "Of course, the people adore my mother. My father always said she cast a spell on them. But there's more to it than that. I've waylaid her messengers and bribed some of the wealthier barons to withhold payment. But if the collection goes on at this rate, Toulouse will be taking the first instalment to Austria before Christmas."

Barbe of Chalus put down his empty tankard and belched. "The King of France is no more anxious to see that ransom paid over than you are," he said.

John fiddled with the Great Seal on his finger. "When Philip Capet came over to see his cat of a sister he used to admire every hare-brained thing Richard chose to do," he recalled doubtfully.

"Well, he's jealous of him now that your spectacular brother has stolen his thunder," Chalus assured him, dabbing at some spilled liquor with the soiled velvet of his sleeve. "Can't you have Toulouse murdered?"

As if to provide suitable accompaniment to his sinister words, a sharp spatter of rain lashed the window shutters and a heavy door banged somewhere in the rising wind. John strode to an archway and jerked aside the leather curtain. But there was no one there. Not even Picot. When he came back he had shed the last shred of pretence. "You know I can't," he said testily. "He's too well connected. I should have old Sancho on my trail. And even Philip wouldn't stand for it."

Chalus rose to his feet unsteadily. "He could be robbed on his way back," he suggested.

John met a shrewd glance from his little, simian eyes and grinned. "Not such a bad idea for a crafty antique collector in his cups!" he approved shamelessly. He walked to the window and pushed open a shutter. A blustering inrush of air extinguished most of the torches. The soft west wind disarranged his smoothly bobbed hair and beat against his face. He didn't mind it. It was all part and parcel of the land he coveted. The sweet smell of damp earth came up to him. It was not yet quite dark and a watery moon bathed her shadow in the winding Wey. The last jovial party of pilgrims had passed over on their way from Winchester to Canterbury, and John could just make out the figure of the ferryman, like a hooded Charon, tying up his boat. Here and there a light from some house in the huddled town warmed the dank and cheerless evening, and from the foot of the steep street leading up to the castle the silent, sleeping woods stretched in a soft blur towards Albury and Shere where he had been hunting all afternoon. "Those woods down there are infested with robbers," he remarked, drawing in his rumpled head and tapping his short, square teeth with a thoughtful finger.

"I know," agreed Chalus, steadying himself against a heavy iron torch sconce. "But most of them are bungling amateurs."

John eyed him curiously. "How do you know?" he asked.

"I was held up by a band of 'em and robbed."

"More fool you to travel alone!" John told him bluntly.

"I didn't want to be conspicuous—seeing I'd brought you a letter from the King of France." Chalus tapped the wallet at his belt secretively. After all, he was far more afraid of Richard than of robbers.

John closed the shutter and fastened it carefully. "I didn't know Philip hated Richard as much as that!" he said softly, padding back into the room like a pleased cat.

They sat down again in front of the fire. The draught of fresh air had cleared some of the fumes from the head of the Duke of Normandy's treacherous vassal. "Your Kentish ale is very potent," he remarked apologetically.

"It makes men talk," agreed his host cynically.

Barbe of Chalus began to talk to some purpose. "Everybody knows Philip is really the cleverer of the two, but all the time we were out there the Cœur de Lion dominated everything," he explained. "Just took everything he wanted—quite casually—and enjoyed it."

John laughed, brushing the wood dust from his hands as he replenished the dying fire. "Poor Barbe!" he mocked. "I prefer blondes myself, but my mother says Berengaria is very beautiful. Now, seriously, what does Philip suggest?" He held out an eager hand for the letter, and Chalus unfastened his wallet with maddening clumsiness. A small roll of parchment passed from his stubby fingers to John Plantagenet's fine ones. Plain and terse ran the suggestion that they should out-bid the English ransom by offering Leopold fifty thousand marks apiece to keep the world's most famous crusader in captivity. Even in the glowing firelight the words stood black as the treachery of Judas. A pretty bargain between a comrade-in-arms and the brother of a man whose name would stand for courage down the ages. The words were written by Philip's pedantic quill for John's eyes alone to read. But the seal had been broken. "Why has it come like this?" he demanded, holding half a waxen fleur-de-lis in either hand.

"I told you," muttered his fellow conspirator. "I was held up by robbers."

John looked up quickly. There was fear in his light-blue eyes. Fear of the fettered lion. "You mean—someone has seen this—besides us three?"

Chalus would have dismissed the matter with a shrug. "They rifled my wallet. But what matter? A lot of ignorant peasants—"

John sat back in his chair. In sterner moods he was beginning to look like his father. "Tell me exactly what happened," he ordered.

There was nothing for it but to describe the humiliating incident. "I was riding leisurely through those woods enjoying the first glimpse of your towers—congratulating myself that my journey was almost done—when a band of home-made desperadoes sprang out on me. They seemed surprised that I should be travelling alone and had to content themselves with the money in my pouch." Chalus chuckled reminiscently. "They were so simple they didn't even search for the gold stitched in the leather padding of my mail. And when I asked for that letter back the fellow who seemed in charge let me have it without much ado."

"What sort of a fellow?"

"Oh, a tall, brownish man—about thirty. An impoverished gentleman of sorts, judging by his speech. Reminded me of someone, if only I could think who…Not in face, you know—just his mannerisms. The way he threw back his head when he laughed—and the crisp, careless way he gave his orders—as if he were cocksure they would be obeyed." The elusive likeness still seemed to worry him. "But there…You wouldn't know the man, even if I *could* remember…"

John smoothed the crumpled letter uneasily. "Some of these swashbuckling ne'er-do-well sons of squires have a smattering of Latin these days," he said. "You don't suppose he could read?"

"Lord, no!" Chalus reassured him. "Why, the fellow held it upside down most of the time and wanted to know what it was. 'Some important business tally, I suppose?' he asked, seeing I was so set on retrieving it. And when I said it was just a record of a private bargain between friends he laughed and said, 'Well, what's a scrap of parchment worth anyway?' and handed it back to me as unconcerned as could be."

"This one may be worth a crown!" chuckled John, relieved.

Chalus leaned forward eagerly to tap the letter on his host's crimson-clad knee. "If you can't manage the whole fifty thousand," he offered, "I can lend you some."

"Sounds as if you stand to get something out of this too!" jeered John, pealing at the pages' bell to annoy him.

"There are other things a man wants out of life—besides gold, and a crown," admitted Chalus.

"Richard's wife, for instance?" suggested John.

The man was too anxious to implicate an accomplice to resent his rudeness. "Then you'll write to Philip?" he persisted, trying to forestall the approaching footsteps of an intruding page.

But John was too clever for him. "No, I will write nothing," he said. "But you can take him what money I have." As the page bowed at his elbow he threw Philip's crumpled letter into the heart of the fire. "Light me to bed," he ordered, stretching himself as he rose. "And tell the Constable we shall be leaving in the morning."

Next morning they rode to London. They stayed at the Conqueror's Tower. And what more natural than that Prince John should show a foreign guest the sights? Among others, the crypt at Westminster which his father had converted into a stronghold for the royal treasure. John showed Chalus the false step and the seven keys. He loved showing people the false step because it precipitated anyone who tried to rob his family down a slimy stone oubliette into the black swirl of the Thames. The seven keys, he explained with a grin, were really supposed to be kept by seven different barons so that no one—not even the king himself—could unlock the great chest and dissipate what was left of the wealth of England without the knowledge and consent of them all. But he—John Lackland—had done away with all that nonsense. Ever since he had succeeded in getting rid of that bandy-legged Frenchman, Longchamps, he had kept all seven keys himself. And whenever a baron started shouting at him, he jangled them jocundly at his belt. It gave him childish pleasure, healing past slights. It was the kind of jest proud barons don't appreciate—the kind of thing that ends up in revolt. But John could not foresee that. And he enjoyed opening the great chest and handing over the remains of his brother's heritage to a money-grubbing, double-crossing rustic count who lusted after a Plantagenet queen. He hated parting with the money, of course, but of what use would it be to him if Richard and Berengaria came back to England and bred sons?

So, having given it into Chalus's keeping to add to the loan of gold stitched into the lining of that miser's mail, John turned to the question of an escort. He had grown a little golden beard since the crusaders brought home the fashion from the handsome Saracen sheiks and, back at Guildford, he plucked very thoughtfully at that beard, considering the size of the escort. He wanted it to be strong enough, but he was still more anxious that it should be inconspicuous. Just in case the barons guessed the crypt was empty—or in case Richard ever got to know. The bare thought of Richard knowing made him err on the side of secrecy. And the night before his guest departed for Austria he lost a good deal of sleep over it, remembering the robbers in the woods. But they were just amateurs, Chalus had assured him. So John rose in a better temper, called for his hunting boots, and rode with him as far as Shere. The miller there had a pretty daughter who had so far eluded him.

It seemed a strange coincidence that the armed convoy had scarcely parted from its royal sponsor when Chalus came upon the tall, brown fellow who had held Philip's letter upside down and handed it back so unconcernedly. He was leaning indolently against a tree fondling a little lame doe, and the faded green of his leather jerkin was so much the colour of the foliage that Chalus was almost level with him before he could think of turning back. But the man had seemed simple enough to outwit before and even if he were not alone, what were a handful of thieving outlaws now one had an armed guard? So Chalus nodded casually and rode past with a slack rein, calling back over his shoulder to the captain of the guard, "That's the fellow I told you about who had the impertinence to rifle my wallet when I came."

But to his surprise the captain of the guard, a gnarled old-timer who had served with the Plantagenets since he was a boy, stopped short in his tracks and crossed himself. And the next thing they knew was a rain of arrows from the thicket on either side. They were so completely taken by surprise that before John's men-at-arms could lift bow-string to cheek each of them had an arrow quivering in his right wrist. The man leaning against the tree just threw back his head and laughed.

"For God's sake, why don't you cut him down?" raged Chalus, drawing his sword. "Can't you see the grinning dolt has nothing but a hunting knife?"

"But he could strangle the life out of you with his bare hands," warned the captain, urging his horse between them like a shield.

"How d'you know? Who is he?" demanded Chalus.

The old soldier opened his mouth as if to speak, caught the outlaw's eye, and thought better of it. And as the rest of the gang closed in from the woods about his helpless, bleeding escort, Chalus let loose a flood of impotent profanity. For amateurs, they had made a pretty good job of it, and all he could do was to threaten them with horrible punishment if they interfered with the property of Prince John. The sacks on his mules contained a present of Wonersh wool, he improvised, on its way to the Duke of Austria. Naturally, the Prince wanted to stand well with him just now in the hope of expediting the release of his brother. A hope which should appeal to all down-at-heel Englishmen who found living conditions so difficult just now that they were forced to take to the woods.

Their leader seemed unimpressed by either threats or blandishments. "If Prince John wants these sacks taken to Austria, to Austria they shall go," he promised blandly. "And if it helps you to sleep more soundly o' nights I swear no man shall tamper with them until they have done the King good service." Still stroking the doe's ear, he rapped out half a dozen orders as if he were the King himself. And when some of his stalwarts were all for setting on Chalus, he looked as if he would forestall them. With the lightning strength of a master wrestler he had him from his saddle, grovelling on the ground in their midst. Then, with a shrug and a laugh, he changed his mind. "Let's give him a year or two more," he decided, looking down at him contemptuously. "I've a friend who may like to meet him, and God forbid that I should deprive him of his kill!" According to his code, that was the sporting thing to do. It did not occur to him that in years to come he might curse himself for not having torn the treacherous wretch limb from limb.

The convoy went on its way with its double set of guards, the tall outlaw riding with careless grace at its head. Only Chalus and the Captain of the Guard were left behind, ignominiously chained to a stake in a cow-shed. "Funny, now that cursed brigand's gone I've just remembered whom he reminded me of!" remarked the badly shaken Count, watching the dwindling cavalcade through a chink in the planking. "What were you going to tell me about him back there on the path?"

But the Captain was suddenly very sleepy. Young Lackland might pay him his wages, but his loyalties went back to the days when Henry the Second's word was law in England. The golden days when he—Giles of Oxford—had taught the Duke of Aquitaine and his foster-brother to ride their first ponies. Days when Oxford castle rang with the pomp and circumstance of a rich, worldly-wise archbishop and the scurfy and laughter of family life. He could remember the black day when words spoken in Angevin anger had murdered the archbishop in his own cathedral; and the awful day at Dover—before he got his commission in the Holy Land—when King Richard, drunk with rage, had sent him to fix a notice on the Reeve Hall. And although the notice had set a price on Robin's head which had never yet been claimed, old Giles began pulling off his boots and making himself a bed in the straw. "Nothing special," he yawned, "except that I've heard tell he's written a book."

He stretched himself out with a great rattling of chains and was soon snoring like an old campaigner. He had nothing to worry about, seeing that Robin himself—who never forgot old friends—had winked when the padlocks were fastened, and told him to let the old skunk go in the morning.

But the Count of Chalus lay awake most of the night thinking of his companion's words. Presumably an outlaw who wrote books could read, even if he *had* held Philip's letter upside down. So instead of returning to face John, Barbe hurried back to Chalus and set about strengthening his own castle. For once, he spared no expense, and he prayed from the bottom of his black heart that Richard Cœur de Lion would never get free.

Chapter Thirty

RICHARD CAME HOME TO England in the Spring. Fit and handsome as ever, with a fine new beard that became him and
a reputation that would outlive him. If he strode about
more restlessly than ever most people supposed it was to make up
for fourteen months of captivity. But those who knew him best
guessed it was because he didn't want to sit down and think, for—
to the mystification of his subjects—he had come back without
their new Queen.

The sleepy Surrey town of Guildford was seething with excitement because as soon as the Dowager Queen heard that he had
landed she hurried there to plan with John a family reunion. As
poor Avisa was not invited to set her husband's house in order,
Eleanor brought old Gregory, who used to serve the late King. He
was so shaky these days that he only retarded the joyful hustle,
but the way a younger son had established himself in the country
offended his sense of decorum. "Where shall we put this, Madam?"
he demanded, when the servants had taken down John's standard
from the hall. And Eleanor had answered indulgently, "Oh, in the
river if you like—it has hung *there* four years too long!" She spoke
absently, out of her own happy thoughts, but the old man had
taken her at her word and had tottered down with it to the River
Wey. And there had been quite a scandal because some respectable
towns-women whose daughters John had seduced had thrown the
gorgeous silk thing in the water with their dirty dish clouts.

The people of Guildford had almost forgotten how splendid Richard looked. As he rode through the town they rushed from shops and houses to cheer him, and if the more thoughtful among them remembered how he had fought against his father and outlawed his foster-brother, the broad red cross on his breast and all he had suffered in its cause argued well for a humbler temper. His was the forthright, openhanded type that appealed to them—and they were proud to have him represent their breed. John was well enough, with his easy accessibility and pleasure-loving habits which put money in their pockets, but Richard's courage had made the name of Englishman something to be reckoned with throughout the world. He had cost them a pretty penny, but in return he had fed that aggravating sense of superiority that they valued still more.

Their enthusiasm knew no bounds when he stood tall in his stirrups to wave to them but—shove and scramble as they would—they could see no queen. There was Johanna, their own beloved princess, with her new husband; and the only other woman they could see was a Greek girl, bright as a parakeet in silks and beads, pricking her mettlesome little Arabian mare close behind the King. At first they wondered if he had brought them back this brazen, bare-headed child as their queen. But of course that could not be—for Berengaria, they had been told, was white as magnolia blossom. An exquisite lady who had refused half the princes of Europe for his sake and who had nursed him devotedly through some pestilential foreign fever. Their hearts were warm with welcome for her—poor Berengaria, who was raging in proud loneliness in Rome!

She ought to have been there at that family reunion when Richard and his party rode in through the barbican and John and his mother came down the castle steps to meet them. But it was for Eleanor the women shed tears of sympathetic joy when Richard sprang from his horse to gather her to his breast—the indomitable old Queen who had lived and suffered with them through the last lean years. With an arm still about her he turned with casual good humour to dismiss them. He had done so little for them, and they adored him. They would tell their children such stories about him that in years to come he would still be the hero of their race. While John, who had revived the Wonersh wool trade and had the men of Chiddingfold taught how to blow glass, and who really wanted their favour if only because it annoyed the barons, stood eclipsed and forgotten. When he turned to follow his family into the hall, he was confronted by the portentous sight of his elder brother's three embroidered leopards crouching where his own single beast had ramped and was aware of the faithful Picot sulkily picking bits of scarlet silk here and there so as to turn their fierce snarls into ludicrous smirks. But he only laughed and wrung his brother's hand. If John hated having to turn out of the best bedroom, or felt like an unsuccessful Judas, he had sense enough to serve expediency with good grace and play the genial host.

Eleanor was welcoming her daughter and, because she was over seventy, it seemed only yesterday that Johanna had been seventeen. "The echo of her voice has barely died away in the rooms at Oxford before you've brought her back to us!" she said, slipping an affectionate hand through her new son-in-law's arm. She asked them to tell her about their journey from Sandwich and all they had done in London, but her eyes and thoughts always came back to the splendid crusader at her side.

"We did try to hurry, darling, but the city seemed to have gone mad," Richard told her. It was the same London that he had once said he would sell.

"Even your peace-loving shopkeepers, John, fought each other to get a glimpse of the man who had killed so many infidels," laughed Raymond. "Richard and I had to ride slowly to avoid trampling on small boys who believed our saddles would be hung with Saracens' heads."

"And every time we pulled up to avoid them," added Johanna, "the women kept kissing Richard's scabbard and fingering Ida's foreign clothes."

Richard suddenly remembered his lovely hostage. He duly presented her as the Emperor of Cyprus's daughter, and was at pains to explain that he had brought her as an insurance against any trouble her father might make for de Lusignon on the island.

As a stroke of policy, the matter was unimpeachable, and the way Eleanor turned from the absorption of her own family to set the little interloper at ease was a lesson in courtesy. But when she had handed the girl over to the care of her ladies she said to Johanna in the privacy of her bedroom, "Why on earth didn't he bring Berengaria?"

"She wouldn't come—as well," explained Johanna, while her women tidied her after her journey. "At first he had a number of important people to see and things to attend to. There was the Emperor Henry and a whole string of bishops waiting to congratulate him on his release. Of course, he meant to go and fetch her as soon as he was free. But in the meantime that horrible Chalus man called at the villa and took care to tell her that Ida Comnenos was with him."

"She *might* be only a hostage," said Eleanor, smoothing the snowy folds of her headdress.

"I pointed that out, but unfortunately Chalus had told her the girl had been at Triffels hanging about for Richard. And Berengaria, who is the soul of kindness, has always been so hard about Ida. So she wrote him the coldest of letters telling him she'd made some very pleasant friends and preferred to winter in Rome. He probably deserved it, but it was the sort of letter that dries up everything decent in a man. I had to take it to him because nobody else dared." Johanna threw down an embroidered towel and replaced the lovely emerald ring Raymond had given her. Wrinkling her adorable nose at an appetising whiff of roast duck, she put an arm about her mother's waist and drew her back to the hall. "All this has meant that poor Blondel has had to come home without Yvette," she whispered as they took their seats. "And probably all four of them are utterly miserable."

They could see John buttonholing Blondel in a window recess. By the wary eye each of them kept on the King's back, it was clear that he was trying to find out if there had been a matrimonial quarrel, and Blondel was being loyally uninformative. Knowing her younger son's hopeful curiosity, Eleanor rescued the embarrassed squire with a beckoning finger. "If I hadn't sold my last jewel, dear

Blondel, I should have liked you to wear it for finding the King,"
she told him, when he hurried across the hall to greet her. "But
I am told you left a very precious jewel behind in Rome, so I'm
going to persuade him to let you wear that one instead." As she
tilted back her head to laugh at his blushing pleasure, her dark eyes
were as vivid as ever in her ageing face, but he thought the lovely,
ringless hand he kissed felt more frail. And even as it slid from his
grateful fingers her attention was caught by the sudden wrangling
of her sons.

They were standing beneath the rich lights of John's new
coloured glass windows. There was no fire, for it was spring; but
their voices rapped across the empty hearth as sharply as the crackling of sticks. John—sulky and defiant—was saying, "Somebody
must keep the castles properly garrisoned. You didn't want them to
go to ruin, did you, like the crops?" And Richard—scoffing, fresh
from foreign conquests—replied, "What d'you suppose I care for
your toy fortifications? Or whether you wanted civil war or not?
It's your friendliness with France—"

John's shifty eyes narrowed at that. He wasn't sure how much
Richard knew. Did he know, for instance, that Chalus had sat in
this very room tempting him to treachery with a proposal from
Philip. A fiendish proposal that they should out-bid the English
ransom by offering Leopold fifty thousand marks apiece to keep
him in captivity. John had wanted Richard's crown, and Chalus
had wanted his wife, and so between them they had raised the sum.
And Chalus, travelling very secretly, had offered to take the money
to Austria. But something had gone wrong, and Richard had been
liberated. Chalus had sent some cock-and-bull story about being
robbed before ever he reached the English coast; but even if the rat
had double-crossed him, John calculated rapidly, it was only one
man's word against another's! And Richard had always stuck up
for him—even against Robin. "You *used* to be quite friendly with
France. And *someone* had to treat with foreign powers, if only to
safeguard our commercial shipping," he countered brazenly.

Richard drew off his gauntlets and threw them on the table,
where they landed with a clatter among the dishes. "That's what I

made William Longchamps Chancellor for," he said, glaring at the filched signet ring on his brother's finger.

John drew it off and handed it to him, negligently. "Then it wasn't particularly clever of you," he said. Men gasped. They all thought it, but no one but John would have had the effrontery to say it. "The people always hated him. You must have known that. They used to call after him in the street 'bandy-legged little Frenchman!' They wanted an Englishman."

"You, in fact!"

"Anyone—who cared a damn what happened to them." Both of them knew that the people had wanted Robin. And Richard had wanted him too, and, hating to part with him—had lost him altogether. John suddenly changed his tone, speaking with effective restraint. "My dear fellow, remember you've been away four years! If I've assumed more power than you intended it has been almost forced upon me. The country was bled white by your war. Trade practically at a standstill. No able landowners left and all the best craftsmen and labourers in the army—"

Richard had been warned about all these things before—by someone whose opinion meant far more to him than John's. He had deliberately ignored them, but he knew them to be true. Had he not gone over them again and again in his delirium at Haifa? "You need not labour my negligence," was all he said. Everyone was astonished at his mildness. And John, as usual, was quick to seize upon the moment of his softening. He indicated with charming diffidence that his guests were waiting to begin. "You know Avisa and I have a son?" he asked eagerly, drawing his brother towards the table. "I've called him Henry after our father."

Richard was glad he had done that. Often of late, sensing the bond between Berengaria and her father, he had felt compunction for his behaviour towards his own. "Splendid!" he approved instantly, taking the chair of state beside his mother. "You two have been luckier than Berengaria and I. Let's drink to the youngest Plantagenet!"

John was all radiant hospitality at once. "It must be the best vintage. None of our boorish ale. There's a special Bordeaux I want you to taste. You'll be surprised how I've increased our wool export by importing more wine." Waving the wine steward aside, he insisted upon going down to the cellars to choose it himself. If only he could keep Richard well amused at Guildford, it might be weeks before he discovered about the rifled coffers at Westminster.

When he had bustled out beyond the serving screens at the far end of the hall, Eleanor sighed with relief. She was growing old, and weary of the quarrelling of her brood. But the others felt cheated. They had expected a real Angevin row. "I can't think how you can be so patient with him!" exclaimed Raymond, who had suffered much veiled insolence and secret circumvention on his last visit and had hoped to see John well and truly shown up.

Richard only shrugged, helping himself with zest to some slices of good red English beef which a page was handing round on a long silver skewer. "He didn't get a square deal over the inheritance, and my father spoiled him hopelessly."

"And, of course, none of us ever takes him seriously," added Johanna. It was one of the things about the Plantagenets that always amazed and infuriated their friends.

"I think you should," insisted Raymond.

"Just as if he knew more about our affairs than we do ourselves!" thought Johanna, feeling aggressively English. She considered her husband was being irritatingly ponderous, but Richard had a wholesome regard for Raymond's common sense. "Very well then," he agreed. "Just to show him—and Philip—that I'm master in my own land, I'll be crowned all over again next week at Winchester."

Eyes were raised and knives suspended in pained surprise. His mother touched his hand reprovingly. "But Berengaria won't be here—" she ventured.

"And you always said it should be at West-min-stair," Johanna reminded him, tactlessly mimicking the way her sister-in-law always said it.

Richard glared at her. "That's why," he said laconically.

Eleanor could see he was in no mood for argument. "It will be a strange sort of coronation," she said resignedly. "You with no queen and me with no crown." When Richard looked up, his mouth too full for questioning, she explained cheerfully, "I had to pawn it to the Jews to help get you back."

He finished his mouthful in silence. Out of the secret welling of his loneliness he wondered just how much good he would be to them now they *had* got him back. He knew he wasn't clever at statesmanship, like Philip. Nor shrewd, like John, about tithes and charters and crops and all the other dull things these English were for ever arguing about. During those first few months after he came to the throne he had had Robin at his elbow, prompting him. Robin, who knew just how far one could push these patient inscrutable peasants, and where one must stop. Who knew just the sort of gesture they loved and could prove, oddly enough, that there were certain gestures they loved more even than money. Robin, who never asked for lands or praise or power—who drew out all one's best with happy laughter and offered sound judgment so unobtrusively that one believed it to be one's own...Richard caught himself looking up expectantly at the banging of a door, and wrenched himself back to the present. He picked up his mother's hand and kissed it gratefully; but, as usual, she repudiated sentiment with common sense. "What is a dowager's crown, anyway, to a woman who has had two coronations of her own?" she asked brusquely. "And a train of fleur-de-lis reaching half-way down the aisle of St. Denis?"

"Vain old woman!" laughed Richard. He looked down at her out of those shameless, alluring cat's eyes of his, and lowered his voice. "You'll look after that ardent little Cypriot for me, won't you, and lead her back into the paths of virtue?" he asked, with sudden irrelevance. It was the same sidelong grin he had been wont to give her as a boy when cajoling her for some excitement forbidden by his father or confessing to some crazy escapade. He had never pretended to her, and she had often wondered humorously whether she should accept his candour as a compliment or the reverse.

She glanced along the table at Ida, wondering exactly what there had been between them. It wasn't the first time she had had to fend off a girl he had tired of or who had fallen too embarrassingly in love with him. But this girl, with her ripe lips and smouldering eyes, had come between him and his wife. Eleanor could not forgive her that. "I suppose I shall have to," she agreed reluctantly. "But it would be easier if I knew exactly how unattractive you've already been making the paths of virtue look!" As Richard vouchsafed no indication, she leaned across him to catch the girl's attention. "How would you like to come back to Oxford with me after the coronation?" she invited, with her most persuasive smile.

Ida looked up from her platter in panic. To be shut up in a castle with an old woman was unthinkable after the freedom and emotional excitement of the crusade. "It is kind of you, Madam," she stammered, in the careful Norman she had improved so patiently for love of Richard. "But I am all alone in this strange country. I beseech you, don't send me away from—from the few people I know."

Since Raymond and Johanna must soon be going back to Toulouse, the cause of her desperate entreaty was obvious. Unable to meet her imploring eyes, Richard plunged into a conversation with a brilliant young theologian, Stephen Langton, who had been recommended to him as a possible candidate for the see of Canterbury.

But Eleanor had no such qualms. "Nonsense, my dear!" she told the girl bluntly. "You can't go following the King about now. In the East it was different. But here he will have councils and all sorts of state business to attend to." She turned to the youngest lady of her household, who was about Ida's age. "We must find room for her at Oxford, mustn't we, Dorigan? Until the King gets her a husband and a household of her own."

And Dorigan, anxious to please, suggested the Tower room. To her it was just a room that was never used. She had no idea that it was peopled with happy family ghosts, and was covered with confusion when the King himself turned sharply and vetoed the idea. And Ida, torn between the twin horrors of Oxford and a husband, thought in her self-absorbed young vanity that he did so to keep her near him. Never once, in the hours they had spent together, had he talked to her of the Tower room or the people he really loved.

"The little boat you were carving for Arthur is still up there," Eleanor told him. "After you left I had it brought from Dover and put on the window seat. But Constance wouldn't let him come while you were out of England."

Richard smiled, seeing his gallant little galley framed in the grey stone arch of the window just where the boy would see it as he came to the top of the turret stair. Outlined against that vast expanse of sky, she would look as if she rode an azure sea. It would be fun to have Arthur there—or even John's youngster. But best of all, of course, to fill the old room with a family of his own. Tall sons to take the place of Henry, Robin, and himself, and that "daughter like Johanna" Berengaria had always wanted. He could almost hear their quarrelling and their laughter, and the eager hurrying of their feet on the stairs. Suddenly, he wanted Berengaria unbearably. What a fool he'd been! Why couldn't he have been big enough to understand her hurt pride? But women exaggerated things so. Just because that poor pretty Comnenos jade had come to him when he was simply starved for the tenderness of a woman…And to whom else could she have gone? All the same, Richard wished he had not taken his wife at the bitterness of her word. Someone had told him since that that swine Chalus had been seen with her in Rome. As likely as not he'd been pestering her. With half his mind still in Rome he asked automatically, "And how is Arthur?"

It was John who answered, appearing round the corner of the screens followed by the laden cellarer. "Remarkably strong, by all accounts," he reported, without enthusiasm. Under either arm he had tucked a cobwebbed bottle of the wine he had been hoarding against the day when Richard's prolonged captivity should make his own son Henry England's heir. Old Gregory hurried forward. It pained him to see a Plantagenet fetching his own wine. He fussed over the serving pages and insisted upon handing the King's drink with his own shaky hand.

"Well, here's to the new Henry—" began Richard, but paused with the wine half-way to his lips. "My dear Gregory, the old horn cups! I don't come home from the wars every day!" he complained, half vexed and half amused at what he supposed to be the old fellow's forgetfulness. "Where are the gold ones?"

He could have bitten his tongue as soon as he had said it. He could see Gregory, his stiffening back still bent apologetically, raising troubled eyes to the Dowager Queen, and was aware of people fiddling with their untasted wine in uncomfortable silence. "I see," he said slowly, "you had to sell those too." He smiled his acknowledgments to Raymond and to his mother, but it was only his eyes that smiled. Somehow Acre and Arsouf didn't look so fine just then. "Well, here's to the way you two bled this blessed island to pay my ransom!" he said briskly, and gulped down John's best vintage with unappreciative palate, his former toast forgotten.

Eleanor heard the angry indrawing of breath that pinched his long, fine nostrils, and looked at the long, firm line of his mouth. There was something she longed to tell him—something that would wipe that bleak look from his face and bring back the laughing Dickon she loved. "It wasn't only us—" she began.

Everyone looked at her. Even Raymond, who had worked with her to raise the money, hung on her words, hoping for some last-minute explanation of the miracle. After all, the wiping out of a fifty-thousand-mark deficit in a few weeks takes some explaining. But one cannot take a secret gift, and betray the giver. All her life Eleanor had had to juggle with divided loyalties. "It was just— the people," she ended lamely. She was thankful when Stephen Langton rose to sign a blessing, and they were all free to push back their stools and drift into little chattering groups.

Only Richard, the hero of the hour, stood alone by the table. He was balancing a knife on the top of a dish of pomegranates they had brought back as a novelty from the East. The servants had already begun to clear and Picot was sprawling in the chair he had just vacated, telling him a funny story. It was something about a miller's daughter who had been brought to the castle and had given John the slip. But Richard wasn't really listening. He was calculating how long it would take people who had been bled white by a war to raise fifty thousand marks. There wasn't as much, he knew, in the Royal treasury, and only a very rich man could spare it and go on living much as before so that the world wouldn't know who had paid it. And he didn't know any man as rich as that. Except Chalus, of course. And Chalus was no friend of his. Why, the miserly old bittern hadn't even made Berengaria a wedding present of the borrowed crown. Probably that was why he'd gone to Rome now—to get the thing back.

The knife jerked downwards in Richard's hand, inadvertently piercing the soft, pulpy heart of a pomegranate and squelching an ugly mess over a tablecloth so finely embroidered that it could only have been the work of Ann. Looking down at the soiled fleurs-de-lis, he remembered her prim fingers and her sharp tongue and the way she had fooled him. He was well out of that. But if ever another woman betrayed him...

He called a passing servant to clear away the mess and, before settling down to tell the family all about his adventures he clapped the misshapen little jester encouragingly on the back.

"Picot seems to be in good form," observed John, pulling forward a chair for his elder brother in the middle of the circle. "Which story were you laughing at just now?"

"I've no idea," said Richard vaguely. "I was just wondering which of us, Picot or I, was the bigger fool."

He laughed again, whole-heartedly, in the way Eleanor loved to hear. Because Ann had been a slut, Berengaria would always be to him as the Holy Grail.

Chapter Thirty-One

JOHN WAS AN EXCELLENT host. He had planned some sort of expedition for each day. Hawking and outdoor sports for the mornings, a visit to the Holy Well at Dunsfold or to Chiddingfold to see the new coloured glass being blown and boating parties on the Wey in the lengthening evenings. After supper, when the torches were lit, he would be in his element producing a really good entertainment with minstrels and mummers from London. And Richard, fresh from the monotony of Triffels, was ready to enter into it all. But just the first morning he cried off John's hawking party. "It's a marvellous morning for it," he said, joining the others in the hall. "But if you don't mind, dear fellow, I think I'll go up to St. Martyr's."

Eleanor was not altogether surprised. There was a new gravity about Richard these days, and sometimes she felt that he was making a belated effort to meet and understand the spirit of his father. This was a source of great comfort to her, for she always felt that these two whom she had loved best might have been friends had they not been goaded by the bonds of relationship.

Ida Comnenos looked about her at all these tall Anglo-Normans standing around breaking their fast with rolls of bread and great draughts of ale. "They are all so healthy, and they must always be doing something!" she thought. Her own idea of breakfast was innumerable cups of thick, sweet coffee brought by a slave-girl to her cushion-strewn divan. She turned to Dorigan, whose hard bed she had shared in the ladies' bower, and asked with perplexity, "What *is* St. Martyr's?"

Dorigan drew her to a window. On the other side of the flat river valley, the morning sunlight was chasing cloud shadows across the slope of a steep and wooded hill. Perched on the top of it, four-square to the winds of Heaven, stood a small, squat chapel. "King Henry built it for the peace of poor Becket's soul," she said reverently.

"And who was Becket?" pursued Ida.

Dorigan looked profoundly shocked. She had supposed that everybody knew about their famous archbishop. "He was King Henry's friend until he became so rich," she explained with unconscious cynicism. "And then they quarrelled. And one evening after supper the King said, 'Is there not one of you knights eating my bread who will rid me of this turbulent priest?' He didn't really mean it, you know. He was just tired and in a temper because the Archbishop wouldn't do what he wanted. But four of them got up and rode to Canterbury and murdered the poor man in his own cathedral...And afterwards, in his remorse, King Henry did public penance before his shrine and had chapels like that built all over the country for the pilgrims who go to Canterbury to pray for Thomas à Becket's soul."

Ida Comnenos watched a party of them coming down the hill. If she half closed her thick lashes they looked for all the world like little black flies crawling down the side of an inverted green bowl. She wasn't interested in shrines and stuffy archbishops. "This king you're talking about was Cœur de Lion's father, wasn't he?" she asked.

Her new friend nodded.

"But I still don't see why he wants to toil up there on a day like this instead of going hawking."

"He too quarrelled with his friend," explained Dorigan, her piquant face all softened with pity.

"And did he have him murdered—like What's-his-name?"

Dorigan implored her, with a gesture, to speak more quietly. "Of course not," she whispered, glancing apprehensively over her shoulder at Richard, who was standing about in a detached sort of way watching the preparations for the day's sport. "He outlawed him. And now a lot of people think he too is sorry. But it's difficult to find out because nobody dares mention Robin's name."

Ida considered the situation, drumming with idle fingers on the stonework of the window. "Then he'll be sure to go up there alone," she deduced. Presently she crossed the hall to the open doorway where John was showing the party his valuable hawks. The steps were crowded with falconers, eager to hear their birds praised. The May morning was merry with the jingle of their little bells, and down in the courtyard the horses were being brought round. Richard had had his mother's chair placed by the door so that she could watch the scene in comfort, and he was leaning over the back of it. Ida curtseyed demurely, lowering her eyes so as not to meet his sheepish grin. "Do you think, Madam, I might go hawking too?" she asked.

"Why, of course," agreed Eleanor. "I hear you are a very clever horsewoman. Have them fetch her mare, John."

John shouted down the order and turned to the girl with a quick, approving smile. Richard was no bad judge, he thought. When she pretended that she had never even seen the sport before he chose a gentle merlin and showed her how to carry it on her wrist. He was just enough like his brother to make the process interesting, but his hands were not so strong and he was so much shorter. Johanna, with the friendly helpfulness of a true sportswoman, lent her a leather glove. And when they were all ready, Richard himself came to the top of the short flight of steps to wish them good sport. He was very plainly dressed after his gorgeousness of yesterday, and the horse his page was walking up and down the bailey was without trappings.

"You won't change your mind and come with us?" John shouted up to him. "There's plenty of woodcock in Wootton Woods and heron down by Shere pool."

But Richard shook his head. He was out of tune with hawking. Snaring helpless birds seemed tame after killing Saracens. Those had been the best years of his life perhaps—keyed up to danger all the time. If only he could have taken Jerusalem! If only he'd attacked once more from Beit Nuba! If only Philip hadn't ratted! Every time he thought about it he hated Philip more. So he deliberately wrested his mind back to the inconsequent present, considering what an attractive young devil John was, laughing and showing off down there in the sunshine and bandying jokes in mongrel Norman with the crowd at the gate. Descending the steps and tousling the head of the very small page who had fought to hold his stirrup, it occurred to Richard that it would be mighty convenient if Ida thought so too!

But brunettes, however beautiful, were safe with John. In the bustle of getting through the cheering town, he did not even notice that his exotic hawking pupil lagged behind. He clattered up the steep street from the river laughing and shouting to Johanna, with the rest of the company pressing hard on their heels to catch the bright threads of their disjointed conversation and to lay bets on the chances of his great hooded gerfalcon killing a deer. He had had it trained to perch on their heads and to peck out their eyes, but Johanna contended that it was an Asiatic form of sport, and horrible. And Stephen Langton, who was of the party, said what could you expect when Christian countries like England still recognised the putting out of a man's eyes as legal punishment? This started an argument, and it was easy enough for Ida to turn her horse unnoticed up a side street. Near Shalford mills she came upon the party of pilgrims she had seen from the castle window. They were resting and regaling themselves rather hilariously at an alehouse and showed her the sandy track that led up the hill to St. Martyr's. "I should hurry, my dear," giggled one of the women. "Such a tall, handsome man has just gone up that way!" Apparently, they had no idea he was the King. "They seem to get plenty of fun even out of a pilgrimage!" thought Ida, looking at their good-humoured, sunburned faces. She supposed it was all part of this peculiar country.

The last part of the climb was so steep that she tethered her little mare to a tree. The scarlet leather shoes which Eleanor had insisted upon her wearing kept filling with cool silvery sand—so different from the golden kind she was used to—so she took them off and went on climbing with them in her hand. The hill-top was deserted save for Richard's horse, contentedly cropping the short grass in the shade of some birches. At sight of the great, glossy beast Ida's red lips parted in a smile. She was glad she had left her mare at the bottom. "The King will have to carry me down on his saddle," she thought. "The way he did that night I first saw him in Limassol."

The little chapel shone new and white in the sunlight. Still panting lightly from her climb, she tip-toed to the open door and peered in. As her eyes grew accustomed to the cool gloom, she could make out the figure of a monk moving about the sanctuary and Richard kneeling very tall and still before the altar. He held his two-handed sword like a cross before him, and the lighted candles made a soft, blurred radiance behind his bowed head. It was like the paintings of new young Christian knights keeping vigil, which had so much impressed Saladin that he wanted to have his nephew admitted to their order of chivalry. Even Ida's pagan soul was awed by such humble reverence in the most famous of them all.

She went back to the place where Richard's horse was tethered and threw herself down on the warm earth, reviewing her new world through a miniature forest of stiffly curled fronds of young bracken. "This will be the first time I have seen him alone since we set foot in this horrible country," she thought. "It's been nothing but cheering crowds and a lot of silly ceremony and his everlasting family. But here, under these gold spangled branches, I will make him remember that it was I—and not his romantic queen—who sweltered and scratched for weeks in that loathsome inn so as to welcome him from prison. He was glad enough to have me that first night he was free!"

To her hot impatience it seemed a long time before the horse beside her pricked his ears and whinnied. Ida sat up. She could hear the harsh grating of spurs on the stone aisle. Richard had to bend his head to pass beneath the low spandrel of the door, and the action matched his mood. She saw him stand there for a moment or two, blinking at the light. Remembering that his sword was still in his hand, he sheathed it with unwonted gentleness and strode to the edge of the hill. He stood there, bare-headed and newly shriven. The sandy plateau dropped away sharply at his feet and all the South of England seemed spread before him in the morning sunlight. Fold upon fold, the wooded hills of Surrey merged into the blue distance of the Sussex weald. The bare Downs were a smudge of purple on the horizon. And somewhere beyond their bulwarks lapped the sparkling sea. Richard expanded strong lungs in exultation, straining his gaze to the utmost limits of his land. How could men breathe, he wondered, who did not live upon an island?

The panorama looked so much like a map that he began trying to pick out places he knew. There was a gap in the faint outline of the Downs that he imagined might be Pevensey, where his ancestor had landed—or Hastings, where the Normans had fought for it. How the Saxons must have hated them! For the first time he knew how it would feel to be a Saxon, and how his father had worked to mend that hatred. Somewhere farther east, he supposed, would be the busy ports of Winchelsea and Rye—and Sandwich, the gateway to his dukedoms on the Continent. And snugly inland, almost at his foot it seemed, the market towns of Worth and Reigate, and somewhere in the middle of the blue distance the manor of Horsted de Cahaignes where Blondel's people lived. He said each name over carefully, trying to pronounce them as John did with no trace of foreign accent on the R's. He always remembered with embarrassment landing from Aquitaine and asking the way to Arundel, and how the Sussex farmers had stared as dumbly as their sheep because he had called it "Hirondelle."

But he had said his first prayers in Saxon at Hodierna's knee. And this was his kingdom, and every castle from Arundel to Alnwick was his. The little English may trees blossomed pink and white around him, and down in the valley the young tops of the oaks were tipped with gold. His foot pressed fragrance from a clump of wild thyme and a lark rose singing to the blue. And when the lark had flown out of sight the clear notes of a hunting horn brought back memories of other Spring mornings. Richard turned and looked down on the tops of the beeches that made a soft mantle for the tower of Shere church and the miller's pond, and suddenly he felt Robin to be very close. It was as if the spirit of England breathed upon him as it had done in boyhood. It could not hold him as it held Johanna and John, but in that moment it mastered him. His mind was empty of ambition. "If only people didn't keep perstering me with what wants doing in the duchies!" he muttered, realising how happy a smaller—or less restless—man might be with just this little, sea-girt land. For the moment he had had a surfeit of war. "By the good heart of God, I'll stay here till my next crusade!" he promised himself. "I'll send Blondel back for Berengaria. And if only I can find Robin we three will go round seeing that these people get decent living conditions, humane game laws, and all the other things my father wanted."

He laughed aloud at the idea and Ida, who had not dared to interrupt his exalted mood, got up and crossed the laced shadow cast by the birch trees. Unobserved, she watched the changing expressions of his face. Would he turn presently, laughing boisterously at her persistence, and kiss her with the careless arrogance she loved? Would he lift her on to his horse as if she were an amusing child, or take her offered womanhood with that half-grudging urgency for which she must always plot and tempt? Gazing at him, hungry for him, the warm-blooded Greek girl tortured herself remembering how his eyes smouldered when he looked down at Berengaria and how the hard lines of his mouth curved into a maddening, secret tenderness. How, even in some crowded room, he would sometimes draw his breath sharply at her touch so that men could not help seeing how utterly his body was hers. Hers—Berengaria's. Everything was Berengaria's. His body and his conquests and his name. The right to sit beside him at banquets and to walk unquestioned into the austere little cell of a room that was usually his bedroom in these grim northern castles. Everything but the proud joy of bearing his son. She, the ignored captive, had seen to that. She laughed cruelly, remembering how she had held aloft the dead Saracen's head and how the poor exquisite Queen had shuddered at the sight.

Ida became aware that she was being watched from the chapel doorway, but it would take more than a disapproving old monk to shame her. With a gesture of defiance she shook back her wind-swept curls and ran to Richard, calling him by some soft Greek love name. He turned with surprise, his mind still bemused with plans for the future and memories from the past.

She weaved her fingers in the fastening of his cloak. "You won this onyx clasp in single combat with that fierce emir at Arsouf, didn't you?" she murmured. "And you value it almost as much as my father's horse? Or the Crescent you tore from the Citadel that day you and Count Raymond galloped almost alone into Jaffa?" She told over his conquests and hummed the wicked little dance tune the native drums were playing that night in Acre. She pressed her warm young body against his until their shadows merged. But the pulsing music of the East had ceased to be a fire in his blood, and the scent of young may trees was more potent than the perfume of her enticing hands. He looked down at her blindly and detached them in a preoccupied sort of way, pushing her from him as if she were no more than any pestering whore. "I thought you'd gone hawking with John," he said.

"That was only an excuse," said Ida. "I had to see you alone."

Had she been content to remain a child in his eyes, she would have retained his indulgent affection. As it was, though Acre and Triffels would stand for great events in his life, she herself was only an incident. "Get back to the Castle," he ordered. "And don't dare to deceive my mother like that again!"

His indifference was more convincing than any anger or harsh words. It shattered her self-fed dreams so that even her envy of the Queen fell to pieces. For the first time she regretted her craven father's defeat. For months she had been dramatising herself as a romantic beauty destined to go on indefinitely moving through the colourful excitement that surrounded Richard's life; and now, quite suddenly, she was made to realise that the best thing that was likely to happen to her was the ordinary humdrum marriage of which Queen Eleanor had spoken. It would be arranged for her and it would set the confines of her life. In the tragic youthfulness of her passion she saw no possibility of second-best, no hope of compensations. Her little bangled wrists slid slowly from his shoulders—slid slowly down over his unresponsive heart. Never again would its strong beats quicken for her. This cold country, with its white cliffs and bracing winds, had beaten her. Ida Comnenos turned, sobbing like a wild thing, and ran shoeless down the hill.

Seeing her go, the old monk offered up a *deo gratias*. He had been the late King's confessor and knew that most of the stories about Plantagenet morals were true, but he often wished a censorious world could see some of their temptations! Presently, Richard went back to him. It was evident that he had already forgotten the girl. "Even if an outlaw came here, you would give him sanctuary and say nothing, wouldn't you, Father Christopher?" he asked.

The monk started in surprise. "Of course, my son."

Richard began tracing some of the crosses that batches of pilgrims had cut in the stone of the lintel. "Nevertheless, if ever my brother Robin should come—will you send word to me?" he asked, with averted eyes. The words came awkwardly because it was the first time for years he had spoken of Robin to anyone except Berengaria.

Father Christopher glanced anxiously over his shoulder in the direction of Shere. He wasn't sure how Richard really felt about Robin. "Why should you suppose that he might come here?" he asked non-committally.

But Richard could think of no adequate reason. "I just felt him near—that's all," he said.

Father Christopher folded his finely veined hands in the wide sleeves of his habit, "Those whom we love are always near—when we remember them before God," he said, beginning to understand the reason for this royal visit.

But Richard did not want that kind of comfort. He wrenched off the emir's treasured clasp and dropped it impulsively into the alms box—but not for Becket's soul. "Pray constantly that I may see him again!" he entreated without subterfuge.

A sigh of relief escaped the man of peace. He stroked the spandrel carving of which he was so inordinately proud. "All these chapels are, in a manner of speaking, monuments to the Angevin temper and the misery it has caused," he said, with a twinkle in his kind old eyes. "Maybe, my son, God will not grant you your heart's desire until you have mended yours."

"That I shall never do," laughed Richard ruefully. "But pray at least that I may know before I die that Robin has forgiven me, and I vow I will stay and mend this country!"

Father Christopher looked at him with the understanding of one who had seen the splendour of Becket, the perfidy of Ann, the homeliness of Hodierna, and the incomparable friendship of her son. "At Matins, at Nones, and at Vespers I will pray," he promised. But he sighed as he watched the man these influences had made go plunging down the hill side on his great, sure horse. He had heard so many Plantagenet vows!

Chapter Thirty-Two

WHEN JOHN'S HEAD FALCONER sounded his horn, it was to round up the hawking party by the mill pond at Shere. After the exhilaration of the first hour's sport they had begun to straggle badly, relapsing into desultory conversation and enjoyment of the May morning. There was so much to talk about. Johanna and John rode over Merrow Down exchanging stories of the crusade with all the latest gossip from London and Oxford.

"And you never see anything of Hodierna now?" enquired Johanna, purposely lagging behind their companions as they made the descent into Shere.

John watched his sister put her horse at a gate and envied her her hands. "Mother wanted her to keep the Tower room in comfort, but she preferred to share Robin's hand-to-mouth sort of existence. She came back once—a few months ago with some sort of message from him, I believe."

"Then our mother must know where he is." As he made no answer, Johanna crowded against him in the narrowness of the miller's rutty lane. "Do *you* know?" she insisted.

John was forced to shrug a denial although he had tried hard enough to find out. "All over England, I should think!" he muttered resentfully.

"What on earth do you mean?" demanded Johanna. But John had caught sight of the miller's daughter milking her goats in a little field at the back of the house. A flaxen girl in a blue gown who had had the bad taste to elude him for weeks. He turned aside at once and trotted across the field to speak to her.

Johanna reined in her horse to wait for him, letting the rest of the party go on. It was a lovely place in which to wait. The woods sloped down steeply on either side, and just below her the mill pond lay like a green jewel, mirroring the trees, with the assembling hawking party making a fringe of shifting colour along the mossy greenness of the bank. For the first time Johanna noticed that Ida was not among them, but she couldn't be bothered to go down just then and make enquiries about her. It was amusing to watch her brother conducting his amours among the goats. He cut a fine figure in scolloped scarlet, making his sturdy grey plunge and rear dramatically as he cut off the girl's virtuous break for the back door of her home. Johanna laughed outright when the great dappled creature, chafed beyond endurance, lashed a hoof at the bucket, surrounding them both in a frothing stream of milk.

But in spite of her spontaneous laughter, she was sore at heart. For the first time she and Raymond had quarrelled and it had been all her fault. The remembrance of it had nagged beneath the morning's gaiety, and she was glad of a few moments' quiet to sort out what had happened. First there had been that solemn sheriff of his arriving unexpectedly last night with endless business to discuss and sheaves of documents to sign, spoiling the first evening of their home-coming. And this morning, not only had Raymond been too busy to come hawking, but he must needs spoil her own sport by reminding her of what the Roman doctors had said. All the time she was dressing he had been urging her to ride gently, to ride side saddle like other married women, so that at the last minute she had thrown her new Turkish trousers into a corner and called angrily to her woman to bring the oldest dress she could find. "You don't care how dull a time I have as long as I can produce an heir, do you?" she had raged, struggling into the old green velvet she had had at Oxford. "It's all you men think of!"

Johanna remembered with compunction how, instead of shaking her as she deserved, her husband had sent the tire-woman away and fastened the gown himself. How he had taken her face between strong, square hands and said, "It's you I think about always—you lovely, vital thing! Of course my people want me to have sons. But if I were to lose you—" And he had turned away because he couldn't put into words what the loss of her would mean.

Because the old green velvet had brought back a dozen precious memories she had shrugged herself out of his arms and told him not to be old-fashioned and intense. And because he was a man and not a foot-mat he had grown angry then and told her straight out, "I've spent the last six months on your crazy family and if I don't bring my bride home soon the people of Toulouse will believe you're pock marked!" They had quarrelled violently, and she had been abominably rude. "I'm not a brood mare to be bartered from one country to another," she had flung back at him. "And I'll *not* go back to Toulouse the moment I've come home, just because that sour-faced sheriff of yours says your negligible little province wants seeing to!" And she had picked up her gloves and banged the bedroom door behind her so that the clang of it must have startled the prisoners down in the dungeons.

And now the sun was shining and the lovely pool she had wanted to show him was a green jewel silent and mysterious with the reflection of many trees. But the silence was broken, and she was roused from her reverie by the urgency of thundering hoofs. She turned to see John pounding across the tender shooting corn in hot pursuit of the miller's daughter. The chase may have begun in fun, but as he made a grab at her flying flaxen hair the hooded bird on his wrist impeded his progress, squawking and beating its fierce wings in his face so that he lost his temper completely. The girl screamed, stumbled, and lost a shoe. The party at the water's edge turned to stare, tittering or aghast according to their kind. But John scattered friends and falconers to left and right, riding her down as if she were a panting deer.

"Don't be a fool, John!" shouted Johanna, knowing the depth of the deceivingly transparent water beneath the banked up mill dam. One summer, when they had stayed at Guildford Castle, Robin and her elder brothers had taught her to swim there. But in all probability this mill girl couldn't swim, and in any case the frightened horse might drown them both. She saw young Langton step forward, a tall, white-clad figure among the kaleidoscope of colours, to catch at the scolloped crimson rein. But John only swerved, blaspheming. His mind was fuddled with the fumes of anger. "By God, I will ride the little white idiot down, and to-night I will teach her to defy me!" he thought. The mounting madness made him blind and deaf to shame. His vision was limited to the frustrations that unleashed his brainstorm. "I am John Lackland," chanted the crazy voices of his breed. "Son of a red-headed Angevin, thrown to the kill-joy priests, cheated of my birthright by proud elder brothers, and I will take what I want—now and always—to make up for it!" The plaything he wanted danced before his brain, just out of his reach, like Richard's sparkling crown. And just as Robin's crisp words used to spoil his play-acting whenever he tried on the crown, so a sharp stab of pain brought him back to his senses now. An arrow skimmed low across the water and stuck quivering in his wrist. It came from nowhere and changed everything.

A moment ago it had seemed that John and his quarry must go headlong over the bank. But his reins went slack. With a roar of rage he felt the great horse rear and slide to a standstill within a foot of the water, its dappled grey neck sickeningly bespattered with his own over-heated blood. For the first time he became aware of men shouting and of women's screams and of a sky darkened by the whirring flight of frightened hawks.

Johanna had not moved from her vantage point at the end of the lane. Her indignant pity rose for the fainting girl. She saw a couple of falconers rush forward to drag her from the danger of the grey's stamping hoofs and lay their limp blue burden among the forget-me-nots and rushes, and was glad when Langton lifted her tenderly against his knee, cupping up some water in his own scholarly hand to revive her. When the other women began crowding round her brother and tearing up their veils for bandages, she felt no urge to help. He had got what he was asking for, making a wild beast show of himself like that! They'd all of them tempers, of course, but her other brothers had never been brutish. By the way some of the servants were crossing themselves, she knew they believed the mysterious arrow to be a judgment straight from God, and without caring much where it came from she felt with disgust that the May morning looked less lovely because John lived in it. "We all tolerate him because he's amusing," she told herself. "But Raymond was right. We ought to take him more seriously." The white-faced girl was carried past her to the house. The miller's wife came to the door. Johanna watched Langton cross the field to speak to her. "Though Heaven knows," she thought, "how he can explain the incident!"

The hawking party was remounting and preparing to go home. They had forgotten all about their wagers on John's gerfalcon but, as usual, he had given them something better to talk about. He rode homewards up the rutty lane, sheepish and sullen, in the midst of them. His left arm was in a sling made from the scented veil of an adoring baroness, and a page was leading his horse. He avoided looking at Johanna. Possibly they both remembered how she had once rated him for torturing a mere dove. Or maybe they both had begun to think the same thing about the arrow.

The woods resounded with shouts as the servants made a great show of beating them for the invisible archer. But once John's back was turned they soon gave it up. Shere woods were known to be infested with men wanted by the corrupt courts of justice and men who had lost their tongues by John's orders because they knew too much, and anyone who wore his livery had good reason to avoid them.

"The horrid felon might have killed him!" some of the women had cried. And the polite fallacy had been left unchallenged. But the men knew well enough that a marksman who could pierce a rider's wrist at three hundred yards could easily have found his heart had he wished.

"Outlaw or no outlaw, the King himself couldn't have bettered the shot!" a hoary old falconer was saying to his mates as they gathered up the last of the morning's kill.

They moved off up the lane, and Johanna was left to stare across the deserted mill pond to the rising ground on the other side. Great king beeches rose there like giants from a dense undergrowth of lesser trees. Suddenly she knew as well as John who must have pulled that bow. "Have any of you seen the Cypriot princess lately?" she called casually after her brother's men, and when they would have turned back she said, "Never mind. I will wait for her." They thought it natural enough that she, who was so kind even to the grooms and chambermaids, should wait for a foreign visitor. And John, she knew, would be in no hurry to ask for her.

As soon as the men were out of sight she set her horse at the plank bridge that spanned the mill race, taking the path round the pond and plunging into the woods they had just been searching. Almost directly the sound of their voices died away and the grassy hunting rides lay deep and still as if no one had ever been there. Johanna tied her horse to a young oak and pushed her way through the undergrowth until she came to an unexpected clearing. Here were the tallest beeches of all, with primroses nestling at their feet and great shafts of misty sunlight piercing their golden solemnity. At her approach a herd of fallow deer rose on slender legs, gazed at her with brown, reproachful eyes, and bounded off. But one lame doe, after an abortive effort to hobble after them, was left behind. Someone had made a rough splint for her leg with two smoothly whittled twigs and a bit of green cloth. Johanna bent down to look at it and smiled. In the private chase of a prince who trained his hawks to pick out the deer's eyes, surely only a crazy reformer would bother about binding up their knees. Cursing the encumbrance of green velvet, Johanna picked up her skirt and began running among the trees. Her heavy plaits came unbound, and she could feel the soft wind in her hair. And as she ran she found herself calling, with delicious excitement, "Robin! Robin! Where are you?" just as she used to do on the battlements at home.

He let her find him under one of the beeches, his bow still in his hand. He stood so still that the faded leather of his jerkin and the violet shadows and the smooth grey-green of the trunk seemed one. She remembered feeling how that quality of stillness used to make the restless movements of her family look cheap. But his face was warm with vitality, his eyes a laughing welcome. "It must have been your smile and not the torches that lighted Oxford Castle," she panted inconsequently, "and all the days of my youth!"

She went straight into his arms, and he held her and kissed the russet of her hair. "It is like the shining beech leaves in autumn!" he teased. But even in that moment he held her as he always had— shielding her from all that was ugly and turbulent in her family, and from his own desires. "My little Johanna!" he said, although the hair he kissed was almost on a level with his lips. "It was a thousand times sweet of you to come!"

She laughed and cried against the faded jerkin and presently drew herself out of his arms to look again at his beloved face. Holding on to his arms, as if at any moment he might vanish, she scrutinised and learned each line of it. "Rough living agrees with you," she decided. "You've changed much less than Richard."

"It's a pretty good life, after all," he said. "And you don't look a bit like a sophisticated woman who has had two husbands!"

In her joy at finding him Johanna had forgotten both of them. She flushed warmly and withdrew her possessive hands. To keep them safely occupied she began picking the bits of bramble from her dress. "Funny I should wear this to-day…"

"You were always loveliest in velvet," he assured her. "And I always think of you in green…"

She looked up, well pleased. "And I you," she said. "But yours is all patched!" There were tears in her eyes for that. She remembered how he had moved becomingly at stately banquets and talked with brilliant men like Becket, and how much her father had thought of him. Johanna's rare tears moved him so that he shook her in self-defence. "Uncurable tenderheart! My mother loves to mend them," he laughed. "Remember how she was always going to make Dickon that shirt that was proof against poisoned arrows? And how she made your wedding dress? And how you enslaved Blondel in this one?"

They laughed unsteadily, with the tenderness that wraps the irretrievable past. The thick woods closed them in, setting them apart from all that might come after. And part of Johanna's heart was crying forlornly, "We are quite alone—and he let me go!" He rolled over a log with his foot, and she sat down on it among the primrose roots. "Were you enslaved too?" she asked. She had to know.

He leaned a shoulder against his tree trunk and lied cheerfully. "Not in the least!" he assured her, for her own good. The lame doe came and rubbed against his knee, and he bent to scratch the top of her head. It was uncanny the way animals never feared him.

Johanna tried to coax her away from him, but she would not come. "Then all I said—and the way I clung to you—that last night in the herb garden, was just—cheap?"

Robin stopped fondling the little dappled beast. "It was the most blessed thing that ever happened to me," he said. "But, don't you see, I owed everything to your parents and I knew their plans for you." He was silent a moment, remembering that awful morning in the King's workroom when he had been told of them, and how he had said, "Yes, Sir," like a dolt and blotted the important treaty he was drawing up. "You were only a child," he went on. "How could I warn you and smash your happiness? But even when we were all happiest together I always knew that our separation must come."

"And so it was easier for you?"

"I had had a long time in which to school myself," Robin answered guardedly.

"And—when you heard William was dead?"

"I didn't—until after you had left Sicily."

Johanna was quick in her elder brother's defence. "Richard tried to tell you. He was out searching the woods all night. But he doesn't know them as you do. And there was a terrible thunderstorm…"

Robin's eyes were shining. "Did he do that?" he kept saying. He came and stood beside her, one foot on the log. "This morning a fellow we outlaws had befriended told me the King was at Guildford, so when I heard the horn I went down to the edge of the pool and peered through the branches. I was hoping to see him."

"Poor Robin!"

He met her sympathy with a ready smile. "I didn't see you either. You weren't with the others. Only that godless brute, John. My men say they've seen him snooping after that girl before. He must pick on just the decent, hard-working sort of family the country needs. You know, I've been following that precious brother of yours about ever since Richard left—trying to restrain his men's cruelty and to undo some of the mischief he does—without letting him get a rope round my neck. And believe me, it was a feast day for me being able to stick an arrow into his pampered flesh!"

"That explains something he said up there in the lane. He feels your influence thwarting him." Johanna bent to gather some primroses and arranged them consideringly. "And yet he loves England too."

"He covets it," corrected Robin.

"But he often does things for the people. He was telling us last night how he had taken the bridge at Godalming away from the Abbots and given it to the town."

"To annoy the Abbots," laughed Robin.

"But they'd been charging the poor market people a toll every time they used it."

"And now the poor market people will probably let it get into disrepair. John loves cheap popularity but he hasn't much foresight."

Johanna pinned her posy in the front of her gown, and Robin dismissed him contemptuously from their conversation. "The man's growing fat," he remarked. "Another six years and the way he's lived will show in his face."

Johanna surveyed his own lean, sinuous limbs with affection. Woman-like, she hoped he got enough to eat. She felt they were both skirting the subject they wanted to talk about, and she preferred to ride full-tilt at things. "Richard has gone up to St. Martyr's," she told him.

His slow, affectionate grin was more telling than any show of sentiment. "They tell me he's grown a beard," he said.

"It makes him look older—and much sterner. It suits him in a way, I suppose—but Berengaria says she's lost the young man with the devastating mouth she fell in love with."

"Why didn't she come with him? Is it true they quarrelled?"

Johanna nodded sombrely, picking shreds of bark from the birch on which she sat. "Over Isaac Comnenos's daughter. Richard was fool enough to bring her to England. As a hostage for the Cypriotes' good behaviour, he says."

Robin flung himself from her with an angry exclamation and began pacing back and forth across the sward, beating one fist upon the other. Except that he was more graceful, some of his gestures were ridiculously like Richard's. "You Plantagenets!" he raged. "Must you quarrel with *everything* you love? Probably he doesn't care two hoots for the baggage, but it's to be hoped Berengaria will be big enough to forgive him. If she came and settled down here and raised a family, there'd be some chance of his stopping in England."

"Why should he?" challenged Johanna resentfully. "Normandy's more important. And he was Duke of Aquitaine before he was King of England." Robin, she knew, thought of them all as servants to his precious island. Whereas they, in spite of their father's precepts, still thought of it as a gift from their great-grandfather—a place to enjoy. That, she supposed, was what Robin meant about the difference between John's love for it and his own. But what did it all matter when she was with him again and had so much to tell him? She sat there twanging the string of his bow as if it were a harp and enjoying his rare impatience. "Berengaria may be unreasonably jealous," she told him, "but at least she sticks to the rules herself. When I was in Rome she was sick with anxiety for Richard, but she refused to buy his release by selling herself to the richest man in Europe."

"Chalus, you mean?"

Johanna looked up quickly, surprised that an outlawed Saxon should even have heard of him. But she hurried on with her tale. "And then, inevitably, she tortured herself, wondering if she had been over-fastidious or mean. You'd like her, Robin." She went on, covering the foul name he called Chalus. "She simply hates war and makeshift living in tents, and yet look how she nursed Richard through all that heat at Haifa!"

"Heaven bless her!" ejaculated Robin.

"She has far more self-control than we have. She never once complained about the dirt and the discomfort although she herself was far from well at Acre."

Robin swung round at mention of the place. "God, what wouldn't I have given to see Richard raise that siege!" he exclaimed. Johanna hadn't realised what it must have cost him to give up his share in such adventure. He came and sat on the log beside her, and she told him the whole long story of the crusade, what people had said and done, how Richard had laughed and fought and triumphed and been frustrated—making it all live for him as if he had been there. It was the best gift she could give him, since for England's sake she hadn't been able to give him herself. He opened his pouch and shared his midday meal with her as he had done many a time beside the Thames, and neither of them noticed how the noonday sun was slipping westward.

"It must have been well nigh unbearable for him, leaving Jerusalem untaken!" he said.

"The thing I regret most was his killing all those prisoners outside Acre. Berengaria begged him not to, but she was too tragic about it. If you'd been there he wouldn't have done it. And you'd probably have stopped him from quarrelling with Leopold. It was funny at the time, of course. And Blondel and I both felt you'd have known how to keep it—just funny." Johanna saw it clearly, how Robin had always been the complement of Richard, keeping him at his best. Richard was the more spectacular, but Robin was the stronger. Richard with his head in the clouds, Robin with his feet on the soil...She turned to him impulsively. "My dear, won't you let me ask Richard if you may come back?"

But Robin was no plaster saint to make the first move. He had been grievously and unjustly hurt. Even now, it was hell to think of them all up at the Castle and he and Hodierna not there. It would be wonderful, of course, to ride back with Johanna now. To take a chance on it. A stab in the back from John's men-at-arms or the chance of a handgrip from Richard. To walk into the hall he knew so well and warm himself at the fires of friendship, to kiss his beloved white-haired Queen and put his feet under a civilised table again...Silks and velvets and napery, coming and going of well-trained servants, the stimulating talk of travelled men, the laughter of well-born women. What right had any man, in maniac anger, to cut him off from these? Robin shook the bitterness from his mind and pressed Johanna's pleading hand. "No, no, sweet. Believe me, it's better as it is. I find there are things I can do—contacts I can make—which were impossible while I lived with you. Perhaps if I believed Richard would really stay...But we both know him so well. The first time he gets another chance at Jerusalem, or Philip casts an eye on a bit of his land...Your mother's getting too old to take an active part when he goes. There'd be just John and me. I'm not even your father's bastard, but the people would follow me. And that would mean another civil war."

Johanna smoothed out a bit of birch bark on her knee. The under side of it was pink and silver like one of Berengaria's beautiful gowns. "I suppose that would be worse than having us conquer you," she admitted.

But Robin was never serious for long. "My dear child," he mocked lazily, "*did* you conquer us? I rather thought we just absorbed you."

"Absorbed us?"

Robin moved to a grassy hummock in the sunshine and sat there hugging his knees. "Haven't we borrowed all your best words and enriched our strain with your haughty blue blood?" he demanded.

"Why do we keep saying 'we' and 'you?'" complained Johanna. "You're really part of everything, with a Saxon father and mother whose people were half Roman. And then being brought up with us. But you ought to love us best!"

Robin answered her with categorical honesty. "I love your swiftness and your efficiency, and even your splendid anger. Sometimes I envy your arrogance. I want these things as leaven to our Saxon stolidness. But I hate your everlasting quarrelling and warmongering. It doesn't give us a chance. I want the people of this country to have years of peace so that they can earn a square meal without stealing some over-fed Norman's deer. I want their fields and their lives to be their own so that they don't have to go and be butchered in your petty foreign squabbles. I want their children to learn to read. You know, Johanna, it would be exciting to write a book, not in solemn Latin, but in this everyday new language we are making—this English."

"So that we should come to think the same kind of thoughts?"

"Imagine the result! Courage welded to good-humour, efficiency to patience. It should produce a breed who would seek peace and ensure it—but who'd fight with their last breath to prevent another Hastings."

It was getting chilly and Johanna stood up, shaking the bark shavings from her lap. "Oh, Robin, you always did want queer, idealistic sort of things!" she said, thinking how utterly different his ambitions were from Richard's. "Don't you ever want anything for yourself?"

With effortless grace he was on his feet as soon as she. "More than anything I want your happiness," he said gravely. "By all accounts you have married a man this time."

Johanna stood curling the last little strip of bark round her finger. She felt that she must pronounce some sort of judgment because he really wanted to know. "He is the sort of man every woman wants to father her children," she said slowly. She didn't know what made her say it. She had never thought of Raymond particularly in that way before. The thought had crystallised only as the words passed her lips, but she recognised it as the truth. And she and Robin stood at a place between two long separations where nothing less than the truth would do.

A sudden shouting and the baying of deep-throated hounds brought them back to immediate reality. Instinctively, Johanna moved to shield him from the direction of the sound. The colour was drained from her face. It had been so lovely talking to him again that she had forgotten he was outlawed, and that by her impulsive coming she had endangered him.

"It's probably you they're looking for," he reminded her.

She smiled, half reassured. "I suppose it is. I expect Richard sent them. But they're John's hounds—and they'll comb these woods." For the first time they noticed how the sun had moved westward, transforming their sanctuary with its slanting shafts of light into an ordinary Surrey wood. "I must go," she whispered.

Robin walked with her to the edge of the clearing. Her heart sang with pride because, although the shouts and baying were drawing nearer, he neither hurried nor looked away from her. "I should tell Richard what you told me—about Berengaria refusing that swine, Chalus," he counselled. "It might bring them together." His last thoughts were for Richard but his smile was for her. He stooped to lift a trailing bramble from her path and watched her go out of his life. His real renunciation had been made when she was seventeen.

Johanna walked swiftly to intercept John's men, and as she walked her hands were cupped against her breast as if she held something infinitely precious. She had a queer feeling that she and Robin could never really be parted again. Like many very vital people, she had always feared death; but now she was sustained by a certainty that when the time came for her to go out alone into the darkness, Robin would be there, waiting for her. And that his smile would warm her desolation…

After all, she found that the search party had not come to look for her but for Ida. And up at the Castle everybody took it for granted she had been doing the same. Her mother and Richard were so worried about the girl and so annoyed with John that they asked Johanna no questions at all. John himself had retired to bed. So presently, when news came that their foreign visitor had been found trying to persuade a party of pilgrims to take her to the coasts, Johanna left the hall and went upstairs to the Constable's room. Her husband was still there working with his sheriff. She closed the door quietly behind her and leaned against it, uncertain of her reception. But although they had parted in anger and she had been horribly rude to him, Raymond looked up from the document he was signing and smiled at her. Quick to meet his generosity, she came and perched on the arm of his chair. She took the quill from his fingers, and he leaned back with a sigh of relief and dismissed the man immediately. "Did you want to tell me something?" he asked, watching her thoughtful face.

She had meant to tell him that she had seen Robin—that, however much Robin may have wanted to, he had not made love to her—and that staying in England did not matter so much now. But suddenly she saw that this would make Raymond feel second-best always. And from the first she had known him to be too good for that. She knew now that she would never tell anybody about Robin. Already, their meeting had begun to take on the guise of unreality like one of those wishful daydreams she used to indulge in when she was first sent to Sicily. "I only wanted to tell you that, after all, I'm glad you made me wear this dress," she answered. Seeing that Raymond looked puzzled, she added evasively, "It isn't many women of thirty who could still get into a dress they wore when they were seventeen, is it? Why, I wore it the day Blondel first came to us. I remember trying to be kind to him."

Raymond pushed aside his papers. "That man gets all the luck!" he laughed. "What with his jaunt to Navarre, and squiring Richard all through the crusade, and that charming girl Yvette falling in love with him, and your trying to be kind!"

"He was very homesick," explained Johanna, sticking the quill through his thick hair and thinking that the way it was beginning to grey just above the temples gave him distinction.

"So, I believe, am I," pleaded Raymond.

It was very still and pleasant in the Constable's room with the westering sunlight warming the round stone walls—rather like the Tower room at Oxford. And when Johanna looked at Raymond she saw him only. His humorous face and his dear, steadfast eyes. Brown eyes, with golden flecks in them, looking with compelling kindness into her own. There was no longer the shadowy figure of a tall, handsome dream lover behind him, dwarfing his charm.

Johanna was pleasantly sleepy after her day in the fresh air. She leaned against his shoulder, and he held her very close. He had a way of doing it that always made her want to laugh because it reminded her of the clenched fist on his shield with the motto "*Je maintiendrai.*" She was emotionally spent and happy in a new, muted kind of way. She even made the rare admission that she thought she must be a little tired.

"Impossible!" he teased.

"Perhaps I won't ride quite so much when we get home," she yawned drowsily.

Raymond held her asleep in his arms until his page called them to supper. He was beginning to savour the full richness of life. It was the first time his wife had alluded to Toulouse as home.

PART IX

Chalus

RICHARD GAVE ENGLAND EIGHT months. Eight months of fair promise and unprecedented popularity. The fame he had brought them was appreciated by the barons. The church—so long jeered at by John—commended his reverent manner, and the people believed their millennium was come.

But Richard wanted spacious action, and there was no one at hand to persuade him that the most difficult fields for conquest would always lie in his own nature. It was all very well dedicating himself to these people of his, but he wasn't so sure that he really understood their needs. If he happened to see a man's rick burn or his horse fall over a bridge he would be quicker than his own servants to help. But he just did not understand their passion for what they called "their rights" and their complicated system of tithes and tenures, and he was neither humble nor patient enough to learn. And John was clever enough to underline his mistakes. Where Robin would have asked him a few leading questions, giving him time to get the hang of things, John would explain each island custom with exaggerated patience just as if he were talking to a foreigner. Although there were men like Langton who would have given anything to help, Richard gave up going to council meetings and assizes. Why be tittered at in stuffy buildings, he argued, when he could quell men's vitals with a sword?

Before Johanna left she told him about Berengaria and Chalus. "She knows I'd rather have rotted in prison than let any other man touch her!" he had raged approvingly. And, as Robin had foreseen, the bare thought of it sent him hot-foot to Rome. He meant to bring her back. But when he reached Rome he learned that Philip had encroached on his land, and that was the moment when England really lost him. After that, even his mother's entreaties fell on deaf ears. His heart was hard with vengeance for Jerusalem. He sent for Blondel and Mercadier, and the best of England's manhood was called to war again. They sailed up the Seine to Rouen. And for five years two Christian kings who had been friends in youth and fellow promoters of the most famous crusade in history fought each other like snarling dogs over every foot of debatable border land.

Berengaria had salved her pride. She had stayed in Rome until the world saw her heroic husband come for her, humbly and without his enticing hostage. Inevitably, their passion flamed again and Berengaria—who so loved beauty and home life—lived up and down the duchies in camp and battered castle for his sake. Perhaps her conscience made an atonement of it for her obstinacy. Determined not to grumble, she grew too self-controlled. Her lips, once so prone to laughter, began to fold too tightly in repose. Everyone who cared for them rejoiced over the reblossoming of their romantic love, but they themselves felt in their hearts that the first bloom had been knocked off it by hard words.

So the years passed—tedious for Berengaria and strenuous for Richard—until, besides his mighty dukedoms and his neglected island, he owned more of France than the French king. So much had Richard's feelings changed that news of the death of their mutual enemy, Saladin, came to him as a personal blow, and he knew now that he would never have heart or interest to lead another crusade. So he went on picking one stupid quarrel after another until finally he stumbled upon the one he had been subconsciously hankering after, and the Anglo-Norman army found themselves encamped outside Chalus.

It was a base enough quarrel about a few pieces of gold. A ploughman had turned up a group of golden statues and a vase full of Roman coins on Barbe of Chalus's land, and the exaggerated rumour of it had spread like wildfire across Maine and Anjou.

Seeing that it was Roman gold, it seemed probable that Chalus had hidden it there himself. A clumsy trick out of which to make a test case, for according to feudal law he was obliged to pay part of it to his overlord. And if Richard didn't bother to claim it, and the correct "due" were once paid to Philip, it might be fairly argued that he admitted Philip's right.

But, contrary to Chalus's calculations, Richard did claim it. Comparatively small as the treasure was, he came hurtling down from Gisors and Chalus had to give it up. He had hoped the Rome incident was forgotten and his furtive visit to England unsuspected. But when he sent out a messenger with the massive Roman ornaments everybody was talking about, Richard claimed his castle as well. So there was nothing for it but to pull up his super-strutted drawbridge and lower his double-pronged portcullis. And the sight of such unexpected defiance provided Richard with more zest than he had felt for months.

"Mercadier says this is going to be a mere practice at the butts compared with Gaillon and Freteval," he said to Berengaria the first evening his batering rams got busy. "And as soon as we've taken the place we'll go down to Toulouse and see this new nephew of mine."

"You're very sure Johanna's going to have a boy!" laughed Berengaria.

"We always have boys in my family," he boasted. "Arthur, and little Henry, and now, I'll wager, another Richard!" Berengaria wondered if he were thinking of his own son, Fulk; but he went on cheerfully with his plans. "My mother should be with Johanna by now," he reckoned, notching off the dates on a tally stick. "We'll stay for the christening and then we can take her back with us. I don't like her travelling alone now. The three of us ought to be in England by Michaelmas."

The castle was much stronger than it appeared, and Mercadier's mere practice at the butts looked like turning into a long, wearisome siege. Richard's interest flagged, and he was depressed by a slight return of the ague which plagued him from time to time. And then, one cloudless summer day, the blow fell. One of Raymond's men came galloping into camp with a message from

Eleanor. Richard and Berengaria sprang up to meet him. They clutched like eager children at the letter in his hand. "It ought to be simply *full* of underlining this time!" prophesied Berengaria, almost too impatient to wait while Richard broke the seal. They were too excited to heed the man's stammered words of warning, and it was quite a long time before they could take in the purport of Eleanor's stark words—that Johanna's little son had lived only a few minutes and that Johanna herself—the best loved of all the Plantagenets—was dead.

"But she was so full of life!" protested Berengaria, hating the mocking sunshine and the movement and the flaunting standards her sister-in-law had so loved. She thought of all the months of precious companionship given to her so ungrudgingly in Rome and wailed, "Dear God, what will poor Raymond do?"

Long after it was dark she could hear Richard tramping up and down outside the tent. She checked her own sobs to call to him, and he came in and sat on the edge of the bed. She tried to comfort him, but he just sat there muttering at intervals, "I can't believe it! I can't believe it!" He could see Johanna again as a laughing child, swinging between his own arm and Robin's, begging them to take her to Banbury fair. And their father pinching her cheek and telling her she was worth the whole bunch of them.

Depression settled on the whole camp. Blondel went about like a man stunned and Yvette, who was now his wife, became secretly terrified because she too was pregnant. She didn't want to die in childbirth. She was terribly upset about the Countess, of course, and sorry if she had ever been jealous and horrid to Blondel about the way he worshipped her, but—being a practical little person— all she really wanted was to get back to Fontevrault, where the kind nuns would look after her when her hour came.

Richard and Berengaria ceased to discuss their home-going plans because, in a world without Johanna, every plan seemed empty. Berengaria walked in the fields behind the lines, listened to Yvette's rosy descriptions of Fontevreult, and wrote long letters to Raymond. And while she hugged her grief, Richard—man-like—turned from his. He left the battering-rams and catapults to

Mercadier and sent for the great iron-bound chest in which he kept his building plans. Hour after hour he would pore over the drawings of Château Gaillard, the great castle he had built to protect Rouen.

"Fair, year-old daughter of my brain!" he called it as Blondel helped him unroll the well-worn parchments, clamping them down irreverently with Chalus's golden vase. Years ago Blondel had watched the great walls and towers grow on parchment beneath a master hand until Richard—haggard in some early dawn—had finally thrown down his quill and cried, "She'll grin defiance across the Seine when you and I are dust!" Until the road from Gisors was black with laden carts and the Isle of Andely alive with toiling masons and the whole splendid dream rose before their eyes in solid stone, embodying all that was known of military science and all that was finest in one man's brain. For—unlike his father—Richard had not dissipated his energies in building a plethora of castles, but had patiently, here and there, added, altered, and experimented until he was ready to fling all his architectural knowledge and all his fighting experience into a stronghold that made all the castles of his contemporaries look like antiquated toys.

And now when one petty campaign drew him into another, when for the first time life was becoming a stagnation, he liked to look back to those zestful days when he had spent himself in such absorbing effort. Retracing the cunningly scolloped defences, and the clever, prow-shaped walls of Gaillard's keep, he forgot about the baseness of Chalus. The afternoon heat shimmered like a skipping rope across the plain, and he had sat inside his tent all day, his linen shirt open at his sunburnt throat. He had not even bothered to put on his mail hauberk. Blondel had picked the thing up and was sitting on a stool just outside the doorway mending a broken thong. He might have called the pages or the armourer, for he was Sir Blondel de Cahaignes now. He was glad of his new title for Yvette's sake. As he bent over the hauberk in the warm sunshine, their shared life stretched peacefully before the fertile garden of his mind. They would call their first son Richard and perhaps the King himself would stand godfather. They would have other children, of course, who would play round the manor at Horsted, and in the evening he would sing to them and teach them to make ballads so that the exploits of Richard and Robin would not be forgotten. He would be glad to be done with war and to have time to look after his orchards and his woods and his good Sussex steer; but when his time came to die they would cross the stone feet of his effigy to show he had been a crusader. Blondel had just reached the proud absurdity of admiring his own tomb when an arrow whizzed so close to his head that it almost necessitated his being buried there and then. It spat onto the trampled soil just behind him and stood quivering in the tent doorway.

Richard glanced up from his plans. "Someone drew a long bow then!" he remarked absently.

"The arrow's well barbed, too!" reported Blondel, leaning sideways from his stool to pull at it. "It's that sniper up there on the portcullis battlement."

"A useful marksman—if it's me he wants!" grunted Richard. "Better come inside, hadn't you?" Like most men who had lived through many emergencies together, they wasted few words.

Blondel's anxious gaze shifted from the wicked-looking arrowhead in his hand to the gateway of Chalus. The sun was getting low, and already the outline of the castle began to look like a bit of black scenery carved against the roseate sky. It always did in the late afternoon and it was just the hour when their own white tents made such an excellent target. "I'm afraid it *is* you, Sir," he said. "The man's been at it all the week. Yesterday, you remember, he grazed your horse when you were inspecting that new battering-ram."

Richard was only half listening. "Send one of our best archers to pick him off then," he suggested, forgetting that the sun would be in the man's eyes. It was so unlike him to forget anything to do with war. It must be because he was thinking of Johanna…Blondel got up to give the order, letting the chain mail fall across the stool on which he had been sitting. The heavy mesh of it slithered to the ground with a metallic sigh, like some spineless, discarded woman…If he too had not been grieving about Johanna, he might have persuaded the King to put it on.

Chapter Thirty-Four

BLONDEL HAD NOT BEEN gone many minutes before Richard became aware of someone blocking out the light. He looked up from his parchments to see Berengaria standing in the entrance of their tent; but he saw her only with the vagueness of long habit. The only thing he really noticed about her was that her arms were full of wild flowers. He was concerned for her safety and, like most anxious husbands, spoke irritably. "For God's sake, why must you loiter just there? An arrow struck the very spot only a few minutes ago."

Berengaria came further into the tent. She moved with a sort of weary indifference. Life had driven her a long way since her girlhood in Navarre when she shrank from a cut wrist at a tournament. "One gets so used to arrows and blood and maimed bodies," she said. She stood for a moment bearing the thudding reverberations as Mercadier began battering at a fresh breach, then relaxed with a shrug and sniffed delicately at her flowers. "But the meadows are still lovely where your war machines haven't crushed the buttercups."

"No sane woman would want to wander about picking buttercups beside a besieged castle," snapped Richard.

Berengaria made a separate posy of a few straggling wild roses and remembered that her rare bush ones would just be coming out in Navarre. "Most women have gardens to keep them sane," she reminded him with bitterness.

He laid down his measure with a sigh of exasperation. "*Must* we go all over that again?" he asked. "I'm only trying to tell you that the castle garrison have found our range. This striped tent is too conspicuous. You'd better use Yvette's and Blondel can come in here with me."

Berengaria had to laugh. It was so like him not even to notice how the sun and rain of innumerable battlefields had faded Johanna's gay wedding gift to the drabness of any other tent. She looked round at the littered interior and wondered where she should put her flowers. "I suppose it would be profane to use the *casus belli?*" she suggested, seeing Chalus's vase perched incongruously on the edge of the table as a parchment weight. She laid her flowers beside it and tilted it to examine its earth-stained interior. Instantly the plan Richard was examining sprang back into an exasperating roll. He disentangled it from the sticky stems of sorrel and dog daisies, and carried the pretentious golden thing across to an uncluttered table for her. "You know very well it isn't the vase itself," he said, viewing the fat embossed figures on it with aversion. "It's the principle of the thing. Chalus should have reported it to me, not gloated over it with Philip."

"But he sent it out to you quite civilly when you came for it," objected Berengaria, briskly swilling out his treasure and filling it with water from her ewer. Much as she loathed Chalus, she had no desire to go on punishing him. All she cared about was getting to some settled and civilised habitation.

"He cheated me," declared Richard, wondering if she had really been flattered by the way the beast had hung round after her. "The ploughman who turned it up swears the ground was cluttered with Roman coins and they carried them up to the castle. For all I know there's enough gold up there to build another Château Gaillard!" It was unspoken knowledge between them that Berengaria hated the place. It had come to mean to him what her children should have meant. But he picked up the main plan and held it aloft. He knew it to be the complete answer to every general's dreams, and it was inconceivable to him that anyone could look upon it without appreciating its perfection. He himself had gazed at it so often, both in stone and on parchment, that he only spoke his thoughts aloud when he said, "When I'm dead this lovely, solid daughter of my brain will stand to protect my land in place of the sons my body has been denied."

Berengaria dropped the gold vase with a crash. It went rolling behind their bed. It might have rolled back to Barbe for all Richard really cared as he swung round and caught her in his arms. Even the parchment towers of Andely rolled unheeded too. "Forgive me!" he entreated. "It was like my clumsiness to say that! I know it's worse for you, sweet. And at least I haven't had to lose you, my dear, my very dear, like poor Raymond lost Johanna!"

Berengaria allowed herself the relief of tears. "It seems so unbelievable that anyone so gay and kind should die!" she cried brokenly against his shoulder.

Richard stroked her hair and said gently, "I am so thankful Mother got there in time—and to be with Raymond afterwards." It was all the comfort he could find.

Berengaria gathered up her scattered flowers and tried to be bright and practical. "You do think she'll come here on her way back to England, don't you? I'm s-sorry about the vase."

Richard picked it up absently and began putting his plans back in the open chest. He was beginning to wonder if all this pother about vengeance was worth the time it stole from one's life. If it hadn't been for this trumped-up business of Chalus, they too might have been in time to see Johanna again. "I'll have every man of them hanged!" he vowed savagely.

Berengaria gave tongue to something which had always puzzled her. "Why do you let hatred for Philip sour your life and yet—even now you know about the money—you can forgive that treacherous thief John?"

"I can go back any time and undo what he has done," explained Richard confidently. "But what Philip did cost me—Jerusalem." He stood staring down at his possessions in the great coffer, but he was really seeing the grey river lapping the walls of Westminster, the homeliness of Oxford, and the windswept sweetness of St. Martyr's. A sudden nostalgia for his island assailed him. He shut the lid with a bang, and went and perched on Berengaria's table, pulling her hands impatiently from the buttercups and daisies. His green eyes were shining. "'Garia, I'll be glad when we get back to England!" he said, with sudden urgency.

Berengaria stared at him unresponsively and pulled away her hands. He was saying it just five years too late. "Back!" she echoed coldly. "You forget I've never been there."

"Then you shouldn't have sent me that crushing letter from Rome."

"You had that Cypriot girl with you." It was all so long ago that she found she could speak of it almost objectively.

Richard reddened beneath his tan. "I told you I was sorry about that," he reminded her. "But still you wouldn't come."

"You seemed to be enjoying quite a blaze of bachelor popularity without me."

"How could I help it if a lot of love-sick women followed me about?"

"Oh, well, you know you adored it all, Richard!" she said, finishing her floral effect and pushing the vase from her. "And if only I had known you were going to cram all the work you owed to England into eight short months, I would have come instead of behaving like a jealous fool. It looks as if I shall be the only English queen who never saw England!"

"No, no, my dear. We're really going this time—as soon as I've exterminated this rat who dared to make eyes at you." He put an arm round her waist and whispered against her cheeks "I promise you—"

But Berengaria turned from his blandishments and sat down on the end of the bed. "For eight years you've been making promises, and I've been trying to live on them," she told him, determined for once to disentangle facts from passion. "Didn't you promise, that blue and gold morning in Cyprus, to love and cherish me? Is this cherishing?" She looked round the tent contemptuously. Each time she moved, discarded pieces of armour clinked together on the bedcover behind her and the rich Persian prayer mats de Lusignon had brought her for a wedding present were kicked askew by the constant tramping of dusty feet. She thought of the ordered graciousness and mental stimulous of life in Pamplona and realised that she and Richard had begun to live inwardly with their own thoughts because they had nothing fresh to say to each other. It riled her to know that, had they lived peaceably in London or Rouen, her own accomplishments need not have been frustrated. "I seem to have no one to talk to but Yvette," she complained. "And I miss Johanna so!" She saw Richard wince, but she was in the state of nervous strain when the very dumbness of his grief annoyed her. "Oh, I know she was yours!" she flared. "But what time have you to fret? Even when you come in to meals you are planning some fresh sortie. I only have the real you when you are too sick to sit in a saddle. Or when you're too tired to do anything but seek oblivion in some woman's arms. Any woman who is fool enough to follow you from one foul battlefield to another!"

Richard gripped her gesticulating wrists. "It's a lie!" he protested, livid with rage.

In spite of her imprisoned hands, she went on hysterically. The dam of her composure had suddenly snapped, and her long-pent grievances flowed over him in full spate, gathering momentum from the lashing of her unconsidered words. "It's true! It's true!" she insisted. "What do you care for my thoughts? What use have you for my leisure? Except that there are silk trappings to this bed and a lot of silly heraldic beasts, how am I different from those bedraggled strumpets following the baggage wagons?"

Such wild talk was so unlike her that Richard's anger turned to bewilderment. "I'd no idea—" he began, letting go her hands. But she interrupted him, mockingly, "That's just the tragedy, isn't it? Two people living together—thinking they know each other—and they've no idea…"

She was right, of course. It had been like that between himself and Robin. Richard saw now that all these years, while he had chosen their way of living, his wife's nerves must have been getting like the ropes of his catapults—more and more taut until they relaxed suddenly and let fly. He noticed how the hands he had crushed so roughly went to her temples as the biggest battering-ram of all thudded against the tough masonry of the outer wall. "Hi, you, Thomas," he shouted to the sentry outside, "tell someone to ask Captain Mercadier to stop that infernal din for a while."

The sentry disappeared, but inside the tent Berengaria's voice went on. The suffering of her sensitiveness must all be laid bare at last. "And what about all your fine promises?" she railed. "The poor people who gave all they possessed to pay your ransom—and lionised you as no hard-working, stay-at-home king has ever been lionised?"

He tried to soothe her—to tell her that it would be only a few days now before he mopped up Chalus's garrison. But she got up—tense as a tragedy queen—and asked with contemptuous vehemence if he had ever considered what it meant to a woman brought up as she had been to live for eight years within sight and sound of his butcherings.

Like most good women driven beyond the limit of their endurance, she was being bitterly unfair. He took her gently by the arms. "That first night in Limassol I warned you that war is my trade," he reminded her.

"As mothering is mine," she countered. She struggled to get away from him and, failing, turned her head aside. Her lovely voice was low and monotonous as if she were repeating an oft-told tale. "That day at Acre—when you slaughtered three thousand bound prisoners—your son turned from you in my womb. And when your light-o'-love held up the Saracen's head to frighten me—he died unborn."

She had not meant to tell him that, and now that she had said the words, nothing could ever recall the knowledge. Richard's horrified remorse was patent. He pulled her close, his unhappy eyes searching her white face. For the first time he really saw her as a tired woman and not as the radiant girl he had married. "'Garia! I didn't know," he swore. "My mind was blind with rage because those Moslems had tricked me. I've dragged you through hell, haven't I? I ought to have taken better care of you. I'm ashamed." Because his passion for her was unquenchable, he began kissing her closed eyelids. "But we've known Heaven too, beloved!" he exulted. "The still desert nights…The stars at dawn…Surely no woman since Eve can have been so passionately loved?" His lips crushed hers. His strength bruised her small, soft breasts. But for the first time she fought the compelling ecstasy for which she had sacrificed so much. Her head went back defiantly against his arm, her eyes met his accusingly. "As an antidote to war," she jeered, hurting him through that part of their love which had been most perfect. "Even under those stars I remembered your arms were brute strong from killing, and between your kisses I've tried not to think about the distorted dead. Don't you suppose your damnably caressing hands have often set me wondering how it must feel to lie helpless beneath your plunging sword? I've imagined the smell of blood on that persuasive mouth of yours until its passion sickened me..." She stopped short, aghast at the things she was saying— knowing them to be only half true. She had been so utterly in love with him that often and often she had forgotten everything but joy in his masterful tenderness. Her eyes fell before his. "Oh, Richard, so much has been spoiled for me!" she added, more accurately. "I wish we could have lived at peace!"

"God forgive me! We will live differently," he muttered, stroking the sable smoothness of her hair. "Only have patience..."

The storm of her self-pity was spent. The lost dimple he loved began, rather tremulously, to dent her cheek. "Perhaps it would have been better if I hadn't tried to be patient for eight years," she suggested. "For now I seem to have none left."

He drew her gently back to the bed, and they sat there side by-side, holding each other's hand like a pair of lost children. "What do you want me to do?" he asked, without rancour.

"Let me take Yvette to the nuns at Fontevrault. She oughtn't to stay here much longer, and she always thinks of that as her home place. In a way it's yours too, isn't it?"

"Yes," agreed Richard, thinking of the solemn abbey with the carved tombs of all the Angevins since his great-grandfather Faulk.

"Yvette says the nuns have a beautiful walled garden with cool, clipped walks—and cloisters and libraries—and fruit trees and rose bushes. The roses will just be in bloom." Berengaria's cheeks were pink again and her eyes shining with anticipation.

"Now you look more like my kind tournament princess," he teased.

She put her arms round his neck and hid her face in shame. "Please, please, Richard, forgive me for all the cruel things I have said—and for leaving you," she implored. "But I just can't stand this tent another day! Honestly, I think if I have to look at another wounded soldier I shall go mad."

He patted her shoulder encouragingly, but without any sort of passion. "You are just worn out," he said, remembering how many of his wounded she had comforted. It never had been easy for him to say he was sorry, but he began twisting the ruby ring on her wedding finger. He had had it made very hurriedly for her in Cyprus, so when he said, "I was fool enough to put a precious stone into a cheap setting," she wasn't sure if he was alluding to the ring or to herself. And, hearing someone singing outside, he got up almost immediately and strolled across the tent. She would never know how much or how little she had hurt him. "Come in, Blondel!" he called. "I want you to take the Queen and that home-sick little wife of yours to Fontevrault."

Blondel needed no second bidding. He had hoped that his son would be born at Horsted de Cahaignes but clearly they would not be home in time, and this was certainly the next best plan. "Yvette will be delighted, Sir!" he said, gratefully.

"Let's tell her," suggested Berengaria.

They called to her through the covered way that had been made between the two tents, and she appeared with some of the Queen's half-folded garments still in her hands. The briskness had gone from her step and her small, round face had the hushed look of a grave Madonna. Directly she heard the good news, she went to where Richard was standing and kissed his hand. "You have always been so good to me!" she exclaimed.

"How soon do you think you can be ready, little lady?" he asked. And when she answered ingenuously that everything was already packed he burst out laughing. It was such a complete give-away for Berengaria. "See how they've been plotting against us!" he said to Blondel. They were still laughing when the sniper on the battlements tried again. Yvette saw the arrow coming and screamed, but before Richard could screen her it had passed clean through her long, hanging sleeve. The next moment she was in her husband's comforting arms and both men, who were used to working unconcernedly in a hail of arrows, were in a veritable fret of anxiety about one that had barely touched her.

"It's that damned sniper again," complained Blondel.

"Hasn't anyone split his impudent carcass yet?" demanded Richard angrily. He strode outside and called to the sentry, "Here, Thomas, lend me your bow and I'll do the job myself!"

"Not without your hauberk, Richard!" remonstrated Berengaria, who had begun gathering up a few favourite possessions to take to Fontevrault. But he waved it away and called back over his shoulder, "I'll be back directly." So Blondel unhooked his long, pointed shield from the tent pole and took it out to him instead, while the two women went to Yvette's tent to finish their preparations for the journey.

All the time Richard was selecting a shaft from the quiver Thomas held for him, he was giving Blondel final instructions for their journey. "Have the horse brought round to the back of your own tent and get the women away as soon as possible. It'll be cooler for them riding now. Take what money you want and go by easy stages because of Yvette." He shot his left arm like a bolt through the leather loops inside his shield and tried Thomas's bow rather absently against his cheek. "And be sure to take a safe escort for the Queen whether Mercadier can spare 'em or not."

Blondel waited long enough to see the arrow fly. Men always did wait to see Richard shoot. It was one of those utterly satisfying sights, like a ship in full sail or a laden hay wain. But this time, although he got the range, the arrow went wide.

Chapter Thirty-Five

THOMAS, THE SENTRY, COUNTED himself a lucky man. He was in for a private view of what promised to be one of the finest duels in marksmanship he had ever seen. Like most Englishman, he was no mean archer himself; but here were two protagonists right above his class who could pick each other off at three hundred yards and more. And it was his own bow that one of them was using. He'd always thought a lot of that bow but now, he reckoned, he'd be able to tell the whole village when he got home, "The King hisself used that there bit o' yew!"

True, the King had muffed his first shot. "The target be high an' the sun be low," chuckled Thomas excusingly. Come to that, the bow wasn't up to the tall Plantagenet's height—but he was too fine a sportsman to mention the fact. He just waited with braced muscles and narrowed eyes for the riposte, and when it came he laughed and caught it on his shield. The arrow point struck the belly of one of his painted leopards and had he not judged the trajectory so expertly it would certainly have pierced his own. "Good shot!" he yelled good-naturedly, for all the world as if he were at some friendly tournament. It was such a remarkably good shot and his opponent exposing himself so recklessly against the reddening sky that Richard stopped to wave his congratulations before turning away. "It would be a pity to finish such a first-class marksman," he said, handing back the bow. "'Fraid my eye's out to-day, Thomas, anyway."

But Thomas hadn't yet had his fill of excitement. Everyone else seemed to be either swarming excitedly round a fresh breach made by the battering rams or hurriedly cleaning themselves up to escort the Queen. "More like 'tis your heart that's heavy, Sir," he ventured, emboldened by their isolation. "There was no one like our Princess Johanna."

Richard glared at him. He may have been touched by the man's clumsy sympathy, but he preferred to keep his troubles to himself. He was half-way back to the tent when the abashed sentry suddenly sprang forward shouting, "Look out, Sir! He's taking aim again."

In spite of his forty-two years and increasing weight, Richard spun round with the instant reaction of a man used to carrying his life in his hand. He laughed in his ruddy beard because the impudent sniper had picked up a battered frying pan to use as a shield. It was the spectacular sort of thing he might have done himself when he was ten years younger. He was in time to shout "Good shot!" again—to wave and dodge behind his shield. But this time, in his enthusiasm for a fellow sportsman, he reversed the process—and dodged a fraction of a second too late. Just a fraction of a second. And the three golden leopards that had crouched and snarled at his enemies through so many bloody conflicts failed to protect him. The arrow pierced the careless opening of his shirt and drove down between the strong muscles of sunburnt neck and shoulder. It drove the grin on his lips into a grimace of agony. "He's got me this time, the persistent dog!" he groaned.

But he wasn't going to let the persistent dog know it—nor any of his less venturesome backers. For all Richard knew that cur Chalus himself might be up there skulking behind the battlements, bribing the man with his filthy gold to get Berengaria Plantagenet widowed. Richard turned on his heel and walked back to his tent as if nothing had happened.

The pride of that day was done for poor Thomas. He threw down his cherished bow and ran after the King. "For God's sake, Sir, let me pull it out!" he entreated, without thought for the grave responsibility he offered to take. But Richard had caught sight of

Berengaria at the back of their tent, so he said hurriedly, "Not now, my good fellow!"

Thomas's crusading training held. Hadn't the Hospitallers impressed upon them all never to leave an arrow embedded in their flesh? "But, Sir, it might be poisoned!" he protested, following at the King's heels like a faithful dog. "Why won't you let me pull it out?"

Richard shook him off; but in return for common-sense, which at any other time he would have commended, he vouchsafed a reasonable answer. "Because it will make a horrible mess, and the Queen hates the sight of blood. She will be gone almost directly, and we can see to it then." The irony of it, he thought, that all these years she should have forced herself to bear such sights and the strain of it should have broken her just as his own turn came! Remembering how she had just said that she couldn't endure the sight of another wounded soldier, he went and stood in the dimmest corner of the tent with his back to her. Under the linen of his shirt he could feel the blood trickling, warm and sluggish, from his left shoulder; but he reckoned that as long as he kept still she probably would not notice anything amiss.

"I've come to say 'Good-bye,'" she announced. Already the prospect of a holiday had restored the old lilt to her voice. She seemed inordinately glad to be going. That hurt unreasonably... Because, of course, she didn't know...He could hear her behind him raking over her dressing chest for some forgotten bit of finery. At Fontevrault it would be worth while making herself exquisite again. "Oh, won't it be wonderful," she laughed gaily, "to sit at a well-appointed table and not get the gravy spilt in one's lap every time a catapult goes off!"

"Yes—wonderful," agreed Richard, without enthusiasm. He wasn't so sure about the trickle—his shirt felt sodden. He tried to cover the protruding arrow head with his left hand, pressing the lips of the wound together. It was agony; but he knew that if she guessed he had been hit she would stay. And he wanted so dreadfully to keep her that if she didn't go quickly—now, while he had enough strength to be obstinate—he would let her stay. "Hadn't you better be starting if you want to reach some decent sort of habitation before sundown?" he suggested irritably.

"Why on earth does he stand there like a dummy instead of taking me in his arms?" thought Berengaria. But after all, she had said things to him that were hard for a man to bear. She lingered, shamefaced and self-conscious, trying to think of something suitable to say. "You have made these two young things very happy, you know, Richard," she told him. "Are you sure you can spare Blondel?"

"Perfectly," agreed Richard, politely. Berengaria had so often heard him speak like that when he was trying to get rid of an importunate deputation that she was almost glad when he added with very human resentment, "It's a good thing I can make *someone* happy!"

She went to him and pressed her cheek passionately against his right arm. "Darling, it was only because my nerves were torn to shreds—"

"I know," he agreed at once. "You've always been good and beautiful and sweet."

He spoke with such low intensity that she said laughingly, "You sound as if you were writing my epitaph!" Almost timidly she slid her palm down his sleeve until it touched his own. But he did not respond—he, whose body had always been like plucked harp strings to her caresses! He just squeezed her coaxing fingers and smiled down at her. "Good-bye, 'Garia. I hope the good nuns will spoil you unconscionably. I shall like to think of you—as I first saw you—sitting among the roses." His voice sounded cheerful enough, but there was a note of finality in the words. So there was nothing for it but to go to Fontevrault uncomforted and unkissed. Berengaria turned away and gathered up her riding cloak. He might at least have offered to put it round her shoulders, she thought. He had a way of tucking her into it which made her feel precious. But he just stood there with his back to her, swaying irritatingly on his heels. She sighed and looked round the familiar interior. Now that she was going each separate furnishing called to her with the heart-break of homely habit. Even the horrible iron-spiked mace at which she used to shudder seemed part of Richard. It was unfair the way the very things she had hated now held her. She must ignore them. She had given years to her husband's warmongering, and now it had broken her and she must go for a little while to rest mind and body in that blessed conventual peace, to forget all the ugly things she had seen, to be with women again and talk of the pleasant things that interested them. But she still lingered, fingering the little bunch of wild roses she had gathered behind the battlefield. "You'll come to me at Fontevrault, won't you, Richard?" she asked.

"Yes," he said.

"No more broken promises?" she insisted laughingly.

"No. Somehow or other—I will come." There was a great weariness in Richard's voice, but this time his promise carried conviction. Berengaria noticed how he passed a hand over his eyes and thought perhaps he too would be glad to be done with war. It would be lovely to have him there, unpreoccupied with affairs of war or state; for in spite of all the gardens and libraries of Fontevrault, the centre of the universe must be for her this faded tent until he came. Glancing down at their bed, her lips curled into a tender smile. She knew just what shape mound his long body would make under the huddled covers, sleeping this night alone; and she tossed the roses onto his pillow. They would be a message for him after she was gone, reminding him of a hundred sweetnesses they had shared.

Chapter Thirty-Six

CASTLE AND MEADOW HAD gone black before Richard's eyes, but he was still listening intently. As soon as he could hear the women's voices and men scuffling with baggage in the other tent his rigid stance sagged—he snatched blindly at a trailing wimple to staunch the blood that would spurt as he removed the arrow. Without waiting to call Thomas he took a firm grip on the head of it and pulled upwards—but the shaft was widely barbed and grated excruciatingly against his collar-bone. He noticed that it was a squat thick phéon, made for use with a cross-bow and—as the experienced old soldier had suggested—it might be poisoned. Fear rose hot within him. He wrenched at it frantically and the arrow-head snapped off in his hand. Steadying himself by the tent pole, he stumbled to a chair.

When he regained consciousness the sweat of agony was clammy on his forehead and Thomas—his face sallow with fear—was leaning across him with a cup of wine. The warmth of the wine crept through Richard's veins, reviving him. "It broke off flush with the flesh," he said stupidly, looking down at the arrow-head in his hand. At first the words had no implication—he merely remarked on the fact objectively. Then his heartbeats quickened. He felt over the mouth of the wound with quick, exploring fingers and withdrew them only slightly reddened because the cavity was sealed by the broken shaft. He let Berengaria's veil fall to the floor. "There's nothing left to catch hold of now," he muttered, and found himself searching Thomas's face for corroboration of his own thoughts.

"Hadn't I better send after Sir Blondel?" the man implored.

Richard recalled the brisk clip-clop of that departing caval-cade, his wife's spontaneous laughter, and the relief of Blondel's anxiety. Suppose the shock of being recalled by bad news were to kill Yvette's baby—just as the brutalities of his warfare had brought abortion to Berengaria's? His cruelties came crowding upon him like the swift recollections of a drowning man, and he wanted to keep his kindness intact. "No, no, not Blondel," he decided. "But fetch the local doctor—I saw him about the camp just now. And Captain Mercadier. And don't let them make any fuss…" It was damnable that this should happen just when they had no proper surgeon and there wasn't a soul of his own about.

Mercadier was the next best thing. Mercadier, whom his father had made constable of Dover Castle and who had been his own right-hand man throughout the crusade. He came running into the tent now, his lean, chain-meshed legs ludicrously outstripping the doctor's portly ones.

"They've got me this time, Mercadier!" said Richard. The black-jowled Gascon jerked a knife from his belt and cut away the shoulder of his surcoat without ceremony, his practised eye summing up Richard's chances at a glance. "You asked for it, going out there without your mail!" was his laconic comment. He always looked fiercest on the rare occasions when he was moved. The fussy little local practitioner pushed between them. "Let me look," he panted consequentially. And, having looked, kept repeating nervously, "Tch! Tch! A bad business. A bad business."

Richard's pallid face flushed with annoyance. "Damn you, I know it's a bad business!" he broke out, trying to endure the man's ineffectual probing. "But surely you can cut away the flesh and pull it out?"

The man was flustered at being sent for to such a famous patient. "It might mean severing an artery," he objected dubiously.

"I've seen it done scores of times in Syria!" scoffed Mercadier impatiently.

"To the common soldier perhaps."

"Meaning you haven't nerve enough to give me the same chance?" growled Richard.

Mercadier said something under his breath about "our all being common soldiers here" and dipped his knife into a bucket of boiling water Thomas had brought. For a moment it looked as if he would take the matter into his own hands and botch up some sort of operation himself; but, seeing the medico's hands dabbling delicately with bowls and herbs and pestle, he allowed himself to be overawed by the mysteries of the profession. At least the old busy-body was able to concoct a poppy extract to ease the pain. So he contented himself with saying to him brusquely, "There's only one man can tell you if the arrow was poisoned or not, Old Cautious, and that's the fellow who shot it." And just then Thomas created a diversion. He had been alternately waiting on the doctor and hovering in the doorway in his capacity as sentry, and now had good news for the King. "Sir," he called excitedly, "our fellows have widened that breach. Those French dogs are lowering their drawbridge at last and the portcullis is going up."

The captain joined him at the entrance. "It's true," he confirmed. "Chalus has surrendered!"

The news had come so suddenly—and so narrowly too late. "If they'd only given in an hour sooner Berengaria and I might have been riding to Fontevrault—together," thought Richard. Realising how his captain must be torn between conflicting duties, he made a feeble sign of dismissal. "And remember—every man's head for this!"

Mercadier crossed himself surreptitiously. "It would be an evil thing to have on one's conscience—" he muttered.

But Richard knew well enough that the ruthless old ruffian thought the order indecent only because it came from a man who might be going very quickly to his Maker. "I have had worse," he remarked with a smile. "A whole neglected kingdom, for instance. So mop up every man of 'em, Mercadier! Except that sniper. Bring him here, will you?"

The little doctor was glad when the Gascon went. He didn't want his shrewd eyes watching everything he did, nor his sharp tongue telling the world afterwards that he really wasn't sure *what* to do. Bandages and a sleeping draught could do no harm, and the surgeons from Rouen would probably arrive before it was too late—providing the arrow wasn't poisoned. So he got Thomas to help him support the King to bed.

"If the arrow is only barbed I will do my best," he promised, in common humanity. "But if your sniper says it is poisoned—" He did not finish the sentence but began arranging some medical paraphernalia for the night.

Richard raised himself on his right elbow. His eyes held unmasked anxiety. "And if it *is* poisoned? Mind you, man, I want the truth."

"If it *is* poisoned," answered the doctor, without looking up from the bowl in which he was washing his hands, "it would only cause you much useless pain." That much, at least, he was sure of.

Richard sank back against the pillows. He was glad when they brought the sniper and, with a great scuffling, threw him to the floor of the tent.

"Get up, chien d'un chien!" ordered Mercadier, kicking the prostrate figure with his mailed boot.

Chalus's man rose slowly to his feet. His clothes were torn from his back and his face was bleeding. He had just seen every other man of his garrison killed, and Chalus's wicked black head rolling into the moat like garbage; and he took it for granted that he himself had been singled out for a far worse fate. But he was still defiant.

Richard was surprised at his extreme youth. "What is your name?" he asked.

"Bertrand de Gourdon," answered the young man, flinging back his disordered black hair.

"You are a very fine marksman, de Gourdon," approved Richard, his voice quiet and steady as if he were presenting a tournament prize. "Was your arrow poisoned?"

For the first time the young man's nerve failed. He looked round at the tense faces of his captors like a trapped animal and passed his tongue over his bruised lips before he could bring himself to speak. His eyes came back to Richard. "Yes," he said distinctly, as if they two were alone.

Instantly, a dozen hands were at his throat, choking the life out of him. But the King himself stopped them. Above the blood beating in his eardrums, de Gourdon heard his voice as if from a long way off asking, "Tell me, de Gourdon, why were you so determined to kill me?"

De Gourdon had been brought up to picture him as a giant of cruelty and evil. He hadn't expected to see an ordinarily good-looking man, human and likeable, suffering as uncomplainingly as anyone else.

"You killed my father and my brothers," he said sulkily, "and I wanted to know if it is true what men say about you—"

"And what do they say?" asked Richard wearily. He had heard most of the fantastic rumours, and at the moment he almost wished some of them were true.

"That no mortal man can kill you because from the devil you came and to the devil you will return."

Richard chuckled weakly at the horror-stricken faces around him. He knew that this bombastic youth had only said to his face what many of his own men half believed in their hearts. The legend provided a perennial source of badinage among his intimates, and he himself never tried to discourage it because he was shrewd enough to realise how it had helped to build up his military success. "If I were you, Mercadier," he said, "I'd let the young cockerel go free. He might teach some of your archers to shoot straight." And that was the nearest Richard ever came to reproaching them all for not picking off the sniper before their slackness cost him his life.

"Do you mean—go free—*to live?*" asked de Gourdon in a croaking sort of whisper, which cracked and ran up an octave. Richard's eyes were closed but the smooth auburn head nodded assent. Bertrand de Gourdon was very young—very emotional. He had been through a terrible ordeal. And now reaction brought him to his knees, sobbing hysterically against the bed. "Again and again I've tried to kill you," he blurted out, between tearing sobs. "I'm helpless in your tent, and you make me a gift of life. Christ Himself must have taught you such generosity!"

Richard patted his shoulder tolerantly. His thoughts were back in Jaffa. "On the contrary," he confessed drily, "I learned it from an infidel."

De Gourdon got up and walked in a dazed sort of way to the doorway. The evening sunlight and the long purple shadows looked like a gift from Heaven. Because he had not hoped to see them again, he turned back to give thanks. "Life is so precious," he muttered apologetically, "when one is young."

"And when one is not so young!" murmured Richard. But no one heard him. They were busy hustling the sniper away to torture him. Mercadier made no attempt to interfere. He went back to his master's bedside, concerned with no other man's pain. When their eyes met the King's were glazing over with weariness. "Good night, my friend," he said, swallowing a sleeping-draught without protest.

"It is still afternoon," said Mercadier gruffly.

"Is it?" murmured Richard listlessly. "But it's getting dark—and cold. And I am tired." He lay for a few moments with closed eyes, then roused himself sufficiently to look with something of his old fierceness at his inefficient doctor. "Oh, I know you're supposed to stay with me because I'm a king and not a common soldier!" he jibed. "But I prefer to be quite alone. I've so little time—and so much—to remember."

He turned on his right side and seemed to sleep almost at once. Mercadier went out without a word. There was the re-garrisoning of the castle to see to, and striking camp for home—even if it all seemed meaningless now. The doctor was only too glad to go. He had been fetched from the first bite of his supper and was hungry.

Thomas the sentry was hungry too. Officially, his hours of guard were over, but the whole camp was so disorganised that they had forgotten to relieve him. He could have appealed to the departing Captain, of course, but he hadn't done so. Very soon now he would be back in his Kentish village and there would be years in which to sleep and eat. But there might not be many hours left in which to serve this famous Plantagenet. Home-spun as he was, he sensed the significance of the brief, high episode of history. So he lit a torch and stuck it in a sconce fixed to the middle tent pole where it vied with the departing daylight. When he had hung the King's shield on the hook below it he fancied, in the fitful light, that the leopards had a shamed and sullen look.

Never in his life had old Thomas slept on anything grander than straw but, in spite of the intimate possessions of royalty around him, he felt in his untutored way that the place looked forlorn—the way his own hovel of a cottage looked when his wife was away from home. If only the Queen hadn't gone—or Sir Blondel...Thomas glanced furtively towards the still figure on the bed and wondered if he too felt the tragedy of their departure. Awkwardly, embarrassed by his clumsy shoes, he began tidying the tent—picking up a chair the guards had knocked over, folding a garment here and putting away a crock there, the way he supposed a woman would. He hung up Richard's jewelled belt and bundled away his bloodstained shirt, and when he came to the bed he caught sight of Berengaria's posy half crushed beneath the patient's ruffled head. And because the stems were sharp with thorns he leaned over to retrieve it. He was still holding its fragility between his hoary fingers and breathing hard with caution when he became aware that the King's eyes were open, watching him. "It be just a few wilting rosebuds, Sir," he explained hastily, with the peasant's instinctive fear of being caught pilfering.

He was about to throw them away when the King stretched out a hand for it. "It smells of Navarre," Thomas heard him say drowsily.

The stars were beginning to come out when the old man-at-arms went outside again. Everything was still and peaceful. No more battering and cursing and shouting. Only from inside the tent he could still hear the King's voice. Rambling, he supposed. But Richard was remembering—with the rose buds pressed to his lips and the far-off perfume of Navarre in his nostrils.

He had more to remember than most men, and Life came back to him in vivid patches. The good warm smell of harness leather—and lances glittering in the sun. A girl's warm, brown eyes and the first strength of manhood—all the intoxicating joy of untried life…"That hulk de Barre ought to have beaten me, but I was straining my heart out for her smile. And afterwards she touched my sweating flesh with her cool hands. 'One day, Richard Plantagenet,' she said, 'you will leave a wound too long. And then—perhaps—you will die.' And, by the living heart of God, she was right. But I didn't mean to die yet. I haven't finished living. I meant to go back—to England…"

Chapter Thirty-Seven

THOMAS KEPT GUARD THROUGH the weary night. Men came and went and whispered; but towards midnight he had his reward. There was a stir of arrival—lights swaying nearer in the darkness—and approaching in the middle of a gesticulating group, the hooded figure of a woman. At first Thomas praised God, thinking someone had defied the King's orders and ridden after the Queen and Blondel. Then a raised lantern showed him that the woman was Eleanor of Aquitaine.

The Queen Mother was nearly eighty and reluctantly travelled by litter these days. Two of her sons had been taken from her in their restless hey-day, she had come straight from the death-bed of her daughter, and now the unthinkable thing had just been told her—that Richard, the light of her heart, must be snuffed out in all his splendid strength before she could slip away in her infirmity. She dispersed her informants with a gesture and approached the tent alone.

"Has he been told I am here?" she asked of the heavy-eyed sentry.

Thomas moved aside and held back the tent flap for her. "No, Madam. He has been asleep for hours. And before that he seemed to be wandering." He followed her respectfully into the tent with a fresh torch, and because he was a person of no account he was privileged to witness their meeting. While he was crushing out the spent torch he saw the King begin to stir and heard him complaining in a thick, drugged sort of voice,

"Didn't I tell you nobody was to come in? Who is it?" And heard the old Queen laugh and say briskly, "The one person who will always come, Richard." Before Thomas went the King had raised himself to stare joyfully at the beloved figure standing at the bottom of his bed.

The sleeping hour was theirs—the faded striped canvas a curtain against the intrusion of yesterday's and to-morrow's world. Eleanor moved round the side of the bed, smoothing the covers and turning his pillow just as she had done when he and Robin were small. "I was on my way up from Toulouse," she explained, striving to speak normally. When he was tidy and composed she added, "You know about Johanna? You had my message?"

He nodded, but waking to find Eleanor there had been so good that at first he could do nothing but follow her movements with vast contentment.

"It was a boy—and they meant to call him Richard," Eleanor went on, talking to cover his weakness. "And Johanna wanted me to tell you that you gave her the best husband any woman ever had."

"Because she was so furious with me at the time," smiled Richard. "Did she—suffer much?" His own pain was much easier for him to bear than the thought of hers.

"If she did, something seemed to sustain her. And when she came to die—she who loved life so much—her eyes were shining and she held out her arms as if she were going to meet a friend. I know she and Raymond were very happy these last years together. Yet when he had laid her back on the pillow he said, 'I only warmed myself at the bright, unquenchable flame of her spirit—I never really possessed her.'"

"Poor devil!"

"I never saw a man so heart-broken. Luckily Ida had begged to come and help Johanna. She herself has suffered and seems to understand how he feels and to be able to comfort him. But when he hears about you—" A good sleep had brought more normal colour to Richard's face so that his mother found it difficult to believe that even the Rouen surgeons would not be able to save him. "You don't *look* so bad, Dickon!" she said involuntarily.

He laughed almost comfortably. "Lift me up a bit so that we can talk."

She sponged his face and gave him a drink and added Berengaria's great embroidered pillow to his own. "Where *is* Berengaria?" she asked, glancing towards the inner tent. She supposed her daughter-in-law to be resting. No one had dared to tell her that he was quite alone.

Richard's finely shaped hands lay outside the coverlet still holding the little wilted bunch of roses. "Half way to Fontevrault, I hope," he said, speaking more strongly.

"You mean—she left you—now?"

"Of course not, darling. I sent her. With Blondel and Yvette. It was all arranged before this happened, so that Yvette should get proper attention. Wish I'd thought of it sooner—Berengaria needed a change, you know…"

But Eleanor wasn't listening to his defence. Her arms went round him suddenly, trying to hold him back. "Oh, why did you send Blondel away?" she cried, in a rare outburst of emotion. "Somehow I feel he would never have let you die!"

Richard held her gently with his good right arm. When she looked up remorsefully she found him smiling at her faux pas. "So they've told you?" he said quietly.

Eleanor straightened herself and pushed back the short white curls disordered by her journey. "I met the doctor outside there," she told him. "He says the poison may take hours. He looks a fool—but probably he's right." She stood for a few moments fingering one of the quaint white stags she had embroidered with such happy care and asked with embarrassment, "Richard, would you like me to go now and have them send you a priest?"

To prevent her doing so he imprisoned one of her hands. "No, dear. Not yet. There will be time enough for priests," he assured her. "And each moment alone with you—is so precious now. Won't you sit where I can see the torch-light on your hair? I would rather make my last confession to the same dear, worldly woman who heard my first."

She took off her cloak and settled herself in his chair. "Oughtn't it to belong to Berengaria?" she said, hugging the preciousness of her hour.

"It is too ugly," said Richard. "I've made her suffer enough."

"What you mean is I'm too wicked to shock!" laughed Eleanor. "But perhaps it's something in the sight of God that you still want me."

"Haven't we all wanted you—always?" he said slowly, brought face to face with the realisation of how much she had shaped his life. "You used to evoke for us such splendid, shining dreams. And now I've lived some of them—and some of them I've tarnished with self-love and lust and hatred. There was Philip—and Chalus whom I hated. And the mother of my fine bastard Fulk—and that little witch Ida—and women whose names I don't remember. All I know about them now is that nothing they gave me was worth the hurt they gave my wife..."

Eleanor sat very still with the light on her hair and her hands in her lap. Every sin was the heritage of her passionate union with Henry of Anjou. And before ever she had met him, while Louis the Saint was at his prayers, she too had known the thrill of Syrian nights. It was not for her to pass judgment. "There were also the splendid battles when you went crusading for the Christ," she reminded him.

"I should have been nearer to Him—if I had been killed in one of them," sighed Richard. "Somehow I never thought of dying like this—in my bed—safely shut in with you." He looked round at the shadows shifting over the familiar table and chests that Thomas had tidied. "Why, it might be the old Tower room at Oxford!"

"With Henry and Johanna and John—"

"And Robin and Hodierna and Blondel." He told over their names slowly as if he were saying good-bye to each. "What Hodierna used to call a Plantagenet party!"

"Blondel will break his heart that he wasn't here."

"Yvette will mend it," prophesied Richard. "Funny, isn't it, how some people are constructive and others just destructive? I seem to have been breaking things ever since I can remember. My father's plans—and Robin's ideals—and Berengaria's happiness…" His voice trailed off into tiredness. "I meant to do so much—but some adventure always beckoned—or I rushed into some silly quarrel."

"And then the charmed life failed," sighed Eleanor, remembering how certain she had been that he would come back from the Crusade. "Well, the old witch kept *her* side of the bargain!"

Richard turned his head so that he could see the gold vase with its incongruous burgeoning of field flowers and raised a hand to flick contemptuous fingers at it. "A paltry thing, Berengaria said, to buy with human lives!" It seemed so short a time since the words were spoken and since her hands were touching it. Her little hands, that he would never again hold against his racing heart. It was unbearable. "I promised to join her at Fontevrault," he recollected with a wry grimace. "And now, I suppose, it will be only my big, sinful body they will take her. Poor sweet, I wonder if her tears will purge it? Will you come—too—and comfort her?"

Eleanor was determined not to mar this precious hour with her own tears. "Of course," she promised steadily. "I was afraid you were going to ask me to go back to restrain John."

"I wish I had done something more definite about Arthur!" muttered Richard. "You've never let anyone down, have you?" He spoke with heavy bitterness. "I let Berengaria down—and Robin—and England…"

But that was more than Eleanor could stomach. "You—a failure!" she exclaimed indignantly. "When you've made for yourself an imperishable name that will stir men's minds after most other kings are lumped together as forgotten dust! Richard Coeur de Lion."

"Robin—and my poor people—would probably prefer me to have been called 'the Peacemaker'!" smiled Richard.

But Eleanor was of her generation—feudal to her fingertips. "Peacemakers soon get forgotten," she snapped. "But the citizens of London will probably build a splendid statue of you so that when John has turned them into a nation of shopkeepers they may still see the inextinguishable spirit of their breed in your uplifted sword!"

"I expect Berengaria would like it put up at West-min-stair," said Richard.

Eleanor suspected that he was making fun of her. "Well, anyhow, Blondel is sure to go back to wherever it is in Sussex and make ballads about us all!" she laughed.

Richard turned his head drowsily on the pillow. "Then I'm sure his children will like best the ones about Robin. About his wrestling at the fair and befriending witches and living in the woods."

Eleanor saw that his strength was ebbing. It could not matter what she told him now. "If I could sing I could make them a better one about him," she said deliberately. Richard's green eyes snapped open and he found that she was not laughing any more. "I've always wanted to tell you but Hodierna made me promise I wouldn't," she added resentfully.

Richard said nothing but just lay there waiting. The pain in his shoulder was becoming an agony again, but he was glad that the effect of the drug was wearing off because it left his head clear and he felt sure that in a few moments he would see the pattern of his life completed with the piece that was missing.

"It's about the last instalment of your ransom," Eleanor began, pleating the velvet of her gown across her slender knee. "It wasn't at all miraculous really. It was Robin who paid it."

Richard stared at her through narrowed lids and the roses slipped unheeded from his fingers. "But he hadn't a groat!" he said. "I had stripped him of everything."

"Don't worry about that, my dear," she said. "He ate your venison every day. And don't let your conscience nag you about the way you've hated Philip and Chalus. That money-grubbing lecher, Barbe, came to England. You didn't know that, did you? And it was the pair of them who tempted John to steal the exchequer money—to bribe Leopold to keep you in prison." It wasn't easy for her to talk about the depth of their infamy. After all, John was still her son and his father had thought the world of him. "We've all been too soft with John," she said. "But Robin caught Chalus taking the money out of the country and appropriated it to pay off your ransom instead."

Eleanor took joy in telling him the whole story, and Richard—who was dying—lay there and laughed. His hand gripped the embroidered coverlet, and across his belly the leopards he was leaving as a legacy to England heaved to the painful movement of his mirth. The story was Robin's gift to him, devised with understanding. Besides buying his freedom, it squared accounts with Philip, who had cost him Jerusalem—and with Chalus, who had dared to lift his monkey eyes to a Plantagenet's mate. And the best part of it was that Robin, whom he had beggared, had done it without killing and without legal status—just by the ingenuity and humour of his breed.

Neither the money nor the freedom mattered much now, but Richard had the assurance of his friend's love to go out with him on a longer, more hazardous voyage than Acre. Eleanor saw the hard lines smoothed from his mouth, leaving it humorous and tender.

"Now, by the compassionate heart of Christ, I know that Robin forgave me!" exulted Richard, remembering with remorse the broken vow he had made to old Father Christopher on the hilltop of St. Martyr. There had been clean wild thyme, the shivering ecstasy of a lark, and the drifting scent of May. The young tops of the oaks had been touched with gold in the valleys, and the weald had stretched in blue loveliness at his feet. Every spring in England the world would look like that, and somehow he and Robin would always be a part of it.

The Tudor Rose

BY MARGARET CAMPBELL BARNES

COME AND SIT BESIDE me, Bess. Margaret Beaufort, Countess of Richmond, has sent us a message, and as it is confidential we will send the others away." With a wave of one bejeweled hand Elizabeth Woodville cleared the parlor.

"The Countess sends me word how gifted and personable a young man her son has grown," she said.

"Naturally, since he is her only son." Elizabeth smiled.

"But all reports confirm the trend of her devotion…and his mother says that it is high time he took a wife," added the Dowager Queen.

"Probably he will marry the Duke of Brittany's daughter," remarked Elizabeth, with polite indifference.

But her mother leaned forward and placed a hand upon her knee. "The message was particularly for you." She said impressively.

Elizabeth came out of her own private thoughts with a start. During her short life she had become accustomed to being offered as matrimonial bait for some political reason or another, but the implication of her mother's words appeared to have no rhyme or reason. "A message for me about Henry Tudor of Lancaster?" she exclaimed. The scornful abhorrence in her voice was as unmistakable as it was purely hereditary.

"Better a well-disposed Lancastrian than a treacherous Yorkist!" snapped the Dowager Queen.

"But my father would never have heard of such a thing,"

stammered Elizabeth, realizing that the suggestion was being made in earnest.

"Were your father alive to hear, there would be no need of such a thing," pointed out his widow. "But times have changed, and we must change with them."

"Have you forgotten, madam, that Henry Tudor is attainted of treason and still in exile?"

"He might be persuaded to come home."

When an ambitious woman's world crumbles about her, she can still meddle in the advancement of her children, thought Elizabeth. "Nothing would induce me to marry him," she said, and having always rendered sweet obedience to both her parents, was amazed at her own words.

The Dowager Queen flushed red with anger. "I think you forget, Elizabeth, that in your father's will he left me charge of my daughter's marriages. Even our enemies who dispute your legitimacy cannot dispute that," she said.

"So you must plot with a Lancastrian? White rose or red, I suppose it can be all the same to you Woodvilles!" accused Elizabeth Plantagenet, for the first time insulting her mother's birth.

Before such rare defiance, the Queen Dowager's vivacity wilted to self pity. "You do not consider me at all," her mother was wailing as Elizabeth dutifully dabbed rose water to her brow.

"It is the boys who need considering," said Elizabeth. "In what way would your proposal benefit them? Judging by what my father told me of Henry of Lancaster, it would not get Edward back the throne."

"No, but it might save their lives. We could make it a condition… you could offer him your precious blood, in return for a promise that he would keep your brother honorably in his household."

"As for promises, has not Uncle Gloucester sworn exactly the same thing? Why should I sell myself in the hope that a Lancastrian's word may prove more reliable than a Yorkist's?"

"Because your uncle has already broken his word. He has not kept them in his household but in prison," pointed out their mother.

Elizabeth stood aside as the solicitous waiting women came to escort the Dowager Queen to her room.

"I begin not to believe much in any promises," she said sadly.

Reading Group Guide

1. This book was originally published under the title *Like Us They Lived*. It was retitled *The Passionate Brood* for its release in the United States. How is each title appropriate to the novel? Which do you prefer?

2. In the early chapters, Barnes gives us an intimate, familiar view of this powerful royal family. How effective was this in drawing you into the story? What were your early impressions of the family?

3. "Peace!" Hodierna cries at the end of chapter 4. "I doubt if you crazy Plantagenets know the meaning of the word!" This marks the major difference between the Plantagenets and Robin and Hodierna. How does this difference play out in their relationships? Do any of the Plantagenets develop an understanding of peace?

4. In chapter 9, Berengaria says of her aversion to the sight of blood, "One has to be bigger than one's dislikes," and Richard is struck by her "unilluminated courage." Which other characters show this sort of courage in the face of things they dislike?

5. In chapter 12, we see a picture of Richard and Robin at liberty in a scene that goes from jovial banter to constructive debate to serious quarrelling and then finally to Robin's banishment. How do Robin's greatest strengths—his love for England, his candid nature, and his devotion to Richard—all play a part in his downfall?

6. How might England's history have been different if Richard had listened to Robin's counsel and not gone on his crusade, but stayed to rule and improve his country?

7. Berengaria gives Richard the nickname *Couer de lion*, the "lion-hearted." How does this name suit him? What are some events that take place in the book in which his lionheartedness is apparent? Does this prove to be a positive character trait or a negative one? Or both?

8. Both Eleanor and Richard believe "love necessarily include(s) understanding," and both are hurt to learn that such is not always the case—Eleanor in her marriage to King Henry and Richard in his friendship with Robin. In what other relationships in the book is there evidence of an imbalance between love and understanding?

9. Even after being outlawed, Robin is never far from Richard's thoughts. How is Robin still a guiding presence throughout the book, even through his conspicuous absence?

10. Richard says of ruling a country: "A man who can't burden his conscience with occasional ruthlessness hasn't the right to rule." Taken in the context of our own time, do you agree or disagree with this statement? Why?

11. How does John's position as the youngest and favorite son of Henry II, combined with his lack of an inheritance, form the motivations that impel him to seize power in Richard's absence?

12. Who was the better ruler: Richard, who was always absent, but had good intentions for his country, or John, who did many things to improve the quality of life in England, but usually for the wrong reasons?

13. *The Passionate Brood* is the story of the establishment of a dynasty (the Plantagenets) and the birth of a nation (England). Barnes does much to show how the individual stories of each are intertwined to form one inextricable history. How might the Plantagenets be seen as the launching point for all of English history that would follow?

14. Margaret Campbell Barnes wrote *The Passionate Brood* during World War II and dedicated it to her son Michael, who was killed during the allied invasion of Normandy. Where in the story do we see both the often noble causes and the devastating losses of war?

Reading Group Guide written by Elizabeth R. Blaufox, great-granddaughter of Margaret Campbell Barnes

MARGARET CAMPBELL BARNES LIVED from 1891 to 1962. She was the youngest of ten children born into a happy, loving family in Victorian England. She grew up in the Sussex countryside and was educated at small private schools in London and Paris.

Margaret was already a published writer when she married Peter, a furniture salesman, in 1917. Over the next twenty years, a steady stream of short stories and verse appeared under her name (and several noms de plume) in leading English periodicals of the time, including *Windsor*, *London*, *Quiver*, and others. Later, Margaret's agents, Curtis Brown Ltd., encouraged her to try her hand at historical novels. Between 1944 and 1962, Margaret wrote ten historical novels. Many of these were bestsellers, book club selections, and translated into foreign editions.

Between World Wars I and II, Margaret and Peter brought up two sons, Michael and John. In August 1944, Michael, a lieutenant in the Royal Armoured Corps, was killed in his tank in the Allied advance from Caen to Falaise in Normandy. Margaret and Peter grieved terribly the rest of their lives. Glimpses of Michael shine through in each of Margaret's later novels.

In 1945 Margaret bought a small thatched cottage on the Isle of Wight, off England's south coast. It had at one time been a smuggler's cottage, but to Margaret it was a special place in which to recover the spirit and carry on writing. And write she did. All together, over two million copies of Margaret Campbell Barnes's historical novels have been sold worldwide.

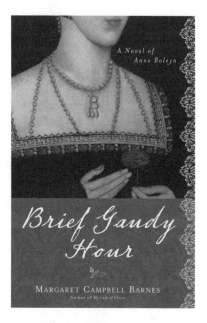

Brief Gaudy Hour

978-1-4022-1175-1 ~ $14.95 U.S./$17.95 CAN

"A moving and life-like portrait…
a thoroughly delightful novel."

—*New York Times*

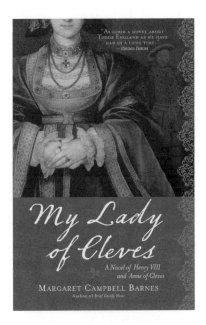

ALSO AVAILABLE FROM

Margaret Campbell Barnes

My Lady of Cleves

978-1-4022-1431-8 ~ $14.95 U.S./$15.99 CAN

"At long last Anne of Cleves gets her day as a noble and high-minded heroine in the lists of historical fiction!"

—*Chicago Tribune*

ALSO AVAILABLE FROM
Margaret Campbell Barnes

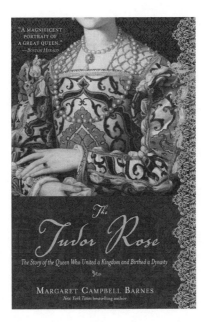

The Tudor Rose

978-1-4022-2468-3 ~ $14.99 U.S./$18.99 CAN/£7.99 UK

"A magnificent portrait of a great queen."

—*Boston Herald*

Also available from

Margaret Campbell Barnes

Within the Hollow Crown

978-1-4022-3921-2 ~ $14.99 U.S./$17.99 CAN/£7.99 UK

"Ms. Barnes captures the flavor, pagentry, and color of the Middle Ages…a distinguished novel."

—*Philadelphia Inquirer*